PENGUIN BOOKS

Little Sister

'Addictive, fast-paced and so expertly plotted that when
I finished I had to read the beginning again, in awe at the twists. I'm a
huge fan of the Sheens series but this is my favourite yet. I loved it!'
Claire Douglas

'A taut, gritty thriller' *Sun*

'*Little Sister* is a smart and devastatingly raw novel of revenge and
manipulation. Brilliantly sharp, and wonderfully paced, it is a
page-turner not to be missed' L.V. Matthews

'Smart, moody, intense and tangled. I loved it'
Gillian McAllister

'Twisting and turning to the last . . . a gripping thriller
that'll keep you engaged' *Cambridge Edition*

'From the pen of a skilled storyteller, this is perfectly paced, with
twists and turns to keep you hooked' Amanda Jennings

'*Little Sister* is a hugely affecting tale of innocence lost and revenge.
Cleverly plotted, perfectly paced, and with the trademark warmth
we've come to expect from this series' Caz Frear

'Intriguing, unsettling and twisty as hell. A great cast of characters
who are brilliantly drawn. Gytha is a classy storyteller'
Neil Lancaster

'Fresh, original and compulsive – I raced through it'
Trevor Wood

'Darkly fascinating, gripping and emotionally intriguing'
Emma Haughton

'I was gripped by this story – so many twists and turns
I was never quite sure who to believe, and it kept me on the
edge of my seat until I reached the last page' Nikki Smith

'Brilliant. Had me hooked from the word go. I loved it!'
Rachael Blok

ABOUT THE AUTHOR

Gytha Lodge is a *Sunday Times* bestselling writer and multi-award-winning playwright who lives in Cambridge. After studying creative writing at UEA, she was shortlisted for the Yeovil Literary Prize and the Arts' Council England fiction awards, and developed a large online following for her young adult and children's writing, with over seven million reads accrued on the platform Wattpad.

She Lies in Wait, her debut novel, was a Richard & Judy Book Club Pick and *Sunday Times* bestseller. With nail-biting cases that hook you in, with heart that keeps you coming back for more, Lodge's highly-acclaimed Jonah Sheens series – which also includes *Watching from the Dark* and *Lie Beside Me* – has kept readers gripped from beginning to end, and Lodge has been acclaimed as 'a gifted writer' by the *Daily Mail*.

Little Sister

GYTHA LODGE

PENGUIN BOOKS

PENGUIN BOOKS

UK | USA | Canada | Ireland | Australia
India | New Zealand | South Africa

Penguin Books is part of the Penguin Random House group of companies
whose addresses can be found at global.penguinrandomhouse.com.

First published by Penguin Michael Joseph 2022
Published in Penguin Books 2022
001

Printed and bound in Great Britain by Clays Ltd, Elcograf S.p.A.

The authorized representative in the EEA is Penguin Random House Ireland,
Morrison Chambers, 32 Nassau Street, Dublin D02 YH68

A CIP catalogue record for this book is available from the British Library

ISBN: 978–1–405–94703–9

www.greenpenguin.co.uk

For Kyn, who provided hugely entertaining childcare while I was writing this one, and only managed to give the boy six wrestling-related nosebleeds during that time.

Prologue

It was far warmer than a September afternoon had any right to be. At four p.m., it must have been almost thirty degrees in the garden of the Spreading Oak. Jonah checked on Milly as one of the waiters deposited a pint of lager on the picnic table. She was soundly asleep under the pram's parasol, soothed by the heat and background chatter.

Jonah lifted the glass of lager, intensely aware of the condensation under his hand and of the very slight breeze that slid across his arms. It was such a rare moment of peace and normality that he felt drunk on it, even before he'd started to sink the four per cent.

Six weeks of Milly had been life-changing. He'd worried, before the event, that the change would be too much for him. That, at fifty, he was too set in his ways to cope with the arrival of a baby, and too old to deal with the lack of sleep.

He'd surprised himself by relishing it. He'd even enjoyed the first two weeks, when there had been no apparent end to his daughter's needs, and no real guidance about how to satisfy them. He had still caught himself watching her with wonder, or grinning stupidly as she looked up at him, slightly cross-eyed.

That wasn't to say that it was easy. Sharing a child with someone months after a messy break-up had built-in baggage, and the added serious sleep deprivation and sudden loss of freedom hadn't helped. There had been moments of complete misunderstanding, and moments where it had all seemed impossible.

He had questioned whether he could really do it. Could he honestly make a life with the mother of his child? A child who had come about through one stupid night of drunken nostalgia. Could he really do it, long after he'd fallen out of love with Michelle? When his heart was so firmly elsewhere?

He'd had to try. That was what he'd realised. Because he couldn't leave Michelle alone to raise a child. Not when she was asking him to try again.

It hadn't been easy, building a new life with his ex-fiancée. The love that he'd felt had been slow to trickle back, but as Michelle's due date had approached, he'd almost felt as close to her as he once had. Perhaps his feelings for her were less intense than they had been, but he hoped that they would continue to grow as they raised their child together.

That wasn't to say that there weren't some genuinely awful moments. Moments when he suddenly snapped out of deep thought with a pounding heart and a feeling as if he'd stumbled into the wrong life. Others when Michelle seemed to be looking at him with total coldness.

But those moments came less often as the months passed. And to be out here, today, with a child who was actually asleep, drinking like a normal human being, felt like a huge privilege. A blessing.

He was two-thirds of the way down the glass before he knew it. The alcohol added its slightly fuzzy halo to everything, and he found himself smiling at a couple with two young toddlers as they walked over to the climbing frame.

His phone buzzed, and he lifted it to read Michelle's message:

Umm, I'm running about 20 mins behind. Fell asleep!! Sorry. Xx

It was a shame. He'd been looking forward to spending some proper time together, unencumbered by bottle washing, laundry and discussions of Milly's sleep schedule. It so rarely happened in this new life of theirs.

But even that couldn't dent his good mood. He messaged back a quick 'No rush!' and then turned to watch the children charging around on the climbing frame. Their parents were right there with them, diving in to tickle them or to help them down the slide.

He felt optimistic, for the first time in a while, that everything would work out all right. That he'd be messing around with Milly like that in a few years, side by side with his partner.

He was still watching them when a figure emerged through the trellised archway from the road. He glimpsed her at the edges of his vision, registering long hair of a brilliant red. Part of him picked up something else – that she looked grubby, maybe – and he turned to look.

Jonah realised that the grubbiness was blood. That her T-shirt was daubed in it; her hands covered in a coating of rust-red almost up to her elbows. For a moment, he wondered whether this was what sleep deprivation did to you. Whether it was blurring the boundaries between the innocence of his family life, and the terrible violence of his work. Whether this might be no more than a hallucination.

But then other diners started to turn, and a quiet began to wash over the garden. After a few instants, there was only the light buzz of music from inside the pub, and noises of effort from the two children as they kept climbing, oblivious.

The blood was real, he thought. And having understood, he tried to work out where it had come from.

There was no evidence that the blood was hers. No

bloom of it to show a source. Just a great river of red-brown down her T-shirt, and daubs of it over her hands. Jonah tried, swiftly, to work out whether she was in trouble. Whether she'd just witnessed a terrible accident.

She was young, he thought. A teenager. And she came to a complete stop a few paces into the garden, as if she'd run out of the momentum needed to keep going.

There was no question in Jonah's mind that he should be the one to step forwards. The moment this young woman had entered the garden, she had become his responsibility. Before that, really. From the moment the blood had been shed on her.

She gazed around at the drinkers with a strangely unconcerned expression. There was no shame. No anxiety. But also none of the signs Jonah had come to expect from a girl who had experienced trauma. None of the usual ones, at least. She looked, if anything, slightly amused.

He got to his feet, and took a step forwards, his hand going to the handle of the pram to keep it near to him.

'Are you all right?' he asked her.

There were hurrying footsteps from the pub. In the periphery of his vision, he saw a waitress emerge from the door with a pair of plates, and then falter as she saw the scene in front of her.

The girl smiled at him, though it wasn't a warm smile. It was almost as if she'd been expecting him to ask, and found it funny.

'I could do with a drink,' she said.

Jonah nodded. 'All right. Come to the bar and I'll get you one.'

He felt very much aware, as he escorted her into the pub, that everyone was now watching both of them. That they were now imagining that he knew her. Assuming that this was somehow his fault.

It was lucky that Jonah had never cared that much about what most people thought.

The young woman moved ahead of him into the pub, and he lifted the pram over the threshold and followed her. He became momentarily blind in the dimness before he shoved his sunglasses up onto his head. The girl was already walking towards the bar.

There was, as ever, no real sense of a queue. Just a mass of people near the bar, all immersed in their menus and shooting each other occasional side-eyed glances in case they lost their place. But they made way for him. Or, actually, for her.

'Lemonade?' Jonah asked, his eyes on the nearest barman. He could see that the guy had understood. That he was going to serve this blood-smeared girl next, no matter who was waiting.

'Sure,' she said. 'A pint with ice.'

Jonah watched her as the barman began to move. He studied the pale eyes as she looked around again. Her tall frame. The lean, strong look of her.

'I'm Jonah,' he said. And then, after a moment, he added, 'I'm a detective. I work with the police.'

She looked back at him, her gaze showing no curiosity. 'Keely.'

'Do you need our help?'

He could hear the lemonade hissing into the glass now. There was nothing else to listen to. The whole room full of people were watching the two of them.

Keely narrowed her eyes at him, briefly, and said, 'I don't. But maybe Nina does.'

'Nina?' Jonah asked.

'My sister,' Keely said, her voice light. Almost merry.

Jonah's eyes moved to the blood coating her arms, and he asked, 'Where is Nina?'

Keely's amusement turned into a brilliant, knowing smile.

'Oh, I'm not going to tell you yet, detective,' she said. 'That would be too easy.'

I

Juliette Hanson was already in the station when the DCI called. She felt caught out, being found there late on a sunny Sunday afternoon. The chief knew perfectly well that there were no pressing cases on their books. Nothing that required overtime.

'Oh, that's useful,' was all he said, but she thought she could hear the slight surprise. The unspoken question about her personal life.

'I need you on something.' There was the brief sound of a passing car, and Hanson wondered where he was. 'I want to know if there's a missing persons report on a Keely Lennox, and her sister Nina. Lennox with two Ns.' Hanson scribbled it down on the big pad on her desk. 'I'll be there in about half an hour, once the uniforms come to assist.'

Hanson paused, her pen in the air. 'Assist with what?'

'With the older sister,' he said, quietly. 'I'm bringing her to the station. I'll explain once I'm on my own in the car.'

Hanson felt a fizz of keen curiosity as she rang off. The DCI rarely came in on Sundays, and it hadn't happened at all since his daughter had been born.

She opened the database and typed in the name 'Keely Lennox'. She was immediately rewarded with a missing persons report, filed on Wednesday morning. Clicking on it showed her two red-headed teenagers, one smiling at the camera, her green-blue eyes warm, and the other, older-looking one, giving it an ice-blue, dead-eyed stare.

There were a couple of brief paragraphs of information

below, stating that sixteen-year-old Keely Lennox had absconded from a children's home with her younger sister, fourteen-year-old Nina. They'd last been seen at bedtime on Tuesday night. Almost five days ago.

There was little else beyond that information and a description. No particular concerns were registered over either of the sisters. Which, she thought glumly, was probably because they were in care.

So the chief has Keely, Hanson thought. *What about the little sister?*

As they lived in Southampton, the misper investigation was being handled by one of Yvonne Heerden's uniformed constables. Hanson decided to put a call through to Heerden's team on the second floor. There should be someone around who could tell her what they'd found out so far. After fourteen months as a detective constable, Hanson knew the drill well enough to get moving without the chief.

As she waited for someone to pick up, she dragged her holdall out from under the desk. She was wearing sports kit, her blonde hair tied back in a sweat-flattened ponytail. If she ended up interviewing anyone, she was going to need her backup gear, which she kept stashed under here for emergency use.

'Alan Jones,' said a voice on the other end. Hanson managed to drag a shirt and jacket out of her bag while straightening up. They were both a little crumpled, but they were clean.

'This is DC Hanson,' she told him. 'My DCI needs some info on a missing persons from last week. Keely and Nina Lennox, on Wednesday the third. The report was filed by a Constable Alsana Meek.'

'OK, hold on,' he said, and she could hear him typing in the background. 'I've got the investigation itself here. I'll send it over, but if you want a quick summary, I can give it to you.'

'Great,' Hanson said. 'I'd like to check what's been done. Were their phones tracked?'

'Yes, on Thursday the fourth of September,' Alan told her, after a pause. 'They'd most recently pinged a mast not far from the children's home in Southampton, on the Tuesday night, but nothing since.'

'Did they check again later?' she asked.

'No, that was the one check.'

Hanson wrote that down with a feeling of slight frustration. It was an unfortunate and inescapable fact that, with stretched resources, a lot of cases simply didn't get the time spent on them that they should. It was a situation that was only worsening, as cuts to mental health and social care services left officers dealing with people who really needed other forms of help but couldn't get it.

But even allowing for that, she was disappointed to learn that two probably vulnerable missing girls hadn't been more thoroughly searched for. Particularly when their phones being switched off might be evidence of something more sinister than a desire not to be found.

'Anything useful from the children's home staff?'

Another pause, and Alan said, 'They interviewed the manager there, who didn't have any ideas.' There was a momentary silence, and then he said, 'She expressed concern for their safety, particularly for the younger sister, Nina.'

'Did she say why?' Hanson asked.

'Er . . . she said Nina is very impressionable, and would do anything Keely suggested,' the officer said, his tone flat.

She thanked him and rang off, curiosity mingling with a slight feeling of unease. The chief was worried enough about Nina to bring her sister in, which implied that the children's home manager might have been right.

She wondered whether she should message Ben and Domnall. The DCI hadn't given her any instructions about that. Presumably because it wasn't clear to him yet whether the whole team would need to come in.

There was no point disturbing either of the team's sergeants on a Sunday afternoon without any real cause. It would be needlessly disruptive, particularly as Ben would inevitably come in the moment she told him about it. The effect of being naturally conscientious.

But she was also in the habit of messaging Ben fairly frequently. It seemed strange not to let him know that something was going on. And sometimes, she thought, it was better to have a heads-up about situations. If she phrased it in the right way, she'd keep him in the loop without making him feel his presence was required.

After a little thought, she sent him a brief text.

> How goes? I'm still in CID and the chief's on his way, too. Interviewing a teenager with a missing sister. Could be interesting. I'll keep you posted.

Ben's reply arrived ten seconds later.

> I'll be there in twenty. I've got flapjack.

Hanson was grinning as she dialled the number for Keely Lennox's children's home. Clearly that hadn't quite been the right phrasing.

Michelle had arrived at the Spreading Oak not long after the two uniformed constables. And just for a moment, as she had climbed out of the car, Jonah felt a drop of disappointment that it wasn't Jojo coming to find him. That it was Michelle, the smart, capable mother of his child, and not strong, irreverent, outdoorsy Jojo Magos who he was now with.

The reaction had made him feel wretched. *You shouldn't be thinking about Jojo. It's not fair. You love Michelle.*

Which was true. He loved her, and he loved Milly. And he'd done the right thing. Of course he had. Jonah had taken a deep, steadying breath, and then had waved to Michelle, gesturing at her to stay put while he helped the girl into the car.

He'd seen the expression on Michelle's face at the sight of the squad car. She had known, immediately, that their weekend together was over.

Jonah had expected her to look irritated. Pissed off that their family time was being bulldozed. But she had looked, instead, slightly panicked. He had seen her glance at the sleeping Milly and away, as though this was too much, and it had both worried him and made his thoughts of Jojo seem inexcusable.

He was still thinking of that expression as he looked in on Keely from the observation room half an hour later. The constables had shown her into one of the regular interview suites, where she was now waiting for the arrival of the on-call social worker to be her appropriate adult.

The impression he'd gathered from Keely was that she wasn't quite normal. While they stood waiting at the pub, he'd tried to get her to talk to him further. He'd asked her about what had happened, and about where she'd come from. About whether she'd eaten, and whether there were parents he could call. She had been totally unmoved by these questions, and had returned them with either a flat stare or one with a trace of amusement. In the end, she'd given a slight sigh and said, 'I'll talk to you at the station. There's no point asking anything now.'

It had been said with incredible coolness. He found it

hard to believe, now it was confirmed, that she was only six-teen. He didn't, in fairness, find it particularly easy to guess the ages of teenagers in general. He had no points of refer-ence as yet. But even allowing for that, it was unsettling to learn that she was so young.

It was her lack of self-consciousness, he thought. There had been no trace of anxiety at the arrival of uniformed officers. No breaking of her silence with mutinous answers. And he couldn't help the discomforting feeling that she'd been weighing him up. Deciding whether he was worthy of being talked to.

He had half expected her to be different once they were at the station. It was inevitably intimidating, walking through CID and then waiting to be interviewed. But now that they were here, he could see no signs of anxiety. Her intent blue-eyed stare was directed straight through the observation window, and Jonah had the rare and uncomfortable feeling that she knew he was there.

Hanson let herself in and shut the door. 'The social work-er's just signing in,' she said. 'I've called the children's home and asked the manager to ring me as soon as she's free.'

'Thanks,' Jonah said.

'Ben's just arrived,' Hanson commented. 'He's got flapjack.'

Jonah shook his head. He should have predicted that Ben would appear.

'Good news on the flapjack. Can you ask him to get up to speed? Tell him to look at what was done during the missing persons investigation, and check to see if Keely has any history of anti-social or violent behaviour. He can field the reply from the children's home manager too.'

'I checked for any criminal record, and she's clean,' Han-son said. 'But she has actually been here before. She was a witness in two possible abuse investigations that were dropped. I've requested more information from the Child Abuse Investigations Team.'

That statement made Jonah's unease step up. If Keely had been abused in any way, it greatly increased the chance of her being violent towards her sister.

'Thanks, that's a good move. And it wouldn't be a bad idea for Ben to find out about any friends the sisters might have confided in. He can do the nuts and bolts.'

'Got it,' Hanson said, scribbling that down.

'And tell him to stop being so keen,' Jonah added, with a smile.

Hanson grinned. 'With pleasure.' And then her smile faded. 'Do you think it's looking urgent, though? It's a reasonable amount of blood, isn't it? I mean, she's not absolutely covered in it, but . . .'

'I've put it through to the kidnap team,' he said, quietly. 'They'll be in to brief us soon. From our side of things, the key thing is talking to Keely and trying to get her to cooperate.'

Hanson nodded, her face sombre. She'd been here long enough to know that he thought this was serious.

Keely's unflinching ice-blue gaze was on Jonah from the moment he entered. As he and Hanson sat themselves down, he found himself reminded disconcertingly of the way his father had so often watched him. It was to do with that sense of being tried and found guilty, and it was strange how it produced an answering kick of anxiety, even when the person looking at him was a teenage girl.

He was glad, for the first time in the last three months, that their interview suite had now been furnished with digital cameras. The old tape machines had finally been removed and replaced with a closed-circuit set in the corner. He'd felt strangely resistant to the idea, after decades spent deferring to incorruptible tape. But tonight, he wanted a record of the interview. He wanted to capture Keely's flat stare. Her composure. The full effect of the blood.

The on-call social worker gave him a brief smile, and then looked down at the table. It was a fairly clear way of broadcasting that she didn't want to get actively involved in this. He wasn't entirely surprised. Keely had barely spoken to her when she had first arrived, and had certainly done nothing to endear herself to her.

He completed the formal introductions for the benefit of the camera, and then said to Keely, 'Are you all right? Do you need anything? Food, drink, painkillers . . .?'

Keely shook her head. Nothing in her expression changed.

'All right. Please tell us if you need anything.' He sat back slightly, a visible cue that this was not going to be a formal interview. 'Are you happy to talk to me now?'

Keely watched him for a moment, and then said, 'That depends on what you want to talk about.'

Jonah nodded. 'I'd like to know what's been happening to you since Tuesday evening.'

Keely gave him a very small smile. 'Why would you be interested in that?'

'It looks like you've been through tough times since then,' Jonah said, quietly. 'I want to know if there's anything we can do to help.'

Keely's smile grew a fraction broader, but she said nothing.

'You left your children's home on Cedar Avenue at some time on Tuesday night,' he continued. 'The staff realised you were gone in the morning. What time did you leave the home?'

Keely did nothing more than blink slowly.

'Were you running from something in particular?' Hanson chipped in. 'Was there something at Cedar Avenue making you unhappy?'

Keely glanced at Hanson. Jonah, watching for a reaction, thought he saw a flicker of something. Interest, maybe. Unease. Though it was almost impossible to be sure.

'People don't generally run from happy situations,' Hanson went on. 'Did the staff treat you well?'

Another silence. And another infuriatingly difficult-to-read expression.

'Is the blood yours?' Jonah asked, nodding towards her hands. They would swab them after this interview and send a sample straight over to the lab, but that was a slow way of finding out the answer. If Keely or – more likely – her sister had been wounded, they needed to know tonight, not tomorrow morning.

'No,' Keely said, lightly. She stretched her arms out in front of her, briefly, and her expression looked satisfied. 'I'm fine.'

Her accent was a lot more middle-class than most of the kids who went through care, Jonah thought. He wondered how long she'd been in the system, and how she and her sister had ended up within it. But those questions weren't pressing right now.

'Is it Nina's blood?' he asked, deciding it was time to bring Keely's sister into proceedings.

He saw her infinitesimal reaction. A dilation of the pupils. A very slight tension in her body. 'So you're actually only interested in Nina.'

Jonah waited for her to look at him again, and then said, firmly, 'We're interested in both of you. In whether you're injured, in whether you've suffered, and in where your sister is and whether she needs our help, too.'

Keely breathed out, slowly, her gaze distant. Jonah assumed she was going to say nothing again, but in the end, she asked, 'Why would you want to help Nina?'

'I believe she left Cedar Avenue Children's Home with

you on Tuesday,' Jonah said. 'Is that right? Were you together?'

Keely's very straight stare flicked back to him. 'You seem to know the answer to that already.'

Jonah watched her for a moment, and then said, 'We know only what other people have guessed. We'd like to hear what actually happened. From you.'

For a full minute, Keely did nothing but look back at him. At the end of it, Jonah nodded, and reached for the camera remote.

'We'll take a break, and let you chat to Kath here,' he said. The social worker grimaced slightly. 'Though we can try and get hold of your regular social worker, if that would help you,' Jonah offered.

Keely shrugged, and Jonah took that to mean that she didn't care either way. It seemed as though Keely cared about very little, except perhaps being the sole focus of their attention.

He stood to let himself out of the interview room. It was only once he'd opened the door that Keely said, 'I'll tell you what happened when you come back. From the beginning.'

Jonah wasn't sure, once again, how to read her expression. There was something more than coldness in it. He thought it might be amusement, or possibly disdain.

In the end, he nodded, and said, 'I'd appreciate that.'

Ben Lightman was waiting for them when Hanson emerged from the interview suite with the chief. He was, of course, impeccably dressed and model-handsome in a shirt and deep blue jacket. Hanson had only ever seen him look less than perfectly groomed when he'd been on his way to a tennis game. But even then, he'd managed to look effortlessly stylish in his Federer shirt and shorts.

'Ben. Just the man I wanted to see,' the chief said, dead-pan. 'Juliette says you brought flapjack . . .'

Ben gave one of his micro-grins and picked up a battered Quality Street tin.

'Home-made by my sister,' he said, easing the lid off and holding the tin out. 'With more calories per square than you're supposed to eat in a month.'

'Let me at them,' Hanson said, reaching in and then real-ising she could have done with a napkin. They were seriously sticky.

'Have you heard from the children's home yet?' the chief asked. He took two flapjacks at once, with no apparent shame.

The team's phone line rang before Ben could reply. He picked up and switched it to speakerphone before saying, 'This is DS Ben Lightman.'

'I'm Magda Becker.' It was a woman's voice, buzzing slightly over the speaker. 'I manage the children's home that – Keely and Nina's home. Sorry, I've only just been told you called. Derek says you have some questions for me.' Magda Becker's voice was tight and slightly unsteady. She sounded, to Hanson, like she was barely holding it together.

'Thanks so much for calling,' Ben said. 'We'd be very grateful for any help you can give us.'

'Has she said anything?' Magda asked, quickly. 'About Nina?'

'I don't have any information about that yet,' Lightman said, looking towards the DCI. Hanson abandoned the flapjack on her desk and started scribbling on her notepad. 'But my colleagues have been speaking to her.'

'Nina shouldn't have gone with her,' Magda said. 'I've tried so hard to – to warn her about just following her sis-ter's lead.'

The DCI took a seat on the edge of a nearby desk.

Hanson held up her piece of paper, on which she'd scrawled the words:

RESENTMENT TOWARDS NINA??

Lightman nodded, and said, 'Were there difficulties between them?'

'Yes,' Magda said. And then she amended, 'They didn't argue or anything. Nina just does everything Keely says. She's so sweet-natured, and Keely's just – she's a strong personality.'

'You think she might have persuaded Nina to do things against her best interest?' Lightman tried. He managed to say it so lightly that it didn't seem like an accusation, a real talent of Ben's.

'Yes, that's exactly it,' Magda said. 'Nina has the chance to be adopted by a wonderful family. They fostered her in the past and she'd been happy there, until Keely messed things up for both of them. We've known for some weeks that it wasn't what Keely wanted, her sister going. I'm sure that's why they disappeared.'

'She didn't want to be separated from her sister?' Ben said.

'Yes,' Magda said, with a touch of hesitation. 'Probably.'

The DCI waved a hand at him, telling him to keep pressing. Lightman nodded and asked, 'Was there any other reason she might not have wanted Nina to go?'

'Well, it's hard to be sure,' Magda said, with a trace of reluctance. 'But I've sometimes thought that Keely resented her sister. Nina is – people warm to her easily. Whereas Keely is . . .' There was a long pause, and Lightman said nothing, letting her go on to fill the silence. 'She's quite difficult to like, sometimes.'

'Does Nina like her?' Lightman tried.

'Oh, Nina idolises her,' Magda told him. 'She thinks she can do no wrong. I'm sure it's partly because Keely is the only family she has.'

'Are they orphans?'

'No, well . . . they might as well be.' She sighed, her breath sounding like a strong breeze over the speaker. 'Their mother died, when they were nine and seven. None of the services has been able to find their father. He walked out on them when Nina was a newborn.'

Lightman glanced at the DCI, who looked thoughtful, but suggested nothing else.

Ben said, 'We may need to talk to you in person. Will you be able to come into the station this evening?'

'This evening?' Magda asked. 'I can't. I have five other youngsters to see to, and two staff members on holiday.'

'We can come to you, if that helps,' Ben offered.

'Thank you. That would be helpful.'

Hanson, deciding which of her various questions was the most pressing, began to scribble again. She could see Ben twisting his head to read it.

Lightman nodded to Hanson: he'd got it. And then he asked, 'Just one last question. Would you trust Keely to look after Nina?'

There was a pause of several seconds, and Magda said, 'I don't think I would. No.'

The kidnap squad arrived a few minutes after the phone call. At least, two of their number arrived. The rest of them were, presumably, engaged in the practicalities of kicking off an urgent abduction enquiry.

The DI in charge was Murray Quick, a man with the air of a military sergeant. In all Jonah's interactions with him, he'd never cracked a smile, but there was something undeniably consoling in his manner. Quick had spent the last fifteen years working with the Red Team on time-critical or danger-to-life situations, and had a near-perfect record of success. Jonah would want him to be involved if anyone he cared about ended up in danger.

Quick had brought with him one of the Red Team's DCs, and the two of them converged near Hanson's desk.

'We need a briefing,' Quick said, with no niceties. 'I'm assuming you're all on board, in which case we can do it here.'

Jonah nodded. 'Here's fine, as long as you don't need a data projector.'

Quick didn't even answer. He just began, 'We've set up checks on Keely and Nina Lennox's phone numbers. Neither pinged any masts between Tuesday night and this afternoon, when Keely's was picked up by a tower in the rough vicinity of the pub. That was at four ten p.m. Nothing from Nina's so far.'

'Sounds like it pinged as she arrived there,' Jonah said. 'Though that doesn't discount her having been in the vicinity earlier, with it turned off.'

'We've already got two constables searching in the immediate vicinity of the pub,' Quick agreed. 'If Nina is within spitting distance, we'll find her. But we're also moving on the assumption that Keely Lennox travelled there from another site. We're looking for other location data now and the superintendent's signed off on a Grade 1 UVA.'

This, Jonah knew from past experience, was an Urgent Verbal Authorisation. It was a rarely used demand that a communications company provided full and complete data on an individual or individuals.

Jonah and his team were not supposed to know the full details of what a UVA could allow access to. The fewer people who knew the force's last-ditch ways of tracing criminals, the less chance there was that criminals would grow wise to them.

But Jonah had been curious when working alongside the Red Desk in the past. And so he had asked an associate of Domnall O'Malley's, a young man named Ziggy, about it. Ziggy, who Jonah strongly suspected was into illegal hacking as well as occasionally helping the police to avert it, had told him that a UVA was probably a demand sent to the manufacturer of the phone.

'There's an awful lot more data stored by a manufacturer than a simple list of mobile phone masts,' Ziggy had said. 'If you want to freak yourself out about exactly what they know about you, just look up how low-energy Bluetooth works.'

Having done so, Jonah had decided to focus on the positives, and hope he never needed to hide from his colleagues.

'I've had a discussion with the DCS,' Quick went on. 'We both think our starting position should be for you to talk to the girl. You've got an initial relationship with her and she's agreed to disclose information. You're negotiation-trained, aren't you, sir?'

Jonah nodded, but felt like protesting. He had spent two years on twenty-four-hour call-out as a negotiator when he had reached the rank of DI, but had ultimately stood down from the role. He had admitted to his then DCI that he was better at breaking people down than at soothing them.

'That's good. But we've got our on-call negotiator on standby in case he's needed.' He gave Jonah an assessing look. 'I'd suggest we check in after an hour and see what the situation is.'

'Agreed,' Jonah said.

He found the dynamics of crisis situations fascinating. Quick might occasionally remember to call Jonah 'sir,' but this was essentially a joint operation. That meant the two of them were, in reality, uneasy equals in the search for Nina Lennox.

'To give my team some idea of where they'll fit in this,' Jonah went on, 'while discussions with Keely take place, I'll need you all to look into her life – and her sister's – in detail. Find the places they're most likely to have bolted to. Work out close contacts to feed to the kidnap squad.' He paused for a moment, and then added, 'And establish, as much as possible, what Keely Lennox's motive behind all this is. Whether she's harmed her sister badly or is doing this for show.'

Hanson moved slightly in her chair and looked thoughtful. 'Do we have phone records from before they disappeared? Messages, in particular?'

'Already requested from Vodafone,' Quick said immediately. 'We'll be looking at them for persons of interest, but we can share that information.'

'Thank you.' Hanson smiled at DI Quick and got only a nod in return.

'What information has Keely given you so far?' Quick asked Jonah, instead.

'Essentially nothing,' Jonah replied. 'She's said she'll tell us everything once I go back in, but given what I've seen of her so far, I'm not sure it's going to be quite that simple. I think we should still make an effort to listen to what she has to say, though.'

Quick nodded to them and left without any courtesies. Jonah saw the Red Team DC's amused expression as she excused herself and followed him. Jonah was relieved that one of the kidnap squad, at least, had a sense of humour.

Jonah returned to the interview room with little idea of what to expect. Part of him was braced for bad news. He had to be ready to hear that Keely had done something awful to her sister.

The other part of him, though, clung to optimism. There was a reasonable chance that Keely had just been playing for time, for reasons of control. The presence of blood wasn't enough to conclude there had been a fatal injury. It always, he had learned, looked like there was more than there really was.

Though a quiet, dark voice in the back of his mind told him that even a little bleeding could be enough to kill someone if it carried on unchecked, or involved internal wounding. He took a breath before he opened the interview-room door, nodded to himself, and entered.

Keely gave him a very small smile as he sat in front of her. He got the impression that she'd already made some kind of decision about him, and that it amused her, whatever it was. It was strangely belittling.

She seemed far less interested in Hanson. Her gaze wandered over her briefly, and then returned to Jonah.

'If you're ready to continue,' Jonah told her, 'we'd really like to hear what happened to you.'

Keely studied him for a moment, and then said, 'All right. And in the true spirit of the law, I'm going to tell you the truth, the whole truth, and nothing but the truth. Every single thing that happened to us since we entered the care system.'

Jonah leaned forwards very slightly, without letting his expression change. 'We'd like to hear all of that. Can you tell us about the last five days first, though? What brought you here?'

Keely's expression hardened. 'No,' she told him, 'I can't. You're going to listen to all of it, or you get nothing. And, believe me, you won't find Nina without me.' That very small smile returned. 'I've made sure of that.'

2

You don't get to choose your story. That's the thing I've really learned. You can warp it a bit, if you're lucky. Twist a few events around and make things better – or not. You can even dress it up in a different way. Like I could tell this as a comedy, if I did it right. Or maybe as gritty YA where everyone matures and learns and gets stronger.

What you can never, ever do is change the genre. You're stuck with that for life. So my story is what it is. A story defined by three men, and the way their desires took our lives and moulded them. Mutilated them.

If you want to find Nina, I have some starting advice for you. It's about understanding that those men are no worse than you are. Not really. We all have the same savage possibility in us. I know I do. Mine got stripped pretty bare by everything.

So, to find my sister, you have to look in the mirror, and actually see what's there. Have a good delve into all the dark places. At all the times you've chosen your own interests over someone else's. All the petty or selfish things you've done.

Isn't it weird how, with all those things, you can still hold it all together and tell yourself you're a good person? That's because you didn't have the same pressure I did.

You know, I'd probably be a lot like you if all the bad stuff had happened later. It wasn't really child-appropriate, any of it.

The trouble is, nobody's overseeing this stuff, and life just does its thing. It has basically no respect for ratings.

When everything went dark for us, for my sister and me, we were nine and seven. Two young girls who thought the world revolved around cake and paint sets and birthday presents. We defined ourselves by things we wanted, actually. In the front of every diary I started and then abandoned would be my name, my age, and what I most wanted in the world at the time (usually some kind of animal but occasionally a book).

We were lucky back then. Our mum would generally get us the things we wanted. She loved to treat us. And back then, I had no idea that the money might run out.

Our dad had only ever been a vague, almost mythical figure to me. Someone who had once been part of our lives, and who'd then just vanished. He existed only as a beardy, glasses-wearing face in two posed photographs, and nowhere else.

My sister, whose memory has always been weirdly complete, remembered more, despite having been only three when he left us. She drew pictures of him, sometimes, or wrote stories where he'd be strict and tough, or where he'd shower the two of us with presents like Mummy did. None of that seemed real, to me.

As far as I was concerned, it was all about Mummy. She was my everything. From the way she spoke and laughed with us, to the cut flowers she brought into our idyllic little single-storey cottage. From the games she played with us to the things she taught us. From the time she woke us gently in the morning until the time when she tucked us into our beds, letting us fall asleep to the sound of her piano playing in the living room next door.

So it was a real kicker when she died, horribly and completely unnecessarily.

In one of those unfair inversions, my sister remembers nothing about that day, where I remember it with total grim clarity.

I really envy her for that. I'd love to forget that spray of blood, and our mum's mangled form.

One of the counsellors we saw told us it isn't always healthy to forget. She said it's better for the mind to remember everything, even the really hard things. Which is great. I'm sure it's really healthy being a small child and having those pictures in your mind every time you go to sleep.

Anyway, I was the one who found our fiercely loved mummy, at just before eight in the morning on a freezing day in late January. I crept downstairs, shivering in the cold air flooding in through the open French windows. I didn't know enough yet to realise that those open windows meant something was wrong. I just thought she'd be out there, gardening, despite the dim dawn light.

I went out there, hoping we'd get a bit of uninterrupted time together before Ninny invaded. Instead I found years of nightmares.

To be clear: what I found on the patio wasn't really Mummy. It was the tangled remains of her, all jumbled up with broken garden furniture.

I saw a sticky, dark red spray across the flagstones, too. And I ran inside to call an ambulance.

With, like, *perfect* timing, my darling sister woke up and stumbled downstairs while I was trying to talk to the operator.

'Mummy just needs a doctor, Ninny,' I whispered to her. 'Stay at the top of the stairs.'

She nodded, obedient with sleepiness, and sat nicely on the top step until the paramedics came.

I thought someone had murdered her. Our mummy. It's what I eventually told my sister, too, a few weeks afterwards. It was only much later that an excruciatingly awkward staff member at the children's home put me right.

'I hear you've been telling people that your mummy was murdered, Keely,' she said, looking like she'd rather be anywhere else. Anywhere but the cramped little manager's office with two red-headed children staring at her.

'It's not true,' the woman said. I feel like her name might have been Tina, but in my memory, all the staff members seem to be called Tina, which is unlikely by the laws of probability.

Anyway, the woman who probably wasn't Tina paused. It was one of those dramatic, unnecessary kinds of pauses people do when they're trying to Let That Sink In.

We both stared back at her until she said, 'It was just an accident. She went out late at night and tripped over. The glass-topped table fell down with her, and the glass cut her in a particularly important part of her leg. It wouldn't have hurt.'

I remember holding her gaze. I knew a bit about pain by then. Not as much as later, but a bit. Like how much it had hurt when I'd put my hand down on some broken glass once. And the rage-inducing hurt of a paper cut. So I knew this woman was a liar. Of course it had hurt.

She could probably tell what I was thinking, too, because she blushed a really deep red and pretended she had to go and do something else.

Anyway. Regardless of the specifics, our mum died. Violently. That's all you really need to know.

Her death hit us differently. Ninny went to pieces at first, and stayed in pieces for several days. But I stayed strong. I felt this weird sense of responsibility. Like I had to be the grown-up, now, because fragile little Ninny needed protecting. Isn't that hilarious? When you think about where we've both ended up?

Some of it probably came, unconsciously, from Mummy. She'd somehow always made it clear that Ninny was breakable in ways that I wasn't. That she needed care and indulgence.

It wasn't just that she told me not to pull her hair or play too roughly. It was also about what we both said to her. The way she was our 'little Ninny', a nickname that was full of affection and indulgence of her slightly dippy ways.

We were also supposed to be really considerate of her feelings. And we weren't supposed to leave her alone. Mummy reminded me of all this with boring regularity. Though I sometimes wonder if that was less to do with Ninny than to do with what she saw in me. I think, sometimes, that Mummy saw the shadow at my centre even back then. I've always understood that it was close to the surface. Stamped down by love and affection, but still there.

I don't think she ever saw it in Ninny. It was buried a long way down in my soft-hearted sister. Which wasn't because she's *better*. It's because everyone looked at her, all skinny and delicate, and they smiled at her. They patted her head, and dried her tears, and let her go on wearing her soft feelings like some kind of friable clothing. She had layers and layers of softness to hide that dark little core.

And then there was me. Built like I was made to last. Strong, and stocky, and incapable of creating those tender feelings in people. I never had a nickname, though I have vivid memories of being called a 'lump' whenever I climbed onto Mummy's lap.

I was the one who was always told to be a brave girl, and to stop crying and get on with it. And not just by our beloved mummy. By all of them. The women in shops. The delivery men. The playgroup leaders and teachers. The parents of our friends.

What they didn't realise, as they gradually moulded us from the outside in, was that I'm also the clever one. A lot cleverer than Ninny. A lot cleverer than everyone, really.

I mean, some of them occasionally seemed to be aware of it. Sometimes I'd start talking in front of them, and they'd look sideways at my mum. She would laugh and say I'd always been very old for my years. And perhaps, mixed in with her pride, was a little bit of what the others felt. That I was unnatural. Old before my time. Wizened, like a kobold. A child-spirit.

I think that's how the staff saw me, too, when we landed heavily in that first children's home. It was a skanky, bleach-smelling place in Southampton with a cat-turd-covered garden and no plants except a large, flowerless rhododendron. Ninny and I were appalled.

It probably didn't help that we were so obviously middle-class. From our floral dresses and prim haircuts to our accents and manners.

I'd never even stopped to think about whether we were rich or poor. Our mummy must have had money, surely. Except that, once she was gone, that money turned out to be imaginary. She'd been living off her inheritance, and then off what seemed to be loans. The title deeds to the house had, at some point, been transferred over to a man who'd lent her fifty thousand pounds. The house was no longer hers, which presumably meant that our mum had never managed to pay him back.

So there we were, two little middle-class girls, suddenly

thrust into a care system that had been designed around children steeped in poverty. Two posh little girls who didn't fit.

And it was probably worse that I took it upon myself to defend my sister's rights. I was my sister's constant champion. I stood up for her in every way.

I also encouraged her to eat the tasteless food they made us, sometimes by playing games with it, and sometimes by talking so much that she ate without noticing. She'd always been a fussy eater, but it threatened to become pathological in that place. Misery made her nauseous. Unfortunately it also made me perpetually hungry, comforted only when I was stuffing my face.

It turned out the one thing I couldn't protect either of us from was the attitude of the other kids there. Having only attended a small village primary school with a head who was zealous about kindness, I wasn't ready for any of it. Not for the way they would gang up and chant 'ginger' at us, or for one of the older girls pretending to find 'one of our pubes' on the couch. Not that I knew what pubes were back then.

By the end of the first week, we were never called anything except 'Ginger One' and 'Ginger Two' by the other kids. Ninny cried over it most days.

I was hanging on for us to move on somewhere, but it turned out Ninny was afraid of that, too.

'Tina says we'll probably go to a new family,' she said to me, about a month in. (I mean, like I said, it might not have been Tina, the name. But that's definitely the way I've remembered it.)

Ninny was hunched up on the undersized bed, the pale skin under her eyes an angry red from crying. 'I don't want to go to a different family. I want Mummy.'

I sat down next to her, and the plastic sheet they'd put over the mattress made a crunching noise. I have stark memories of the rubbery smell of those things. How it would leech through the sheet on top, and how on warm nights the plastic would create a gradual build-up of sweat that would start to soak into my pyjamas. Multi-sensory misery.

'It's all right,' I told her. 'We'll find a new mummy. Maybe a new daddy, too. Wouldn't that be nice, Ninny?'

I put my arm round her and rested my head against hers. 'What if it's as horrible as here?' she sobbed.

'It won't be horrible,' I promised. 'Mary said she'd find somewhere nice.' Mary, by the way, was our social worker. Social workers evidently aren't all called Tina. 'They might have a big garden with a swing. And a dog. And a ginormous fridge with loads of ice cream.'

I carried on for a while, and Ninny started joining in with the imaginings, and then eventually fell asleep. I moved back to my bed. For hours, I lay there and tried to think about a perfect new home, and not about my mum's blood sprayed across half the garden. In the end, it was thoughts of my sister being cuddled up to a new mummy and looking as though she might be happy again that soothed me enough to sleep.

I know these are the thoughts I had that night. I can remember, clearly, having them, if not how they tailed off into dreams. But that naive girl seems like another person entirely. I don't recognise myself in her at all.

3

Jonah waited for a moment for Keely to continue, and when she didn't, he said, quietly, 'That must have been more than tough. Losing your mum like that. Losing your home.'

Keely looked back at him flatly, and he thought he detected a flicker of derision in her expression.

'Oh, I moved on, detective chief inspector,' she said. 'Don't you worry. That's what you learn to do. Keep looking forwards, away from the torture that's behind you and into the torture that's ahead.'

It interested Jonah that she called him by his full title. Most of his interviewees forgot it, no matter how many times he repeated it for the camera. He was often called detective, or chief inspector, or sometimes just inspector. Some of them probably got it wrong deliberately, as a mark of disrespect. Keely, on the other hand, somehow managed to make the full rank sound like an insult.

He matched her look, and said, 'But moving on from this stuff doesn't mean it doesn't leave marks.'

Keely leaned back in her seat, and stretched, her arms up behind her head.

'I'd like a break now, I think.' She yawned widely. 'I could use a Starbucks, if you're going.'

Jonah felt like telling her she could have instant coffee and get on with it. But he guessed that a show of power would have no effect on Keely. She didn't seem to be intimidated by him, or by anyone else. And despite the clear urgency of the situation, he had to go gently. To work out the lay of the land.

'Sure.' He rose and gave her as warm a smile as he could. 'Just tell us what you'd like.'

Despite it now being seven p.m. on a Sunday – and a Sunday that she had mostly spent at work – Hanson felt full of energy. The urgency of a missing fourteen-year-old had pushed everything else aside.

It was an unmistakable relief. Not to have to think about the twice-postponed court hearing involving her abusive ex, or about the countless messages he still sent her through anonymous accounts, was something of a lifeline.

She'd hoped to be free of all this by now. After catching Damian on camera throwing a Molotov cocktail through her kitchen window, she'd been able to act at long last. And in acting she had felt in control for the first time in months. In control, and strong.

But things had become a great deal more tense once she had. Her initial assumption that Damian would be charged with vandalism and stalking offences had been, when she thought about it, a little stupid. After assessment within the uniformed division, the case had been passed over to her own colleagues in CID, and had been investigated as Arson with Intent. It was this much more serious crime that Damian was now awaiting trial for, with a few stalking charges thrown in for good measure. There was a chance that, if the prosecution proved he'd intended to kill her in the blaze, he would face life in prison.

It was little wonder, given this, that Damian had decided to continue his campaign of harassment. With the stalking charges of so little weight in comparison, it was worth the risk to get some sort of revenge while he could.

But his incessant disruption to her life bothered her a lot less than it had, and one very strong factor in that had been having Ben Lightman on her side. It had been humiliating to break down in front of him when everything had been at its peak, but it had both unburdened her and given her an ally. She was still profoundly grateful that Ben had taken her side without question.

Unlike her then-boyfriend, in fact. Jason Walker was another DI and worked in the same big, open-plan office. He had been fed a pack of lies about her by Damian and had believed it all without question. It had been hard for Hanson to forgive it, even when Jason had asked her to consider exactly how manipulative her ex was.

While the database was loading, she found herself glancing at where Jason usually sat. It was fortunately a lot further away than it had originally been. Dealing with a break-up with someone on the next desk over would have been agonising.

She hoped that his chair would remain empty until the morning. His constant helpfulness and civility in the aftermath of it all filled her with guilt. She knew he wanted her to try again, even though she'd realised it was impossible. She guessed that Jason thought it was all about trust, when, in fact, it had turned out to be more about what was left when trust was taken away. Jason didn't fascinate her. He didn't even make her laugh all that often. He'd always been more reliable than he was interesting, and that meant there wasn't much left when the reliable side evaporated.

Her screen finished loading, and she opened up Keely's previous police interactions with a bubble of the odd happiness that this job still brought her. It was just her and the evidence for now. Which was just as it should be, she thought.

Keely's children's home was in many ways less depressing than Lightman had been expecting. Before today, he had only ever visited a large home on the fringe of the impoverished Thornhill estate. That had been a brutalist block with small, flimsy-looking windows and yellowing plastic frames. Most of the sparse equipment inside had been broken. The kids there had been universally obnoxious towards him, and he'd taken away a heavy-hearted impression that they were all lost already.

The Lennox girls were in a home of a very different kind, at least at first sight. It was on Cedar Avenue, not far from Lightman's parents' house in Shirley, and was made up of two suburban semis merged into one. The front garden had been converted into a large paved driveway with a few shrubs in circular holes, and one of its slope-roofed porches was clearly given over to storage. It was crammed with equipment, and Lightman could see a miniature football goal and a number of inflatable balls in among the chaos.

Heat radiated up off the paving as Lightman climbed out of his Qashqai. The sun had only just vanished in a dazzling orange display, and evening birdsong drifted from back gardens. It was, Lightman thought, strange to have an underlying sense of desperate urgency on an idyllic September evening. These mismatches happened often in policing, but he felt particularly aware of this one, perhaps because of the age of the missing girl. And because of the blood.

There was a lamp on in the bay window next to the door, and as Lightman rang the bell, he glimpsed a girl curled up on a sofa, reading. This, he thought, was what Nina should have been doing. This, or talking, or watching TV in company. Not languishing somewhere, alone, possibly injured, and probably very frightened.

It was Magda, the manager, who answered the door, her

movements tense and her expression concerned. She was in her early fifties, he guessed. A short, strong-looking woman with a round face and thick, greying blonde hair in an untidy bun.

'Are you the police officer?' she asked him, and then went on, before he could answer, 'I can give you fifteen minutes before I need to start getting the younger ones to bed.'

He followed her down the plain white hall, which had clearly been carved out of the two separate houses by knocking through part of each front room. They passed a big kitchen to the left, where a thirty-something man and a boy of about twelve were elbow-deep in washing-up, and then a games room on the right where three children of a range of ages lounged on bean bags. One of them was absorbed in a rally simulator on an Xbox.

Magda's office was at the furthest end of the house, and was a larger and tidier space than he would have expected. A pair of comfortable chairs sat opposite each other, with a big, shaded lamp to one side of them. There was a view of the very green garden through the window, and seascapes spread over the walls. He suspected that the space doubled as a counselling room.

They rattled through Lightman's initial questions quickly. There were no parents or grandparents, aunts or uncles who might know where Nina was.

'Her mother was an only child, and their grandparents had her when they were quite old,' she said. 'No sign of the father since he ran off thirteen years ago.'

'What about friends?' Lightman asked. 'Are there any children who have moved on from the home, into assisted living? Anyone like that?'

Magda considered for a few minutes. 'That's a more difficult one. I don't really know if any of them would be close enough to take them in. As I think I mentioned, Keely can be quite difficult, though I'm sure she doesn't mean to be.'

Lightman studied her face for a moment, trying to interpret what looked to him like slight embarrassment. 'Did she fall out with any of them? Any big arguments?'

Magda looked more uncomfortable. 'She didn't really. Not here. Some of the others complain from time to time that she's taken their turn or been unkind to them. And I've sometimes had to talk to her about quite harsh things she's said to them.'

'But in the past?' he said, gently. 'Have there been big arguments before?'

'Well, yes,' Magda said, flushing slightly. 'But I don't think you should assume she's a bad person for it. Sometimes people . . . sometimes people just don't get on, for one reason or another.' She put her hands out to the arm of the chair, as if bracing herself. 'But when they were being fostered, with another boy, she beat the boy very badly. It's the main reason the two girls ended up back in care.'

Jonah occupied himself with data gathering while Hanson did a run to Starbucks. He'd told her to buy one for everyone. If Keely was getting expensive coffee, the rest of them should have it too, including the on-call social worker. He'd also asked Hanson to get food to go with it. Jonah had realised long ago that a team working out of hours is infinitely happier when it has a ready supply of carbs and caffeine. He'd handed her the cash to cover it.

A year ago, he might have winced slightly at the expense. But he felt a lot more affluent these days. Since his mother had been taken under the wing of the local church, he no longer had to pay for her to have company several times a week. Michelle was also sharing the bills on his house now that she'd moved back in. She was on full maternity pay from her decent communications role, and had been definite about contributing. So even with lots of baby paraphernalia to buy, Jonah still ended up considerably better off each month.

With food sorted, Jonah's first action was to put a call through to the emergency duty team at Southampton social services. The call handler was pleasant and positive, and promised to get both the Lennox sisters' care records to him within the hour.

Jonah bit down on his frustration. If Nina was seriously injured, a delay of an hour could be disastrous. But it was clear that the call handler now needed to go through her colleagues and get the information sent over, so there was little he could do to hurry it.

After the call, he rang the last member of their team at long last. He'd hoped he might leave Domnall O'Malley to enjoy his weekend. They had other pressing work to do tomorrow, including continuing an arson investigation, and it would have been good to have at least one team member rested and alert. But with no immediate sign of Nina, he needed everyone here.

Domnall was the oldest of his team, a warm, insightful but haphazard man in his late forties who had a whole previous career in the military behind him. That previous career was hard to compute in light of O'Malley's chaotic desk and his eccentric working hours. But Jonah was more than happy for him to work in whatever way suited him. He was brilliant at unlikely connections, and had a charm that disarmed all but the most difficult of witnesses.

'A good evening to you, chief,' O'Malley said on answering. 'I'm assuming I can help you with something.'

'Sorry,' Jonah said. 'Missing teenage girl with a high

possibility of violence. But if you come in, I'll get you a crap dinner to make up for it.'

'Ah, that's pretty tempting,' O'Malley said. 'And I was after sitting around all afternoon, so it's not too brutal. I'll be with you in twenty-five.'

'Thanks, Domnall.'

He felt a little better knowing that he would have his whole team assembled soon. He could feel time draining away, even while he started skim-reading the original missing persons reports from four days before.

It was clear that he had to simultaneously look for pointers as to where Nina was and get the measure of the older Lennox sister. He couldn't just blast in there. There was a risk, and a strong one, that pushing her would result in her refusing to tell them anything.

The missing persons report had been circulated with a flyer, he saw. It had been made for distribution online and around Keely and Nina's area of Southampton. He opened it up, interested to see what they'd included.

Jonah found himself looking at two very different photographs. On the left was Keely Lennox, immediately recognisable despite her hair having been pulled into a high bun, hiding much of its colour. That same direct gaze was there as she stared straight at the lens. She looked, in fact, as though she wanted whoever was taking the photo to shrivel up and die. It was disconcerting to look at for long.

The image on the right was starkly different. Nina was sitting at a café table outdoors, smiling widely at the lens. Her hair was loose and fell in perfect curls that might even have been natural. She was slimmer than Keely, with lean legs and arms and a delicately defined face. There were some resemblances, though. Nina was red-haired and pale-skinned as well, with Keely's rounded cheekbones. But there was none of Keely's flat defiance. Nothing disconcerting. She looked like an ordinary, slightly self-conscious teenager.

Lightman called as he was looking between the two images.

'I'm still at the children's home,' he told Jonah. 'The manager had quite a bit to say.'

The sergeant's tone was as unhurried and neutral as ever as he went through Keely's attack on her former foster brother.

'The manager was given extensive information about it before taking the girls on,' Lightman said. 'She said Keely had felt betrayed by the boy, and had been angry with him.'

'The violence could be significant,' Jonah said, feeling another brick of worry about Nina click into place.

'Yes, though Magda – the manager – impressed on me that most of the kids they take have had some violent episodes,' Lightman said. 'She says there's a big difference between a troubled child momentarily giving in to frustration, and real sadism.'

'I suppose that's fair,' Jonah agreed. Though he wondered, thinking back to Keely's total self-assurance, whether she was the sort of person who even felt strong emotion. 'Was the boy badly hurt?'

'Enough that he needed stitches on his head and his nose setting,' Lightman said. 'She used a tennis racquet.'

Jonah brooded on this for a moment, before asking, 'Have you spoken to anyone else there?'

'I've asked to talk to some of the other kids, but the manager is a little resistant. Possibly for a few reasons.'

'See if you can persuade her,' Jonah said. 'Keely isn't giving up much, and there are things the Lennox sisters could have said to their friends that the staff wouldn't have known.'

He rang off, feeling an increased weight of responsibility. It was quite possible that this previous violent episode was a one-off, as Magda had said. It didn't necessarily mean that Keely was likely to attack anyone else. But there was the blood to account for, and something about the image of Keely with a weapon made his concern for Nina jump upwards.

Lightman eventually persuaded Magda to let him interview Nina's one real friend. She turned out to be the girl he'd glimpsed through the window, and she was still reading on the sofa with her feet tucked up under her by the time he was shown in.

It was hard to judge Samantha's age. The jeans and hoodie could as easily have belonged to a twelve-year-old as to an eighteen-year-old, and her face had a real young-old look to it. Her eyes were wide and a little vulnerable behind her big glasses as they moved over the pages. She barely took up any space, her slight frame dwarfed by the sofa's big, slightly discoloured arms and back.

'The police would like to ask you a few questions, Samantha,' Magda said. 'Just about Nina and Keely.'

The girl only looked up slowly, clearly reluctant to leave her book. She glanced towards a clock on the wall and back, and Lightman felt the need to say, 'It won't take long.'

'It's a long way off bedtime,' Magda said. 'You can have until ten.'

Samantha's sombre expression warmed into a smile. 'OK. Great.'

Lightman gestured for Magda to keep the door open as she left, and perched himself on the arm of the sofa opposite.

'Sorry. I know time to yourself is precious.'

Samantha glanced down at the book, and then put it carefully onto the sofa cushion, face down to keep her place. Lightman twisted to read the cover, and saw it was one of Frances Hardinge's.

'My older sister is obsessed with those books,' he said. 'She's thirty-five and still loves them.'

'They're not children's books, really,' Samantha said, sounding thirty herself. 'They're quite complicated. And quite dark.'

'That's what my sister says,' Lightman agreed. 'She's a Samantha, too,' he added. 'Sammy.'

'I'm normally Sam,' the girl told him. She tugged at her sleeves, and shifted slightly. 'Magda's the only one who says Samantha.'

'Nice to meet you, Sam,' he said.

Sam peered at him, and then asked, 'Are you here about Nina and Keely?'

'Yes. Has anyone explained why?'

'Magda said you'd be coming,' Sam told him. 'She said you might have tracked them down.'

Lightman paused for a moment. It was always a difficult balance, choosing what to say to potential witnesses. He knew that Magda's chief concern, as manager here, was to shield these kids from anxiety about their friends. These kids who had probably already been through the wringer.

He understood it, but without explaining that they were worried about Nina, he doubted that Sam would take his questions seriously.

'Well, we know where Keely is,' he said, in the end. 'She seems fine. But she hasn't told us about Nina, and we really want to find her.'

Sam's eyes sharpened on him. 'Weren't they together?'

'They left together, as far as we know,' Lightman said, neutrally. 'But Keely has now come to the station.'

It was clear that this news hit Sam hard. Lightman could see an odd flush across her cheekbones, and she put a hand out to the arm of the sofa as if she felt a little unsteady.

'I thought they . . . I thought Keely would be with her.'

Lightman watched her for a moment, and then asked, 'You're close to Nina, aren't you?'

Sam shrugged, and shifted. 'We're friends.'

'What's Nina like? Is she a big reader, too?'

Sam nodded, immediately, and made eye contact. 'We share a lot of books.'

'Do you talk about them with her?'

'Yes,' Sam said.

'What about other things?' Lightman asked. 'Like how you're finding it living here?'

Sam shrugged again, but she kept looking at him this time. 'Sometimes.'

'She didn't say anything about running away?' Lightman asked, and then he added, swiftly, 'You aren't in any trouble if she did. There are lots of reasons not to pass that kind of thing on.'

Sam shook her head, but said nothing. Her eyes had slid away, to the cover of her book, but she didn't seem to be looking at it.

'Nina didn't talk to you about it? Or say anything that made you suspect?'

There was a slight pause, and then Sam said, in a very quiet voice, 'I don't know. I thought something . . . was going on. But . . . I didn't think they'd run away or anything.'

Lightman leaned forwards, and said, 'Even if you just had a feeling, it might be useful to tell us why. Something unimportant could give us the clues we need.'

Sam shook her head. 'I don't know.' She paused. 'They were just a bit secretive, I guess.'

Lightman gave her a moment, and then nodded and got to his feet. 'Maybe you can think back over last week, and then let me know if anything strikes you.'

He pulled out one of his cards and gave it to her, and then left her to her book. He walked to his car with an uneasy feeling that Sam had a lot more to say, if only she wanted to say it.

Jonah checked the team's email while he waited for Hanson to return. She'd had to head all the way to the drive-through on the M27 to meet Keely's request for a Starbucks.

He was gratified to see that the Child Abuse Investigation Team had sent through full details of the two cases Keely had been a witness in.

He started with the first summary and skimmed over it to find out who had been involved. Keely had been the one putting forward the complaint, along with her sister. They had accused a Sally and Henry Murray-Watt. They were listed as the Lennox sisters' foster parents.

He had only skim-read the summary by the time Hanson returned, but he had gathered, by then, that the claims were based on harsh punishments and emotional abuse. Claims that the CAIT had found no grounds for.

He broke off at the end of the overall findings and went to bolt down a sandwich. He told Hanson to do the same.

'Eating all together feels a bit too like a friendly picnic, to me,' he said. 'Which isn't the vibe I'm going for.'

Keely then surprised Jonah by thanking the two of them for the food and drink. It wasn't effusive thanks, but it didn't seem sarcastic, either. She set to eating a tuna sandwich with quiet enthusiasm, then wiped her hands and picked up the takeaway latte.

'Is that all OK?' Jonah asked her.

Keely nodded, and drank, before saying, 'I'm ready if you are.'

It almost, almost seemed like a gesture of cooperation.

The social worker started hastily mopping up crumbs from her paper bag, not quite finished with her panini. Jonah gave her a smile and did the introductions for the benefit of the video. And then he said, 'I'd like to ask you something, Keely. It isn't about Nina. It's about Callum.'

Keely became quite still, and her expression became harder.

'Why do you want to ask about him?'

'Because the manager of the children's home explained that your time in foster care had ended because of an altercation between the two of you.'

Keely gave him a very stark look. 'If that's an indication of your investigative ability, I'm not impressed.'

Jonah gave a small smile. 'I'd like to hear what happened.'

She looked towards Hanson, and then back at Jonah. 'First of all, there are files on this stuff. I mean, they're not going to be that much help, but they'd tell you a lot more than that I was thrown out after a fight.' For a moment, Jonah thought Keely might be getting angry, but then she smiled again. 'If you want to know what really happened with Callum, you're going to have to let me tell it once I get there.'

Jonah nodded. 'But perhaps in order to be listened to, you need to reassure us that Nina is actually all right.'

Keely's gaze didn't move for a very long few seconds. It was impressive, Jonah thought, how still and unresponsive she managed to be.

And then she said, 'Nina will be safe for the next few hours. I made sure of it.' She smiled very slightly. 'And before you ask any specifics, nobody's going to bleed to death. And even in weather like this, nobody dies of dehydration for a good two days. I'm not saying it won't be uncomfortable, but I think a little discomfort is good for the soul sometimes, don't you?'

She's enjoying this, Jonah thought. *Having fun with all of us.*

And as he swallowed down a gulp of coffee as casually as possible, he felt a trickle of cold run up and down his spine.

4

For almost a year, we waited desperately for a foster family. Anything, we thought, would be better than where we were. Better than the tattiness, the taunting, the fights between the other kids, and the irritable response we had from the staff to any questions or requests. On one occasion, I saw a keyworker laughing when a boy called Ninny a 'ginger whore'. I didn't know what a 'whore' was at that point, but I knew it was bad.

School was even worse. After we finished the term, we were taken from our lovely little New Forest school and thrown into the ugly, run-down Gale Park Primary. Which wouldn't have been so bad if the staff hadn't clearly given up on the pupils who went there. The teachers seemed to limp from lesson to lesson, happy if they got through one with nobody throwing a chair across the room or bashing another kid's head onto a table.

It was absolute torture for Ninny. She cried every morning before going, and would arrive to meet me afterwards wide-eyed and white-faced. I knew she wasn't eating at lunch. After hunting for her days in a row, I had eventually found her during her year's allocated time to eat, wandering around the playground boundary with her hands in her coat pockets. It had broken my heart to watch her, and to see that nobody came to talk to her once they'd all spilled out from the lunch hall.

The only thing that made any of it bearable was the arrival of a new keyworker eight months in. A French-born but very English man named Jared, who I now realise must have been no more than eighteen. Barely an adult.

He was actually kind to my sister. Not brusque or stiff or apathetic like the others. He would make time to play with her, and would gently insist that other kids included her.

It was wonderful to see the effect it had on her, his kindness. Her cheeks would start to dimple the moment she saw him, and it was as if she'd pulled the persona of the sunny, appealing girl back on, out of storage. Which in itself made things easier for her with the other staff members and kids.

The only thing it didn't solve was school, where she was the subject of constant bullying. There was a terrible month when I honestly thought she might starve herself to death. It started when she wet herself one night and two of the staff let on to some of the kids. It meant everyone at school found out, too, because we were all there at Gale Park together. She became known as 'Pissy' for that whole month, and in spite of Jared's efforts at cheering her up, it almost broke her.

As it turned out, there were worse things than Henley Road Children's Home, and even than the god-awful Gate Park Primary.

Terrible places don't always look terrible. Another thing I've learned. They can look beautiful. Lush. Seductive.

In our case, they looked like a gorgeous house back in the New Forest and a couple called Sally and Henry Murray-Watt.

There were a lot of great visuals from the start. We were treated to a rush of them when we visited in early winter. The big, perfectly kept house; the sculpted garden; the huge TV; the farmhouse kitchen; and Sally Murray-Watt herself.

I remember her crouching down, soon after we'd arrived, to ask anxious little Ninny if she'd like some banana cake.

Sally's warmth and trace of shyness made her immediately appealing, and the rush of floral scent she wore conjured up immediate memories of Mummy. It all made me ache to be cuddled, and I reached out a hand to touch her trousers, rubbing the linen between my fingers and remembering the texture from our other life.

I found myself searching out all the similarities between Sally and our mother while she introduced herself. Her height. Her clothes. She had a squareness to her face that was even similar, though there were differences, too. Her blonde hair. Her slight squint. Her thinner build. They seemed insignificant, those points of contrast. She represented *motherness*, and I wanted to have her as mine.

I wasn't so sure about her husband. Henry Murray-Watt was a tall, very rectangular, slightly stooped man who didn't seem to like looking at any of us. As we stood in front of him to be introduced by our social worker, he gave a funny smile and then looked somewhere else while the conversation went on.

Our social worker, Mary, left for a while to give us some space. Sally set us up with some toys in the large, lushly furnished living room, and then vanished somewhere into the house with a breezy, 'I'll be right back.'

I approached the toys carefully, conscious of Henry being in the room. He sat in an armchair and picked up a book, making no effort to speak to us now that Sally and Mary had gone.

Ninny was less worried by him. She began to pull toys out of the box, and when she gave a gasp of excitement about a doll, I remember clearly the disgusted noise Henry made. As if we were getting in the way of what he wanted to do.

It unsettled me. I wanted to believe that everything was perfect, and that noise cut through it.

I felt definite relief when Sally came back, but I was startled to see that she wasn't alone. She had a boy with her. He was tall and lean, with side-parted hair, and he carried resentment like a black cloud above him. It seeped through the smart chinos and shirt he wore, and I was immediately certain that he was really a scruffy jeans and T-shirt boy. The sort of boy who set things on fire. A wild, unpredictable thing.

'Callum, this is Keely, and that's Nina,' Sally said, in a gentle voice. 'They might come and stay, too, and give you some company.'

Callum said nothing. He looked at us from under his side-swept fringe, and somehow the strength of his dislike seemed to settle on me. In the face of Callum's silence, Sally went on, 'Callum's about to turn twelve, girls. Nearly grown-up, hey?'

I could have done what Ninny did, and smiled at him. Told him it was nice to meet him. But I found myself staring back instead, as aggressively as he was staring at me.

Henry rose swiftly, and told Callum to try a civilised greeting, and then left the room without waiting for an answer.

'It's nice to meet you,' Callum said, in a voice as grudging and furious as possible.

Sally, seemingly oblivious, said, 'I think you'll get on really well as a three.'

A few minutes later, she opened the door into the garden so Ninny could try the swing set. I moved to the window to watch them, happy to stand back and enjoy my sister's delight. She glowed with it. It was so clear that she was happier with Sally than she had been since our mummy died. Happier, even, than she was when Jared goofed around with her.

Callum came to stand next to me, bringing with him a

peppery aroma and the sound of stiff fabric brushing against itself. I could feel the hairs standing up on my arms, but I didn't want to show him that I was afraid of him. I'd learned enough in the last six months to understand that showing fear would set the tone for everything.

There was a long silence in the room, while Ninny chattered away out in the garden about the swings we'd once had at home. And then Callum said, 'You'd better tell them you hate it here. Tell them you hate it, or you'll regret it.'

I felt unease turn into crushing disappointment. If Callum hated us, we couldn't be happy here, could we?

But maybe, I thought, he just hated *me*. I looked at Ninny, who was now laughing as Sally pushed her backwards and forwards on the swing, and I decided it might be all right. I was strong enough. It didn't matter that he was older, or bigger. I was strong.

'I'll tell them exactly what I want to,' I said.

I turned to face him, refusing to back away even though he was uncomfortably close. Close enough for me to feel the warmth coming off him. To see the way his jaw hardened in anger.

'What you want doesn't matter,' he said.

When the social worker picked us back up, I told her how much I'd love to live there. So I suppose everything that happened was my fault, in a way.

The first few days in our new foster home felt like paradise. Or as close as I've ever come to it. To spend time with Sally was almost as good as having our mummy back. Except now we really knew to be grateful for it. For every cuddle, and every conversation. For being tucked into bed at night, and for having our own rooms with our own comfortable beds. Our own toys.

There were a few niggles even then. I remember Callum glowering at me from the doorway of my room on that very first day. He watched in silence while I unpacked my clothes into the pretty yellow chest of drawers. I'd been enjoying every part of the process up until then, from the smooth slide of the drawers to the feel of the painted wood under my hands. The scent of varnish inside. The satisfaction of putting everything into the right order.

But I could feel the anger radiating off Callum, and the sour note creeping into my perfect day irritated me.

'Why are you standing there?' I asked him, getting to my feet and staring back at him.

'I told you not to come,' Callum said, darkly. Being an older boy, and taller, I supposed he thought he was intimidating.

'But you don't know us,' I replied, folding my arms. 'You'll get to like us, if you stop being mean and talk to us.'

Callum made a disgusted sound. 'I didn't say anything about liking you.'

'No, you just don't want us here.'

Callum went silent for a little while, and turned his head away, but he didn't go anywhere. He stared at the doorway as if he hated it, and I was about to go back to my unpacking when he said, 'For your own good. I said it for your own good.' And then he walked away.

If I hadn't already been angry with him, or if I'd been a few years older, I might have thought a bit more intelligently about what he'd said. But instead, I felt like he was ruining everything. Our dream new home. Our shiny, fresh lives. And I hated him for it.

5

Keely had come to a stop, and Jonah sensed that she was waiting for some kind of response. Some acknowledgement that what she was saying was significant. Perhaps a round of applause for her excellent memory.

It was frustrating when she'd told them so little. Even more so that she was so clearly building up the Murray-Watts as the big bad guys, when an investigation into them had concluded otherwise.

He was searching for the right tone when Hanson said, 'So Callum didn't want the two of you there.'

'Well,' Keely said, looking at her thoughtfully, 'I'd say he was fairly mixed up about the situation. Despite not wanting us there, we offered fresh meat.'

'So he was a bully?' Hanson asked.

Keely gave her one of those very level looks. 'He was a very unhappy eleven-year-old boy. Unhappy eleven-year-old boys tend to lash out.'

This answer genuinely surprised Jonah. It was abundantly clear that Keely was sharp. Perceptive. Piercingly so. But he hadn't expected her to show empathy. Particularly not towards someone who seemed likely to have victimised her.

'Have you struggled with that, too, Keely?' Hanson asked, gently. 'With the effects of unhappiness?'

Keely gave a long sigh. 'I don't really struggle with it, no. I made peace pretty quickly with the darker side of myself. I'm a little smarter than Callum is.'

Jonah tried not to give in to frustration. The speed with

which she had undermined a momentary gleam of humanity was infuriating. She was immediately back to callous arrogance. It almost seemed deliberate.

But frustration wasn't going to help him. He needed to cut through the coldness, if he could. To touch the more human side of Keely, which had clearly been there once, and persuade her to tell them where her sister was.

'This stuff happens to a lot of people,' Jonah said, quietly. 'And it unquestionably leaves a mark. We see the outcome of that quite often. Nobody gets away untouched, but I think you have more power to move on than you think. And to make choices. To decide whether to be what they made you or not.'

Keely gave a very slow smile, one that made Jonah feel cold.

'You know, I think you might actually be right,' she said. 'I did have a choice. And I wouldn't be sitting here if I hadn't chosen, would I?'

'What choice was that?' Jonah asked.

'Really?' She laughed. 'I thought you'd kept up a little bit better than that.'

Jonah wondered, briefly, if this was how most parents with teenagers felt. Helplessly furious in the face of a total disregard for you and everyone else, all from someone with almost no life experience. Though even the worst teenagers he'd interviewed hadn't managed Keely's level of condescension.

There was a tap on the interview-room door. Lightman appeared round it, and Jonah experienced a rush of relief at being able to stand up and walk away from Keely Lennox for a few minutes.

Lightman waited until they were in the corridor outside with the door closed before saying quietly, 'Her care record has come in, and I've dived into it.' He glanced towards the door. 'It might be worth talking it through before you go back in.'

Ben's expression was, of course, calm. But if there was enough in the report for him to interrupt the interview, then Jonah knew he needed to hear it.

He ducked back inside to call a brief break, and to bring Hanson back out.

'The reason for Keely's removal from her foster home was a little more complex than we thought,' Lightman told them.

The group now included Domnall O'Malley, who was making his way through a blueberry muffin with evident satisfaction. O'Malley often admitted that eating self-indulgent food was his favourite part of policing. He balanced it out with a fair amount of walking, both recreationally and while working, and so was comfortably padded rather than huge, but Jonah knew that O'Malley's partner worried about his health.

'On the day of Callum's attack, social services got a tearful call from Keely Lennox to say that all three kids needed to be rescued. She said that their foster parents, the Murray-Watts, were abusing them, and had now beaten Callum badly. She said she was frightened for all of them.'

Jonah looked at him blankly. 'Keely said her *foster parents* had done it?'

'Yes, and social services kicked into immediate action. They brought in the police and arrived at the house to find Callum locked in his room. The Murray-Watts claimed to be mystified over how it had happened, but found the key and let him out. He looked in a bad way, and he backed up the story that it had been the Murray-Watts, initially.'

'But only initially?' O'Malley asked, screwing up his muffin wrapper and throwing it into a nearby bin.

'For the first few minutes,' Lightman agreed. 'When they brought Callum downstairs, Sally Murray-Watt spoke kindly to him, and Callum Taylor then broke down and admitted that Keely had beaten him up, not his foster family.'

'Wow, OK,' Hanson said, sitting up in her chair. 'And he stood by that later?' At Lightman's nod, she went on, 'Did the officers give him an opportunity to talk to them alone?'

'They spoke to him at the hospital alongside a social worker, and again at a children's refuge, where he was taken for the night,' Lightman told her. 'The three of them were given a few nights in a refuge, and a DI from the Child Abuse Investigation Team interviewed Callum separately with his social worker present. Callum said he'd been doing what the girls wanted, and was sorry he'd lied at first. When they asked why the girls had told him to lie, he said it was because they were very unhappy living with the Murray-Watts and wanted to be moved.'

'Did the couple get interviewed too?' Jonah asked.

'Yes, the girls' social worker visited with one of the CAIT constables.' Lightman glanced over at his screen. 'He reported that the Murray-Watts seemed to care about the children. But I'd like to look at the whole thing in more detail. The social care report doesn't have a great deal of information on the abuse team's procedures after the initial interviews. I think it's worth looking at the full investigation.'

'The Murray-Watts are the people who want to adopt Nina, aren't they?' Hanson asked, swinging slowly back and forth in her chair. 'And Nina seemed more than happy to go there. Maybe she had regrets about what she said before, and has been trying to get away from Keely.'

'Do we think Nina could have been directly in touch with the Murray-Watts after leaving?' O'Malley asked. 'Trying to reforge a relationship there? It'd be worth talking to them directly, I'd say.'

'I wouldn't want to assume that Keely and Nina's original allegations were false,' Lightman interjected. 'They wouldn't be the first kids to be let down by a failure to prosecute. It's also possible that the two girls lied to get away because only one of the household was violent towards them. Henry Murray-Watt alone. Or possibly even Callum Taylor.'

'I guess there are different forms of abuse, too,' Hanson said, thoughtfully.

It was all of it, Jonah thought, decidedly muddy. But it was part of their remit to look into it, while the kidnap squad did their thing. All of it had some bearing on Keely's mindset, and as hard as it might be to establish whether or not abuse had taken place, it would be enormously helpful for them to know.

At the same time, his team needed to keep sight of the places Keely and her sister were associated with. It was hard to know for sure, but he suspected that Keely would have chosen to hide her sister in a place of significance. The dilemma for Jonah was deciding how much to focus on the past, and how much to look at what Keely was saying now.

'OK,' he said, coming to an initial decision. 'Juliette and Ben, I'd like you looking at the girls' past history. Talk to the foster family, and go through those care reports and the investigations from the CAIT side. There was a second case where Keely was a witness, wasn't there? Pull all the files and go through them.' He paused for a moment. 'We're still looking for significant places, so don't lose track of that. But we also want whatever you think might help give us insight into Keely's thought processes. O'Malley, why don't you head in with me? Give Keely a little of the kind uncle effect.'

'Sure,' O'Malley agreed. 'I'm good for that.'

'You're sure you don't want to try the heartbreakingly handsome young sergeant effect instead?' Hanson asked, and grinned at Lightman.

'You can eff off,' Lightman said, good-naturedly.

'I'm saving Ben up,' Jonah said, rising. 'For when I decide to go for the jugular and there's a kind, attractive officer for her to tell everything to.'

'Can you do "kind", do you think?' O'Malley asked Lightman.

Lightman considered. 'Probably. But I'd better practise in the mirror for a bit.'

'This is Detective Sergeant Domnall O'Malley,' Jonah told Keely, as they re-entered the interview suite. 'He's going to come and chat things through for the next while.'

'Ooh, a promotion,' Keely said, with a mocking smile. 'What happened to your constable? Couldn't she hack the pace?'

O'Malley laughed, easily. 'She's a busy woman. I, on the other hand, have plenty of free time, and I love a gentle Sunday-evening reminiscence.'

Keely looked uncertain for a moment. It was clear that she wasn't sure how to take O'Malley's humour. While Jonah had intended to make her feel more comfortable, confusion was a potentially interesting effect.

Thinking of Keely's upbringing, he wondered whether gentle teasing had simply not been a feature of it. If what she'd said was true, then bullying had been commonplace, but that was a different thing entirely. Perhaps, as much as she liked to give out mocking humour, she had little idea of how to take it.

Jonah decided to start straight in with his questions before Keely had a chance to get comfortable again.

'We've had your case notes through from the office of social care,' he said. 'I'd like to know why you claimed that your foster family had beaten Callum Taylor up.'

Keely shifted, and then slowly looked back at him with one of her signature flat stares. 'Why do you think I told them that?'

'For the laugh?' O'Malley tried. It seemed that the sergeant had clocked her discomfort too and had decided to prod it. Thank goodness, Jonah thought, for having a smart team of officers around him.

Keely gave him a quick, uncertain look. She looked as though she was considering some kind of reply, when O'Malley carried on, 'Or because it was a way of demonstrating some control over all of them?'

Keely sounded almost frustrated as she replied, 'Or, in fact, because it was true. The simplest solution is generally the right one.'

O'Malley tilted his head. 'Well, actually, the simplest solution is that you girls were telling fairy stories. Callum himself said you were the one who beat him up. Why would he lie about that?'

Keely made a noise that sounded almost like a snort. 'Ah, yes. Why would a troubled young man who was himself a victim of abuse lie about it?'

O'Malley gave a slight shrug, as though he wasn't much convinced, but was allowing her the benefit of the doubt. 'Your social worker said they seemed to care about you. Your foster parents, I mean.'

'They cared? Yes, they did care,' Keely said, and it seemed

as though she might actually be angry. Jonah wondered why this was getting to her when everything else had failed to. Was it O'Malley's cheerfully mocking tone? Or was it simply that Keely disliked someone else being in control of her story?

'They cared an awful lot. Just not about us. What they cared about was how they looked to social services when they were suddenly under scrutiny.' She gave a twisted little smile. 'Wouldn't you pretend to care, under those circumstances?'

She stared at O'Malley, fiercely. But he shot back, 'Like you pretended to care about your sister?'

Keely looked away, and Jonah had the keen sense that she was getting herself back under control. 'There are some things you don't get to choose in life,' she said, after a moment. Her voice had returned to its flat, slightly scathing tone. She looked up at him. 'And one of those things is your family.'

Hanson struggled, at first, to concentrate fully on the case notes. They were a series of individual reports provided by Keely's various social workers. They weren't always in a logical order, and some of them were no more than a few lines long. Others were lengthy and involved, and sometimes seemed entirely without a point. They documented illnesses. Arguments. Complaints in various directions. Changes of keyworker.

She skimmed through them until she found the batch of files from 2011. The ones that referred to the incident with Callum Taylor.

She began to read a transcript of a recorded interview between Keely and Mark Slatterworth, the girls' social worker. Within seconds, she was suddenly having no trouble concentrating at all.

MARK SLATTERWORTH: I wanted to talk to you about Callum's injuries. Callum is very insistent that you were the one who hurt him.

KEELY LENNOX: Of course he is.

MS: Is that because you were the one who attacked him? You won't be in any trouble for it, Keely. We just need to know what really happened.

KL: [REMAINS SILENT]

MS: It's honestly all right to tell the truth. Whatever's happened, we need to get to the bottom of it. And with Callum saying one thing, and you another, it's hard to know what we should be doing about it.

KL: All right. I did it.

MS: Why was that? Were you angry with him?

KL: No. I don't get angry.

MS: But you hit him quite hard.

KL: I had to, or his injuries wouldn't have been serious enough for you to take us away.

Hanson could well imagine the cold factuality of Keely's statement. The lack of emotion. It sent a little trickle of cold down her back.

MS: You wanted to be taken away?

KL: Yes.

MS: Why didn't you just tell me at one of our meet-ups that you weren't happy?

KL: Because I was afraid that you wouldn't believe me, and that the Murray-Watts would punish me for telling you the truth.

MS: But we're here to protect you. You can talk to us about your worries, and we'll take them seriously. We always will.

KL: Really? I mean, you don't believe me now, do you?

Hanson could well imagine the reaction of the social worker. The awkwardness. The feeling of being put on the back foot. She was certain Keely had been good at it, even three years ago, at the age of thirteen.

MS: I just want to hear from you about what happened. Can you tell me what led you to this? What was it that made you so unhappy at Sally and Henry's?

KL: [PAUSE] They aren't nice people. Not nice people at all. I thought they were at first, but then they started to give us punishments, for tiny things. Like being too noisy or too messy. Not eating enough. Eating too much.

MS: Punish you how?

KL: It depended on how they were feeling. Sometimes it would be a harsh remark. Telling us we were stupid, or ugly. But it got worse, gradually. They would deny us food if we'd been what they called cheeky, or clumsy, or – anything, really. Then they started taking me – us – down to the cellar. They'd make me – or Nina, or Callum – put a blindfold on. And then Mr Murray-Watt – Henry – would whip us. And then they'd lock us down there.

MS: In the cellar?

KL: Yes. There was nowhere to sleep except a mattress on the floor. And there were spiders, and rats, and cock-roaches. You could beg and scream to be let out, but they would still leave you there. In fact, I learned not to scream, because they seemed to relent earlier if you didn't.

Hanson could feel her forehead tightening as she read. It sounded convincing. Realistic. The work of genuinely con-trolling people.

Lightman had said that the CAIT had decided the accusations were baseless. Had there been no truth to them, or had the investigation failed to prove it?

MS: They both did this to you?
KL: Yes. Well . . . Henry did the worst of it. And he would tell Sally what to do. She would just send us to our rooms if we'd been bad, and then wait for Henry to decide. Sometimes she wouldn't tell him. I think sometimes she felt sorry for us.

And that, Hanson thought, was another resoundingly convincing part of it.

After Damian, she'd spent hours researching how abuse worked on a partner, in an effort to understand how she'd let it happen. She'd dug up articles and read messages in forums, and many of those accounts had included people manipulated into actively participating. Mothers or occasionally fathers who had been gaslighted to the point where they would abuse their own children for the sake of their partners.

She finished reading, took a very large breath, and then opened up Nina Lennox's account. Had Nina disagreed? Is that what had happened?

MARK SLATTERWORTH: Tell me what life is like with Sally and Henry.
NINA LENNOX: It's not great. They aren't nice people.
MS: Can you tell me what you mean by that?
NL: They like to punish us. Sometimes it's just a harsh remark. Telling us we're stupid, or ugly. But it's got worse gradually . . .

Hanson stopped there, her mind feeling like it was spinning uselessly. She looked back at Keely's account.

But it gradually got worse . . .

The two sisters had said the same. But they hadn't just given the same information. They'd used almost the same words.

They rehearsed it, Hanson thought, feeling a rush of something close to anger. *Keely was controlling everything Nina said.*

6

My relationship with Callum didn't improve over the next few days. I found myself responding to his presence with fury, and he seemed to feel exactly the same. I could tell that we both itched with it whenever we were around each other, but it was one of those irritations that needs to be sought out. To be scratched, over and over again.

I remember getting dressed early on the third morning just to go out and watch him kick a ball around the garden, unable to ignore him and find my own occupation. He was doing keepy-uppies and I grew more and more irritated the longer he went without dropping it.

Eventually, of course, the ball went out of his control. It shot towards me. I put a foot out to stop it, and then bent to pick it up.

'Why don't you try?' he asked, and I knew he wanted me to fail at it.

'Not today,' I said, and kicked it back towards him.

It wasn't a good kick. It went hard, straight across the lawn, and into an evergreen clematis that was growing up the back wall.

'Not at the bloody flower beds!' Callum said, chasing after it and retrieving it.

'I didn't mean to,' I said, my cheeks warm.

'Don't kick it so hard if you can't control it,' he said, his expression furious.

I expected him to ignore me after that, but instead, after a moment, he rolled the ball towards me.

'Gently,' he said.

I did as he said, that time, and Callum was able to run for it and kick it just as gently back. This went on for a little while, until he said, 'We should get your sister to play, too. She's quite good at football.'

I don't quite remember why this angered me so much, but the next kick I gave was deliberately hard. Hard enough to hurt my foot.

The ball lifted this time and sailed straight over the side wall and into the old allotments next door.

I stood watching in defiance as Callum turned to follow it with his eyes, and then turned back to me in fury. 'It's going to be bloody lost,' he said. 'What's wrong with you?'

I turned to stalk away, furious with him, stung by guilt, and wondering why he couldn't just try to be nice.

He was different, however, with Ninny. He would talk to her normally, and show her occasional kindness, like reaching up to get cups out of the cupboard for her when Sally wasn't around to help, or showing her his tamagotchi, which she fell in love with immediately.

But the kindness grated on me. She was *my* sister, not his, and he had no right to try and console her.

And there was, of course, pure jealousy, too. The kind that I didn't want to acknowledge at the time. The kind that asked in fury why he seemed to like her better.

Watching the two of them in their burgeoning affection for each other took over from simply hating Callum. It became my favourite, most-hated occupation.

All I consciously saw at first was him intruding on our lives. Chiselling away at the bonds between us and trying to steal some of her love from me. But gradually, Ninny's actions started to have an effect, too.

There is one occurrence between them that I remember keenly. It was a milestone for me, because I felt a surge of anger at Ninny, too. And anger was something I had never felt towards my sister.

Sally had offered to walk the neighbour's dog for her, a huffy little Scottish terrier who made the three of us laugh with his mood swings. I could see the way our neighbour, a woman who seemed impossibly old to me, thanked and praised Sally profusely as she handed the lead over. I felt proud to be Sally's foster daughter just then. It was clear how kind and well liked Sally was.

We all climbed into the Land Rover, and Sally drove us to the opposite end of the village, where the old allotments lay. The dog spent most of the journey barking and trying to jump out of the boot, and Sally shook her head over the noise but never told him off.

We climbed out, all of us in wellies and winter coats though the sun had come out. The allotments were full of long, dried grass that had somehow clung on in the cold, with a deep rutted track vanishing into them. Off to one side was a little stand of bushes clustered around a few taller, overgrown trees.

'You can play in the trees for a little while, if you like,' Sally said. 'I'll just walk the dog up and down.'

Ninny was off almost before Sally could finish, hurtling into the bushes and calling that we should make a den. Callum and I followed more cautiously, neither of us speaking to the other but neither of us moving away from the other, either.

It took Ninny less than two minutes to get herself into trouble. By the time we emerged from the almost leafless bushes into a little clearing, she was already calling for help.

I felt my heart squeeze in my chest as I saw her, a good ten feet up in an old apple tree.

'I'm stuck,' she said, and her voice sounded on the edge of tears. 'It's hurting my foot.'

I could see the problem immediately. Her welly had become wedged in a deep V-shape between a branch and the trunk, and her weight was only pushing it further in.

It had always been my job to rescue Ninny. But before I could even think about what to do, Callum had swung himself into the tree, pushed up off a lower branch and got a hand onto her boot.

He tugged, hard, and the boot came free. But the force of it unbalanced Ninny, and my heart felt like it had stopped altogether as her other foot slipped off the branch.

For a moment, she was hanging from her arms, legs flailing wildly. But Callum just reached out and grabbed her around the waist. He pulled her back onto the branch, and then held on to her while she found her footing properly and relaxed enough to gradually release her grip and start to climb down.

Watching them, I felt a sick worry begin to grow in me. The way Ninny looked at Callum afterwards, her smile shy and grateful, made me dizzy, and then furious.

I turned and walked away from them, running to catch up with Sally, and leaving them to do whatever they wanted.

I don't need them, I told myself.

It wasn't really true. Not back then.

There was only one other thing that made me worry about our new home, and that was Henry Murray-Watt's oddness. He was still distant. Cold.

Sally explained, early on, that Henry found new people hard, but that didn't mean he didn't love us all. She also told us that Henry liked structure and routine and order, so we should do our best not to disrupt that when he was there. We should try not to make a mess, or be too loud when he was in the house. And he was working hard each day to support all of us, she said. So we should support him and show our gratitude.

But we were largely shielded from Henry for the first fortnight. It was Sally who drove us to school for our last few days at the awful Gale Park, and who played with us once we were home. She was the one who made us dinner, and who tucked us into bed. We only saw Henry once each day, at the dinner table. And while Sally insisted on perfect table manners in front of him, and no talking unless we were talked to, it was the only really restrained part of our day.

But then our second Saturday in the house arrived, the Saturday before Christmas. Sally fed us breakfast and then asked us to occupy ourselves quietly for a while in our rooms.

'Henry has some important work to do,' she said, in a very quiet voice. It was almost as though speaking in a normal voice would disturb him, and I felt a squeeze of worry. I'd promised Ninny a game with her dolls, and that usually meant putting on silly voices that made her laugh.

I turned to Ninny once we were in her room, and put my hand on top of the toy box to stop her immediately removing the dolls.

'We need to be really quiet today, Ninny,' I told her. 'We need Henry to like us too, don't we?'

Ninny gave me a wide-eyed look, and glanced down at the box as if I were denying her food, or oxygen.

I glanced towards the door, and went to close it. 'We could pretend we have to keep quiet because of

pirates,' I said, unable to deny her the fun of our promised game.

Ninny didn't look keen. She wasn't really into pirates. But
to my relief, she managed to keep her voice down. She even
laughed quietly. At one point we heard footsteps coming
upstairs, and the two of us froze. But they moved off
towards the other end of the landing, and we heard Henry
talking to Callum. He wasn't coming to tell us off.

Henry went out a short while later, and Sally came to
fetch us downstairs, her smile broader now and her movements more lively.

'Henry bought a Christmas tree last night and he's put it
in the living room. Do you think you can decorate it for
me?' she asked.

It gave me a sudden, sick feeling. The Christmas tree had
always been a huge event back when our mummy had been
alive.

We were going to do it without her. We were going to do
Christmas without her.

Ninny didn't seem to feel any of this. She beamed at
Sally. 'I'd love to,' she said.

Sally looked at me, expectantly.

'OK,' I said.

I saw Sally's expression. The slight drop of disappointment. I tried smiling, and that seemed to help a bit.

I made a point of saying to Ninny, 'This is going to be
fun,' as Sally left us with boxes of silver, red and gold deco-
rations. But they weren't like the ones we'd had at home.
There were no purples and pinks and blues. No homemade
ones made out of baked dough. I could only half pretend to
enjoy it.

It was only halfway through that I wondered why Callum
wasn't helping us. I imagined him sneering at anything

Christmassy, as if he was too good for it, and it made me angry just thinking about it. But Callum didn't appear at lunchtime, either. And when Sally said nothing about it, I eventually asked where he was.

She had just returned to the table with three freshly baked mince pies, and she put them down with a slightly sad smile.

'Callum won't be joining us for lunch,' she said, her voice full of regret. 'He was extremely rude to Henry this morning, and is now in his room, thinking about what he's done.'

I remember the shock of that. Did he not want his lunch? Or had Sally and Henry decided that he didn't deserve any?

I looked at the mince pies, which were filling the room with a smell that meant Christmas and laughter and self-indulgence. Sally had returned to the table with a jug of cream, and I could already imagine the hot and cold gorgeousness of them together.

I felt a momentary pang of guilt. Surely Callum wanted a mince pie.

But then I wondered what he'd said to Henry, and exactly how rude he'd been. Maybe he'd sworn at him, or tried to hit him. Maybe he'd deserved it.

Sally put the jug of cream onto the table with a gentle clack and gave me a warm smile. 'I'm so glad you girls are here now. It's going to really help him having such good examples to follow. You'll make sure you're good, won't you?'

I nodded and sat up straighter. I wanted her to think I was different from Callum. And I could see Ninny doing the same. Dissociating herself. Signalling that *she* was good.

I made a point of thanking Sally for the delicious lunch, and then asked to get down from the table. Her eyes crinkled as she smiled at me, and she drew me into a hug once my feet were on the floor. 'What wonderful manners you two have. Why don't you watch a Disney film together while I get things tidied up?'

I considered saying that I wanted to go outside after a whole morning spent indoors. That what I really wanted to do was to play in the garden. But the film was obviously being packaged as a treat, so I nodded and thanked her. I didn't want to be rude, like Callum.

She tucked us up on the sofa and put *Hercules* on, which I hadn't watched before and actually started out enjoying. But my attention wandered. I kept finding myself thinking about Callum, shut up in his room and hungry.

There was satisfaction in those thoughts. Callum was a bully. He was mean to me. He deserved it.

Yet there was unease, too. I couldn't quite think of him going without food and not feel sorry for him. And alongside all that, I felt a burning desire to know whether he was sulking, or crying, or reacting in any other emotional way.

Midway through the film, I told Ninny I was going to the toilet, and I slipped out of the room. I listened to make sure Sally was busy in the laundry room before I crept upstairs quietly. I found myself nervous of being found up here, though I wasn't quite sure why. She'd never told us we couldn't go to our rooms, or anywhere else upstairs. Only Henry's study was out of bounds.

But my heart was still pounding as I tried to walk silently along the landing towards Callum's room. It seemed to take hours to get there.

I paused outside the closed door, and suddenly wondered what I was going to do. Was I going to knock? To go in?

There were no sounds coming from the room. Callum wasn't crying right now, or shouting or complaining. There were no noises to suggest he was playing with any of his toys, either. Maybe, I thought, he'd gone to sleep.

I considered retreating downstairs, but for some reason that wasn't enough. I wanted to see his face. Maybe to feel satisfied that he was sorry for what he'd done.

So I turned the handle very slowly, and pushed the door open.

It swung back more easily than I'd been expecting. I flinched, expecting Callum to shout at me. But as the door opened further and further, it became clear that Callum wasn't there. His bed was perfectly made, his toys all tidied away, and the room absolutely empty.

It disturbed me in a way I couldn't quite explain. Even now, I can't say whether part of me suspected the truth at that point. I remember the sudden acceleration of my heart, anyway. The tipping feeling.

I closed the door in a rush and hurried downstairs, anxious to be back on the sofa with Ninny.

It was only later, when I knew Sally was running on her treadmill out in the garage, that I risked looking further for Callum. But I failed to find him. I checked every room in that house except for Henry's study, and Callum was nowhere. It was as if he'd vanished.

7

Keely had paused again. It was clear that she saw herself as a storyteller from the way she rounded off each part and then waited for a reaction. The whole thing felt, to Jonah, strictly stage-managed, and that made it harder to listen to.

He thought he knew where her story was going. She was leading them towards the Murray-Watts as abusers, just like she'd told her social worker. And if he had needed to tell a story of abuse, this is how he would have started: with unsettling suggestions of something wrong.

Despite what the CAIT had decided, Jonah knew the story might just be true. Keely might be here to describe the abuse that had happened to the three of them. She might have threatened Nina in order to be listened to.

How far might someone go to be believed? he thought. *Far enough to harm their own sister?*

It was hard to know what to ask her next. Keely clearly expected questions, but Jonah found himself unwilling to ask the obvious ones. About whether she'd found Callum in the end, and what had been happening to him. Whether Henry Murray-Watt had genuinely become violent.

They seemed the wrong questions. However much Keely might want to be heard, the key to everything was still how she felt about Nina, and whether she would let them find her.

'It seems like you had a good relationship with your sister at that age,' Jonah said, having decided what line he wanted to take.

Keely gave a shrug. 'There was no reason to dislike her back then.'

'But later?' Jonah asked, with as little judgement as possible.

Keely gave a small smile. 'I came across a lot of reasons to dislike her, pretty soon after those events.'

'How do you feel about her now?'

Keely's eyes moved towards O'Malley, and she shook her head slightly. 'He loves to jump ahead, doesn't he? When what he should be doing is listening, actually listening, and realising that I'm giving him all the answers, one at a time.'

Jonah watched her, trying to assess the truth of this statement.

Keely seemed to be giving them very little on the surface of it. A story from years ago that bore no apparent relevance to what had happened to Nina this week.

But was Keely actually doing more than it seemed? She was clearly leading them towards Henry Murray-Watt now, and she had already told them that there were three men who had taken her life apart. Was all this some kind of elaborate game to bring them all to justice via a series of clues? And if so, could he afford to wait to hear about all three?

'Maybe you need to make it a little easier for him,' O'Malley said, suddenly, with a cheerful shrug. 'Help the poor man out.'

Keely gave a sigh, and looked away from both of them, as though they were boring her. 'Maybe you both just need to try a little harder.'

The remark was clearly designed to irritate, but it slid off Jonah. He was trying to bring to mind everything she had said so far. To process it. Crunch it.

Keely glanced towards the door. 'I need to use the facilities now, please.'

It was such a strangely coy, adult phrase, that Jonah wondered where she'd got it, and whether she was deliberately imitating someone. It bothered him more than he wanted to admit that Keely so often spoke so strangely. Like someone of forty or fifty instead of sixteen.

Where, he wondered, was the slang? Where were the phrases that were guaranteed to make him feel old? Did she talk to her friends like this?

And then he wondered, briefly, whether Keely actually had any friends.

'A comfort break is fine,' he said, after a moment. A pause at this point might be no bad thing. He wanted to get his team together again. To talk through the reports they had read, and Keely's odd hints.

His eyes went to the clock as he rose, which now read five past nine. They wouldn't be able to keep Keely here much longer tonight. She was a minor, and had rights.

Keely's temporary social worker would also be entirely within her rights to demand that Keely go home to sleep at any time after ten. He might push that to eleven, but that was less than two hours away. Two hours, and then a whole night where they could ask her nothing. A night that might mean Nina was lost for good.

With this urgent thought in his mind, he called out, 'Keely,' before she could leave the room. He saw her turn, her eyebrows slightly raised, but he ignored the ironic gesture. However cold she might seem, she was still human. There must be appeals she would respond to.

He tried to make his tone direct. Vital. Hard to deny. 'We're against the clock here. I know you're positive that your sister will be all right, but there are some things that are too important to risk.'

Keely lifted her arms up over her head in a shoulder

stretch, giving him a look that was at once amused and challenging. 'Really? And what are those?'

'Two lives,' Jonah said, returning the challenge. 'The life of your sister, and the life you're about to screw up for good if this goes wrong.'

Keely's smile faded. She dropped her arms to her sides, and for a moment she seemed troubled.

And then she leaned forwards, and spoke as though each word was being carefully lowered out of her mouth. 'In what way do you think my life hasn't been screwed up already?'

O'Malley gave a brief laugh. 'Well, you're not in jail,' he said, and then shrugged when she looked over at him. 'I'd say that's a pretty big plus.'

Keely's lip curled slightly. 'You haven't been listening to me at all, have you? That isn't even a fucking threat.'

'Well,' Jonah said quietly, as he and O'Malley made their way to the kitchen for a top-up of coffee. 'That was one victory, anyway. You finally managed to get her to swear.'

O'Malley gave a low laugh. 'Were you uncomfortable without bad language? Or just missing what goes on at home? I bet Milly swears like a trooper.'

Jonah felt a sudden, strange pang. For the first time in months, he'd actually managed to park thoughts of his baby daughter almost entirely. Except for briefly reflecting that he would do anything to keep Milly out of the care system, he hadn't thought of her once in the last two hours.

He felt bizarrely guilty about that, and instinctively checked his phone for any calls from Michelle. He was relieved to see that there was nothing, and then tutted at himself. Michelle was perfectly able to look after their daughter. She had Milly every day while he was at work.

At that point, he thought briefly of her expression back at the pub. Was it different today? Had she needed his help?

But surely, if she *did* need help, she'd ask for it. She could always message or call. They were good at communicating.

'She's not all-out swearing yet,' he told O'Malley, putting his phone away, 'but I'm confident her first words will be four-letter ones. And don't you think it's something teenagers should do? Have a good healthy lack of respect for authority, that kind of thing?'

'Oh, I'm confident Keely Lennox has that,' O'Malley said. 'Lack of respect oozes out of her.'

'It does,' Jonah agreed, thinking back to her taunts. 'Let's take five minutes to talk.'

They collected Hanson and Lightman from their desks, and the team trailed into the big meeting room.

'So. Take me through the abuse allegations,' Jonah said, once they were all seated.

'I've been looking through the interviews,' Hanson began, 'and it's fairly clear why the CAIT decided the girls were lying. Nina's account is just the spit of Keely's, like they were lines they'd learned for a play.'

'The child abuse team had a few other concerns,' Lightman agreed. 'One of those was the description of a cellar they were allegedly locked into, which doesn't seem to exist on any plans of the house.' He paused for a moment, glancing at his iPad. 'The Lennox sisters' social worker was also confident that there was no abuse going on. But that said, the investigation could have been more thorough, in my view. Callum Taylor was only interviewed twice, and then released back to the Murray-Watts. They seemed to then approach the interview with Nina Lennox from an assumption of her having been coerced by her sister. Nina ultimately backed down and agreed that it wasn't true, but it's hard to tell whether she decided to tell the truth or just gave up.'

Hanson nodded, a little dubiously. 'Though there's been nothing negative reported about the foster parents from Callum Taylor since then. He always said he was happy to be there when interviewed by his own social worker. They've actually adopted him now, and he seems to have been enthusiastic about the process.' She sat back in her chair. 'They have no criminal record, either, and no hint of any issues before the Lennoxes moved in. You'd have to be squeaky clean to be allowed to adopt. The Murray-Watts will have jumped through huge numbers of hoops to get there.'

'And they wouldn't be allowed to adopt Nina if she'd objected,' Jonah agreed, nodding. 'Though we can't rule out that she was still open to coercion from them.'

'No,' Hanson said, with a sigh. 'We can't. I'll try calling the Murray-Watts again. I think it would be useful to talk to them.'

Jonah thought for a moment. 'Keely touched on suggestions of abuse a few minutes ago. She talked about Callum vanishing, and being denied food. I wondered whether this might all be about being heard. If the Murray-Watts were abusive in some way, even some milder way, then they got away with it scot-free. It's possible that everything Keely's done over the last week has been a way of making us listen to her.'

'I wondered about that, too,' Lightman agreed, quietly. 'If you'd been denied a voice, you might find a way of shouting.'

'There's something else to throw into the mix, too,' Jonah added. 'In this last interview, Keely said that the answers are there, in what she's been saying, and that we just needed to listen.'

'Hmm. I've just started reviewing the videos of your first

conversations,' Hanson said, thoughtfully. 'I think it's credible that she's giving us information in a way that guarantees her control. But if she is, that information's hidden somehow.'

There was a brief pause, and then O'Malley sat forwards, and clapped his hands together. 'OK. So we look for hidden clues. Anyone any good at crosswords?'

Hanson left the briefing with a feeling of satisfaction. O'Malley had volunteered her to keep looking at Keely's tapes to find clues.

'Why not you?' she'd asked, both pleased and a little embarrassed.

'Ah, I quite fancy looking at the investigations that went before. Nothing like pointing out my colleagues' mistakes to warm my heart on a Sunday evening.'

'I think we should be talking to Callum Taylor, too,' the DCI had said, thoughtfully. 'Ben, can you track him down, and think about visiting him? Callum and the Murray-Watts are currently our best bet for finding out more about Nina. The kidnap squad are in desperate need of more information. So if we can't raise the Murray-Watts over the phone, I think we should go and see them, too.'

'Sure,' Lightman agreed. 'Callum Taylor is on Waverley Road, so not far away. The Murray-Watts will take a little longer, but the traffic should be good.'

The chief had wrapped up the meeting and left them all to get on. Ben had picked up his phone to call Callum Taylor the moment they were back in their seats, and O'Malley had cleared some room on his haphazard desk and positioned his notebook on it.

Hanson put her headphones on and loaded up the video file of Keely's first interview. The view was slightly top-down but caught a lot of Keely's expression. Or, Hanson thought, lack of expression.

The phone on the team's desk rang a few moments into the interview, and she saw Lightman pause with his car keys in his hand as she paused the tape and picked up. He was presumably off to see Callum Taylor and the Murray-Watts.

'Sorry, I hope I'm talking to the right . . . This is Sally Murray-Watt,' the woman on the line said. Hanson nodded to Lightman, and put the call onto speakerphone. 'An officer left us some messages . . .'

'Thank you for calling back,' Hanson said, quickly. 'You're through to the right team. We wanted to ask you a few questions –'

'Is it about Nina?' Sally asked, cutting in. 'Have you found her?'

She had one of those ageless voices that could have belonged to a girl or a sixty-year-old. Sally was somewhere in her forties, though, Hanson remembered from the file.

'We haven't got anything definite to report yet,' Hanson replied, guardedly, glad that she wasn't having to explain the situation in full just yet. It interested her that Sally was only asking after Nina. The messages Hanson had left had been deliberately vague, and hadn't explained that Keely had now reappeared.

'Are you looking for her?' the ageless voice asked.

'We are,' Hanson said, firmly. 'We now consider it to be an urgent missing persons case, and as part of that I wanted to check in with you about anywhere on your property that might hide someone. Any outhouses? Sheds?'

'We checked the sheds and the old pigsty when they first went missing, and we've gone in there a few times since,' the woman told her. 'There was nothing, and no sign of anyone having used them.'

'That's useful to know,' Hanson said. 'But can you think of anywhere Nina might have gone to hide? Perhaps somewhere she would have felt particularly safe?'

'I . . .' There was a pause, and Hanson could imagine Sally trying to gather her thoughts together. 'We've been trying to think of places all week. I've put posters of them up all around the place here. I hoped she – they might come here.' There was a noisy swallow. 'But I'm not sure Keely likes either of us that much.'

'It's possible that Nina might make her way to you now,' Hanson said, with a glance at Lightman. 'The two of them have gone their separate ways, so it's possible that Nina might now be free to go where she likes.'

'They aren't together?' The question was sharp. Immediately anxious.

'No,' Hanson confirmed.

'How do you know?' But there was barely a pause before she went on. 'Have you found Keely? Is that how?'

Hanson glanced at Lightman again, thinking that Sally Murray-Watt was in no way stupid.

'Did they argue?' the woman went on.

'I'm afraid we don't know as yet,' Hanson said. 'But if you can think of anywhere that meant anything to them. Anywhere that they might have gone to hide . . .'

Hanson could hear a distant man's voice in the background. It sounded as though Sally's husband was calling to her. There were rustling noises. She'd clearly put her hand over the phone, but Hanson could hear her calling, 'Sorry. I'll be there in a minute, darling.'

After a brief pause, Sally's voice came more clearly again. 'There's a branch half down on one of the trees near the house. We've been out trying to remove it. I think he needs me to foot the ladder again.'

'I won't keep you much longer,' Hanson said, quickly. 'I just wondered whether you thought . . . is Nina definitely happy to be going to you? To be separated from her sister?'

'Of course she is,' she said, and for the first time there was a note of steel in her girlish voice. 'It's the best thing that could happen to her, to get her out from under Keely's spell.'

'So she's really enthusiastic about it?' Hanson pressed. 'Looking at her care record –'

'If you're thinking of bringing up all the nonsense about abuse again, you can tell it to my solicitor,' came the reply, and there was more than just a note of steel now. 'Nina admitted that it had all been fabrication.'

'Why do you think she said it in the first place, then?' Hanson asked, refusing to be flustered by the threat of solicitors. She was well aware of her right to ask questions.

'I would have thought that's obvious,' she said, a little harshly. 'If you have her records, you must be able to see that Nina would do anything for her sister.' She took a deep breath, as if calming herself. 'Sometimes you meet people who are just . . . powerful. I don't know if it's because they're obsessed with power, or whether they become obsessed with power because they realise how easy it is for them to wield it, but, whichever one, they are magnetic, and they generally get exactly what they want.'

'You think Keely is like that?' Hanson asked.

'You tell me,' she replied. 'You're the one who's interviewing her.'

Hanson hung up feeling as though Sally Murray-Watt had thrown down a strange sort of challenge. Was there something she thought Hanson should have understood by now?

She glanced up at Ben, who looked thoughtful.

'What do you think?'

'She sounded anxious to do what her husband wanted,' Lightman said. 'And possibly like she was trying to tell us something.'

'I thought so, too,' Hanson agreed. 'The powerful people stuff. She might just have meant that Keely is manipulating everyone. But she could have been saying something coded about her husband.'

Ben nodded. 'It would be useful to talk to her in person, away from him.'

'I don't know whether time is on our side on that one,' Hanson said. 'But I'll send her a text message.'

O'Malley had added a piece of flapjack to his arsenal of carb-heavy food and was making his way through it as he read the Child Abuse Investigation Team reports.

Lightman had already covered the basics of the first investigation in the briefing. The CAIT had been brought in by Callum's social worker. The first officer to step in had been DI Elliot Turner, who O'Malley knew had ultimately moved to London to join the Met.

Turner's work seemed to be reasonably thorough but not exhaustive, as Lightman had said. As well as interviewing everyone concerned and getting as much info as he could from their social worker, the DI had also spoken directly with the Lennox sisters' schools. Keely was in year eight at Southampton High by the time the incident with Callum Taylor had happened, while Nina was in her final year at Godshill Primary. Neither school had expressed any concern about the girls' welfare, though O'Malley was interested to note that Keely's school had raised some concerns about the girl herself.

She has trouble making friends, O'Malley read in a transcript from a chat with her form teacher. *She doesn't seem to find empathy all that easy, and the other kids find her cold, and a bit weird. Several times over she's become very close to a particular student, one who seemed to hero-worship her in each case. But it always ended in a big falling-out.*

O'Malley sighed slightly, well able to believe that Keely found friendships hard going. He wondered whether it bothered her that she couldn't gel with people, or whether she was simply uninterested. Or, in fact, toying with them all for her amusement. He could easily believe that of her.

He scribbled down a few notes, and then opened up Keely's care file, looking to see what had happened to the sisters after their allegations against the Murray-Watts had been dismissed.

There was very little information covering the time directly after the Lennoxes left the Murray-Watts' house. A note described how the two of them had been returned to their original children's home on Henley Road. There were also a few details of Nina's prospective move to Southampton High School, and a brief report about her catching influenza and being hospitalised for two days.

After five months, they had been fostered again. The new family was a couple living in Ashurst. They were called Frank and Evelyn Pinder, and were in their mid-thirties. The Lennoxes had been positive about the move after meeting them a few times, and had moved in during September 2011.

O'Malley read on, and felt as though he were only seeing a small part of the picture. There was nothing to suggest whether Keely had been offered counselling after their failed fostering. Nothing, either, about her friendships at school and whether they had improved. Just a quick note that they had remained at their existing school and were being driven to and from by Frank Pinder, who worked not far away.

There was a gap, and then a report about a detention that Keely had been given for smoking on school grounds. Her social worker made a routine visit afterwards, and noted that Keely had been very uncommunicative. The social worker had asked the Pinders whether she was struggling with friendships once again. The Pinders thought not, but said she was going through a classic teenage rebellious phase, which they trusted her to grow out of.

And then, in November of 2011, there came a curveball. Though, of course, it wasn't such a curveball when you'd read the basics of the investigation that had followed. Keely had asked to meet her social worker after school, and had announced that she and her sister were being abused by their foster father.

O'Malley read through the transcript as Keely told, in direct, disturbing language, how Frank Pinder had begun grooming her almost from the moment she arrived at the house.

KEELY LENNOX: I thought he was so nice. He used to buy me things. Well, he bought things for both of us, but they were different. For me, it was short skirts. Tight tops. He'd grin and say, 'I'm told girls of your age like this kind of thing.' And I felt so grateful. You know I . . . I was teased, before, for my clothes. When we were with Sally and Henry. All that Boden stuff. Now everyone at school envied me. They wanted the kinds of clothes I wore, and the alcohol I was given to share out. For the first time, I became cool.

MARK SLATTERWORTH: He wasn't unkind to you?

KL: No. The opposite. He was overwhelmingly kind. Always making sure we had 'us' time. He drove me to every party with a bottle of vodka or a load of beer, and picked me up from the park if I wanted to stay out late. He was great, I thought. The best possible foster father. Until it suddenly turned out I owed him something.

MS: What was that?

KL: [AFTER A PAUSE] First it was lying cuddling for a while, because that's what dads do with their daughters. And then it was a kiss, because Evelyn and he don't kiss any more, he said. And I felt – really grateful, at that point. So I did it. But then suddenly he was telling me to touch him. Or asking me to let him touch me. And I didn't want to do that at first. [PAUSE] Frank told me it was all right to be scared. But it was real love, what we had, and sometimes that could feel like fear. Nervous excitement, he called it. We loved each other. And he was so kind to me, and told me such amazing things, that I thought maybe he was right. So I . . . let him.

MS: Did you think you loved him?

KL: I don't know . . . Probably. I was confused about it. There was something that . . . he kept telling me how wonderful I was, and how he'd never met anyone like me. And how he was going to find a way of leaving Evelyn for me, but then I just felt guilty, of course. And very confused. I wasn't sure if I wanted him to. But all that time, I thought it was just happening to me, so it was all right.

MS: You mean you didn't think your sister was being treated this way?

KL: Yes. But by the time she was twelve, he was buying those clothes for her, as well, and driving her to parties, and . . . and I just suddenly knew that he was grooming her too. When I asked her, she told me everything. It was just the same. He'd said all the same things to her. She thought it was just her, too.

MS: He was asking her to touch him, too?

KL: Yes. And more.

MS: How much more?

KL: He's been having sex with her for months. Just like with me.

MS: Can you be clear . . .?

KL: I mean full penetration, all right?

8

Callum eventually returned from his mysterious absence twenty-four hours later. Sally had made pancakes for the three of us, and once they were ready, she turned to call Callum.

I froze in the act of sitting at the table, waiting to see if she'd forgotten that he was gone. He hadn't appeared the night before, and so I'd asked her, at bedtime, where he was. She'd given me a brief, very hushed reply about him needing his own space for tonight. It hadn't been an answer, but I saw the way she'd looked towards the corridor. She looked, for a moment, slightly frightened, and that had been enough of a warning for me.

It turned out that Sally had forgotten nothing. Callum was returned to us, announcing his presence by walking silently into the room, his eyes on the floor. He looked pale, and every line in his body seemed beaten.

Sally, poised at the counter with a pan in her hand and a tea towel over her shoulder, smiled as she saw him.

'You must be starving,' she said.

Callum came to sit opposite me, never once looking up as he pulled his chair out and then tucked himself under the table.

Behind him, at the counter, Sally loaded three pancakes onto a plate, threw halved strawberries on top, and brought all of it over to him like a gift.

'Have some maple syrup, darling,' she said, watching the top of his head.

There was a pause, while Callum sat absolutely still, and then he reached a hand out and opened the maple syrup bottle. 'Thank you, Sally,' he said.

Sally suddenly reached for him and pulled him into a hug. She kissed the top of his head, and said, 'There. You be a good boy now. No more cheekiness, and everything will be fine.'

'Sorry, Sally,' Callum said, in a quiet voice.

It was only after Sally had turned away to serve up more of the pancakes that Callum raised his head. He looked directly at me, and the pretence that he was sorry, and broken, fell away. The expression he gave me was direct. Angry. And full of something I didn't understand.

I remember feeling horrified at the rebellion still in him. How could he be like that when Sally was being so nice to him?

And I felt a surge of anger, too. I'd started to feel really worried about him.

I looked away, towards Ninny, who was drawing a farmhouse scene in a notebook. It was for Sally, she'd said.

Ninny has always been a gifted artist, even if her subject matter was a little repetitive at that age. She loved birds and butterflies, and drew them everywhere she could, in stylish, intricately shaded ways. I knew Sally was going to love the new picture. She'd already found Ninny a private drawing teacher: a soppy, enthusiastic woman called Daniella who ran the community art centre in the village.

A heavy tread came in the hallway, and I felt all of us stiffen. Henry must be joining us for breakfast today. I disliked it when he did. His presence seemed to loom over us like a blackening cloud, one that might pass by leaving us untouched, but might bring a storm.

'Yours is just ready, darling,' Sally said, rushing over to

the oven, where she seemed to have been keeping a plate warm just for him.

Henry said nothing. He walked past her with a frown set deep into his forehead, and sat down at the table.

I could see Sally's expression drop slightly, but she breezed over with a plate for him and one for Ninny, who beamed at her and put her pen away obediently. I waited, as patiently as possible, for my own plate. The pancakes smelled wonderful, as all Sally's cooking did, and my stomach was rumbling from waiting until so late in the morning.

The plate was actually on the table in front of me when Henry's voice rang out from the head of the table.

'I don't think so, Sally,' he said. And although he was talking to her, his eyes were fixed on me. 'She needs to lose some weight. She can have fruit.'

There was utter silence, and then Sally said quickly, 'Of course, darling.'

She took the plate back, tipped the pancakes off, and brought it back with only a handful of strawberries on it.

I can still remember the dizzy horror of that moment. If I tried to describe it to someone now as a cruelty, they would probably laugh. Ask me if I thought getting fed pancakes is some kind of human right.

Of course it isn't. And yet what Henry did was terrible. He had deliberately waited until I had been on the point of enjoying them, and then snatched them away from me, and only me. And, more than that, he had humiliated me so casually in front of Sally and my sister and Callum. I had been told, publicly and for the first time in my life, that I should be ashamed of my body and who I was.

I know that I blushed, furiously. Callum kept looking at his plate, but I imagined he was triumphant. I could feel Ninny's gaze on me. Hers soft. Anxious.

'She can have one of my pancakes, Sally,' she said, not grasping what Henry had said.

Sally held a hand out to her and stroked her hair, hurriedly. 'I know you're trying to be kind, but you heard what Henry said. It wouldn't be helping your sister. Letting her get fat, so nobody likes her, isn't being kind, is it? To be kind, we need to help her to lose weight.'

I thought about running away from them all. About going to my room and slamming my door and never speaking to any of them again. It was only Henry's looming, fearful presence that kept me where I was.

Sally went to fetch the bowl of strawberries.

'You can have a few more strawberries, if you like,' she said, once she'd sat herself down. 'I think that would be all right, wouldn't it, Henry?'

Henry looked up from his mechanical chewing, stared at my plate, and then said, 'A few.'

I felt unable to accept. As if it showed that I couldn't manage without food. So despite my stomach aching for something more, I shook my head. 'I don't need any more, thank you,' I said, with my eyes on my plate.

I was so fixed in my own misery that it took me a while to notice Sally's own plate, which had only a few strawberries on it, too. No pancakes. No syrup. And I realised that she was watching the other three eat with an expression that was close to desperation.

And for some reason, that only made me feel worse.

Before you ask, I'm not telling you this because it's the worst of what they did. I'm showing you the warning sign. The first sting that warns you you've settled yourself on an ants' nest. A short, sharp pain that you think you might have imagined, until the stings come more and more often and begin to overwhelm you.

We only had three more days of school that week, at the awful Gale Park. It's strange to think how much I dreaded going there, when only a few days later I would find myself longing to go back. Desperate to be anywhere but at the house.

Christmas was almost on us. On the Monday, a day after Callum had returned and the pancakes had been snatched away, we all gathered together to play Uno in the living room. All of us except Henry, that is.

If you could have drawn or photographed us just then, we would have looked perfect. The Christmas tree in the background, festooned with lights, and the matching runner over the mantelpiece. The seductive effects of pretty furnishings and an apparently perfect family. Despite my misgivings about the last two days, it almost seduced me. Even Callum was playing nicely.

We must have been talking when the front door opened and closed, because the first I knew of Henry Murray-Watt returning from work was a loud tread in the hall outside. I remember tensing slightly, hoping that he would carry on towards his study. But the footsteps turned onto the thick carpet of the living room, and Sally rose, hurriedly.

'Hello, darling,' she said, moving to kiss him on the cheek. 'How was your day?'

This was their ritual. The kiss, and the enquiry. For some reason Henry never asked how Sally's day had been. He would tell her whether his day had been good or bad, and then Callum and Ninny and I would chime in with saying hello to Henry in turn, and he would nod at each of us, his eyes running over us and then away as if he wasn't quite satisfied with what he saw.

'Why don't you sit down, and I'll make you a coffee?' Sally asked. And this was the other part of the ritual. Sally had to do something for him. Take his coat, or his briefcase. Fetch him food or drink. She'd told us several times how tired Henry was when he arrived home. How we mustn't irritate him.

'Thank you,' Henry said, and folded his lanky frame into the armchair.

It was clear to the three of us that the game was now over. Callum started to pile the cards up, his head lowered, as usual. He seemed to take particular delight in grabbing mine from me, as if I hadn't been trying to get rid of them for the whole game.

With Uno cleared away, there was nothing for us to do. We knew we shouldn't talk in front of Henry. And though Ninny seemed happy enough turning to gaze up at the Christmas tree, I couldn't focus on anything. I was too aware of Henry watching us.

Henry's gaze must have followed Ninny's to the tree at some point. Just as Sally was returning, I heard him say, 'What in God's name is that?'

He leaned towards the tree, and I felt as though my heart was dropping into my stomach. He reached out and pulled off it the hand-painted, glittery star I'd made at school that day. The one my teacher had told us to hang on our tree at home. I'd enjoyed making it, and hadn't worried that the glitter was uneven or that I wasn't very good at cutting.

There was a silence, as Henry looked from the offending item to each of us in turn.

'I'm so sorry, darling,' Sally said, quickly. 'I didn't know it was on there.' And she turned to us, her voice suddenly sharp. 'Who hung that up there?'

It felt like the room was tipping as I whispered, 'I did.'

Henry's gaze fell on me for a moment, and I felt like an insect. Like a grub.

'Take it from Henry, please,' Sally said, quietly.

I stood, slowly, not wanting to go any closer to him. I was suddenly afraid that he was going to grab me and hit me. But he sat absolutely still as I took the painted star back off him.

'Now,' Henry said, 'you're going to put it in the waste-paper bin, where it belongs.'

I could feel tears threatening, but I wasn't going to cry. I wouldn't, *wouldn't* cry in front of Callum. So I did as I was told, in silence, and took it over to the bin in the corner. There was nothing in there except the cellophane from the Uno pack we'd opened, and my cheerful little star fell onto it and seemed to look back up at me with reproach.

'You should have asked, shouldn't you?' Sally said, in a voice that was less harsh than Henry's. I saw her glance over at Henry, and then add, 'It's not your tree, is it?'

'No,' I whispered. 'Sorry.'

'Sorry, *Henry*,' Sally said, in a low, warning voice.

'Sorry, Henry,' I said.

Henry said nothing. But I could feel anger radiating off him.

'Why don't you go and tidy your room?' Sally said, after that. And although it probably seemed to Henry like a punishment, I think she meant to help me. It let me leave them all and hide myself away to cry.

Later, Sally came to see me, and spoke earnestly to me. About how we mustn't ruin things for Henry. How he tried very hard to be patient, but we had to be obedient.

'And I think we should work on your drawing, too,' Sally said, once she'd finished the lecture. 'Girls *should* be able to draw. It's one of the things Henry liked most about me, the beautiful handmade Christmas and birthday cards I painted him. Why don't we get you some lessons at the community art centre, too?'

'I'd like that,' I whispered.

Sally smiled at me. 'It's clear you haven't got the same talent as your sister, but you can work on it at the central art centre, with some help.'

And that was the first time I felt it. The sudden little burn of resentment towards Ninny. Not jealousy because Callum and she were getting on. Not protectiveness. Resentment.

It's not like I'd never had an uncharitable thought towards my sister. I'd been annoyed with her at times, like any other sibling. Back when it had been just the two of us and Mummy, I'd often wanted her to leave us in peace.

But I'd never felt bitterness like this. The spark of envy was new, and hot, and uncomfortable. And it began to consume me.

It became painfully clear that I was the lesser sister in my foster parents' eyes. The flawed one. Henry would sit and read with her, his expression soft in a way I never saw it at any other time. He would praise her appearance, and tell her how wonderful her manners were. He was almost human in those moments.

And although Sally seemed to feel for me, she had clearly taken Henry's thoughts to heart. She would tell me, casually, how I should try to look more like my sister. How if only I would brush my hair more carefully, it would be more like hers. This despite brushing and brushing it until it was a frizzy mess, while somehow Ninny's hair fell into perfect ringlets. And she would point out that Ninny had said 'thank you' beautifully, when I had not. That she smiled so nicely, while I always looked surly.

'It isn't an attractive quality, my dear,' she told me, on more than one occasion, her expression sympathetic. 'If you ever want your own husband one day, you're going to have to learn to smile. Henry gets angry if I don't greet him cheerfully, and he's right to. It's the least I can do, when he gives us so much.'

I once brought a swear word home from school and let it slip from my mouth in front of her. I was profoundly lucky that it hadn't been in front of Henry, and that she decided not to tell him in the end, but I could see how appalled she was.

'You will never have any respect or liking from anyone of worth if you speak like that,' she said. 'And I will warn you now that Henry would have flown into a towering rage if he'd heard it.' I later found out just how angry he would have been, after Callum stubbed his toe and let out a vicious curse.

In fact, swearing was something Henry was so incensed by that I can barely bring myself to do it even now. It's been trained out of me, leaving me clean-talking and formal, despite the darkness of the thoughts in my head.

But I was talking about Ninny, wasn't I? Their perfect foster daughter. She was held up to me as the ideal of slim girlishness, too. I was told that the only way I was going to be half so beautiful was to lose weight.

My portions had become half the size of my sister's. I would end each meal staring longingly at Ninny's plate, my mouth full of saliva and my stomach somewhere between aching and sick with anxiety. Ninny would sometimes try to give me some of her food, but Henry caught her doing it once, and blamed me. His lacerating words were so awful that even Ninny cried, and she never tried again.

And then came Christmas morning. I'd been so excited

for it, in part because Callum had told us that it was a day of treats. The cat was out of the bag for us about Santa, so it was no surprise to hear him talking about what Henry and Sally would put in our stockings. I'd watched Sally making an enormous Christmas cake over the past week, too.

I spent several days beforehand dreaming about the food I'd eat. About the sensation of being full once again.

We all took our stockings down to the living room to open, and even as we walked downstairs in line, I could feel something in me sinking. Callum and Ninny's were clearly bulging with presents, where mine was limp and half empty.

It took no time at all for me to open my four presents: three toys and a skipping rope, which Henry made clear was 'for exercise'. Callum and Ninny, in contrast, opened package after package of chocolate and sweets. It went on, and on, and I was mortified to find myself crying in front of all of them before it was finished.

I saw Henry's gaze settle on me, and I knew I was in real trouble.

'You're being unbelievably ungrateful,' Sally said, her cheeks flushed. 'What other child would be given wonderful gifts and sulk about it?'

'Go to your room,' Henry said.

'I'm sorry,' I said, in desperate appeal. 'I love the gifts. I'm sorry.'

'*Go to your room,*' Henry repeated, his voice ringing out in a way that I sometimes still hear in my sleep. It wakes me sweating, that booming tone of his.

I ran from the room.

And so I spent Christmas morning on my own upstairs, while the others played with their new toys and gorged themselves on chocolate, and Sally put carols on the sound system. It's amazing how long you can cry for in circumstances like those.

Midway through the morning, there was a quiet tap on my door. Ninny, coming to check on me, I thought. But when the door creaked open, it was Callum's voice I heard.

'Here,' he said, in a whisper. 'That's half my stocking chocolate. I've taken the wrappers off so you won't get caught with them.'

I sat up, quickly. My face felt hot and ugly as I turned it to him, and I couldn't quite believe it when he deposited a slightly melted handful of wrapperless coins and Quality Street into my lap.

'You'd better have it all now, and wash your face and hands when you're finished,' he said.

I felt undone by this gesture of kindness. I didn't know what to say. I think, looking back, that I'd latched on to my anger at Callum as a way of surviving. And I didn't know what I would do if I had to let go of it.

'Thank you,' I said to him, in the end. 'You didn't have to.'

Callum gave a shrug, and a half-smile. 'We have to look after each other.'

I ate the chocolate after he'd left, and for some reason found myself thinking of my sister again. My own sister, who hadn't come up to share her food. Who hadn't come to see me at all.

And a little sliver of my floating anger found a home.

9

Lightman left his Qashqai next to the kerb on Waverley Road and walked up to the square, seventies block of flats that Callum Taylor now lived in. Social services had informed him that Callum had been living there for the last three months.

It was a quiet enough road, Lightman thought. At least on a Sunday evening in summer. There was a little traffic noise from Mountbatten Way and the sound of a TV drama drifting out through an open window, but little else.

Overall, this was a pretty good address for someone moving on from care. The advantage, he supposed, of having been adopted by a wealthy couple. Even if Waverley Road wasn't the most affluent street, and looked cobbled together from a dozen different architectural styles, it wasn't within any of the violent parts of the city, and it seemed safe enough for an eighteen-year-old boy on his own.

Lightman couldn't imagine having to live alone at eighteen though, even here. He'd had a base back at his parents' house right through university and his first year of policing. The thought of managing without his parents still terrified him now, at thirty. But he was now facing the reality of it, starkly, with his father's accelerating decline from cancer.

He gave the buzzer for Callum Taylor's flat a lengthy push, and looked around for signs of life while he waited. When nothing happened, he buzzed again, and then moved round to the back of the block. It was hard to tell which Callum's flat was, though from the number, he suspected it was one of the top two. Only one flat had lights on, so Callum might not be here.

Deciding that he could live with himself if he disturbed Callum's neighbours, he pushed the buzzer for what he guessed was the adjacent flat. After some time, an elderly woman's voice came over the intercom to ask who he was.

'I'm Detective Sergeant Lightman,' he said, speaking close to the microphone. 'I'm actually looking for your neighbour, Callum Taylor, but I hoped you might be able to help.'

'You're the police, you say?' she asked. 'I'd appreciate it if you could hold your ID up to the camera.'

Lightman did as requested, slightly surprised that they had a camera system here at all. The resident buzzed him up.

The hallway and stairwell were basic but clean. There was no smell of urine, and the dark blue carpeting was comparatively free of stains.

The owner of Flat Four was waiting for him on the top floor. She was a tiny woman. Wiry of build, she had a piercing gaze through a pair of outsized glasses. The delay answering had led him to expect some kind of disability, but she seemed nimble enough as she let him into a small living room, where *Midsomer Murders* was paused on a boxy television screen.

'Sorry, I was just trying to restrain the cat when you buzzed,' she said. 'She likes to make a bolt for freedom when anyone comes in, but she's hiding somewhere.'

'I shouldn't need to take up too much of your time,' Lightman said. 'I really only wondered whether you knew where Callum was, or when I might be able to catch him.'

'Can I ask, first, why you want to find him?'

Lightman nodded. 'There's no trouble involved. We're just hoping he might be able to tell us more about one of his friends, who's missing.'

'Oh, well,' the woman said. 'That sounds all right.'

'Sorry, I didn't ask your name.'

'Gaynor,' she replied. 'Gaynor Richardson.'

'Thank you. So would you be able to help? Do you know him well?'

'I know him reasonably well,' Gaynor said, her eyes drifting around the flat, presumably in an effort to spot her cat. 'He's quite helpful about carrying things upstairs for me, and he's been in for a few cups of tea. He gave me his mobile number. In case I needed anything.'

'He sounds a nice lad,' Lightman commented.

'He's a good boy,' Gaynor agreed. 'Quiet, polite and considerate.'

'Do you know where he might be at the moment? Does he have a job of some kind?'

'Not on Sunday evenings, no,' Gaynor told him. 'He's taking a year out before university. He works at the big Tesco's most days, but they're closed from five on a Sunday.'

God bless sharp-minded people with lots of free time, Lightman thought.

'Can you think of anywhere else I can check?'

'If he's out,' Gaynor said, thoughtfully, 'it's usually the cinema or something with his girlfriend.'

'Right,' Lightman said, pulling out his iPad in order to make a note. 'You presumably don't have the girlfriend's number or address?'

'No, I'm afraid not,' Gaynor said, apologetically.

'And you haven't seen him around today?'

'Not today, no,' Gaynor agreed. 'He probably went straight out after his shift.'

'Well, thank you,' Lightman told her. 'That's been very useful.' Which wasn't strictly true, but was good practice.

*

'There's a lot of detail in what Keely had to say about Frank Pinder,' O'Malley was telling Jonah, his chair turned half away from his screen and a thick pad of paper balanced on his lap. 'The way she talks about him is pretty reminiscent of a number of grooming scenarios we've witnessed.'

Jonah had delayed going back in to speak with Keely. He wanted to know about the two abuse allegations, and was particularly interested to learn that the claims against her second foster father were of a sexual nature.

'And Keely claimed that Nina was also a victim?'

'Yes,' O'Malley agreed, reading from his notes. 'And Nina backed her up once again, though this time she stuck to her story.' O'Malley looked up at Jonah. 'I'd say it's worth talking to the foster father, Frank Pinder. If Keely's aiming to get revenge or justice or whatever against the Murray-Watts, then she may want to do the same with him, the other foster parent, who was never prosecuted.'

Jonah nodded, thoughtfully. 'See if you can get hold of him. And a brief summary of the investigation would be useful, too. I'd like to know the details of why they didn't prosecute.'

'Sure,' O'Malley said. 'I'll have it with you in ten.'

Jonah returned to his office, feeling increasingly uncertain about what Keely Lennox wanted. Part of him was inclined to view her as a victim. He wasn't going to assume that Frank Pinder was innocent, no matter what the investigation had concluded. It was more than likely that Frank was one of the three men Keely had talked about. One of the three who had effectively put an end to her childhood, according to her own account.

But there was another side to him that wondered whether everything had been about game playing, right from the moment she reported the Murray-Watts. And although the root cause might still lie with the death of Keely's mother, it was also just possible that Keely simply wasn't born with the ability to empathise. In short: that she was a sociopath.

And if she really was, then she might not care about what happened to her sister. It might, in fact, already be too late for Nina.

Hanson's feeling of urgency was stepping up with every minute of video she watched. It was more than just the passing of time; it was Keely herself, and the unrelenting coldness of her. The sense of calculation behind everything she said.

There was already a scribbled list of locations on Hanson's desk jotter. Keely had mentioned multiple places during the various interviews. Their childhood home. Their first children's home on Henley Road. Their primary school. The allotments. The Murray-Watts' house.

She was now listening to the recordings again, trying to work out how a girl like Keely might decide to leave them a clue. The most obvious way was frequency, though Hanson strongly suspected that it wasn't that simple. She had begun writing tallies of the numbers of mentions next to each place in order to keep track anyway, while the rest of her mind looked for something else. For some kind of hidden sign Keely might have given. For a hand gesture. A tone of voice.

She was halfway through the second tape, trying to watch Keely's feet as well as her hands and still tallying, when she found herself hitting the pause button.

'Was that . . .?'

Hanson realised she had spoken aloud when O'Malley glanced across at her, so she gave him an apologetic smile and hit the rewind button. She listened again, her eyes on Keely's mouth now as she spoke.

'. . . *As it turned out, there were worse things than Henley Road Children's Home, and even than the god-awful Gate Park Primary.*

'*Terrible places don't always look terrible. Another thing I've learned. They can look beautiful. Lush. Seductive . . .*'

Hanson stopped the tape with a mixture of triumph and doubt. She pulled her headphones out and said to O'Malley, 'I think I might have something.'

Jonah was moments from going back into the interview room when Hanson tapped on his door. Her slightly over-bright expression was familiar.

'What have you got?'

'I'd like to show you, if that's OK . . .'

Jonah followed Hanson to her desk. O'Malley had drawn his chair up close by and was waiting.

'OK,' Hanson said. 'Listen to Keely talking about her primary school.'

She ran the tape, adjusting her speakers so that Keely's voice was clear, and Jonah frowned.

'Did she call it two different things?'

Hanson nodded, smiling as she paused the tape. 'She's called it "Gale Park" every other time. It *is* called "Gale Park". But here, just here, she calls it "Gate Park" instead.' She glanced back at the screen. 'Anyone else might have made a mistake, but I don't get the impression Keely Lennox makes mistakes.'

Jonah found himself agreeing. 'It's a Sunday evening. The school will probably have been empty for most of the weekend.'

'Should we get out there?' Hanson asked.

'Yes,' Jonah agreed. 'And take some of the kidnap squad with you.'

*

CID was empty when Lightman arrived back. He checked his phone and saw a message from Hanson explaining that they'd gone to Keely's primary school. Lightman took his coat off and sat to write up his report, but was almost immediately interrupted by the team's phone ringing.

'This is Mark Slatterworth,' a warm voice with a strong Edinburgh accent said. 'I'm Keely and Nina Lennox's social worker. I think you wanted to talk to me?'

'Thanks, yes,' Lightman said, picking up a pen.

'Sorry for taking so long to call back,' Slatterworth said. 'I was at the cinema. *Star Wars.*' He gave a short, good-natured laugh. 'I'm hoping this means you've made some progress with finding them.'

'Yes, we've tracked Keely down,' Lightman replied, neutrally. 'We're concerned about Nina's whereabouts, and wanted to ask you a few questions about the two of them.'

'Oh,' Mark said, his cheerful voice much flatter. 'I see. Is there – what's happened?'

'We picked Keely up at a pub, but she's unwilling to tell us where her sister is.'

Mark let out a long breath. 'Well, I understand you being worried. Keely isn't the easiest to get to grips with. But I think . . . I've known her a while now, yes? And I have a lot of sympathy for her. The death of her mother hit her very hard, and I've sort of always suspected there were other things that have made it difficult. I think perhaps she's a little on the spectrum. But fiercely smart, you know?'

'You think she shows autistic traits?'

'Oh, aye, I'd say so,' Mark said, and then he laughed. 'Sometimes she just doesn't seem to react at all to big events. Or not like you'd expect. Other times she's about ten steps ahead of you and you're left running to catch up. She's definitely unique.'

Lightman made a brief note, and then asked, 'Do you think this caused her problems with her foster parents?'

'I don't doubt it,' Mark confirmed. 'She struggled to gel with people. I'm positive that having lost her mother violently made it much harder for her to let people get close. And she was that bit older than Nina when it happened. That much more affected by it, even if she doesn't remember much about it.'

'Would you mind telling me about the accusations she made against the Murray-Watts?' Lightman asked. 'What was your feeling about those?'

Mark gave a sigh. 'That was all really hard. It was only six months after I'd started this job and I felt quite out of my depth, if I'm honest. I didn't know what to think for a lot of it. I obviously took her seriously from the off, because you have to. These kids only have you to protect them. And her story was more than convincing.'

He went on to talk through how he'd alerted the Child Abuse Investigation Team, and his suspicion that Keely had schooled Nina in what to say. 'And then there were factors like their living conditions at the Murray-Watts'. They had lovely rooms, clothes, toys . . . And all this stuff about the cellar that didn't exist. And that was aside from what Callum said.'

'That it had been Keely who beat him up?'

'Yes,' Mark agreed. 'And, more than that, that he was never locked in his room, and had never been beaten up by them.'

'But Keely insisted she said it because they were being abused in other ways.'

'Yes, I know,' Mark said. He gave another sigh. 'And that kept me up at night. It really did. I went back several times to the house while Callum Taylor was there, hoping to witness something that might make sense of Keely's claims, but there was nothing. And the conclusion I came to in the end was that the death of Keely's mum had left its mark on her.'

Lightman wrote this down, and then asked, 'Those weren't the only accusations that Keely Lennox made, were they?'

'No,' Slatterworth agreed, 'they weren't. I'll say now that I was really disturbed by what she had to say about Frank Pinder. The details were extremely convincing. It sounded like textbook grooming, and I was horrified.'

'So what led that investigation to find him innocent?'

'It was a lot of things together, really,' the social worker said. 'Some of the dates she claimed abuse had happened on couldn't have happened. And Frank's wife queried other elements of her story, like gifts he had apparently given her. Though I think, overall, it was more about the way she talked about it, in the end.'

'How so?' Lightman asked.

'It was all just . . . wrong,' Slatterworth said. 'When I looked back over how she'd described it, she actually talked about him "grooming" her, as if she was aware of the process. She was able to identify that he had used her desperation to be popular as a method of making himself indispensable to her, and had played on her fear of losing his support.' The social worker made a tutting noise. 'It honestly sounded, when you thought about it, like someone who'd read all the literature without ever having experienced it at all.'

Lightman considered this for a moment, and then asked, 'But why would she do that? What would her motivation be to accuse her foster father of something so extreme?'

Mark made a slightly protesting sound, but then said, 'She might simply have been a very unhappy girl looking for revenge.'

'Revenge?' Lightman asked.

'Frank had a falling-out with her just before the accusations,' Mark explained. 'A big one. He found out she was dating a lad he thought was trouble. He went in a bit heavy-handed, you know, and banned her from seeing him. And then when she said it was none of his business, he grounded her.' Mark sighed. 'It was really badly handled on his part, but it was just fear, and he would have calmed down about it. But Keely got incredibly angry, and I think . . . well, that the accusations were the result.'

There was something uniquely sinister about public buildings in darkness, Hanson thought. Gale Park Primary was probably a perfectly ordinary-looking place during daylight hours, if a little gothic. It had clearly been built a long while before the scruffy houses around it, probably before the city had ever spread this far. Hanson imagined schoolchildren in Victorian dress lining up to walk inside, which unhelpfully brought to mind all the Edgar Allan Poe stories she'd inhaled as a teenager.

Hanson had parked her Nissan on the zigzag lines out in front, unconcerned about the legality given the time of night. The wide front gates blocked any access to the school car park, but there was a pedestrian footpath that let on to the front of the school, and it looked as though they'd be able to walk around the place with ease.

Quick's second-in-command appeared a few moments later, and hitched her Ford up onto the pavement. She'd brought a heavyset constable with her.

There had been some discussion about bringing a method of entry team to force any doors open, but DI Quick had suggested taking a plastic shim for now, and seeing whether anything else was needed. They might not have to access the school itself, as it was unlikely that Keely had a key to the place. Though Hanson wouldn't put it past her to have obtained one somehow.

The four of them approached the large, arch-shaped front door. O'Malley pulled at the wrought-iron door handle, but nothing happened. Hanson shone a flashlight through the windows, but there was nothing to see apart from an empty office and corridor.

Without speaking, they moved off in pairs around the building. O'Malley and Hanson moved right, a route that opened on to a concrete playground. The huddled shapes of play equipment over a rubberised surface occupied one corner. Hanson pulled out her baton and moved straight towards the equipment, while O'Malley continued on down the building.

Close to, the apparatus proved to be a set of monkey bars and balance beams. There was only shadow between them. Beyond, an expanse of empty concrete went all the way to the fence.

She heard a quiet call from O'Malley and turned. He was at the door to a small, boxy room that had clearly been added during more modern times. As she approached, he swung the door fully open.

Hanson made her way over. She could see nothing beyond the door. It was pitch-black inside. Impenetrable.

O'Malley moved into the darkness before she could switch her flashlight on again. She saw him reach a hand round to the wall, and light suddenly blazed at the far end of the room.

It was a drama studio. The lights were stage lights, set up to shine on an acting area at the back. Wings were marked with thick drapes, and there was a screen of floor-to-ceiling curtain right at the back.

Her eyes went straight to the centre of the illuminated area, drawn to a single figure. A red-haired figure slumped in a chair.

Keely's expression was triumphant as Jonah let himself back into the interview room alone.

'Ahhh, another one bites the dust,' she said. 'Did the poor sergeant get scared off, too?'

Jonah found himself instinctively wanting to argue. To tell her that O'Malley was a military man who had seen things that would turn her pale. But he knew that rising to her digs would allow her to win her little game.

'Absolutely,' he said instead, with an easy smile. 'I'm going to have to ask you to stop scaring my officers, or I'll be the only one left. And god forbid I have to do any actual work around here.'

Keely narrowed her eyes at him, and then looked away. Jonah felt a quiet note of satisfaction. A point to him.

He had considered what to raise with her now. In particular, whether or not to bring up her old primary school and the four officers on their way over there.

Mentioning it would make her feel that they were playing along. It would make her feel in control. Which had its definite downsides, Jonah thought, even while it might keep her sweet.

He also wasn't quite sure they'd worked her clue out right. It would be a mistake, he felt, to tell her about it until they were certain. But if they'd got it, it would potentially earn a little of her respect.

In the end, that had been the deciding factor for Jonah. He shouldn't be trying to earn the respect of a sixteen-year-old girl. He should be solving this case, and that meant treating her like any other suspect.

'So,' he said, as warmly as possible. 'You were going to tell me about your relationship with your sister, back when you lived with the Murray-Watts.'

'Oh yes, I was,' Keely said, and her eyes grew momentarily distant. Her lips moved into a very small smile. 'Little Ninny. What a doll she became.'

10

Punishment became part of our routine. A graded scale of it that would be applied at intervals. And it was meted out with such casual randomness, too. A big crime might get us a sharp word and then nothing; but a forgotten 'thank you' or some moment of clumsiness might mean lacerating criticism of everything about us and banishment to our rooms.

I didn't understand the power of that until later. Now that I look back, I can see it was part of what kept us under their control. That constant fear that we'd done the wrong thing without knowing it.

And the bias of it. That was almost worse. Callum and I were constantly in trouble over those first few months, but Ninny seemed to glide over it all, buoyed up by her status as a sweet little girl.

I tried to feel happy for my sister. Sometimes I would tell myself that this was what I'd wanted. It was, wasn't it? The most important person in my life was being cherished as she had so badly needed.

But it was impossible not to resent it. Not to crave that status for myself, instead of being viewed as a sullen, lumpish child without charm. And that was at best. On the worst days, Henry would call me a spiteful, unpleasant person. An ugly brat. And Sally would look down and say nothing in my defence. At times, she would even go over to Ninny and hug her, maybe to remind herself that Henry approved of one of the children she was bringing up.

I would watch her with a burning feeling in my stomach.

I wonder, now, whether actual hunger fed into my resentment. I was so often denied treats, and even whole meals, that I was constantly ravenous. Emotional. Hangry.

Henry would come to inspect me once per week, on a Sunday evening, to see if I was thin enough to be allowed food yet. It was the single worst part of every week. That mixture of hope, dread and humiliation.

The result was always the same. He would curl his lip and tell Sally that I was still too fat, and Sally would look like she was fighting back tears as she promised to help me get thinner.

My new school, a place I had yearned to escape to, turned out to be no escape at all. In spite of the fact that it was cheerful, well moneyed and full of a Church of England ethos, I fitted in there as badly as I had at Gale Park.

Each morning began with bitter embarrassment, from the moment we caught the bus from the stop on Purlieu Lane. Ninny, all smiles and likeableness, would jump on board and immediately be invited to sit with three of the other girls, taking the last seat in their little four. They would already be laughing about something by the time I trudged past on my way to one of the unoccupied seats halfway down.

I did my best to avoid looking too hard at the two boys and one girl from my year who were spread across the back row. I had only once asked to sit with them, and the burning humiliation of being told that the final seat was taken – when it remained empty each and every day all the way to school – had been enough to stop me ever asking again.

It would remain hard for me during the day, too. A few of the teachers were kind enough to insist that some of the other girls keep me company at breaktimes, but I could see that the girls themselves resented it. So I would bring a book, instead, and I would fill my time with reading. It was one of the few things I did that Henry approved of.

Naturally, retreating behind fiction only increased the problem. I was that strange girl who read books and never talked to anyone. They would avoid me, only looking at me sideways. And there were honestly some days when, if I wasn't asked a question by a teacher, I didn't speak to anyone from the moment the bus picked me up until it dropped me back at the Pearl Lane shelter once again.

I'll admit that I didn't help myself. I would make it obvious in class that I thought they were all stupid. My small revenge for the thousand hurts I'd suffered. And I made no effort to keep up with the TV shows they were watching, even when Ninny was watching them all and made room for me on the sofa. Maybe I had too much pride even then.

But Sally and Henry didn't help me, either. They sent me in with a packed lunch every day, to stop me 'pigging out' on school dinners, and it would rarely have more than fruit and a yoghurt in it. Totally aside from my ravenous hunger, that lunch box marked me as an immediate outsider. Where the other pupils would trade their jam sandwiches, crisps and chocolate bars, I would eat my lunch from my lap, to hide its meagreness. I would work my way through it slowly, too, to make it look like there was more than there was. But I'd still end up finished and staring desperately at all the treats around me. I must have looked like some sort of desperate stray dog.

In the end, my hunger got the better of me. I'd watched Sarah Phillips, a small but noisy girl in my year, pull a Mars Bar out of her school rucksack one breaktime. As she did it, I'd seen that there was a whole packet of them in there. A whole pack of glorious, filing chocolate bars. She then slung this bag full of wonderful riches back onto her peg as if it were nothing and ran outside to the playground.

I couldn't think about anything else for most of the morning. My mind kept going back to that bag, and the more I thought about it, the hungrier I felt. It seemed, just then, like I might die unless I ate one.

Inevitably, I gave in to the temptation. I stayed behind at break to go to the loo, and then ransacked the bag. I wanted, so desperately, to take all of them. To gorge myself on each and every Mars Bar in that pack. But I knew I could only take one. If it was just one, Sarah might not notice. She might think she'd miscounted.

The bliss I experienced opening and eating that Mars Bar was almost worth the fear of being caught. But it turned out it wasn't worth the consequences that came later.

Arriving back at home with Sally, Ninny and I dutifully took our coats off in the hall to be hung in the closet.

'What's that?' Sally asked me. She'd gone very, very still, and I could feel the room tipping. My heart twisting.

'Sorry?'

She strode towards me and pulled my slightly baggy white school Aertex out towards her from the bottom hem.

'This is chocolate,' she said. 'Isn't it?'

I couldn't say anything. I felt frozen with fear. With shame.

'What have you been doing?'

I tried to come up with an explanation. To say that everyone in my class had been given chocolate, and I hadn't wanted to say no. I could feel Ninny's wide eyes on me as I stammered and tried to apologise.

Sally looked crushingly disappointed. 'I know you want to eat, but you can't, darling,' she said. 'You just can't. Nobody will like you if you're fat.'

No amount of chocolate was worth the shame I felt then. It was as though it was bubbling up and pouring off me, but Sally seemed unable to see it. Her usually soft, understanding face began to harden.

'You aren't even sorry, are you?' she said.

'I am,' I said, quickly, my head down. 'I'm really sorry.'

But when I looked up at her, there were traces of tears in her eyes, and I knew what that meant. I knew.

'I'm really sorry, Sally,' I gasped.

'I'll have to speak to Henry about this,' she said.

'Please don't,' I said. 'I'm sorry. I'll say no next time. I'm sorry.'

I could see that she was torn. Part of her wanted to accept my terrified apology. To move on. But part of her was too much under Henry's spell.

'Go to your room.' Her voice was shaking, but she turned away from me.

I was in my room for half an hour. I wanted so much to climb into bed and hide, but I was too afraid of messing it up. Henry sometimes came round and inspected our rooms, and unmade beds were the worst of crimes. So I sat on the floor, my back against the wall at the far end of the room.

There was a tiny tapping at my door after a while and Ninny opened it, her expression full of horrified sympathy.

'Are you all right?' she whispered, from the doorway.

I didn't answer. I didn't want to cry. I knew Henry would be angrier if I'd been crying.

There was silence, and then my ever kind-hearted sister said, 'Sally says it's to help you. It probably feels horrible at the moment, but if you get thinner, then people will like you more, won't they? And you'll be better at sports and happier.'

I'd never hated Ninny before, but I hated her just then. I wanted her gone: out of my room and out of my life. I stared at a point on the floor not far from her and I waited for her to leave.

'Would you like a hug?' she asked, after a full twenty seconds.

'No,' I said, taking some small pleasure in being as harsh to her as I could be. 'I want you to get out of my room.'

I did look at her then, and I enjoyed her hurt expression. I even enjoyed it when she turned away, and went hurrying off down the stairs. I felt a twist of fear at the thought that she might tell Sally. But part of me almost wanted her to.

Henry arrived home twenty minutes later. I knew he had Callum with him. He'd picked him up from his cross-country training after school. But I heard nothing from Callum at all. The only sounds were of Sally and Henry talking in quiet voices.

I wanted to run down and howl that I hadn't meant to. That I was sorry. That it wasn't fair.

But I'd started to understand that none of that would help. Not now that Henry was involved.

Sally appeared a few minutes later, her eyes wide and slightly tearful. Her chest moving. She looked afraid, and it sparked a surge of fear in me so great that I thought I might vomit.

'Henry's waiting for you downstairs,' she said.

My legs were shaking hard as I walked down behind her. Henry's gaze was on the floor, but I felt as though he was watching me anyway. He seemed impossibly large as I walked towards him, and I tried to stop some distance away. But Sally pushed me forwards, into his shadow.

'What's this Sally tells me about you disobeying us?' he asked. I felt the room tipping as he looked at me. 'About you being a greedy pig, and ruining the clothes we've bought for you?'

'I'm so sorry,' I said. 'I didn't mean to.'

I didn't see the blindfold coming until it was over my

eyes. Sally must have had it in a pocket. I gasped, and tried to pull it off, until Henry snapped, 'Keep still.'

And then I felt a sudden, hard grip on my hand. Hard enough to hurt me. He was dragging me forwards, towards somewhere I couldn't even see.

'Stairs,' Henry's voice snapped from close in front of me, and I flinched, expecting to trip on them. But when I put my foot out and up, it met nothing, and I gave into a real scream as I felt myself falling forwards.

The hand that had been dragging me jerked me roughly upwards and, with a stagger, I found myself standing on something solid once again.

'Stupid girl,' Henry said. 'Just walk down the bloody stairs.'

The stairs were going downwards, not upwards. But there *were* no stairs that went down from the ground floor.

And yet we were descending, my shaking legs finding steps and the air growing colder.

At last, we stopped, and I felt a moment of wonderful relief. Until Henry said, 'Now you need to learn to do as you're told.'

And there was a whistling sound, and a crack, and pain bloomed across the back of my legs like fire. It came again. And then again.

I could only think about it being over while I begged Henry to stop. *Please, please to stop.*

It turned out that the beating wasn't the worst of it. The worst thing came after a few sounds I didn't understand, as I stood there with the back of my legs burning and throbbing. It came when they left me down there.

I didn't understand what was happening until I heard the door close. I pulled the blindfold off the moment I heard it, desperate to work out where I was and what was happening. But after a second of bright illumination that left only a vague image of an almost-empty space, the lights were shut off, and I was in total, profound darkness.

I don't know a child in the world who isn't afraid of the dark. Not one who doesn't have a primal fear of it. And I can tell you that what I felt then was a terror that drove right down into me. The fear chimed with the darkness that had been quiet in me for a long time, and it began to stir.

I'd seen, in the moment of illumination, that this basement was a place of stone and cobwebs, with only a few piled-up boxes in corners. But there was a mattress on the floor not far from my feet. With my hands held out in front of me, I crept towards it, and I was so frightened of what else might be down there with me that I gave a tiny scream when my foot connected with it. But it stayed still. Just a mattress, not a rat or a cockroach. I slowly, carefully, lowered myself down onto it.

The bedding was cold, but it was dry. There was a thin duvet over it and I climbed underneath, trying to cover every square inch of my skin in case there were spiders down here. Rats. Insects. My mind made imaginary horrors out of every sound.

Some endless while later there was movement above, and the door opened. The light was switched on and it felt like it had pierced into the back of my skull. I threw my hands up to protect my eyes.

It was Sally, her movements hurried. She closed the door behind her and kept glancing behind her at it as she made her way down. I wondered whether Henry knew she was there.

She was holding a tray. My initial, grateful thought was that she was feeding me. But as she approached, and placed it on the floor, I saw there was only a cup, and a bowl, and my toothbrush and toothpaste.

'You'd better do your teeth,' she said. 'And I'll leave the water with you overnight.'

I felt myself crumbling, then. She was going to leave me there. In that cold, terrible place, in absolute darkness. All night.

'Please,' I said, my voice strangled by tears. 'I'll never – do it – again.'

'Now, none of that,' Sally said, taking the cup off the tray without looking at me. 'Henry's made a decision, and he doesn't do these things lightly. You won't learn without punishment. You won't get better.'

I don't think I'd ever felt such a surge of misery. I couldn't seem to breathe past the crying.

I somehow cleaned my teeth when she held the toothbrush out to me, while my whole body felt like it was collapsing as I cried. When I was done, she leaned forwards, briefly, and kissed me on the top of the head. And then, even while I begged her not to leave me there, she climbed the stairs, and left. The lights went off a second later.

By the time Sally came to let me out the next day – blindfolding me again and then spinning me around repeatedly before leading me upstairs – I had changed. I could sense the shift in me, as I drifted up to the kitchen on what felt like someone else's legs. It was as though the softer part of me had fought a battle during the dark and had lost. And for the first time, as I looked at my perfect sister, sitting demurely at the table and telling Callum about the horse riding lessons that Sally had promised her, I could only feel pure, unadulterated hatred.

The stage lights made the far end of the room, and the figure on the chair, look unreal. An overexposed, artificial-seeming addition to the studio. The redness of the hair was part of it, Hanson thought. The long curls too bright against the black curtain.

Hanson felt a slight tremble in her legs as she made her way towards it, her shoes desperately loud in the empty space. It took her a few steps to process the shape fully, and to realise that the unreality was in part because of the figure.

'It's a dummy,' she said, trying not to wince at the sound of her own voice.

Domnall moved up alongside her, his eyes scanning the rest of the room and the curtain behind for signs of movement.

Hanson halted just in front of the doll. It was a simple shop mannequin, she saw. Keely – or someone helping Keely – had dressed it in a pair of jeans and a white hoodie and slumped it forwards to look as though it were captive. The slightly-too-large wig sat just off-centre, the red hair covering the face in a lopsided curtain.

Hanson's eyes moved to a second splash of colour: a slash of liquid red across the front of the white fabric.

'I think it's supposed to be blood,' she said.

There were a lot of things Jonah found himself wanting to ask Keely, but in the moments after she'd finished speaking, Lightman tapped on the interview-room door.

'I'll be right back,' Jonah said, and shut the door behind him.

'Sorry, chief,' Lightman said. 'I thought you'd want to hear Juliette and Domnall's update.'

'I do,' Jonah agreed.

'It looks like she did mean for us to go to the school,' Lightman said. 'She left a dummy posed in the drama studio.' He gave a small, slightly wry smile. 'No sign of Nina, though they are searching the rest of the building.'

Jonah felt a rush of genuine anger. So Keely really was playing games, and not the kind that guaranteed any prize if they won.

'Did they say if there was anything significant about the dummy? Anything that might actually be useful?'

'It was tied to a chair,' Lightman said. 'And posed. Do you want to send scene of crime down there?'

'I think that would be good,' Jonah said. He knew this was probably a wild goose chase of Keely's devising, but they still needed to take it seriously for the small chance that there was more to find. 'And I'd like photos as soon as possible. Ask Juliette and Domnall to take some.'

Lightman nodded. 'I also had a call back from Keely's social worker. He had a few observations about the abuse cases, and said he was happy to come in if we want him to. Would you like to see him?'

'I would,' Jonah said, without hesitation. Getting insight from someone who had worked with Keely for years would be invaluable. And it might also, he thought, be worth asking him to talk to Keely directly. Despite her apparent lack of concern over which social worker she had in interviews, there might be some kind of bond there. 'Ask him to come as soon as he can.'

*

By the time Lightman had called asking for photos of the scene, Hanson had already snapped the setup from numerous angles. The two officers from the kidnap squad had moved straight on to the main building to continue the search for Nina, though none of them really believed that she would be found onsite. The dummy was what they had been sent to find. Hanson was certain of it.

She approached the dummy more closely now, and took a close-up of the small black bag that was clutched in its lap. It was a cheap-looking handbag of the kind Hanson had sometimes worn on nights out as a student. A simple black rectangle with a chain, large enough only for a phone and wallet.

'Should we wait for crime scene, or have a look inside that?' she asked O'Malley, once she'd finished her photographs and checked that they were in focus.

'Does it look like there's anything in it?' O'Malley asked.

Hanson reached out and lifted the flap of the bag with a gloved hand, thinking momentarily of booby traps as she did so. Which was, she thought, ridiculous really. Keely might be an intelligent and manipulative young woman, but she was no bomb-making mastermind.

'Nothing I can see,' she said, a little disappointed. 'Though there could be something small.'

'Let's let forensics at it, then,' O'Malley answered. 'I'm sure McCullough will find it if there's something to be found.'

Hanson shared all the photos with Ben and the chief via email, and then stepped back to look at the scene again.

'She said she'd been telling us what had happened to Nina.' Her voice sounded dull. Brittle. 'If she's – if this is what she's done to her, and it's a wound like that which caused the blood, we need to find her quickly, don't we?'

*

Jonah looked over the photos in as calm a frame of mind as he could manage. This was supposed to make him angry, he thought. This deliberate trail of breadcrumbs with its hollow, infuriating prize. Keely was playing with them, and the only way to win her game was to refuse to get riled.

It was difficult going, though. The sight of that figure, with its tied hands and its wounded stomach, brought out a surge of protective fury.

He wondered whether he felt this more keenly now that he had his own daughter. He'd found the world a more horrifying place since she'd been born, he had to admit. News stories of disasters now hit him hard. Bus crashes or typhoons made him imagine Milly as one of the lost, and it was sometimes bad enough to make him switch off the news, or stop listening to a briefing about an RTA.

He had never met Nina Lennox, but that wouldn't stop him from fighting for her life. And it felt, increasingly, as if he really were fighting for it. The clues. The figure. The deliberate sense of danger. They all told him to be very much afraid for Nina.

He wasn't sure whether he felt relief or worry that he'd been told to keep interviewing Keely. Quick's on-call negotiator had reviewed the tapes and felt strongly that Jonah was making progress, even building up a relationship with her.

Jonah wished he felt the same.

He placed the photographs down after a few minutes, and went back to the interview room. He saw the way Keely's eyes lifted to his face as he entered, and her small smile. As if she knew that they'd found her clue.

'Let's continue,' he said, in as calm a voice as he could manage.

'Gladly,' Keely said, leaning back in her chair.

Jonah sat in front of her, took a breath, and said, 'Tell me about the drama studio.'

Keely's smile broadened. 'Did you like my little set piece?' She glanced towards the on-call social worker, and added, 'It's a shame you didn't get to see it, too. I was pleased with how it came out.'

'It was very striking,' Jonah said, refusing to rise to this. 'But I'd like to know what the point was.'

Keely gave a very small shake of her head. 'You need to work it out. That's your job, isn't it, detective chief inspector?'

'Well, not really,' Jonah countered, keeping his voice amiable. 'My job does have its deductive moments, but you'd be amazed at how much of it involves trying not to die of boredom in meetings with senior staff.'

Keely shook her head, still smiling. He wondered, momentarily, whether she might have actually found him amusing, but she went on much as before, her voice that perfect mixture of coldness and condescension.

'So really, I'm doing you a favour, aren't I?' she said. 'Letting you do some real police work.'

'You could do me a larger favour,' Jonah said, slightly more seriously. 'You could help me find your sister.'

Keely gave a long sigh, her smile disappearing. 'I'm really not a fan of these circular conversations,' she said. 'I think I might have another break.'

Jonah leaned forwards. 'If Nina is injured,' he said, 'like the dummy in that studio, then she needs our help. Not in a few hours, when you get round to it, but now.'

Keely's gaze focused on him once again, and it was as flat, and piercing, and unemotional as ever. 'Then you'd better sharpen up and start listening,' she said.

Jonah felt a sudden wave of weariness. A sense that all of

this was for nothing. He leaned away from her again, and looked down towards his hands.

'You look tired, detective chief inspector,' the girl said, after a moment.

Jonah looked up at her, in spite of himself. He wasn't comforted to see that the small smile of hers was back.

'Has the little one been keeping you up?' Keely asked. 'She's a scamp, that Milly. I hope Michelle's coping with her OK on her own.'

And Jonah, looking back at her, felt a wash of cold slide down his spine.

'She knew who I was before she arrived here,' Jonah told Lightman, his voice low. 'There's been nothing in any of our conversations to tell her either Milly's name or Michelle's. And I made sure to be well away from her when I talked to Michelle at the pub. She can only have known because she'd looked me up beforehand.'

Lightman made no effort to argue or tell him he was being paranoid, for which Jonah was profoundly grateful. Instead, he asked, 'Do you think she went to the pub because she knew you were there?'

'I think it's highly possible,' Jonah agreed. 'Though exactly why she wanted to end up talking to me is anyone's guess.'

Lightman considered for a moment, and then said, 'If she only knew you from the news, which is likely, then it might be about the complexity of the work you've done.' He gave a shrug. 'The cases you've been in the public eye about have all been unusual and complicated. She might have wanted someone who was willing to follow her clues.'

Jonah couldn't help but appreciate his sergeant's diplomatic way of putting it. His most recent high-profile case had been referred to the Independent Office for Police Conduct after the violent death of a culprit. Though the inquiry had found in his favour in the end.

He was interrupted in these self-lacerating thoughts by a call from DI Quick.

'Just updating you,' he said, without preamble. 'We've not managed to secure any location data on either of the two phones. Which implies either they've been in a rural location, or that the girls know how to avoid getting picked up, which I would consider unlikely.'

Jonah didn't argue. He wasn't willing to sound like a conspiracy theorist to Quick, but if Keely Lennox had known where he would be on Sunday afternoon and had planned all this around it, then he felt there was no information that would be beyond her reach.

'So,' Jonah said, instead, 'that presumably makes persuading her or working out her game all the more important.'

'Yes,' Quick said. 'I have some other ideas on our own lines of approach, but I'd like a full list of close contacts from you to do that. And I'd appreciate it if your team could see any contacts as soon as possible. If she's been to see someone at any point and we can pin down her location on any given day, that's data we can use.'

'On it now,' Jonah said.

Jonah ended the call and told Lightman what Quick wanted. 'I would include all the foster parents in that,' he added. 'If she's got some kind of a vendetta against them, she may have approached them at some point this week. Possibly with a view to threatening them.'

He returned to his office after that, and called Hanson for an update.

'The rest of the school is empty,' she told him. 'McCullough's here. She says it should be quick.'

'Good. I'd like you and Domnall to track Frank Pinder down,' he said. 'I want to know whether Keely visited him this week.'

'Are you wondering if she threatened him?' Hanson asked.

'Yes,' Jonah agreed. 'Though it's also possible that she approached with a pretence of friendship. I wouldn't assume anything with her.'

'OK,' Hanson said. 'On our way.'

Frank and Evelyn Pinder lived in one of the ugliest buildings Hanson could remember visiting. It had clearly been one of the many identikit brown-brick bungalows along the road before it had been extended lopsidedly to the right, with different tiles and windows. Someone had also, for reasons known only to them, painted all the window frames in a lurid yellow that in no way complemented the brown of the bricks.

'Oh my God,' Hanson said, as they climbed out. 'This one doesn't even need thought. Instant demolish.'

O'Malley grinned, even though keep, sell, demolish wasn't really his game. It was what she and Ben now did when visiting witnesses and suspects. It had arisen a year ago, when a casual conversation had led to them realising they were both obsessed with other people's houses. The numbers in the 'keep' category were still in single digits, and Hanson was acutely aware that her own run-down house would not have made it.

She was pretty sure Ben would agree with her on this one, anyway. They were neither of them fond of bungalows on the best of days, and this, Hanson thought, numbered among her least favourite of all time.

She was relieved to see light spilling through the glass at

the top of the door and from the side of the house, anyway. Despite not answering the phone, it looked like the Pinders were at home and still awake. She guessed that they'd made a point of not answering an unknown number late on a Sunday evening.

Getting visited by the police was unquestionably going to be worse than a call. It was gone ten thirty, much later than they would usually turn up to talk to a potential witness. But there was a fourteen-year-old girl out there somewhere, and that meant none of them were getting a cosy Sunday night.

Hanson decided not to knock as hard as she usually did, purely out of respect for the Pinders' neighbours. The effect was still swift, however. A door banged somewhere, a brighter light clicked on in the hallway, and there were quick footsteps towards the door.

It was Frank, she assumed, who opened the door to them. A short but trim man in a polo shirt. He had a lot of compact muscle, and looked in his late thirties. He also had the tan of someone who spent a lot of time outside. She wondered whether his work was something physical.

Frank didn't open the door all the way, and he looked both irritated and slightly anxious at their presence.

'Frank Pinder?' Hanson asked, moving so that she could see a little more of him. 'I'm DC Hanson and this is DS O'Malley. I'm sorry for calling so late, but we need to talk with you quite urgently.'

She saw his face tighten, a very familiar stress reaction to the presence of the police.

'Of course. Is something wrong?' He was clearly trying for laid-back, and failing.

'We need help rather than anything else,' Hanson said. 'Do you mind if we come in?'

There was a pause before Frank said, 'Sure.'

He let them into a hallway with a slightly shiny purple carpet that had one of the deepest piles she'd seen. She tried not to grin, imagining what Ben, the ultimate hater of deep piles, would be thinking.

'Evelyn's on night shift,' Frank told them, walking towards the rear of the bungalow. 'She's a stroke nurse.'

'Sounds tough.'

'It is, but she does a lot of good,' he said.

Hanson saw him glance towards the door at the very back of the house, which was shut, before turning left through the one open doorway. 'In here.'

He led them into a living room that featured a very bulky suite in cream leather and floor-length floral curtains. The windows presumably looked onto the garden, but with all the curtains shut there was no view, and thanks to the size of the furniture and a lot of colour, the place had a very claustrophobic feel.

Hanson wondered how the Lennoxes must have felt living here. It was clearly nicer than the children's home, but it was undeniably a step down from the pretty country cottage they had lived in with their mother, and miles from the manor-house existence Keely had described with the Murray-Watts.

Might the lowly living conditions have been one of the reasons for Keely's accusations? Hanson knew from case studies that kids could do pretty extreme things when they were unhappy and powerless.

Frank waved his hand at the three-piece suite, which up close looked grubby and worn. He sat on the very edge of the armchair and shifted several times, reminding her of a rugby player readying himself to kick a conversion.

'We need as much information as you can give us on Keely and Nina Lennox,' Hanson said, easing herself onto the sofa next to O'Malley. She studied Frank's face for his reaction. 'I don't know if you're aware that they went missing?'

None of the tension left Frank's expression. He nodded, as though he'd been expecting this question.

'Someone called my wife a week ago,' he said. 'I wish we'd been able to help. But it's been a long time since we've seen them.'

'So they've not been in touch at all since they moved out?' O'Malley asked.

'No.' Frank rubbed his thumb against his forehead and then tried to smile. 'It was all a bit of a shitstorm, because of how angry Keely got.'

Hanson gave him a sympathetic smile, and let O'Malley answer. It was clear to her that Frank was the kind of man who would warm to Domnall's chatty style.

'Ah,' O'Malley said. 'It must be difficult building up a relationship with a teenager. Did you have a falling-out, like?'

Frank rubbed at his forehead again, glancing from O'Malley to Hanson and back. 'Well, that's a bit of an understatement, actually. She said all sorts of things . . . really horrible things.' He grimaced, and sat a bit further forwards. 'The worst thing was, I really cared about those kids. I tried hard – really hard – to make them feel like this was their home. And I did my best when they had problems at school.'

'Friendship problems?' Hanson asked.

'Yeah. They didn't . . . fit in easily. Keely particularly.' He sighed. 'I told her how it all worked. That you had to give these kids something if you wanted something from them. And I probably shouldn't have encouraged her to sit and drink with them all, but it really helped. She suddenly had friends. But then she kind of ran with it, and –' he glanced up at O'Malley, uncertainly – 'she went a bit wild. Which was probably my fault, to be honest. Evelyn thought it was.'

'Wild how?' Hanson asked.

Frank got up, abruptly, and went to fiddle with the curtains, adjusting them to cover some imagined gap.

'She was suddenly staying out late, and coming back really drunk. She got pretty mouthy, too.' He shook his head. 'I probably should have guessed she'd got herself a boyfriend. And of course she'd gone for some complete lowlife.'

Hanson hesitated for a moment, and then said, 'Do you think it was attention-seeking behaviour? Maybe a cry for help based on her own difficulties?'

Frank gave a snort, and turned back to face her. 'Not Keely. She's not like that. She knows exactly what she's doing, and how to get what she wants. Honestly, she had me wrapped round her little finger. Until I found out about Dev, and I just . . . I really saw red.' He returned to his chair. 'What was she doing? Messing around with some drugged-up scumbag? Possibly throwing her life away? I mean, she was fourteen, and sleeping with him. She could so easily have got pregnant . . .'

It was clear that Frank still felt the anger that had first possessed him. His voice grew louder and his movements were jerky as he went to sit down again.

'Did you confront her about it?' Hanson asked.

'I confronted both of them, but separately,' Frank replied, rubbing at his head again. 'I told Dev to stay away from her, and I told her that she wasn't seeing him. End of story.' He shook his head. 'I know that wasn't necessarily the best approach. Her social worker said I should have talked to them about it. Been understanding. But I'm supposed to try and be a parent, you know? And I wanted what was best for her.'

There was a slight noise somewhere in the house, the kind of noise that a heating system might make clicking in. Frank's eyes darted towards the hallway, and Hanson wondered why he looked quite so ill at ease. Whether it was the memory of that time or some present worry.

'How did Keely react?' O'Malley asked.

'Jesus, she flipped out,' Frank said. 'I mean, at first, she just looked at me really coldly, like she wasn't human any more. It really freaked me out. She'd always seemed ... troubled but sweet. A bit over-emotional, you know? Not, like, really cold.'

Hanson was half listening to him, while part of her focused on the back of the house. She could hear no other sounds.

'Fourteen-year-olds can be pretty difficult,' O'Malley said, with a very warm smile. It was amazing to Hanson how easily he could come across as a parent himself, when he'd never had kids of his own. Domnall somehow possessed a unique ability to make people feel like he was one of them. Like they were in this together.

Frank shook his head. 'What she did isn't normal teenage behaviour. Accusing me of ... of ... And, you know, I should have seen it coming and protected myself. It would have been so easy for her to destroy my life. She nearly did. I was just bloody lucky the police were on the ball.'

'So you think she said those things out of anger?' Hanson asked, clicking back into the conversation fully.

Frank shook his head. 'Not even that. Revenge, I think. When I'd finished having my say, she stood up, and came up to me, and she said, really quietly, "If you do this, I'm going to make your life hell." And then she smiled at me.' Hanson could see a sheen of sweat on Frank's forehead now. 'She fucking smiled at me.'

Hanson felt a chill run up her spine. Without meaning to, she found herself picturing the scene, and it was only too believable. The coldness. The absolute belief in her own superiority that Keely had exhibited throughout their interviews.

She wondered, for the second time that evening, whether Keely was playing them for total fools. With the clues. The staged setup.

'What about after they left?' O'Malley asked. 'She didn't try to get in touch with you?'

'No,' Frank said, stiffly.

'And you didn't try to speak to her?' Hanson pressed.

Frank gave a slight laugh. 'I was strongly encouraged not to contact them and, to be honest, I was only too happy to be out of their lives. The thought of them just reminded me of all that shit, and the four days I spent going between a cell and an interview room with my life in pieces were . . .' He shook his head again. 'It's a shame, because Nina's a nice kid, and I think she liked being here. It was just her sister. And I don't know whether she was born the way she is or something pushed her, but there's something really, really wrong with Keely.'

Hanson nodded, with her carefully honed neutral smile. No agreement, and no disagreement. And then she asked, 'Would you mind if I just use your bathroom while my sarge asks a few more things?'

'I . . . no, that's . . . that's fine . . .'

Hanson rose, and before Frank Pinder could direct her to a particular bathroom, O'Malley took his cue and asked, 'Did you see that side of her at other times? The cold side?'

Hanson was already out in the corridor by the time he had begun to reply, and was turning left towards the back of the house. As quietly as possible, she opened the last door on the corridor, to find a bedroom dominated by a super-king bed. There was low lighting coming from a bedside lamp, but most of the illumination was created by a large, wall-mounted TV.

Hanson glanced at it, and saw that it was frozen on an image of two immaculately dressed teenage girls. She recognised the two with slightly embarrassing ease: Leighton Meester and Blake Lively from an episode of *Gossip Girl*.

There was another door in the room, through to an en-suite bathroom, which was in darkness. No sign of anyone here.

Before she could register anything else, Frank Pinder appeared in the doorway.

'It's just down here,' he said, waving a hand down the hallway towards the front door.

Hanson smiled, and said, 'Thanks,' as though she hadn't just intruded on his bedroom.

Jonah had spent some time in his office, his mind spinning over everything Keely had said and done. So much of it, he thought, was designed to cause a reaction. The dummy. The disdain. The casual mention of his daughter and partner.

Keely seemed to delight in prodding. In finding an exposed nerve and hitting it. But the story she was telling seemed to run at odds with that. It wasn't about unsettling him or his team so much as affecting them emotionally.

If you stripped everything else away, he thought, then it was just a terribly sad story of abuse. One that had at times drawn him in.

And he needed to hold on to that, he realised. He needed to shelve all the frustration and the looking for clues, and for a little while just do as Keely had asked and listen. He gave every witness that opportunity, and in spite of everything she was doing to make it difficult, he wanted to give Keely a chance to talk.

He breathed out, imagining all the irritation and urgency leaving him. It was surprisingly effective. By the time Jonah rose and went back to the interview room, he felt a sense of calm that had eluded him for the last few hours.

Settling himself in front of Keely with a smile, he said, 'I'm ready to carry on with your story when you are. I'd like to hear it.'

And for the first time, he thought he might have caught a hint of surprise on Keely's perfectly controlled face.

I 2

As painful as Sally and Henry made my life for three years, I actually owe them something. It was the two of them who pushed me to the point of snapping, and through them I began to understand the power it's possible to have over people if you're only willing to use it.

It took several months for those lessons to really hit home. Several months, and a lot of suffering. My initial resentment of Ninny only made me less attractive in the Murray-Watts' eyes, and my desperate appeals for mercy – or at times for food – seemed to produce nothing short of loathing.

By contrast, Ninny grew ever more happy and grateful. I could practically see her halo. And it was easy for her to be full of charm. She glided over every punishment, and her artistic abilities and her – admittedly extraordinary – memory for stories filled the Murray-Watts with vicarious pride far more than my brilliant academic results. And then there was the horse riding, Sally's one true love, which of course Ninny was also a natural at.

I actually found myself missing Henley Street Children's Home during those months. Even the blandest of food was better than the constant gnawing of my stomach, and the teasing of a few kids had no power to make me feel desolate or terrified like Henry's disapproval did.

The only thing that made any of it bearable was the discovery that my much skinnier frame had its uses. Despite the hunger that sometimes made me feel weak, I flourished as a sportswoman. By the end of cross-country season I was already a strong contender, and with athletics beginning in the summer, my lightness combined with my bitter determination to prove myself gave me a lead over all my peers.

And that in turn led to popularity. Our little primary school was very big on sports, and I became something of a hero as the kids in my house realised I could help them win the end-of-year house points trophy. I no longer had to sit alone at lunch and was often asked to come and chuck a ball around at breaktime.

I think the fact that I was thinner helped my popularity, too. They looked at me and saw someone appropriately spindly and girlish, instead of the solid lump I had once been. I started to find all my interactions easier, and that encouraged me to play up to it all. To be the laughing, delicate girl.

It makes me cringe, looking back. Not that I played the girlish one, but that it took me so long to understand it all. To see how easy it is to control people if you give them what they are expecting to see; or if you unexpectedly withhold it.

This was, of course, long before the other two men moulded us so completely. The two men who would make it clear that we were not just under their control but were their toys. That we existed to gratify them.

My relationship with Ninny went the other way. I could no longer look at her without feeling furious, and I could see how hurtful she found it when she tried to spend time with me. I remember her creeping to my room one night, her face pale and pinched, and asking if she could get into my bed.

'I had a nightmare,' she said.

'I'm trying to sleep,' I told her. 'And you don't have any reason for nightmares.'

She stood holding the door. Although I couldn't see her face, with the dim landing light making her a silhouette, I knew that I'd hurt her. But instead of leaving, she stayed where she was, and in the end asked, 'What's it like? When you disappear? Where do you go?'

I remember sitting up just to stare at her. 'You mean they don't tell you?'

Ninny shook her head. 'No.'

For a moment, I forgot about being angry with her. I just wanted her to know. To believe me, and to feel for me. She was still my sister. Still Ninny.

'They lock me in the dark, Ninny,' I said. 'In the cellar. It's so dark you can't see anything at all. And you can hear insects, all around you. And you're so scared you think you might die, but you don't. It just keeps going on and on.'

Ninny came to sit next to me on the bed. I made room for her, and I found myself remembering the nights when we used to do this, back in the children's home. Back when we'd been real sisters.

There was a pause, and then I could hear Ninny sniffing. She was crying, on my behalf. 'I'll ask them not to. They shouldn't do that.'

'You could try,' I said. 'But they might be annoyed.'

'They don't get annoyed with me,' Ninny said, simply.

I felt the bitter, stinging truth of it. And all the tender little thoughts that had been creeping back vanished in a moment.

'They will,' I told her, quietly, wishing it was true. 'And then they'll do it to you, too.'

Ninny stood up in a hurry, and walked away, quickly.

'They won't, because I'm *good*,' she hissed, loudly enough that I was afraid Sally or Henry would hear.

'No, you aren't,' I whispered. 'You're pretty. That's all. You're no better than I am. And you're nowhere near as clever.'

She ran away from me, and I could see, as she turned towards her room, that her face was all crumpled with the effort of not crying. It made me smile.

From that night onwards, any chance of us being real sisters again disappeared. When I was locked in the darkness, I started imagining that Ninny was there instead. That it was her crying and whimpering. And it made me more and more determined to be strong. Not like weak, pathetic little Ninny.

It was different with Callum. He was punished too, though less often than I was. So instead of being enemies, we became awkward comrades. If one of us had food and the other one didn't, we would find a way of sharing it. It was dangerous, but it kept us from that terrible, intense hunger that made it impossible to sleep. It kept us from going to pieces.

The strange thing was that the irritation with each other was still there, too. We could immediately go from allies to enemies.

I found it impossible to relax when he was around. I felt too aware of his physical presence. Too keyed into it. I would sometimes imagine digging my nails into his skin, or pulling his hair, just to relieve the itchiness, and there were times when I saw the same urge in him, too.

But Callum didn't seem to mind Ninny. Once, when he and I were slung across the lower branches of a beech tree at the far end of the garden, I told him that I hated my sister.

He stared at me, and asked, 'Why would you hate her?'

'Because she's Little Miss Perfect,' I said, rubbing my hand across the smoothest part of the bark. It gave off a faint smell, like wet days in autumn. 'And because she used to care about me, but she doesn't any more. And because the more she sits looking all pretty and well behaved, the more they get angry with me.'

Callum picked at a piece of bark for a little while. I knew he was thinking. He often did this before he spoke. It was what made people think he was slow. Stupid. Witless. But I'd started to realise that Callum was none of those things. He was a deep thinker, and sometimes – just sometimes – he understood things better than I did. And when he did, it would both impress and infuriate me.

'Why do you hate her when they're the ones who are hard on you?' he asked, in the end.

I felt irrationally furious with him for doubting the people I wanted desperately to be loved by. For doubting Sally.

'They'd love me if she wasn't here,' I said, and as tears stung my eyes, I turned away from him.

'They wouldn't,' Callum said, simply and harshly. 'They were the same to me before you came.'

I wanted to argue again. I thought about saying that that was because Callum wasn't good, like I was. He was cheeky sometimes. He took things he shouldn't. Whereas I . . . I tried.

But for some reason, as blunt as he was with me, I couldn't quite bring myself to say it. So I asked him, belligerently, 'So why do you stay? You could ask to be taken away.'

Callum gave a shrug. 'Because other places would be worse. For someone like me.'

'What do you mean?'

He looked at me, with an expression that for some

reason sent a strange thrill through me, and then turned away and shifted on the branch. I remember the exact sound his jeans made as they scraped across the bark.

'I did some bad things, where I was before,' he said. 'No *good* foster parents will have me. There are some terrible places you can end up. At least here I'm at a good school and they help me to learn. I'm going to make my future better.'

I watched him, thinking this sounded like something he'd learned somewhere. Looking back, it's obvious where it came from. They were the words of the Murray-Watts, drilled into him until he believed them. They weren't the thoughts of a troubled twelve-year-old.

He moved again, this time sliding his legs off the branch and jumping down onto the bare earth. 'Maybe you can make your future better, too,' he said to me, before walking away.

13

Jonah let Keely have another break at ten forty-five p.m. It was frustrating to lose more time with her as they approached the potential eleven o'clock cut-off, but at the same time, he found himself wanting to look further into Keely's care records. To see what had become of her in the years since the incidents she was describing.

Abuse and trauma often, he knew, left an obvious imprint on people's lives. A pattern of dysfunctional behaviour. Victims were often incredibly self-destructive. They would do things that made it difficult for them to build relationships with others, or that tore those relationships apart.

He had seen it time and again in the people who committed crimes. And to a certain extent he had lived it, too. Both in watching his mother's decline into alcoholism, and in the powerful urge to wreck everything he had felt at times as a teenager. He was very lucky to have been drawn to the idea of the police. It had offered him a system to play into, and a motivation to keep control. It had been the saving of him.

And then he thought, momentarily, about the night less than a year ago when he had gone home with his ex-fiancée and essentially taken a wrecking ball to the happiest part of his life. When he had torn himself away from Jojo Magos, only months after he'd at long last been able to pursue a relationship with her.

In the face of that, he wondered whether he was entirely free from the effects of his childhood.

You don't have time for that, he thought to himself, and opened Keely's care record with determined concentration. *Look at Keely. Look for who she is, and why she's doing this.*

The care record included frequent references to friendship difficulties before Keely's time at the Pinder house, but Jonah was surprised to note that those fell away once she had become settled with her second foster family. Her social worker reported that she seemed to be managing well, with numerous friends who seemed to all but worship her.

Mark Slatterworth had also noted a few incidents where Keely had clearly picked up and then discarded a close friend, however. He had tried to open up a conversation with her about it on more than one occasion. Some of her responses made Jonah feel twinges of unease, most notably in a conversation that had taken place only eight months ago.

MARK SLATTERWORTH: You were very close to Samantha a little while ago. But you've stopped mentioning her. Is there any reason?

KEELY LENNOX: You've clearly already asked my key-worker about this.

MS: I don't want to know what he thinks. I want to know how you're doing. What you're feeling.

KL: All right. Samantha started making friends with Nina. And I was happy to let her. There's no point in sharing a friend. Splitting their loyalty.

MS: I wouldn't agree with that. I think you three could all be close friends together.

KL: That's not how it works.

MS: For you?

KL: For anyone with any sense. Why settle for half of someone?

The conversation had moved on, her social worker clearly feeling that he was making no headway. But it had its effect on Jonah. He didn't read those comments as a troubled young woman talking. They sounded to Jonah like the remarks of a sociopath.

But then he turned a page and found something that made him momentarily forget his worries about Keely.

The DCI called them into the briefing room as soon as Hanson and O'Malley had returned from Frank Pinder's house. Hanson sensed increasing frustration and urgency from the chief.

'I want to establish what is and isn't worth our time,' he said, half sitting on the table while he spoke. 'We've so far made little headway, despite a lot of hard work, and time is obviously pressing.' He looked towards Hanson and O'Malley. 'Tell me about Frank Pinder.'

O'Malley didn't immediately jump in, so Hanson began, 'I'm not quite sure about him. He seemed nervous, and when I strolled into his bedroom, he reacted with anxiety. It seemed like he wanted me out of there, though there was nothing that would immediately get him in trouble. I was interested to see that he was in the middle of an episode of *Gossip Girl*, though.' She glanced at Ben and Domnall. 'Anyone might be embarrassed getting caught watching a teen drama, but I wondered . . . Could he be getting off on it? Watching it because he's attracted to teenage girls, which was why he was jumpy about it?'

'The investigation into Frank Pinder was fairly thorough, though,' O'Malley argued. 'Names and dates checked, and found to not quite line up. Frank and his wife interviewed exhaustively. He was suspended from his job while this went on, and given he works as a football coach to teenage girls, he'd have have been mad risking something with his foster daughters. He had a lot of supportive witness statements from girls and parents within the club, too.'

'There's some data to suggest that those with a predilection for young girls or boys will gravitate towards roles of authority over them,' Lightman countered. 'I would also discount any testimony from parents or teenagers as irrelevant. Unless they experienced his behaviour directly, their experiences lie outside the scope of the investigation.' He glanced at the DCI. 'Given the fairly low prosecution rate for sexual assault, I would say it's still more likely on the balance of probability that Frank Pinder was guilty.'

Hanson was surprised to hear Ben giving such a forceful opinion. He was usually the neutral one. The one who took even more time to form a definite theory than the chief, which was saying something.

She shot Ben a grin. 'But to be fair, you haven't met her yet,' she said. 'You'll probably come down on the side of it all being manipulation if you do.'

Ben shrugged. 'That just tells me she has an unfortunate manner, which is possibly what's stood against her in the past. To be really objective about it, it's better to discount her personality altogether.'

Hanson had the momentary and distinctly uncomfortable feeling that he might be slightly angry with her. He didn't return her smile or make any effort to soften his words.

'I think something else is worth adding in,' the chief said. 'Keely actually made three accusations of abuse, rather than two.'

'She said, right at the start, that there were three men who'd wrecked her life,' Hanson said, trying to think about Keely and not about Ben's reaction.

'She did,' the chief agreed. 'And it's entirely possible that she's here to get some kind of revenge on them for getting away with whatever they did.'

The chief distributed copies of a pair of printed sheets: a report written by Keely's social worker. Hanson started scanning it, but paused to listen as the DCI went on.

'The third accusation was eighteen months ago, at Henley Road Children's Home. That's four months after the situation with Frank Pinder. Keely Lennox had a keyworker named Jared Boula, who she seemed to get on well with, until she asked to see her social worker and explained that he had sexually assaulted her.'

'Keely mentioned him,' Hanson said. 'He was Nina's keyworker at one point, wasn't he? The one she adored.'

'That's right,' the chief confirmed. 'Though there's no suggestion in the investigation of Nina being involved this time.'

Hanson found the description of the assault on the printout. Boula had apparently forced Keely into a corner, kissed her and put his hand up her skirt.

It was not an unheard-of situation, Hanson thought. She could well imagine a man with power over a teenage girl taking advantage. It was depressingly common.

'After his interview with her, Mark Slatterworth spoke directly to the manager of the home, and to other witnesses there,' the chief said. 'It seems Jared Boula had already raised concerns about Keely. He suggested she should work with someone else, because she'd become obsessed with him.' As Hanson glanced up, she saw he was looking at his team very intently. 'He'd reported to the manager, only three days before, that she'd tried to kiss him.'

Hanson sighed. It never seemed to be simple when it came to Keely Lennox. Everything had another side to it.

'Presumably she didn't succeed in kissing him,' O'Malley said.

'Not according to Jared Boula, no,' Jonah agreed. 'He said that he rebuffed her firmly and attempted to remove himself from the situation. Mark Slatterworth's report was critical of the home's manager for not intervening earlier. He raised concerns about the girls staying there, and ultimately got them moved.'

'Any reason to think the keyworker was lying?' O'Malley asked.

'Nothing obvious, but Keely dropped her accusations the following day, asking her social worker not to pursue them.' He paused for a moment. 'But I'm going to ask for more information from Mark Slatterworth once he arrives. His report is fairly brief, and it's possible he felt there was some truth to her claims. I'd also like to talk to Jared Boula directly.'

'So where do you think this leaves us with how to find Nina?' Hanson asked, doubtfully. 'Should we assume that if we follow her clues, we'll find her sister?'

'That,' the chief said, 'is the biggest question. And it's a tough one to call. I feel that Keely both deserves to be listened to and has her own agenda. It's quite possible that her trail of clues is a deliberate waste of time.'

There was a brief silence, during which Hanson felt neatly torn in two. The more she found out about the older Lennox sister, the more she believed that this was not a well-intentioned game. But Keely was a troubled sixteen-year-old, and so it was also inevitable to want to help her.

The silence was only broken when Lightman said, 'I'd like to keep looking for whatever trail she's left. There are other things we should do, but we have a witness who is asking us to listen to her, in a way that other officers possibly haven't. I think we should prove that we're taking her seriously.'

'Even if it takes more time than we have?' O'Malley asked, quietly.

'So we're ignoring cases of sexual assault now, are we?' Lightman shot back, immediately.

Even the chief looked slightly surprised at his tone. It was unusual for their team meetings to become even remotely confrontational, and, more than that, it was profoundly unlike Ben, who was all but impossible to ruffle.

It was possible that something else was bothering him, and Hanson realised with a rush of guilt that she hadn't asked how things were going with his dad. Ben's father had been given a terminal prognosis for his stomach cancer, and had been slowly losing both weight and strength as he grew less and less able to eat. It was in the nature of these things to go from a slow progression to a fast one, and Hanson felt a squeeze of anxiety at the thought that things might have escalated.

Ben seemed to realise that he'd spoken a little harshly. After a brief pause, he added, 'Look, what I mean is – if this is the only way she's going to let us find Nina, and if there are clear cases of assault, we ought to listen.'

'Thanks, both of you,' the DCI said, and went on with the utmost diplomacy, 'I agree with Ben that we need at least one member of the team following the trail. If we fail to find Nina, having ignored it, I think we'd all feel hugely responsible.' He paused for a moment. 'But we also need to look hard at the places we think Nina might be hidden. That means all the places associated with the people she knows. I'd like to talk to Henry Murray-Watt himself. If he's one of the three men she wants brought down, then he might have something interesting to say about recent interactions with Keely. There could be conversations his wife doesn't know about.' He stopped to take a drink. 'We also need to talk to Callum Taylor, who we've still not successfully got in touch with, and who doesn't seem to be at home.'

Hanson nodded. 'She's talked about him a lot so far, and it sounds like their relationship was complex.'

'I'd agree with that analysis,' O'Malley said, wryly. 'Alongside beating him around the head with a tennis racquet, it sounds to me like she was interested in him. I wouldn't be at all surprised if the two of them had ended up romantically involved, despite the beating. And I'm told some people actually quite like that sort of thing, so, you know . . .'

Hanson laughed, relieved that O'Malley was back to a little light banter. Ben seemed to feel the same, as he offered, in a much lighter voice, 'Callum Taylor's neighbour mentioned a girlfriend. They could be seeing each other now.'

'Keely must have had some help,' Hanson chipped in. 'She doesn't drive, but she somehow managed to set up a scene in the school, leave Nina somewhere, get to the pub, and presumably leave a trail in numerous other places.'

'Agreed,' the chief said. 'I've already passed his details on to the kidnap squad, but I'd also like you to try his flat again, Ben. Take Juliette with you, and if any of the neighbours are awake, talk to them. It's possible one of them has seen something, or that he's actually been hiding out there while he holds Nina.'

'Do you think he really would?' Hanson asked. 'Keely said he was kind to Nina. He doesn't seem likely to want to harm her.'

The chief nodded. 'I would agree, if it were all about his own actions. But from all we've heard about Keely, she's manipulative as hell. It's quite possible Callum has become a victim of that.'

'OK,' Lightman said. He didn't, to Hanson's mind, sound entirely happy still. But he was at least agreeing to the chief's plan.

'If you have no joy,' the chief added, 'we'll get a method of entry team out to you. I think we can justify it on the basis of danger to life. But see if you can get Henry Murray-Watt to come in before you go.'

The briefing broke up, and Hanson and Lightman made their way to their desks. They put calls through to the Murray-Watts' landline, and then to each mobile. They all went to voicemail, and Hanson left messages asking for Henry to attend the station.

'They're probably at home and ignoring the phone,' she said. 'They were in earlier. And that could be deliberate avoidance, or just the fact that it's a Sunday evening and they resent the intrusion.'

'Sally seemed concerned for Nina, though,' Ben replied.

'But maybe Henry isn't,' Hanson said. 'And it sounds like Henry calls all the shots. Though it's possible Keely was lying about that.'

They headed out, in what was an unusual silence. Hanson was still thinking about Ben's snappish responses in the briefing, and waited until they were in her little Nissan Micra to ask, 'Are things OK with you at the moment?'

Ben glanced over at her, his expression as unreadable as ever. 'They're all right.'

'Is your dad . . .?'

There was a pause before Lightman said, 'He's not in a great way, but . . . he's with us.' After a few moments, when Hanson said nothing, he added, 'Sorry for being a bit . . . tetchy.'

Hanson started the engine. 'You're allowed to be. You've got a lot to deal with. And to be honest, if you weren't grumpy sometimes I'd worry.'

Lightman gave a slightly crooked smile. 'I'm happy to fabricate bad moods for your reassurance at any time. Just say the word.'

Hanson grinned back at him, but felt a familiar surge of

disappointment at how little he'd been willing to say. Ben had become better at sharing over recent months, but it was still something he struggled with. It was hard not to imagine that it was her fault each time he skirted a subject. That she was either pressing too hard or that he didn't trust her.

Part of her concern was that he might distance himself from her again if she pushed too hard. He had suddenly gone cold on her the previous year, an episode that she was pretty sure had been triggered by her hugging him for a good while after a tense situation.

He'd hugged her too, of course. It had been a strangely long and emotional clinging together that made her cringe every time she thought of it. It had also come just before she'd started dating Jason Walker, and it was hard to sort out in her mind what had gone on.

Ben had never actually explained his retreat, either. Or, in fact, his sudden return to warmth and banter several months later. And although Hanson had badly wanted to ask him on numerous occasions, she also found herself unable to. It was a subject swathed in embarrassment and the potential for uncovering unwelcome facts.

So instead of saying anything else, Hanson lapsed back into light-hearted banter, which carried them through the rest of the short journey.

Alone in his office once again, Jonah found himself checking his phone for a reply from Michelle. There was still nothing to suggest that she was struggling, but his message showed as being read but not replied to, and this evening it worried him slightly.

He knew the root cause was probably what he was hearing and reading about Keely. However unclear he was on what had really happened, it was almost impossible to avoid thinking of his own daughter. Specifically, about what would happen to her if something befell both him and Michelle.

He felt a squeeze in his chest at the idea of Milly left alone in the world. She wouldn't be left penniless like the Lennox sisters, he told himself. But she would also be without any family to step in and help her. Michelle had lost her mother and was estranged from her father, and Jonah's own mother was an alcoholic who hadn't been a real parent since he'd reached double digits. If he and Michelle suffered some terrible fate, Milly would have nobody, being as thoroughly without godparents as she was without family.

From thinking about this, it was hard not to imagine that something had happened already. He wanted to check on his partner and daughter. The lack of reply was creating a slowly increasing wave of anxiety.

There was another side to his worry, too. And it was a side that he felt instinctively to be overdramatic and ridiculous, but it was there, and it had been triggered by Keely's smiling questions after his family.

The fact that Keely had done her homework didn't, he knew, mean that she represented any threat to his partner or child. That she had laid a careful trail elsewhere made it, if anything, less likely that she had sent anyone after them, not more. She – and whoever was helping her – was unlikely to have had the time for anything else. But the gnawing worry was still there. He opened up his call list and paused with his thumb over Michelle's number. He could so easily just check in.

The problem was that this was a key time for Michelle to get some sleep. Milly generally slept for a good two hours from ten until midnight, and it was often the longest uninterrupted time they got out of her. They had both learned to snatch at that sleep while they could, as that generally made the rest of the night bearable.

If Jonah called now and woke Michelle, there was no question that she would struggle. Or, in fact, struggle more than usual. It wasn't as though the lack of sleep was easy at the best of times.

He closed the calls list down, and sent another message instead, asking her to drop him a line once she was awake. If she had her phone on Do Not Disturb, as she usually did, she would only see it if Milly surfaced for a feed. A much better scenario.

O'Malley tapped on his door as he was putting his phone away.

'Mark Slatterworth is here,' his sergeant said. 'The social worker.'

'Bring him in.'

He felt a surge of relief at having Keely's social worker here at last. He had a lot of questions for him, both about the various abuse allegations and about Keely as a whole.

Mark looked like a good resource to tap. His reports were sympathetic but on the whole, Jonah thought, balanced. Mark had also, according to the care file, last spoken to Nina and Keely less than a fortnight ago. If Keely had been busy setting up her plan at that point, she might have given him some indication of it. And, in particular, of anyone who'd helped her.

Beyond that, Keely's social worker was the most likely person to persuade her to talk. If Mark Slatterworth could somehow get her to abandon the games and let them know where Nina was, then everything else she had to say could come afterwards.

O'Malley reappeared with Slatterworth, who was exactly Jonah's vision of social workers everywhere. He was probably somewhere in his late twenties, and possessed of a very round, very good-natured face. His checked shirt and large, black-rimmed glasses were complemented by a hooded cardigan. He had a swift, slightly bouncy walk, and an air of being able to take whatever was thrown at him and keep smiling.

'Thanks so much for coming in, Mr Slatterworth,' Jonah began, while O'Malley went to find them both a cup of tea.

'Oh, I'm definitely a Mark,' the social worker said, with a laugh. 'I can't pull off anything formal.'

Jonah gave him a smile, finding it easy to warm to the cheery Edinburgh accent.

'You were a great help to my sergeant over the phone,' he began. 'I just had a few other questions for you. I wondered if you could give me your observations on Callum Taylor.'

'On Callum?' Mark asked. He considered for a few seconds. 'I suppose ... I mean, his own social worker will know a lot more, so all I can give you is what I saw when visiting Keely and Nina.'

'How he interacted with Keely and Nina is one of the things I'm especially interested in,' Jonah replied. 'But tell me your thoughts on him as a whole. Was he particularly troubled?'

'I think he was,' Mark said, carefully, 'though he calmed down a lot. At nine, when he was living with his parents, he went after another kid with a knife. I mean, the other kid punched him first, but the reaction was extremely violent.'

'Problems at home?' Jonah asked.

'Yes, absolutely,' Mark agreed. 'An alcoholic father who didn't mind using his fists now and then and a mother who had basically checked out. They were living in poverty. Being fostered was the best thing that could have happened. This other life got offered to him, and he totally turned round. Became a straight-A student, and a calm and willing one.

And I don't think it was just that he saw this big house, and the Porsche on the drive,' the social worker added, with a laugh. 'They were clearly putting in a lot of work with him.'

'So you didn't feel there was any abuse there?'

Mark shook his head, firmly. 'No, I didn't. And I approached the whole thing with as open a mind as you could, but I work with a lot of these kids and you just . . . you just don't see kids achieving like that when they're being beaten at home.'

'So why do you think Keely made those accusations?'

'Because she had a lot of undiagnosed trauma over her mum, and because she was deeply unhappy at school,' Mark said. 'She was being bullied, and ostracised, and she'd not let on. That came out later from the school itself. They'd barely raised it with Sally and Henry, so they were culpable, I think.'

Jonah let all this percolate for a moment, and then he asked, 'Are you aware of any ongoing friendship with Callum Taylor?'

'You mean between him and Keely?' Mark asked. 'Ah, I don't know.' He made a tutting sound. 'I did think, once, that I'd seen the two of them together out in town. This would be, I don't know, a year ago or so. I was on a bus, going down Queensway, and I saw a couple who looked like them. Though when I asked Keely about it she denied it.'

O'Malley returned at that point with two cups of tea, and Jonah paused to let Mark drink a few mouthfuls.

'The investigation seemed to conclude that Callum was being manipulated by Keely while at the Murray-Watts,' Jonah went on, once they'd both taken a drink. 'Did you think that was happening?'

'I think it's quite possible,' the social worker agreed.

'Do you have any idea of what he's up to now?' Jonah asked.

'Ah, he'd be in independent living by now, unless he chose to stay on with Sally and Henry,' he said. 'But, like I said, you'd want to talk to his social worker for more on that.'

Jonah nodded. 'What about the Frank Pinder case? What do you think happened there?'

Mark took another slug of tea, his face thoughtful. 'I've been thinking about this since your sergeant rang,' he said. 'And you know, looking back, I think she fell for him, actually. Frank's a good-looking guy. Sporty, and really kind. He set about helping her become popular at school, which worked really well, and I think a lot of girls of that age confuse these relationships.'

'So why did she end up accusing him of rape?' Jonah asked.

'As far as I could make out,' Mark said, 'nothing was happening with Frank like she wanted. So she started sleeping with some kid at school to make him jealous. And instead of getting her what she wanted, it got her banned from socialising for a while. Frank didn't handle it well, but a lot of parents would worry if their kids were sleeping around at fourteen or fifteen.'

'I know you expressed to my sergeant that you found her summary of the experience bizarre,' Jonah said. 'You and the investigating officer both commented that she seemed far too aware of the mechanics of grooming to be a victim of it. But was it not possible that she'd just looked it all up after the event, and made sense of it that way?'

'I did wonder about that,' Mark admitted. 'But it would be incredibly self-aware for someone of her age. I'd dealt with a real abuse case by then, and there was no way the kid could stand outside herself and see what had happened.' He gave Jonah a slightly anxious look. 'But I don't want you to think I blamed her for any of it. Nobody does this stuff to be destructive, however it might seem. Keely was deeply unhappy. She had no father figure, had fallen for someone who represented that but still rejected her, and she just – she struggles with understanding the effects of her actions.'

'So overall,' Jonah concluded, 'you'd say the results of the investigations were right.'

'Aye, I would,' Mark said. 'Particularly after the business that blew up with her keyworker last year.'

'Talk me through it all,' Jonah said.

'Sure, no problem,' Slatterworth agreed. He took another gulp of tea. 'So Keely had seemed quite happy for a while. She said the kids at Henley Road had started to treat her better, and her keyworker was being very supportive. It all looked good and I was relieved. So I was more than surprised when she called me and asked for a chat, which she insisted had to be outside the house.'

'That was unusual?'

'It was. And Keely genuinely seemed worried about being overheard, which was also unusual. Actually embarrassed, which in itself convinced me a bit. She talked me through how Jared Boula had apparently pinned her against a wall and kissed her, before forcibly inserting his fingers into . . . well, her genital area.' He grimaced. 'She said she'd asked him to stop, and he ultimately did but laughed at her and told her she was clearly enjoying it. So,' Mark said, with a deep breath, 'I told her I would go and talk directly to the home's manager, and obviously halt any keyworker meetings. And then I asked her to go and have a think about exactly what she wanted to say in a statement, and whether or not she might be confused, because she'd been through two investigations and I doubted she wanted to be mixed up in a third without reason.'

Jonah nodded, slowly. 'So you spoke to the manager?'

'Yes,' Mark agreed. 'Grand Ferris. He's been in the care

business a good while. He's experienced. Level-headed, you know. And from him I had a very different story, as I'm sure you're aware. He said Jared Boula had approached him days before with concerns about Keely being interested in him romantically. He showed the manager text messages in which Keely told him she'd been fantasising about kissing him.'

'Did you see those messages?' Jonah asked.

'I saw screenshots,' Mark agreed. 'And they looked like someone who was obsessed. I really felt for her. But then, well . . .' Mark placed his mug down on the corner of the table and gripped the front of the chair. 'So it also turned out one of the boys at the home had been to see the manager about Keely, too,' he said, his expression tight. Uncomfortable. 'A fifteen-year-old called Brandon. He said Keely had approached him, aggressively, offering him oral sex. And when he'd freaked out about it, she'd laughed at him, and threatened to report him if he told anyone.'

Jonah felt a twist in his stomach, a stronger feeling than the previous rushes of unease he had experienced. 'That paints a slightly different picture,' he said.

'Aye,' Slatterworth agreed. 'I spoke to the boy, who was awkward as hell about the whole thing, but I believed him. He just described that coldness of hers so perfectly. And then at the end of the interview, as I was leaving, he begged me not to let her ruin someone's life. He said he knew she was planning on getting one of the staff in trouble, because he'd seen her rehearsing her speech about it in the mirror.' His expression was pained. 'She was practising looking anxious, and embarrassed, and running through it again when it didn't go right.'

Jonah sat back in his chair, nodding to himself. At long last, he found his doubts evaporating, to be replaced by cold anger.

14

I want to make it clear, in case you were wondering, that I didn't talk to anyone else about what was happening at the Murray-Watts'. I shared the full truth only with Callum, and even then only at first.

It was held against me, later, that I hadn't said anything earlier. But I want you to understand why I didn't.

Any child can be manipulated, and Sally and Henry were masters at it. They both conspired to hide the cruelty, even if one was merely the willing tool of the other.

I remember, clearly, how Sally sat down with me the day before our social worker's second visit. It was during the days when I was constantly hungry.

I'd begun to feel that almost anything was better than where I was right then. I wanted to tell Mary, our patient, slightly patronising social worker, everything that had happened. I imagined breaking down in front of her and asking to be taken away.

But, of course, Henry had thought of that. I heard them talking in Henry's study, and waited in terror for a telling-off.

Instead, Sally emerged and asked me kindly to come into the kitchen. She gave me a smile that was somehow both warm and sad, and told me she was worried. 'Henry and I . . . Henry thinks I should tell your social worker about all the times you've been disobedient,' she said, her eyes very wide. 'I'm supposed to. It's part of what we agree to.'

I felt a rush of sudden fear. It hadn't really occurred to

me that telling our social worker I was unhappy might mean admitting to having done bad things. And Henry seemed to think a lot of what I'd done was pretty awful.

'But I think it would spoil everything for you, if I did,' Sally went on, her forehead creased. 'Children who behave badly get taken to really awful foster carers. Ones who live in tiny, mouldy flats and like to give their children housework all day. It's for their own good, I know, but we've – Henry's looked into it, and it's happened to some of the kids we had, and I don't want that for you.' She put a hand up to stroke my hair. 'You are a good girl, underneath it all. I know you're going to turn everything round. So maybe they don't need to know about it. We can keep everything about bad behaviour and punishments secret, and just focus on the happy stuff, hey?'

I found myself nodding. Thinking that I could change and be what she wanted. What Henry wanted. I melted into a rush of grateful tears. 'Thank you, Sally.'

She pulled me towards her for a rare hug, and kissed the top of my head. 'I know you'll get there soon. You have a good heart. You've just been struggling recently.'

I felt such warmth towards her just then. That prospect of being *almost good enough* buoyed me up all through the social worker's visit, and I was so pathetically thankful that Sally said I was a lovely girl that I didn't even think of spoiling it.

Naturally, it came as a shock to me when the very next day she let Henry punish me again for looking surly. I wanted to protest. But the memory of her hug and her softness with me still lingered. I still thought I could persuade her to become my champion. I was too naive to understand quite how well Henry had her wrapped in his web, and how strong the strands of it were.

The odd thing is how I started to recognise his techniques of manipulation. Not when they were used on me; not yet. But when Callum fell victim to them, it was somehow obvious. I started to recognise the way Henry would say just the right thing to tear him down whenever he expressed too much independence, or grew too loud or boisterous. And how he would keep Sally desperate to please him by giving and then withholding praise.

I also saw the difference in the way Callum and Sally responded. Callum would become introverted and sullen, where Sally would try ever harder to please.

I started to realise that neither reaction was attractive. It struck me, however grudgingly, that Ninny was far more appealing than Callum was, and actually more appealing than Sally. I could see it for myself, however much I hated it.

Because she had no fear of punishment from Henry, she was able to smile at him. At both of them. She'd ask them how their day had been and listen with wide-eyed interest. Offer to fetch things for them, but not *too* often. Laugh at herself if she made mistakes, before Henry could grow angry or Sally disappointed.

I began to understand that I had been doing everything wrong. Not just at school, where I was slowly finding acceptance, but at home, too.

This became blazingly clear on sports day, a gala event held on the village's big grassy recreation ground. I went out and won the eight-hundred metres, the fifteen-hundred metres and the hurdles.

Instead of being disinterested, my foster parents were suddenly delighted with me. They were right there on the sidelines, picnic things forgotten on the grass as they stood and cheered.

As I finished the third event, they came to collect me, beaming with pride, and asked if I'd like an ice cream. They barely seemed to notice Ninny. Her middle-of-the-road achievements had finally been eclipsed.

I had a whole two-scoop ice cream to myself and got to eat it all with heady satisfaction as Ninny looked hungrily on.

I had been worried, up until then, about the summer holidays. Faced with six long weeks with no escape from my foster parents, I had begun to think seriously about running away. But as I finished the ice cream, it dawned on me that I might be able to fix this. I just had to be bold.

My first experiment was met with extraordinary success. It came five days after sports day, on the penultimate day of school. The glow of my sporting achievements had clearly begun to fade in their minds. They were dissatisfied with me again. For my lack of smiling; my clumsiness; my gracelessness.

I had been planning my actions for hours, having woken up at five. I'd rehearsed, both in front of my mirror and to myself, exactly what I would say. How my face would look. The movements of my arms and hands.

So I felt like someone acting a role as I sat down in front of my breakfast plate of toast and jam. I smiled, and said, 'This looks absolutely delicious, Sally, thank you.'

I waited for her to react. I watched carefully for the effect of it all. I noted the surprised smile, and the way she seemed to glow as she said I was very welcome.

She came to sit with us, with her own tiny bowl of fruit, and I asked, 'Would it be all right if I ate just half of it, though? I'd really like to stay slim for my running. I thought I might go for a run after school later, if that's OK. I should keep my training going.'

The surprise she had shown before was nothing to her expression now. She opened her mouth, and then beamed at me, her eyes slightly bright. 'Of course, darling,' she said. And then she added, 'Though if you're running, perhaps you'll need the extra energy today?'

'Might we see how I feel afterwards?' I asked, pretending to consider it. 'I'd really like to get a little thinner if I can. It'll really help with my long-distance times.'

Sally agreed, and the intense hunger I felt throughout the morning was more than made up for by the way she hugged me as I left to go to school. And it was doubly made up for when, that evening, she came to watch me run three miles on the same Astroturf where I'd had all my victories, and then handed me a large ham and cheese sandwich that she'd made for me specially.

I remember with an almost sensual joy how good that sandwich tasted. How it felt to bolt it down, and to let crumbs cascade extravagantly down my clothes and onto the grass, without Sally saying anything critical at all. Instead, she hugged me once I was done.

'Well done, darling,' she said. 'Henry will be so proud when I tell him.'

And with that, my career of manipulation began.

I began to look, constantly, for ways of ingratiating myself. I would wait until Henry was there, and tell Sally that she was beautiful. I would ask if I could take Henry cups of tea, and began asking him questions about his work with feigned fascination. And strangely, after a while, with *real* satisfaction, as I quickly understood the nature of his research.

I would ask Sally if she might do my hair like hers, or if I might help her cook or tidy. And I smiled and smiled until my face ached.

Ninny seemed genuinely pleased. It was as though she'd just been waiting for me to be good, and was now delighted that I'd become the sister she'd wanted.

The only person who didn't like the change was Callum.

It took me a little while to recognise it. It wasn't simply that he knew I was faking, though I'm sure that irritated him too. The real problem was that my lift in status had corresponded with a drop in his. Suddenly Callum was taking most of the punishments, and I watched with a feeling of squirming guilt as he was sentenced to starvation or to the cellar time and time again.

I tried to speak to him after a few particularly terrible days. I crept into his room after he'd been let out of the cellar, and sat on the bed beside him. He wouldn't even look at me.

I explained to him that he could make them love him, too. I told him that he just needed to play their game. To smile more. To help Henry in the garden. To be their image of everything a young boy should be.

'It doesn't work like that,' he told me, scrubbing at his eyes to hide that he'd been crying. 'They always need someone to be angry with.'

I sat in silence, as I realised the profound truth of this. It felt like a gong sounding somewhere nearby, a vibration that my body reacted to. It was uncomfortable and true and it woke me.

And it was then that I realised what needed to be done. Because the only way we would ever be happy was if Ninny became the hated one.

15

Jonah had been waiting for Keely to finish. Something in him had decided to give her one last chance to open up and tell the truth. And so he'd listened, all the while almost willing her not to change her tune. Mentally daring her to continue on with her lies, so he could tear into her as he so badly wanted to.

Though, in fact, he found himself wondering. Perhaps there were truthful elements in what she'd said. Because what Keely was really telling was the story of how a psychopath was made. That much had become abundantly clear.

When she was finally done, he did nothing more than stare back at her. He watched her with the same flatness and intensity that Keely had shown him. Mirroring her, quite consciously.

For whole seconds, she returned his gaze. She seemed as unconcerned as ever. But then, as time went on, something shifted, and it was Keely who, at last, looked away.

Jonah felt victorious, though it was the smallest of successes. A chink in her armour, and no more. But one he was ready to exploit.

'I want to know where Nina is.'

He said it harshly. Not just flatly or scathingly, but with all the terrifying power that his father had used so often against him.

It was a strategy that had its risks. He knew that. The camera was running, and Jonah couldn't look like he had bullied a minor. But if they didn't manage to get to Nina in time, his lack of action would be questioned far more.

'Not next week, by the time you've finished talking,' he said. 'I want to know where she is right now.'

There was no obvious change in response from Keely. She gave one of those infuriating smiles, and said, 'Well, clearly.'

'We've listened patiently to what you have to say, all of it, and now we'd like to know what happened to your sister.'

Keely sighed. 'You haven't listened, though, have you? If you'd listened, you'd have found her by now.'

'Oh, I don't think we would,' Jonah said. 'I think we would have danced to your tune, and played your game, and made you feel wonderful about yourself. And we would have got not one step closer to finding Nina.'

Keely's smile faded, very slowly. The look she gave him was flat once again. It felt like he was looking at the lizard part of her, the part most people had the decency to hide.

'You sought me out at that pub,' Jonah said, with his own smile this time. 'Surely you knew what that would entail? I have a reputation, and it isn't for kid gloves. You should have expected some kind of an interrogation.'

There was a pause, and then Keely asked, 'Who says it was you I wanted? You have a whole team of officers around you, any number of whom are probably the only reason you get cases solved.'

Jonah felt tempted to laugh. It was such a childish effort at an attack. So much less smart and controlled than her usual retorts.

Which meant he was getting to her at last.

He sat back. 'All right, then.' He opened up the case file and put it on his lap. 'Let's talk about your story, like you want us to. Is there anything you'd like to revise slightly? A few minor edits?'

'Why would I want to change anything?' she asked, sounding bored.

'Well, I can think of a few reasons,' he said, with a humourless smile. 'One would be if you'd thought of anything you'd missed. The other would be if you were fabricating the entire thing.'

Keely didn't react for a moment, and then she slowly shook her head. 'I thought you, of all people, would understand that not finding enough evidence of something doesn't mean it didn't happen.'

'My colleagues went to huge lengths to find evidence,' Jonah said. 'They checked your first story with Callum Taylor, who told them it had all been a scheme to get away from the Murray-Watts. Then again with your sister, who eventually admitted that none of it had happened. They found no cellar, and no sign of poor living conditions. And when you made further allegations against your second foster father, Frank Pinder, they started a new, thorough investigation. In each case, you told a very convincing story. It just didn't tie up with anything anyone else was saying.'

Keely said nothing. She continued to watch him with that direct, piercing gaze. Jonah refused to feel unsettled by it.

'But those weren't the only allegations you made, were they?' he went on. 'You had another try at convincing everyone your keyworker was abusing you. One of the staff at the Henley Road Children's Home. Abuse that he denies. And strangely, it seems that you yourself subjected one of the other boys to abuse of a similar nature.'

He looked up at her, waiting for something. For some kind of response. But Keely might as well have been marble. She was absolutely still, but also, he was certain, absolutely unafraid.

'It's strange, how this sort of abuse seems to follow you – and only you – around,' he said. 'Wouldn't you agree? Your younger sister was clearly influenced in her thoughts about Frank Pinder by you. It was then you, alone, who claimed that a keyworker named Jared Boula had sexually assaulted you.'

There was another pause. Jonah glanced at Keely's social worker, half expecting her to step in. He knew he was pushing it. Keely still had all the rights of a child, no matter how unchildlike she was. But the social worker seemed to have checked out for the evening. She was sitting back from the table, her arms folded, and her eyes fixed on her own shoes.

Keely was still staring at him when he looked back, and he could feel his blood rising still further. Part of that was rooted in being made a fool of. He'd begun to believe Keely's story, and that was a source of shame, however convincing she'd been.

But he was still intensely aware of that camera, taking all of it in. He needed to give her a chance to respond.

'Do you have anything to say about any of that?' he asked, in a quieter voice.

Keely tilted her head very slowly to one side. 'What *is* strange, is how certain everyone's become about what happened to us.' She glanced towards her disengaged social worker. 'Social services, the police, our keyworkers.' Her gaze went back to Jonah. 'It's become, "But you've made these allegations before, and it wasn't true." Or sometimes, "We recognise a pattern. This is destructive behaviour, and you need to stop." And in a really pretty horrific irony, it's become like a criminal record for *me* to carry around.'

Jonah stayed silent, experiencing a trace of discomfort that didn't do much to calm his frustration.

'You know,' Keely added, 'it should be a blindingly obvious point, and I hoped you were smart enough to see it, but just because there are multiple accusations, that doesn't mean they aren't all true.'

She kept that intense gaze on him for some seconds. For long enough, in fact, for him to feel his frustration start to ebb, and uncertainty rush in to take its place. And then she dropped her eyes to the table and said, 'I'd like to go to bed now.'

Waverley Road was absolutely still when Lightman and Hanson arrived, with the exception of a small black-and-white cat that slunk away as they climbed out of the Nissan Micra. Even the perennial traffic of Mountbatten Way seemed to have stopped for the night.

The block of flats was in darkness except for a covered security light over the door, and Hanson sighed as she saw the buzzer system.

'Which floor?' she asked Lightman, quietly.

'Top, unfortunately,' he answered, following her towards the front door. 'And it doesn't look like anyone in the other flats is awake.'

Hanson glanced up at the windows, all of which were in darkness, and nodded. This could end up in a wait for the method of entry team, and the buzzer system was going to be a complicating factor.

She leaned on the button anyway. She winced slightly as the sound reached her, even all the way down here.

There was no reply, and Hanson scouted round the building a little way. There was, it turned out, a fire escape at the back of the building, an ugly metal structure bolted onto the external wall. It led down to the first floor, from which there was a ladder that presumably could only be unlocked and lowered from above.

Lightman had followed her silently, and she gave him a small grin as she asked, 'Can you give me a leg up?'

*

Jonah had nothing immediate to do. He had updated DI Quick with the reports into Keely, and had passed on Jared Boula's name to him along with Frank Pinder's, however unlikely it was that either of them would have been anywhere near Nina. He'd left a message asking Jared Boula to come in to the station, and the process of sending Keely home was now in O'Malley's court, with calls to be made to the children's home and social services. The on-call social worker had now left the building, too.

So Jonah found himself with time to think, something he always placed a high value on. It let him plan, and consider, and form links. It allowed him to reflect on the best use of his team. That capacity to keep everything in his mind and twist it around was an ability he knew to be rare. It was one of the qualities that made him a good DCI.

And in the hunt for Nina, it was clear that real thought was needed. There was a lot to weigh up, and they needed to find a way forward now that Keely's testimony would be unavailable to them for the next eight or ten hours.

But he felt restless. Unable to focus. He found himself checking his phone repeatedly for a response from Michelle. Which was an intrusion of his personal life into his professional one that he rarely allowed to happen.

To his tired brain, it felt almost as though Keely had found a way of poisoning his thoughts. As if she had intentionally made him start to doubt his partner.

But those thoughts were ridiculous. Apart from anything else, there was no way Keely could know that he and Michelle were having any issues at all. Almost nobody knew.

In fact, the only people he'd opened up to were his friends Roy and Sophie. He'd gone to see them when Milly was three weeks old, having negotiated with Michelle so they could each have an evening out. He'd found it hard to be away from Milly, but he'd been desperate to talk to someone.

So he'd told Roy about how things were between them. About their struggles to find any conversation, and their often tetchy interactions. About how Michelle would largely just avoid him when they were at home together, and how it had become something of a relief.

Roy had been sympathetic. 'I think that level of sleep deprivation would get to anyone. And I'm saying that as someone who's actively planning to have kids. I can totally imagine getting irritable and finding it difficult. And not feeling much like a partner so much as a childcare provider.'

'Yes,' Jonah had agreed, with a smile. 'That's pretty much exactly how it feels.'

But then Sophie, Roy's cheerful but extremely direct wife, had asked, 'You don't think it's partly that you've gone into all this half-heartedly? I mean, literally half-heartedly. With the other half of your feelings tied up with Jojo?'

He'd felt those words slide into him like a scalpel and open up a part of him that he'd worked hard to partition off.

'I don't . . . know,' he'd told her. 'I don't – I try not to think about her. I really want to be a good father to Milly, and a good partner to Michelle.' He looked steadily at Sophie. 'And I think . . . I feel like a lot of the distance comes from Michelle. Maybe she senses something from me, but I'm not sure.'

Sophie tilted her head and asked, 'Does Michelle have a Jojo in the background too? Someone she was seeing?'

'Not really. A guy she'd been on a couple of dates with.' He shrugged. 'I don't think that's the issue. Perhaps more . . . that she feels let down by me, still. With how I was in the past. Maybe she's just waiting for me to be an arsehole to her again.'

'Do you kiss each other still? Touch? Cuddle up when you're in bed?'

Jonah had found himself shifting, uncomfortably. 'Well, I mean ... there's not much opportunity ... Not yet, anyway.'

'You need to find an opportunity,' Sophie had said, firmly. 'You're never going to feel like a couple if you don't. It's that kind of physical contact that breeds closeness.'

Jonah hadn't wanted to admit to Sophie that they weren't even sleeping in the same bed. He'd realised that she was absolutely right, though. That nobody felt like they were a real couple without touch. And so he'd made an effort to touch Michelle as often as possible the next day. To kiss her.

His partner had submitted to it as if he were some unwelcome relative, but hadn't reciprocated. And when he'd once tried to draw her into a hug from behind and nuzzle her ear, in a way they'd once done, she had removed his arms and walked away.

That had been three weeks ago, and his attempts since had been met with a similar response. They were only a month and a half into parenthood, he'd told himself. It was going to get easier. They'd get something back.

But now, in the late hours of a Sunday night, when he should have been thinking about Keely and Nina Lennox, he found himself wondering if the current situation was as close to a relationship as he was going to get.

Hoisting herself onto the fire escape had turned out to be a lot more challenging than Hanson had expected. She'd ended up having to essentially stand on Ben's shoulders, apologising at a whisper the whole time for him having to lift her entirely, and wondering whether it was possible to tell a woman's weight from the pressure on your shoulders. But the pose had meant she could reach high enough to grab the railings of the escape and, incredibly awkwardly, get a foot up onto the floor of it.

By the time she'd staggered over the railing and stood, she was shaky and sweating. But she'd made it. And getting down should, theoretically, be a lot easier. If she couldn't release the ladder, at least gravity would be her friend.

The metal had let out a few clangs as she'd climbed, and she spent a moment braced for a light to come on in the nearest flat. But when nothing happened, she turned to give Ben a thumbs up over the railing. His face was hard to read in the darkness, but she could see him shaking his head at her, and assumed he was grinning as he did it.

She started to move as quietly as she could towards the staircase, and then slowly trod up it until she was on the top floor, outside Callum's flat. She hesitated outside one of the windows, and pulled her baton out before getting closer. There was no point being unprepared.

It was slightly skin-crawling, moving up to the un-curtained windows. There was both moonlight on her from above and street light from below, whereas the interior of the flat was in darkness. She would be incredibly obvious to anyone inside.

She approached the glass, and rested her head against it in order to look in. None of the windows were open, she noticed, which was odd on a hot September night. It implied that Callum wasn't here. Or possibly that the windows had been closed for a reason.

As she peered in, she began to make out the details of a living room. It was sparsely furnished, featuring an off-white sofa, a TV and little else. There was also nobody in it, unless someone was hiding on the floor behind the sofa.

She was going to go right ahead and assume that nobody was. There was no point, the DCI often said, worrying about the things you couldn't help.

She moved along to the corner of the building. The metal walkway of the fire escape only wrapped a short way around, presumably taking in the bedroom and living area of each flat and then stopping.

She felt her nerves rising again as she approached the window of the next room, but it, too, was empty. A bedroom with a small double bed, a row of cheap-looking varnished wardrobes and a desk.

But this room had a little more decoration, Hanson saw. On the bedside table, there was a photograph, and as she shone her torch onto it, she could make out a couple looking towards the camera. The figure on the left had curly red hair.

Keely, she thought, immediately, with a sense of satisfaction. Callum and Keely were an item as they'd guessed.

She let the light of the torch travel onto the wall, where there was a large map stuck up with what looked like Blu-Tack. She peered at its outline, and then realised it was an old map of the New Forest.

Hanson strained to see whether the map was marked in any way. There were no obvious pins. She was poised like that, with her torch shining full on to the wall, when a wash of light flooded into the bedroom from the hall.

Someone had just entered the flat.

Keely Lennox's departure became complicated.

The manager of her home refused, point-blank, to take her. Jonah picked up the phone to her after O'Malley had failed to get anywhere. He was keen to know exactly what her concerns were.

'I'm sorry,' Magda said. 'I don't want to abandon any of the kids in my care, but until we know what happened to Nina, I would feel extremely uncomfortable having her back in the home.'

'Has she ever presented a threat to any of the other kids, before today?' Jonah asked her, quietly.

'I didn't . . . I wouldn't have said so, strictly. But she's . . .' Magda made a slightly frustrated sound. 'She finds it extraordinarily easy to manipulate people. There have been times, before now, when . . . well, there are impressionable kids here, and a few of them have fallen under her spell before.'

'So you're saying she's persuaded them to do bad things?' Jonah asked, his whole body still as he waited for her reply.

'Sometimes,' Magda agreed. 'One of the girls here clearly worshipped her and was caught vandalising the car of Keely's previous foster father. She claims she acted on her own, but it was Keely who held a grudge against him.'

'Was that Henry Murray-Watt's car?' Jonah asked, with interest.

'No. This was the second family that took the girls in. The Pinders.'

Jonah considered this. 'Is the girl still staying with you?'

'Yes,' Magda said, guardedly. 'But she's – your officer already talked to her, and I don't think she knows anything that will help.'

'Can I have her name anyway?' Jonah asked. 'I doubt it's important, but it should be noted.'

Magda sighed. 'Samantha Wild. And, look, she fell out with Keely in the end. She started spending time with Nina instead and I don't think Keely liked it.'

Jonah remembered Mark Slatterworth's notes about a Samantha. How Keely had cut her off because she wasn't single-mindedly devoted to her.

The heavy feeling that had been growing in him increased a little further. Every outside view they had on Keely was of a cold manipulator. Of someone who liked to see others dance to her tune. And of someone who could become implacably angry when they didn't.

He wanted to know just how much Keely had begun to resent Nina. Because even in the stories that looked to be nothing more than fabrication, the one consistent note had been her growing hatred of her younger sister.

He felt suddenly weary of the whole conversation, and said, 'OK. We won't send Keely back to you tonight.'

'Thank you.'

'It might be useful for us to talk to Samantha and the others tomorrow, if we haven't got anywhere by then.'

'I'm sure we can arrange that,' Magda said, with clear relief that the issue of accommodating Keely had been dropped.

Jonah hesitated for a moment, and then said, 'Some of Keely's accounts have been . . . quite convincing. I was wondering whether you'd ever had any doubts.'

'I felt the same about it all, when the girls first arrived,' Magda told him, with a sigh. 'I asked Keely for the truth, and she told me what I imagine is much the same story she told you. And I believed her. I felt for the two of them.' There was a momentary pause, and then Magda went on, in what sounded like tired resignation, 'But there was just too much that didn't add up.'

'You mean because Nina backed down? And Callum?' Jonah asked. 'You don't think they could both have been too much under the spell of their foster parents?' He said it

178

in a last, desperate stab at saving something of Keely. Perhaps something of his own pride. 'It wouldn't be uncommon for victims of abuse to side with their abusers. And even the boy from the Henley Road home, Brandon . . . even he could have been manipulated by the keyworker.'

'No, I know,' Magda said, a little impatiently. 'But I've seen how Keely is, underneath it all. Day-to-day. I've seen the expression on her face when she's been thwarted. She just . . . loses the pretence of human feeling. And it's abundantly clear that she likes to get revenge.'

Jonah was silent for a few seconds, remembering Keely's comments about the shadow inside her. How it had risen thanks to suffering. And, god knew, those girls had suffered. From the moment their mother died, they had endured hardship.

If you'd listened, you'd have found her by now . . .

He felt his stomach twist. He hoped, fervently, that Keely's story wouldn't turn out to be a tale of revenge against her younger sister. But he felt, increasingly, that it might be.

Hanson ducked, her heart pounding as she tried to hide herself below the window frame. She could already have been seen. Whoever had entered Callum's flat would have caught sight of her if they'd looked into the bedroom.

There was a sudden increase in light on the fire escape, a bright rectangle appearing as whoever had entered turned on the bedroom light. She half expected the window to open. To feel a pair of hands dragging her inside. But there was only a faint call, in a slightly quavering voice.

'Poppy! Poppy, are you here somewhere?'

With a faint feeling of ridiculousness, Hanson shifted until she could raise her eyes above the window ledge. And then she sighed.

The intruder into the flat was an elderly woman. She was stooping awkwardly to peer under the bed.

Hanson waited until the woman had left the room and switched off the light, and then she scooted over to the edge of the fire escape and called softly, 'Ben. Try the buzzer. I think we might be able to get in.'

Having finished arranging Keely's accommodation for the night, O'Malley settled in to watch the videos of Keely's interviews. He was ready for the hunt for more clues to be lengthy and frustrating. Keely didn't strike him as someone who'd make anything easy.

Hanson had found an inconsistency during the second interview, and O'Malley had taken note of how it had worked. It had been an apparent error that had turned out to be deliberate.

None of them had spotted anything else in that particular piece of her story, and O'Malley was inclined to think that this was for a reason. The way Keely rounded off each part of her tale so deliberately, as if she had rehearsed it, made it all seem like an intentional series of episodes.

So O'Malley went to the very first of the tapes, reasoning that there was probably something to find there, too. The first clue, which he hoped would be a little more significant than the second.

With his ears tuned for errors, it took him only one repeat of the interview to hear it.

. . . *the cut flowers she brought into our idyllic little single-storey cottage . . . the living room next door . . .*

He listened onwards, smiling to himself as he heard Keely say:

I crept downstairs . . .

He went to find the chief.

Gaynor seemed unfazed by the arrival of two police officers late on a Sunday evening, even when one of them was slightly red in the face from the effort of climbing back over the fire escape. She let them up into Callum's flat, for which she had a key.

'He thought it would be useful in case he got locked out,' she explained, welcoming them into Callum's home as though it were her own. 'I'm around most of the day, so it seemed a good idea. Then this evening I heard a noise through here and thought Poppy must have ended up sneaking in. But there's no sign of her.'

Hanson smiled. 'Cats are terrible for wandering off, aren't they? Is she a house cat?'

'She is,' Gaynor agreed. 'Though recently she seems to have become obsessed with getting outside. Last week she made a bolt onto the fire escape, jumped onto the railing and fell off. My heart was absolutely in my mouth. Luckily she was fine.'

Hanson nodded, and wandered through into the bedroom. She came to a stop in front of the pinboard, and peered at the map Callum had stuck to it.

It showed only Southampton and the New Forest, and it was too large a scale for any detail. The city was no more than a pale brown shape with a few major roads marked. There were no markers. No pins. It looked, in fact, purely decorative.

Hanson sighed, and glanced towards the living room, where Gaynor was telling Ben about Callum's supermarket job and his determination to study law.

'It'll be difficult for him, of course,' she said. 'He has no family to back him financially. But he's had excellent results for his A levels and he's a hard worker.'

So Callum hadn't been entirely truthful with Gaynor, she thought. He'd hidden the fact that he had an adoptive family now and could ask them for the support he needed. And she momentarily wondered why he felt the need to pretend, and to take a gap year in order to work. Was he determined not to ask for his foster parents' help? Or had they been unwilling to give it?

Gaynor glanced over, smiled and walked into Callum's room too.

'I suppose he must be staying with his girlfriend tonight,' she offered.

Hanson nodded towards the photo on the bedside table. The flame-red hair was one of the only notes of colour in the room. 'Is that his girlfriend?'

'Yes, that's Nina,' Gaynor said.

Hanson found herself staring at Callum's neighbour. 'His girlfriend is called Nina?'

'Yes, that's right,' Gaynor agreed. 'She's a sweet girl. She really seems to bring out the best in him. He tells me they've known each other for years.'

Hanson moved over to pick up the photograph, and then turned to show it to Ben, who was now standing in the doorway. He loomed over Gaynor, head and shoulders taller.

There was no question that Gaynor was right. The beaming figure next to Callum was Nina Lennox. Their missing girl.

Gaynor went on talking. She told them about Nina and Callum coming and doing her hoovering for her. About how Nina had brought her flowers.

Hanson was only half listening. She was still, internally, trying to understand this. She'd been so sure that Callum had ended up with Keely. It had been the strong implication from everything Keely had said.

So how on earth had he ended up with Nina?

She found herself gazing at the photograph with a slightly odd feeling. It was a close-up, and captured more warmth and certainty in Nina than the missing persons report. There was something in it, in fact, that made Nina look suddenly familiar.

Hanson looked away, and then back, wondering whether what she was seeing was a similarity to her sister. But the more she looked, the more she felt as though she knew this face. That she had met Nina Lennox somewhere before.

O'Malley came to find Jonah just as he got off the phone to social services. They'd found a solution to Keely's accommodation, at least.

'I think we need to go to the Lennox family home,' the sergeant said, with a slight smile. 'Keely calls it a single-storey cottage with a living room next to their bedroom, and then claims that she somehow walked downstairs the morning she found her mother dead.'

Jonah took that in, and then nodded at him. 'How far is it?'

'Not too far at all,' O'Malley said cheerfully. 'Furzley Lane.'

Jonah tried to keep his expression neutral. To show that the simple name of a road hadn't been a gut punch.

He needed to be stronger about all this, he thought. He shouldn't be so knocked back just because a house lay on the same road as Jojo's. And he definitely shouldn't be thinking how much he'd like to go there himself, just to drive past his ex-girlfriend's home. None of that was fair on anyone, least of all Michelle.

'We can work out who should head there once Keely's on her way,' he said, as if nothing had happened at all. 'I'd like you to come along while I explain the situation to her.'

O'Malley said nothing to indicate that he was aware of Jonah's thoughts, or that he remembered exactly where Jojo had lived. He merely followed him in equable silence to the interview suite.

They stood just within Room One, indicating that they weren't attempting to start interviewing her again. Whatever he felt about Keely, he was going to do this right. If the worst had happened to Nina and this came to a prosecution of her sister, her defence was going to find nothing to criticise. Nothing to stop a conviction.

He started out by explaining that she couldn't go back to the children's home tonight. He wasn't without hope that the reasons might have some effect on her, though he wouldn't have gambled anything on it.

'The manager feels some concern about the safety of the other young people there,' Jonah said.

Keely said nothing, but Jonah, watching her intently, saw something change in her attitude. A slight dullness seemed to come over her. It was almost as though this had disappointed her. It was the same small change he'd seen in her expression when he had stopped asking her about Frank Pinder and tried to question her about her sister instead.

It was hard to know what to think of it. Hard to tell whether this was all part of Keely's game, once again. But he had to respond as though he bought it.

'Keely,' he said, choosing to sit down now. 'If you could just tell us about Nina. Where she is, or what happened . . .' He watched her as she looked down towards her hands.

'I can bring in another social worker, and you can tell us. You wouldn't have to be dragged off somewhere. You could go back to your own room. Your own bed.'

Keely looked up at him, after a while. She looked tired, and it was the first time he'd seen any trace of fatigue in her.

'You can stop worrying about Nina,' she said. 'She doesn't need anything right now. All right?'

'When did you last see her?'

Keely let out a long sigh. 'Lunchtime. She doesn't need anything.' She sounded bored by the conversation. 'I'll sleep wherever I have to sleep. It doesn't make any difference.'

Jonah nodded, and said, 'Social services have offered a self-contained refuge. It'll be safe, and there will be someone in an adjoining room if you need them.' He waited for her reaction. 'There are beds here, but I don't think you'd be as comfortable.'

'A refuge will be fine,' Keely said. She looked away, clearly waiting for him to leave.

O'Malley returned to his computer with slight relish. Whether they were playing into Keely Lennox's hands or not, there was no denying that there was something satisfying about hunting for the clues she'd left.

O'Malley was far from being a details man, but this game wasn't really about detail. It was about putting the intuitive part of his brain on alert, and recognising a mistake when he saw one. It was more like spotting a pattern, in reality, and that was O'Malley's kind of work.

He skipped forwards to the third tape, where Keely had described the gradual rise in abuse, and her strange relationship with Callum Taylor. He listened to her describe kicking a football over the wall of the garden, and he found himself grinning.

'I think I'm getting to grips with this now,' he said to himself.

It was almost midnight by the time social services arrived to take Keely to the refuge, and although she said nothing about being tired, she looked pale and distant.

Jonah asked the short, greying woman from social services to return her at nine in the morning, but Keely interrupted to say, 'We can start again at seven. I don't need much sleep and we wouldn't want to leave Nina waiting for too long.'

She gave him a slight smile as he turned to look at her. He somehow knew that she was thinking of him and his team, who would all of them be up until the early hours. That she wanted them tired and on the back foot.

The joke was on her, he thought. Milly never let him sleep in past six anyway. She was always wide awake, gurgling and making proto-speech sounds, which turned into wailing if she wasn't taken out of her cot quickly enough.

Jonah smiled slightly in return. 'Seven is fine. I'm usually up at six anyway.'

'I suppose you are,' she said. 'I hope you get a few hours in.' She departed, but still turned at the door to CID to give him a last, cold smile.

16

'Chief.' O'Malley was at Jonah's door, and Jonah had the impression he might already have knocked without him hearing it. He had been brooding on all this, his tired thoughts cycling through everything Keely had told them, and on Hanson's discovery that Nina was seeing Callum Taylor. 'You've got Jared Boula here,' O'Malley told him.

Jonah nodded, trying to keep from sighing. It would obviously be useful to talk to Keely's former keyworker, particularly when he was one of the people she had accused of abuse. It was just difficult to summon up the required energy this late in the day.

Jared Boula was a lean but strong-looking man with a distinctly Mediterranean appearance. Dark eyes and hair and tanned skin were exaggerated by what Jonah still liked to think of as designer stubble. He was casually dressed in an olive-green T-shirt, and had a small stone pendant tied on a leather cord round his neck.

Unlike Keely's social worker, he looked uneasy, and didn't respond to Jonah's smile of greeting.

'I hope this is quick,' he said. 'I got your message while I was travelling back from a weekend away, and I came straight here. I've been driving for the last three hours.'

Jared Boula's voice was almost straightforward South-ampton, but there was a touch of French intonation in the vowels.

'It's good of you to come in,' Jonah said. 'I'd just like to ask you a few things about Keely Lennox.'

'I haven't seen her for ages,' Jared said, quickly. 'She moved homes. I don't even know where she is now.'

'Yes, we understand that,' Jonah agreed. 'But we're interested in how she was when you were her keyworker.'

Boula gave a strange laugh. 'Well, that was a mess, as I'm sure you know.' He cleared his throat. 'She got obsessed with me, and then flipped out when I turned her down.'

'How did that obsession manifest itself?' Jonah asked.

'Messaging me all the time,' Boula said, immediately. 'Either to flirt or for no reason at all.'

'When you say to flirt, can you give me some examples?'

'Well, she . . . shortly before she tried to kiss me, she said she couldn't stop thinking about me,' Boula said. 'She said she dreamed about me. I showed the messages to the home manager and her social worker.'

Jonah nodded. 'And also to the boy who said she'd made advances on him, Brandon,' he commented, careful to keep his tone somewhere between a question and a statement.

Jared Boula shifted, and then said, 'I – yes. Well, not those messages.'

'What did you show him?'

'The ones I showed him were more . . . aggressive,' Boula said. 'Quite sexual in nature.'

'Offering you sexual favours?' Jonah asked.

'Yes,' Boula said. 'Exactly.'

Jonah nodded, glancing down at the printouts he'd made of Keely's case file as if finding some answers there. 'And in what context did you show these to a fifteen-year-old boy?'

There was a pause, and then Boula said, 'I – well, he'd approached me because Keely had . . . had made suggestions to him. And I was trying to . . . to reassure him that it was just how she was, because she was troubled.'

Jonah remained silent for several seconds, and was aware of Jared Boula gradually growing more on edge.

'So your response to a troubled young woman making advances towards this fifteen-year-old boy was to share absolutely personal details that potentially humiliated her, rather than to approach the children's home manager immediately?' he asked.

Jared looked away, trying for slightly amused outrage. 'Come on, that wasn't . . . I was trying to help. Maybe . . . maybe I didn't get it quite right, but this was a new situation to me.'

'What happened to those other messages?' Jonah asked. 'The sexual ones?'

'I deleted them,' Boula said, immediately. 'Obviously. I didn't want anyone seeing those.'

'Except for Brandon,' Jonah replied. There was no reply from Jared Boula, except an increasingly dark expression. 'Well, I'm sure these messages would show up on your phone records, at least.'

Jared shifted in his chair, his face hardening further. 'Look, I came here to help find Keely's sister. If you want to question me about all of that shit, then I can call my lawyer in.'

Jonah gave him a small smile. 'You are very welcome to call your lawyer if you like, but I have only a few more questions. These are about the relationship between Nina and Keely.'

Jared's posture relaxed slightly after a moment. 'That's not too hard to answer. Keely was jealous of her sister. Really jealous.'

'Did she tell you that?' Jonah asked.

'She didn't need to,' Jared said. 'She could barely talk about her without getting angry, and when she found out her younger sister was dating the guy she liked, she locked her in the shed at the end of the garden.'

'Would this be Callum Taylor? Their former foster brother?'

'That's the one,' Boula said. 'Dickhead with a motorbike.'

Jonah nodded, determinedly showing no reaction to the way he spoke about Callum. 'Was Nina upset about being locked up?'

'Of course she was,' Boula said. 'It was fucking freezing. Keely didn't care if she froze to death. But Nina wouldn't report her for it. She kept saying it was her own fault.'

'That's very interesting. Thank you, Mr Boula,' Jonah said, making as if to rise. 'Oh, and out of interest, how did you know we were looking for Nina?'

There was a brief silence, and Jared Boula said, 'You said something in your message.'

'I explained it was part of the missing persons investigation into the two girls,' Jonah said, lightly. 'So I'm wondering how you'd latched onto this idea of Nina being missing.'

There was a pause, in which Jared looked down at his hands with a strange, tight expression. 'No idea,' he said, in the end. 'I probably just forgot they were both gone.'

Jonah showed him out, finding himself thinking increasingly uncomfortable thoughts.

'So what do we think?'

The DCI was leaning against the table in the big meeting room, his expression expectant. He had summarised Jared Boula's interview, including the unsettling story about the shed, and the way he had spoken as if only Nina had gone missing.

'I'm surprised Jared wasn't investigated further,' he went on. 'Some of his behaviour seems frankly indefensible. Sharing explicit messages with a teenager. The clear dislike for Keely. And interestingly, what seems an equal dislike for Callum Taylor.' He shook his head. 'I'd work on the assumption that he's hiding quite a bit. His actions make no sense as it stands.'

'Showing sexual messages to a teenage boy to "help him" sounds incredibly unlikely,' Hanson said. She and Ben had returned from Waverley Road, and from a frustrating trip to Godshill, where the Murray-Watts had clearly either been out, or in bed and ignoring the banging on the door. 'I'd be inclined to think they'd made an agreement together to take Keely down,' Hanson went on, finding herself suddenly a lot more on Keely's side in all this.

'Or he might have been bragging,' Lightman put in. 'Which in no way negates the point about an agreement, but a young keyworker who wanted to look good in front of the lads is believable.'

Hanson grimaced. It was entirely believable.

'The trouble we have,' the chief said, 'is that we aren't investigating Jared Boula. If Keely wants revenge on him, then it's debatable whether it's worth our time looking into that. He may or may not have abused her, but either way, he doesn't bring us any closer to Nina. Though,' he added, a little more hesitantly, 'his comments about only Nina being missing are a bit concerning.'

'Do you think there's been a little too much chat going on at social services?' O'Malley asked. 'If we don't think he's got anything to do with her disappearing, that's the obvious answer, isn't it?'

'It's the most likely explanation,' the chief agreed. 'But he could also be involved somehow. The question is whether to prioritise him.'

'It's possible that Keely will only release her sister once the people who've wronged her have been brought to justice,' Lightman offered.

'Yes,' the DCI agreed, 'though knowing who the three

probably are won't help us in the short-term. Not with Keely out of touch for the next eight hours, and no way of telling her we're doing our job.'

'Unless Callum or someone else is watching our progress,' Hanson pointed out. 'If they know where the clues are hidden, it might be possible to keep an eye out, using technology or in person.'

The DCI was silent for a moment, and the three of them waited for him to work through whatever thoughts he had. Eventually, he nodded. 'We need to talk to the Murray-Watts again. We still haven't interviewed Henry, and they could also help us find Callum Taylor. The kidnap squad have nothing from Callum's phone since Tuesday, which is odd in itself. If anybody's helping Keely, it's still likely to be him, even if he supposedly was Nina's boyfriend.' He paused. 'And, O'Malley, you've got another location for us to look at?'

'I've found two,' O'Malley said, quietly. 'The first is the house the Lennox sisters grew up in, which she calls a single-storey building, but then she talks about it having an upstairs. The second is the allotments that are next to the house the Murray-Watts own. She recounts kicking a ball over the wall into them, but then says they had to drive to the other end of the village to get there.' He glanced over at Hanson. 'It's almost easy now you've worked out what we're looking for.'

The DCI thought on this for another minute, and then said, 'All right. I think we should pursue these leads for now, and hope that Keely is being updated on our progress. Domnall, you and Juliette can head to the allotments. I'd like you to tie it in with another visit to the Murray-Watts. If they're holed up at home, they'll probably decide to answer the bloody door if we keep disrupting their peace. I'll take

Ben to the Lennox house. I know it's late, but with eight hours elapsed since Keely turned up, it's more urgent than ever that we find Nina.'

Hanson rose, almost able to hear the words he wasn't saying.

If it isn't too late already.

Jonah went to update the kidnap team on their efforts, and to hear about their own incremental progress. They'd made the decision to access Keely's phone records, and were confident that she wasn't contacting anyone at present. They were monitoring it for any other calls in and out, and Quick hoped to find out who she was cooperating with once she thought herself safe in the refuge.

Which was assuming, of course, that Keely was stupid enough to use her own phone to do the contacting.

Jonah went to find his keys, feeling an odd twist of guilt at having chosen the Furzley Lane clue to follow rather than the Godshill allotment. He reflected, though, that it didn't really matter whether he drove past Jojo's house during the early hours of the morning. She would be asleep, and out of sight.

Almost as if it had been designed to prick his conscience at this point, a message arrived on his phone from Michelle.

> Am fine. Milly awake. Trying to settle her.
> Let me know when you might be back.

He felt some of his anxiety ease. But as he scanned the message again, he imagined Michelle writing it, and felt a twinge of worry for her. It sounded like the kind of message someone would send when struggling. When they were waiting for the other person to come and rescue them.

He messaged back a quick hope that he would be there in

an hour or so, and then put his phone away in a determined move.

Keely followed her escort from social services in silence. Veronica was determined to give her a tour of the flat they would be staying in tonight. It was totally unnecessary. There were only two bedrooms, one kitchen-diner and one bathroom. It wasn't exactly hard to navigate.

Her bedroom was at the back of the flat, past the door to the living room. The bedroom was a decent size, she thought. And the furniture in there looked newer than the tatty stuff in the living area. The bed might be just about comfortable.

The social services woman, Veronica, handed her a hold-all she didn't recognise.

'Magda sent this. Toiletries and clothes for a few days. She's tried to pack your favourites.' Keely took it from her. She let it fall to the length of the nylon strap and watched as it swung backwards and forwards.

'I'm in the one by the door,' Veronica said, unnecessarily, smoothing her shirt down. She was a shirt-and-patterned-trousers woman, and Keely was willing to bet she had a series of these trousers, all of them in bright prints. That she was known for them.

Keely had already seen the smallest bedroom, which was next to the even smaller bathroom, and was relieved that Veronica would be the one sleeping in it. But of course she'd taken that room. She would want to be between Keely and the door.

'Do you need anything?' Veronica asked, her expression determinedly kind. It was quite impressive to keep being so cheerful when Keely was saying nothing. Refusing to react. 'There's bread in the fridge, and butter, and I can order in if you're hungry.'

'No, thank you.' Keely relented and gave her a small smile. 'I just need some sleep. That's all.'

'OK, that sounds a good idea.' Veronica moved to stand in the hall. 'Though . . . perhaps you want a wash, first?'

She gestured at Keely. And for a moment Keely just looked back at her, having become so accustomed to the blood smeared over her that she'd forgotten about it. And then she looked down at her arms and shrugged. 'I suppose so.'

'Good,' Veronica said. 'You use the bathroom for as long as you need.' She paused, and then added, 'It shouldn't be too noisy here. Let's hope you get a good night's sleep and I'll see you for breakfast at six fifteen.'

Keely showered, using a towel she found folded on the bed, washing until the last little rivers of red had disappeared down the plughole. She wondered if she ought to feel something, watching it flow away, but felt nothing at all. And then she pulled on pyjamas, transferring a small phone from beneath her grubby jeans to sit under clean socks, and returned to her room, closing the door on Veronica's concerned expression.

She turned the main light off, and then moved to sit on the bed. She kept the curtains open. They were four floors up in a single block that stood higher than all the surrounding buildings, and she could see right out over the south-west of the city from here. A mass of retail spaces and, huddled somewhere within them, the gleaming construction of the central police station.

She took her smartphone out of her pocket, and then pulled the basic burner phone back out of her sock.

She turned it on and opened her messages. For a few minutes, she looked at one of the threads from an unsaved number, and then she started to type.

Safely in social flat. Is she still screaming for help?

There was only a ten-second wait before the reply came.

She went quiet at ten. Haven't seen them
moving on anyone yet. Anything from your end?

Keely sent a swift answer.

No. But maybe you should get out and about. Just in case.

The reply was almost as quick.

Will do. Be careful.

Keely smiled, and typed a final reply.

When am I not?

Jonah was able to drive to Furzley Lane on automatic pilot. He had made his way here after work numerous times during the months he'd spent with Jojo.

For all that he'd decided not to think about her, his tired mind kept returning to Jojo, before tacking guiltily towards Milly and Michelle.

Lightman was his usual quiet self during the journey and Jonah was thankful for the peace. It gave him time to gradually get his thoughts under control. To focus them back onto the Lennox sisters.

Keely's departure from the station was still bothering him. It was all bothering him, really. But his most troubling thoughts related to the wisdom of playing Keely's game. Whichever way he looked, there was doubt. Whether it was about how Keely felt about Nina, or how Callum Taylor might be involved, or why she so particularly wanted to tell her lengthy story.

Having become convinced that she was a manipulative psychopath who had tried to bring down everyone who'd stood in her way, he had found himself doubting even that in the last hour. Even as someone who generally cleaved to indecision in order to avoid jumping to conclusions, Jonah was finding the uncertainty a strain.

By the time he turned onto the long stretch of Furzley Lane, he'd been over the same ground in his mind a good dozen times. He found himself slowing just before Jojo's driveway on autopilot, and tried to cover the slip by asking Lightman how far down the house was.

'It's quite a bit further,' his sergeant told him. 'I'll let you know once we're close.'

Jonah nodded, and let his eyes wander briefly over the cottage as he sped up again. He took it in at a glimpse. The perfectly designed garden. The Jeep sitting on the driveway. The low-hanging eaves. But it was clear even from a glance that the house was in darkness. All the curtains were drawn and there was no sign of movement. Jojo had probably been in bed for hours.

He did his best to supress a rush of disappointment, asking himself what he had even wanted. To see her? To catch a glimpse of the woman he'd had to walk away from? The woman who might still be angry with him, and might, still worse, have moved on?

You're an idiot, he told himself. Something he seemed to have told himself a lot over the past few months.

He drove on down the lane more quickly, until Lightman told him to pull in. They were outside another cottage, this one overgrown and in what looked like a poor state of repair. As the lights hit the whitewash of the walls, he saw patches of moss, and a large stain where it looked like one of the gutters had become blocked.

O'Malley had passed on several interesting facts about the house. Jane Lennox had purchased it eighteen years ago, using money left to her by her father. But two years before her death, it had been sold to a Southampton banker, and then, after her death, sold on to a local builder, with the apparent intention of building multiple homes on the acre of garden attached to it and selling them for a profit.

Planning permission had not been easy to get, however, and the scheme seemed to have stalled. The cottage had ended up sitting empty for the last seven years.

Jonah climbed out of the car, leaving the headlights on for a moment as he scanned the cottage. There was no sign of any life here. No gleam of light in the window, or sign of anyone having entered recently. The curtains were drawn back; the windows blank. Empty.

There was also no sign of a second storey. No dormer windows or anything similar. No stairs for Keely to have climbed down.

He killed the lights, and he and Lightman made their way across the wildly overgrown lawn, where a series of stepping stones were just visible. Though despite all the obvious signs, it was still possible that somebody lived here. Jonah had found people living in much greater devastation and disrepair than this.

He tapped on the door and waited a full thirty seconds for some sign of life. And then he pressed the handle. The door opened without effort.

He glanced at Lightman, who already had his baton at the ready. They both stepped inside.

The door opened straight on to a living room, which even in the dim light from outside showed signs of being as rundown as the outside of the house. A navy sofa was topped with what should have been bright cushions, all dulled with dust. A chunky TV sat on a unit that had clearly been bought long before flatscreens had emerged. A child's miniature oven made of wood rested in one corner. A bookshelf overflowing with novels, picture books and encyclopaedias was in another.

None of it looked lived-in. And yet the front door had been unlocked. Somebody had been here.

It was darker further into the house. Two doors opened off the living room. One, to the right, showed a small room with a bed in it. At the back, a door led through to what looked like a hallway and then a kitchen. Jonah moved that way and could hear Lightman's soft steps behind him.

There was very little light coming into the kitchen. Jonah decided it would be better to be able to see, even if it made him a target. If anyone was here, they knew someone was coming anyway. The car engine and headlights would have been enough of a warning.

He pulled out his phone and switched it on to flashlight mode. The beam fell on a kitchen that was noticeably tidy and free of dust. The surfaces and tiled floor were all clean and reflective.

Jonah caught a glimpse of green light in one corner. It was a charging light, he saw. An iPad plugged into a wall socket.

As he approached, he saw that there was a handwritten note on a Post-it attached to the iPad.

Here you are, Detective. Just press play.

Godshill looked still and pretty as Hanson steered the Nissan towards the Murray-Watts' house. It was one of the many New Forest villages where sodium street lights had been replaced by white, lantern-style lamps, giving it an oddly Victorian air. Hanson approved of them, while wondering whether that orange wash would start to become nostalgic in itself as it disappeared from place after place. A brief, lurid feature of her childhood and early adulthood.

She had a strong sense of déjà vu as they parked up out-side Sally and Henry's pristine house. It was still in darkness, with only a yellowish light shining in the porch. And after four decidedly loud knocks – loud enough, in fact, that the curtains were drawn aside in the house opposite for them to peer out – there was still no reply.

Hanson sighed. 'Looks like it's time to get the kidnap team looking for them.'

They put a call through to Quick, and then got back in the car in order to move it round the corner to the aban-doned allotments. They were, as Keely had first described, right alongside the house, screened from the road by riot-ous hawthorn hedges. Hanson turned the Nissan down what looked to have been a farm track, and they found themselves in a large, open field of waist-high dry grass. A clutch of trees and bushes off to the right were the only real feature, but with the moon now set and the lights pointing further down the track, Hanson couldn't make a lot out.

The Nissan tipped and swung its way over the hardened ruts, jolting the two of them uncomfortably. She drew it up only a short way in, relieved not to be doing this in winter.

O'Malley, who had been chatting cheerfully most of the way there, looked out towards the trees.

'So I'm sure you're aware, but anyone there will have seen and heard us coming,' he commented. 'And they'll be less night blind than we are, too. It's possible Nina is alone, whether here or elsewhere, but it's also possible that Keely's got someone watching her.'

Hanson couldn't help smiling. It was so rare that Dom-nall sounded like the ex-soldier he was, and it was like a total shift in persona. The quiet, humourless voice. The way he examined his surroundings like he was planning on fighting there; and on winning.

'I'll bring the flashlight,' Hanson said. 'Mixed blessing, but at least we'll be able to see a few feet in front of us.'

'Agreed,' O'Malley said, and climbed out of the car. Despite his heavy frame, he was on his feet more quickly than she was.

A slight breeze stirred the dry grass as she moved outside, and Hanson hesitated for a moment, wondering if she'd heard something else over the top of it. But as it dropped away, there was silence.

She fetched the torch and locked the car, then spent a minute making sure the keys were securely in her pocket. It wouldn't be a good time to end up hunting through undergrowth for them. Only then did she switch the flashlight on, making sure to keep it pointing downwards as she led O'Malley towards a cluster of bushes.

She felt sure the little stand of foliage was where they should be looking. Both because of Keely's story of Nina and Callum in the tree, and because it was the only place that really offered any shelter.

The beam turned the grass a dramatic bleach-white ahead of them, exposing deep cracks in the soil. It looked as though it had been ploughed in an earlier incarnation, leaving it treacherously uneven in its current dry state.

A moth suddenly flew into the beam, making her jump. The effect reminded her powerfully of camping with her parents, back when her father had been part of their family, and she started to move forwards with a slightly unreal feeling.

'Keely mentioned an old apple tree, didn't she?' she asked Domnall, quietly, trying to break the spell a little. 'It should be somewhere in here.'

As they drew closer, Hanson could make out one tree that stood higher than the others. The path they were following seemed to be aiming for it.

They followed it into a passage through the thicket, squeezing past tall nettles and brambles on each side. Hanson was still trying to keep the light low, which meant the brambles that stuck out into the path seemed to jump out at her at the last minute. Several snagged on her suit, requiring her to unpick herself from them, and she tried not to react as one pinged back and caught her across the back of the hand. O'Malley, behind her, seemed to be moving without difficulty. Which she supposed was either training or learning from her mistakes.

She tried to keep her focus ahead. Were there sounds there, too? A movement of branch over branch? The noise of someone breathing?

Without warning, the path became a small clearing, and Hanson reacted by stopping immediately. Fortunately Domnall was alert enough to stop too.

Hanson took a breath and shone the flashlight fully into the clearing. It was no more than ten feet across, tucked under the trunk of the apple tree that had for some reason veered sharply over as it grew before continuing up. In the centre of the clearing sat the remains of a campfire, and close by it a small backpack.

But no people. No Nina. Nobody lying here, captive.

Hanson took a step and felt her heart lurch as something moved under her foot. She lowered the torch sharply, shakily, to illuminate her feet, and realised it was nothing but an old piece of corrugated plastic that had levered up as she stepped on it. It was moss-covered. Ancient. The remains of a greenhouse, she thought. Not a trap.

She crouched down and put a hand towards the fire, and then she was turning to O'Malley, and saying, 'It's still warm. We need to start searching.'

17

Hanson could feel a crawl of anxiety across her skin. She trod as quietly as she could through the long grass, full of an awareness that there was someone close by. That they might be waiting to clobber her with a weapon or to jump her.

The fire could just be someone camping out, she thought, as she made her way along the overgrown path. With the torch switched off, travelling through the fruit trees and bushes was hard going, and she could feel her heart jolting at every sound the two of them made. *It could have just been a bunch of teenagers who've gone home for the night.*

But the largest part of Hanson's mind was certain that the fire was Keely's doing. That they had found their clue. And that awareness made every shadow and rustle of leaves threatening. As though Keely's flat stare was on them, somehow.

She couldn't help feeling a rush of relief as they emerged into the open grass again. With only starlight, it was far from bright, but it was better than thick shadow and dense foliage.

She scanned the field and felt her heart kick up into overdrive. There was a figure out there, clothed all in black, their face a pale smudge between their dark clothes and headgear.

'Domnall,' Hanson said, warning him. But even as she said it, the figure began to run.

Hanson was moving only a second later. The rough,

uneven path was a nightmare to run on, and her third step landed her half in a rut. Her ankle turned, and just recovered, and she was pretty confident that it wouldn't be comfortable later. But she ran on anyway.

The form ahead of her paused, suddenly, and Hanson faltered and then pushed onwards. She could hear O'Malley's heavier steps somewhere behind her and it gave her a sense of security she might not have otherwise had.

A piercing motor noise cut across the sounds of her breathing, and a bright white beam of light stabbed out across the tops of the grass. Hanson only understood what the figure had been doing as they began to move.

'Shit,' she said. 'They're on a motorbike!'

She turned, trying to angle her path so that it intersected with the vehicle track that ran along the edge of the field. She was taking repeated steps totally blind now, her feet landing at angles under the long grass and occasional brambles whipping into her.

What she would have done if she'd been able to get there in time wasn't clear even to Hanson, but it was a vain effort. The motorcyclist shot past, standing in the saddle with their arms braced against the uneven progress.

They were going too quickly for her to see more than an impression of pale skin underneath a raised visor. Hanson grabbed for her phone, and staggered onto the track. She just needed a clear shot of the licence plate.

But there was no plate. Just an empty slot where one should have been. And a moment later, the motorcycle was gone, heading out into the New Forest and away from the Murray-Watts' house.

Jonah was still poised in front of the iPad, thinking tangential thoughts about Alice in Wonderland and a label that said *Eat Me*, and then about some kind of elaborate trap that would be tripped by pressing the button.

He had photographed the setup already, including the note, and sent Lightman to check the remaining rooms of the house. It hadn't taken his sergeant long. There was little to the place. Two more bedrooms and a bathroom off the hallway. Nothing further.

'Are you recording?' he asked Lightman.

Ben nodded. He'd set up his phone to film the first play of the video, in case Keely's message was only able to be viewed once. It was hard to see, from the blurred white, yellow and grey shapes on the thumbnail, what the device was about to play, but they were determined to capture it.

'OK,' Jonah said, and pressed the play button.

The blurred shapes moved and then sharpened, becoming a view of a darkened street with a set of tail lights close to the kerb on the left. There was a figure on the pavement, he saw. Someone with bright white above and grey below. A girl in school uniform, it became clear, as the view swung round slightly.

'Looks like it's filmed from a motorbike,' he muttered, realising that whoever was filming was also on the road itself, and that there was a gentle engine purr overlaying it. But moments later, that sound cut out, and there were bumpy movements as whoever had been riding the bike clearly dismounted.

There was nobody else on the road, which looked to be a dark residential street, the houses set back behind gardens and driveways. The only movements were the girl, the car up ahead, and whoever was filming.

As he watched, it became clear that the driver of the car was keeping pace with the girl, and that the girl was more than a little alarmed by it. Their view moved forwards,

closing the gap a little and making the girl's hurrying movements all the clearer. She was attempting to look straight
ahead, but throwing occasional glances towards the car.

Jonah focused on the rear of the vehicle, trying to identify it. There were no lights over the licence plate, however,
and it was clearly caked in mud. Which might have been
simple laxness, or a deliberate attempt to obscure it.
The low, slightly square shape might have matched a few
different cars, and he found himself thinking of Henry
Murray-Watt's Jaguar and Frank Pinder's Escort, then dismissing them both.

The view drew in a little closer again, and Jonah could
suddenly hear a male voice emanating from the car
window.

'I said you have nice legs in that skirt. It's a compliment,
beautiful. Why aren't you saying thank you?'

The girl looked further towards the car this time, turning
to crane over her shoulder towards the driver. Her face was
very white in the reflected light from the car headlights, and
Jonah could see that she was really afraid.

'I'm just going home,' the girl said, her voice high and
tight.

'I didn't ask you where you were going,' the male voice
called, loudly. 'I asked why you weren't saying thank you?'

The girl scrabbled in her pocket, and from the way she
bent forwards, it was clear she had pulled out a phone.

Jonah could hear the man's laughter.

'Are you going to call for help? I could get out of this car
and drag you into it before you'd even pressed call. You're
on your own, darling.'

The view suddenly became unsteady, as whoever was
filming began to jog forwards.

'Excuse me!'

The call came from the person filming. A young man's voice, with what sounded like a fake Eastern European accent.

Jonah wasn't quite sure why he was certain that this was Callum Taylor talking, but he was.

The girl swung round, wildly.

'Sorry, my dear,' the voice he was sure was Callum's said. 'You know where number eighty-seven is? You show me?'

For a moment, as he drew closer, Jonah thought they would get a sight of the man in the car. But before their view could draw level with the window, the car suddenly accelerated. Jonah was left staring at a pair of tail lights, just before the video cut off.

There was no clear identification. No view of the driver's face or physique, and not even a clear view of his victim. But Jonah had one thing, gleaned from the sound of the engine as it had accelerated away. As distinctive a sound as he knew.

It had been the sound of an old Volvo, the kind his father had driven during Jonah's childhood. And it presumably belonged to the third man Keely was trying to point them towards.

Hanson's adrenaline was still up as she and O'Malley returned to the campfire. She could feel the back of her neck itching the moment she turned away from the open field.

Her mind was half full of accomplices, and half full of wild cats coiled up on grassy savannahs, watching. Waiting.

At O'Malley's suggestion, they checked the clearing again and then took the rucksack over to the Nissan, where the light was better. While O'Malley watched their surroundings, Hanson gloved up and began to reach inside.

It took her a couple of goes to get a grip on a slim metal water bottle to pull it out. Other things were easier. A cereal bar. An apple. A box of matches.

And right at the bottom, a card purse with a bank card and several folded five-pound notes. Probably three or four of them.

She pulled the mouth of the bag open further and saw that there was a wad of folded paper resting against the side of it. She eased it out and opened it.

The paper was clearly a letter. It was covered in large, slightly scruffy handwriting.

'Can I have the flashlight?'

O'Malley brought it over, and she held it up in her left hand as she started to read.

G Girl,

I'm still missing you. Still dying to feel your hands and your lips on me. It's too long. It's too fucking long.

But I'm going to find a way of being with you. Fuck what anyone else says. You, me — we're the only right thing in this world. I don't care what I have to do to make it happen. Who I have to hurt. Any of it.

I love you, and I know you love me. I know. Your being drawn back to me as strongly as I'm being drawn to you.

I'll find you soon.

C x

'Any thoughts?' she asked O'Malley, once she'd finished reading.

'Literally none,' the sergeant said. 'And I think that might be the point.'

*

Jonah and Lightman were almost at the top of Furzley Lane when the Mondeo's headlights caught a figure making its way down the near side of the road. The beams turned a short-cropped head of fair hair almost white.

Jonah had slowed to a crawl before he'd made any conscious decision to do it.

'Do you . . .?' he said to Lightman, and then stopped. 'I might need a minute.'

Lightman glanced at him, and back at the figure. 'No problem.' He pulled out his iPad and began to scroll through something.

Jonah pulled the car to a stop and climbed out, wondering whether Jojo could tell who it was. She had her hand up to shield her eyes, and he leaned in quickly to switch the powerful LEDs to side lights. He saw her wry look as she moved out into the lane towards him.

'If I'd wanted an X-Ray, I'd have booked one, Copper Sheens,' she said.

It was so much like the normal banter between them, the banter that had happened before he'd found out that Michelle was pregnant, that he laughed. In spite of the painful squeezing of his heart. Of the strange, sick and excited feeling in his stomach.

'Noted,' he said. He closed the door, painfully aware of Lightman sitting in the passenger seat. 'Are you all right?'

He saw Jojo's eyes narrow at him before she shrugged, a little unevenly. She was drunk, he realised. Which both did and didn't explain why she was walking down a very empty road at one in the morning wearing a silver halter top and trousers. There was no sign of any bag or warm layer on her.

'I'm fine. I don't even know why you'd ask.' She raised an eyebrow at him.

He nodded, finding it hard not to smile at her. And equally hard not tell her how much he missed her.

He felt tempted to tell her that he'd been seeing her in every short-haired or strong-looking woman for months. Stopping to look, and at times close to calling out to her, before realising that it wasn't Jojo.

This time, he'd known it was her. There was an inevitability to him being here, close to her house. And it being now, a night when Jojo wasn't in bed, as she would normally have been. When she was inexplicably out prowling the lonely roads of the New Forest.

'Are you on your way home?' he asked her, even though there were a lot of things that were more important.

'See? He's a brilliant copper. Powers of deduction,' Jojo replied.

'Did you break down . . .?'

Jojo tutted, as if irritated at having to discuss this. 'Just didn't have quite enough cash for the cab. So I got him to drop me before it got too expensive. Anyway, I'm not really that keen on talking to you now.' She started to move past him.

'I'm sorry,' he said. He'd said it to her an awful lot of times before, but he still felt it wasn't enough.

Jojo gave him a wide berth, and he wondered if he should let her go. But he found himself taking a few steps after her.

'You don't have to talk to me,' he said. 'But I'd just like to make sure you get home OK.'

'Oh, screw you, Sheens,' Jojo said, rounding on him. 'You've seen nothing of me for six months and suddenly you need to look out for me? I'm *fine*,' she said, loudly and pointedly, her chin jutting towards him. 'I'm always fine.'

'I know,' Jonah said.

He wasn't sure if he was relieved that she was angry with

him at last. Part of him had wanted her to shout at him and tell him exactly how much his decision was hurting her. It might have given him a strong enough reason to do the wrong thing.

Though it was too late now. And maybe he would have been tough enough to do what he'd done anyway, only with more hurt. With a greater sense of tearing them apart.

Jojo started to walk again, and then turned again to ask, 'Why aren't you at home? Looking after Milly?'

'I'm trying to find a teenage girl,' he said. And then, with a slight smile, he added, 'I promise I'm not stalking you. Her childhood home is just down the road.'

Jojo frowned at him. 'Which one?'

Jonah didn't hesitate before replying, 'It's the cottage with the roses over it. Empty now. Once owned by the Lennoxes.'

'The one where the woman died,' Jojo said, and nodded. 'Two red-haired little girls.'

It felt strange to hear her talking about them. To find his working life connected with his personal one. Though he should have expected it. Jojo had lived here for twenty-five years, and liked to walk everywhere. Of course she would know her neighbours.

'You haven't seen anyone going in or out of there recently, have you?'

Jojo looked thoughtful, and then shook her head. 'No. It's seemed empty.'

Jonah nodded, and when she started to walk again, he fell into step with her once more. It was only a few yards more to her cottage, and he had a wretched sense of not wanting the walk to end. This despite how pressing it was to find Nina, and despite how much of a betrayal it was. None of this was fair on Michelle. None of it.

Jojo walked in silence, and then turned to face him again in a resurgence of anger. 'You need to leave me alone now. Go back and cuddle up to Michelle. You chose her.'

Jonah nodded, glancing towards her house and then back up the road to his Mondeo. 'All right,' he said.

He began to tread back towards the car slowly. And then Jojo called out to him, 'Why did you choose her, Sheens? I still can't understand it.'

Jonah looked back at her; the alcohol or the time of night or just her anger making her shake slightly. She looked glorious.

'I never chose her,' he said. 'I just chose . . . the result of my stupid decision. The right thing.'

'You chose to be unhappy,' Jojo said, drawing her arms together in front of her stomach. 'You chose to self-flagellate by getting back together with the humourless idiot who you'd somehow ended up engaged to.'

Jonah shook his head, that awful feeling of betrayal dropping on him again. 'Please don't be angry with Michelle. None of this is her fault.'

Jojo's head jerked upwards as if he'd hit her. 'I'll be angry all I bloody want, Jonah.' It almost felt like a blow for him in return, the way she'd used his real name. 'You can't ask me not to be angry when she has everything I want. *Everything* I want but can't have.'

Jojo turned away again and began to walk quickly up towards her front gate.

Jonah didn't pursue her. He waited in the lane until he saw the lights go on inside the house, his mind trying to process what she'd said.

Lightman was silent as he climbed back into the Mondeo. He simply nodded and put the iPad away. As calm and non-judgemental as ever.

By the time they'd arrived back at Southampton Central, Jonah still wasn't sure about what Jojo had meant. But he had a heavy suspicion that she had wanted children of her own and been unable to have them. During their brief relationship, they had never talked about kids. He had thought her too independent for them, somehow.

He had also thought her too independent to be hurt for long. He had guessed that she would move on from him. Find herself another partner, or not, and be happy either way. Ferocious, capable Jojo would be fine. Which he'd both wanted for her and hated all at once.

But seeing her drunk and angry had undermined all of that. It had left him feeling that he hadn't been the only one to feel a hollowness ever since he'd left her. And he wondered whether what he'd ended up doing had been profoundly cruel.

They gathered again back at the station, the big meeting-room table now cluttered with mugs and plates. It was one thirty, and to Hanson's eyes even Ben looked like he might be flagging slightly.

The chief looked better than might be expected, though. He seemed thoughtful, perhaps a little troubled, but not exhausted as far as she could see. Given that he was already short of shut-eye, she'd would have predicted he'd be asleep on his feet by now, but perhaps he'd just become used to chronic lack of sleep.

'So,' he began. 'Our two puzzle pieces.'

He pressed the data projector remote, and brought up a still of the video from Keely's iPad. He'd already shared the video with them and requested they watch it in full.

The image that appeared was the back of the Volvo, in all its grubby glory.

'The first and most obvious question: who is this?' he said. 'We know that the driver is male, has a Volvo, and has a predilection for scaring young girls. Possibly even a history of harming them, judging by what he says to the victim here.'

'There's nothing to suggest Henry Murray-Watt has ever driven a Volvo,' Lightman commented. 'His last car was a Porsche. Frank and Evelyn Pinder have an Escort and a Polo and have owned them for six and eight years respectively.'

'And Jared Boula has a Golf,' Hanson commented. 'Prior to which he drove an ancient BMW into scrappage. I mean, a car could be rented or borrowed, but this looks too old and dirty for a rental, so that would leave borrowing from friends or family as the only option, if it's one of the three we've been looking at.'

'There's a time and date stamp on the video,' O'Malley commented. 'It's from four months ago. And they go past an electric substation at one point. I could try to work out where, and then see about some CCTV. Though it's residential, so . . .'

The DCI nodded. 'So there's no easy way of IDing them. I agree that it could be a borrowed vehicle, but it also might belong to the driver. In light of that, I think we need to think on the three men Keely talked about. She accused three men of abuse, but are those the same three she's apparently trying to prove guilty? It's possible that they aren't the same three.'

'I think we can assume that Henry Murray-Watt is one of them,' Lightman said. 'She's spent a lot of time detailing his effect on her life. He and his wife are also mysteriously off-grid at the moment. Quick's team says there's nothing from their phones at present, and they last pinged a mast a couple of days ago.'

'Let's hope he can find other ways of tracking them down,' the DCI said.

'I'd also guess that Frank Pinder was the second man,' Lightman went on. 'Though that's not definite yet. The seriousness of her allegations points that way. But Jared Boula may not be the third one. She hasn't mentioned anything against him to us, and she dropped the charges.' He nodded to the screen. 'This could well be the real third man on her list, and this is her way of asking us to find him.'

'There are easier ways of getting us to look into someone than a video of a car with no number plate,' O'Malley objected. 'She could have brought the iPad in with her and explained who he actually is.'

'Except that the last time she tried that, she wasn't believed,' Lightman countered, in what was an unusually strong tone. It made Hanson feel uncomfortable, and it clearly surprised O'Malley.

'Maybe she thinks we enjoy the chase,' Hanson said, instinctively trying for humour to smooth the situation over.

The DCI gave a small smile. 'True. I'd say we can't be sure exactly how much of our time this is worth, but we clearly can't ignore it.'

He pressed the button on the projector again. The image changed to a photo of the letter they'd found in the backpack at the allotments.

'The letter is equally mystifying,' the chief went on. 'The only individual we've heard about with the initial C is Callum Taylor. But the contents of the letter don't fit with Callum writing to his girlfriend. There was nobody keeping them apart, as far as we know. It seems strange, in addition, that he would address it to "G Girl" if it was for Nina.'

Hanson looked at those words again, and suddenly found some sense to them.

'What if he was addressing her as "Gossip Girl"?' she said, slowly. 'An in-joke in case someone ever found the letters. In the series, Blair's long-term love interest was named Chuck.' She gave the chief a grin. 'Don't ask me how I know that.'

'Which means it isn't Callum Taylor,' O'Malley said, immediately. 'It's Frank Pinder.'

Hanson nodded, looking at the chief. 'Frank was watching *Gossip Girl* in his bedroom this evening, and was really worried about me going into that room. What if that's because Nina was there, maybe hidden in the bathroom, and Keely never took her at all?'

The DCI glanced over at the letter, and then back to Hanson.

'I think we should get over there.'

As he spoke, his phone began to buzz, and he pulled it out and immediately put it on to speakerphone.

'I'd like some of your team ready to accompany my squad,' Quick's voice said. 'We've had a trace from Nina Lennox's phone. It's been switched on, and it's showing up on the street where Frank Pinder lives.'

Hanson was already on her feet by the time the DCI said 'We're on our way.'

18

There were no longer any lights on at the Pinder house, which wasn't exactly surprising. It was after two in the early hours of a Monday morning.

It was still unusually warm as Hanson and the DCI climbed out of the Mondeo and nodded to the four kidnap squad officers who had met them there. The other team was headed up by Murray Quick, with his DC as second-in-command. Both were wearing their dark work suits.

The other two officers were in black and were armed. They had all arrived quietly, engines running gently and sirens off.

Hanson had never been at what was essentially a raid before. It all seemed strangely overblown.

The six of them drew together a little way from the house, out of any sight lines. The chief nodded to Quick to kick things off, a clear sign that this was the DI's show.

'DC Hanson and DCI Sheens will knock and try to gain ordinary access,' Quick said. It was barely above a whisper, even though they were some distance from the house. 'Are you aware of any rear exits?'

'Yes,' Hanson told him. 'There are French windows opening onto the garden. I'd guess there's also a back door of some kind at the far end of the house.'

'All right,' Quick said. 'Casho, Mark and Finlay will be at the rear of the building.'

One of the black-clad officers nodded. There was something quite surreal about the casual way he had a machine gun slung across his torso. Without another word, the three of them moved off down the side of the building, blending quickly into shadow.

Hanson walked up alongside the chief, who seemed calm. Confident. It was reassuring.

He nodded to her before ringing the doorbell, and then followed it up by giving the loud, uncompromising knock of the police.

Somewhere towards the rear of the house, there was the sound of movement. Hanson looked towards Quick, whose gaze remained fixed on the door.

There was a long, tense pause, and then a light flicked on in the hallway. Hanson could see a figure approaching through the frosted glass. She felt a terrible squeeze of fear that they'd got everything wrong. That Nina wasn't here.

And then there was a shout from inside the house. A call of, 'We've got a young girl here!'

The chief had shimmed the door open in a moment, and Hanson was running ahead of him into the house. She could see the double bed in Frank's bedroom, and a pair of bare feet were just visible beside it.

She barely heard the constable explaining to the chief that Frank Pinder had run, presumably out of the open back gate. She was hurrying into the room, towards a small figure hunched on the edge of the bed. She had blankets wrapped round her, held bunched at the front, and it was clear that she was naked underneath. Made clearer by the skirt, leggings and silver-printed top that were piled on the floor.

The girl raised her head, and Hanson saw, in a rush, the honey-blonde hair. The hazel eyes. The flat cheekbones.

It wasn't Nina.

*

'She's frightened of telling us what happened,' Hanson told the DCI, quietly.

Sarah Mallard, the teenager they'd found in Frank Pinder's bed, was now sitting with a PCSO in a comfort suite, a place that looked as little like an interview room as possible. There was no observation room here, but Hanson had carried a vivid mental image of the panicked girl back outside.

Like many victims of grooming, Sarah was incredibly confused, believing all at once that she was in love, that she was sick and wrong for what she had done, and that her abuser should be left alone.

The only definitive information they'd had out of her so far was that Frank had gone outside a little while before the police arrived. He'd gone to investigate a buzzing noise. He hadn't returned, and the next thing Sarah knew, armed officers were entering the back door that he'd left open.

It seemed that Frank Pinder hadn't been tipped off. Instead, when Nina's phone had been planted outside the house and switched on, it had connected to the network and started to receive bursts of text messages in the patchy signal down the side of the house.

The phone had been close enough to Frank's open bedroom window for him to hear it buzzing and to go out to investigate. He had then presumably heard the arrival of the police, showing that however quiet they'd been, they hadn't been quiet enough. After that, he'd let himself out of the back gate and got away.

Although it wasn't absolutely clear who had left the phone there, the chief and his team were certain that it had been Keely's doing. That she had led them to Frank in order for them to arrest him, and had only been thwarted by a warm evening and an open window.

To the huge frustration of all of them, Frank remained

at large. He had left his phone behind and disappeared into the network of alleys. Despite the kidnap team's best efforts, they hadn't been able to find him, and hadn't picked him up on the very few cameras scattered around Ashurst either.

Evelyn Pinder was still at the hospital, on her shift, and had been there all evening. It was clear she hadn't helped him to get away. She was now on her way to the station, too, desperately confused and alarmed by the apparent disappearance of her husband. Hanson was hoping she wouldn't have to break the news to Evelyn that her husband had been sleeping with a teenager.

Though, in fact, Sarah Mallard had yet to confirm explicitly that they had been sleeping together. She wouldn't answer direct questions about whether or not he had touched her, or what she'd been doing in his house in the first place.

'It's the thought of her parents finding out that seems to be making her most anxious,' Hanson told the chief. 'They're on their way in now. They thought she was at an overnight training camp with some other star players.' She shook her head, not needing to add how grim it was that Frank Pinder's role as a coach had given him access to this girl and many others. 'I don't know whether we ought to suggest a different responsible adult so she feels she can talk freely.'

There was a pause, and then the chief said, 'If we can get her agreement, let's do it. And ask her parents to wait a short while. I think it would be kinder on her to let her talk it out before she has to see them. We probably won't get to handle her case ourselves in full, but I'd like an initial statement.'

Hanson nodded, a little disappointed. She'd been aware

that they were thinly stretched as it was, and that their priority was Nina. But she still wanted to be part of bringing Frank Pinder to justice. The fear and shame Sarah Mallard was currently experiencing had made her burn to hunt him down and charge him.

'This changes things, doesn't it?' she said, after a pause. 'If Frank Pinder was sleeping with a young girl, then it makes everything Keely said about him look a lot more likely. And if she was telling the truth about him, then she was probably also telling the truth about the Murray-Watts and Jared Boula.'

'It definitely opens up the possibility,' the DCI agreed, quietly.

At ten past three, Sarah Mallard's parents arrived. There was still no sign of Frank Pinder, despite CCTV being requested from the surrounding area.

But the teenager had, by the time her parents were shown up to the comfort suite, admitted that this wasn't the first time she and Frank had slept together. Under very gentle questioning by one of the Child Abuse Investigation Team, she had also explained that she'd deleted all their messages. He'd asked her to, and she had obeyed.

Hanson, sitting in on the interview, had seen how torn Sarah was at telling them this. She still felt like she was betraying him. That much was abundantly clear.

With the interview done, Sarah agreed to see her parents. Just before they walked in, though, Sarah ran for the en-suite bathroom, and they could hear her being sick even through the thick wooden door.

Hanson found herself hating, really hating, Frank Pinder just then.

*

'I'm calling time,' Jonah told his team, the moment Hanson returned to CID. 'There's nothing in Keely's clues so far to point the way to Nina, and with some indication that Keely might have been telling the truth about some of the abuse, then it's doubtful that Frank Pinder is in any way involved in holding her. It's also possible that Keely's intentions are good, and that Nina is all right for now.' He paused for a moment. 'Unless anyone has anything that seems like a strong lead?'

There was silence, and then Lightman said, 'The most I've done is confirm that Callum Taylor has a motorbike. He could have been the biker at the allotments. I put his reg plate out to be tracked on ANPR, but he hasn't been picked up on any cameras since last week. The bike you guys saw had its plates removed, didn't it? So there's no obvious way forward there.'

'I've got nothing on the Volvo, either,' O'Malley added. 'I've found the substation on the video, which is in Totton. But there's a total void of CCTV around there, and obviously without a reg ANPRs are going to be pretty useless.'

Jonah nodded, feeling slightly relieved. After a surge of energy with the raid on the Pinder house, he was now feeling drained and in dire need of some sleep. The revelation of Frank Pinder's guilt had turned a lot of his thinking on its head, but it wasn't at all clear to him whether it meant they could fully trust Keely. A desire to take revenge on her former foster father might not equal a healthy frame of mind.

They needed, he thought, to do this right – even if that meant taking a few hours to rest. Though even as he thought it, he felt his stomach squeeze in anxiety for Nina Lennox.

Three thirty a.m. Not the best time to be driving back to an empty house, Hanson thought. Not when Damian so clearly thought he had nothing to lose any more.

'Shall I give you a lift?' Ben asked, as she looped her handbag over her neck.

Hanson turned to grin at him, realising that he'd read her mood without her needing to say anything. She made an effort at protesting, though. 'Don't make yourself later to bed. You're going to need every minute.'

Lightman shrugged. 'You're forgetting that I'm a robot. I don't actually need sleep.'

'True,' Hanson agreed. 'Well, if you're sure . . . I'd probably trust your driving more than mine right now.'

'I'll swing by and pick you up in the morning as well,' he offered. 'There won't be any traffic at that time.'

She followed him to his Qashqai and wondered if he'd mind if she dozed off during the journey. But as she settled herself in, she thought once again of how much more easily provoked Ben seemed to be than he normally was. And so, as soon as he'd started the engine, she asked him, 'Are you doing OK at this end of the day?'

There was a brief pause before Ben said, 'I guess so. It's all a bit . . .'

He broke off, and let out a brief, sharp sigh. Hanson looked at him sideways and saw with a fascinated sort of empathy that his eyes were unusually reflective.

He rubbed a hand over his face, and Hanson turned back to the road again. She knew, without needing him to say, that it was mortifying to him to be emotional in this way.

'Sorry. Pretty knackered.'

'That's OK,' she said.

Ben shook his head. 'It's not the right time for a chat. Let's get through this next day or so.'

'Sure,' Hanson said, feeling a drop in her stomach. It was both the fact that he felt unable to talk to her, and a rush of worry that she and the rest of the team had done something wrong. 'But I'm always happy to talk. If you want to. Even at a stupid time in the morning.'

She glanced at him. Saw his half-smile.

'I know,' he said.

They drove in silence to Hanson's house, though she no longer felt like dozing. She was going back through the last day in her mind, trying to work out what was up.

As he pulled the Qashqai up outside her house, Ben said, much more lightly, 'I'll bring pastries in the morning. I have some in the freezer.'

'How is anyone that organised?' She undid her seat belt and tried to hit a light-hearted note. 'Here's to another day of riding the sugar highs. Just don't tell my mum.'

'Does she worry about you?' Lightman asked.

'She thinks my diet is a diabetic disaster waiting to happen,' she said, with a slightly forced grin.

'God, please don't cut down,' Ben replied. 'I don't think we'd survive if you were tired, overworked *and* sugar-deprived.'

Hanson laughed. 'Do you think I'd get grumpy?' she asked. 'Or go all-out insane, like a gremlin when you give them water?'

'Gremlin,' Ben told her. 'Definitely gremlin.'

Jonah found Michelle asleep on the sofa on his return, with Milly conked out in her carrycot on the floor. Neither of these were a good sign, and he felt a crushing sense of guilt that she'd probably been struggling with Milly while he'd spent time talking to Jojo. It wasn't that he'd had any sleep himself, but there was something uniquely exhausting about a child who wouldn't sleep, and the constant reawakenings when she was restless. It was undeniably worse than working late.

He took Milly up to their bedroom, leaving Michelle an explanatory note. He dreaded having his few hours disrupted, but it would be worse to wake Michelle and then leave her to cope with Milly all day.

They needed a babysitter, he thought. It was highly likely that he'd be held late at work tonight, whatever the outcome of his next conversations with Keely Lennox. There were too many strands to all this to pull at. Too much to arrange.

Given that Milly was already combination fed, it shouldn't be too hard to get someone to take her now and then. Jonah found shoving a bottle down her fairly easy, with no prior experience.

But they suffered from a lack of nearby (rational) parents and an equally lacking network of young things. There was no obvious choice to help them out. Perhaps Sophie and Roy might be willing to step in. It was good practice for their next arrival, surely?

He undressed himself as quietly as he could, and eased himself into bed. Despite all his best intentions, he drifted off thinking of the way his headlights had struck Jojo's blonde hair.

19

Keely was up long before Veronica. She moved silently to the bathroom and washed, with as little running of the taps as possible, and then brushed her hair. She coiled her hair up into a high bun in front of the mirror and pinned it into place before returning to her room. She tucked the wash kit they'd sent from the home back into her suitcase. She wouldn't be staying here another night if everything went to plan.

She dressed in her diamanté Superdry T-shirt and jeans, and once Veronica had been up for a while, she went to eat breakfast with her. She smiled slightly to see that her social worker had made scrambled eggs, a big slushy pile of them, and had laid out jam and toast and hot cross buns. As if there were six of them to feed instead of just two.

She took a single piece of toast and let Veronica pile it high with eggs. She ate slowly, and listened politely as the social worker prattled on, and then went to her room to collect the holdall and slide on her padded jacket. She paused, once she was ready, to send another message.

Time for round two. I hope you're sitting comfortably.

Veronica tapped on her door before any reply had arrived. 'The car's here,' she said.

Keely slung her bag over her shoulder and headed out into the hall.

Hanson's alarm had gone off way, way too soon. She felt as though she'd only just managed to get comfortable, never mind get any sleep. Though at least she hadn't been mulling over what Ben had said, as she'd been expecting to.

There wasn't much time for thinking things over this morning, which was probably a good thing. She'd only just managed to get herself dressed, vaguely spruced up and armed with a travel mug of coffee by the time she heard the Qashqai's engine.

Ben looked, of course, perfectly groomed and well rested. There was no sign of tension today. He laughed at her as she climbed in and hunkered down with her coffee.

'I'll have the last laugh,' she told him. 'I'm going to fake a family emergency at midday and go back to bed.'

Ben considered this. 'I've got my family emergency lined up already, so I might beat you to it.'

'That's not fair. You can't steal my idea.'

Ben grinned at her. 'All's fair when you've had three hours' sleep.'

Milly had slept without waking, and Jonah deposited her back in the living room with Michelle at just before six. His partner was still asleep on the sofa, her dark hair half covering her face. Her legs were bunched up in what looked like defence.

He decided to skip morning coffee out of fear of waking either Michelle or Milly, and instead wrote a short note promising that he would try to find some childcare today.

He wasn't sure why he was suddenly certain his partner was struggling. It felt like a series of impressions: her panic at the pub; the short reply to his message; the sofa; and his own guilt at being out late.

But the realisation might, he thought, have come about thanks to Keely Lennox. He had been confronted with her story; one that had made him think a lot about being a parent. Many of those thoughts had turned out to be uncomfortable.

Before he left the house, he crept upstairs to the bathroom to have a wash and change of clothes. He would have given a lot for a hot shower just then, but the heating system in the elderly house was archaic and noisy, and it would be guaranteed to disturb both Michelle and Milly. So he stripped off and washed himself over the sink with a flannel, and then straightened up to see how his hair was faring.

As he spent a few moments sorting it out, he found himself imagining Keely standing in front of her own mirror. Practising what she was going to say about Jared Boula.

He saw, suddenly, not a manipulative sociopath, but a young woman who had been disbelieved twice over. A young woman who had been telling the truth about at least one of her abusers. And he realised that everything, every part of what she had done, had been about fighting to be heard. To be trusted. To be protected.

It was somehow absolutely as expected that his phone vibrated at that point, with Linda McCullough's number flashing up. The least surprising part was that she was working at six a.m. Their forensic scientist was an undeniable workaholic.

He answered as quickly as he could and muttered a greeting.

'Glad you're up,' Linda said, her voice as dry and as brisk as usual. 'I've been looking at the contents of your school crime scene, and there's a lot more to it than first appeared.'

'That doesn't surprise me,' Jonah said.

'In the handbag the dummy was holding, there were photographs,' she said. 'The first few are of someone's desktop computer, and then some zoomed in on a particular folder. The rest are of the contents of that folder and they're ... well, they're not exactly nice viewing. Pornographic and violent images involving children, all of them.'

Jonah felt a squeeze of anger, and then a surge of sadness for Keely. For his own lack of faith in her.

He promised McCullough that he'd be in shortly and left the house. As he climbed into his Mondeo, he found himself looking forward to talking to Keely. The first thing he'd tell her was that he was going to help her.

It was six-thirty-a.m. quiet on the street outside the refuge. Veronica could hear distant traffic but nothing close by. And no cars drawn up at the kerb, either. Just a four-wheel-drive a few yards down and someone on a delivery motorbike talking across the street.

'He said he was here,' she said to Keely, glancing along the road. 'Maybe he's parked around the corner.'

Veronica sent a message to the driver asking where he was, and then, as time passed and it showed as still being unread, she started to walk along the pavement towards the nearest side street. She felt slow and heavy. Her hip, which was still supposedly months away from an op, was increasingly stiff and painful. On some mornings, she wondered whether it would even hold her weight, but it usually loosened up as the day went on, only to decline once again towards the evening.

She looked at her phone again, where the driver had messaged her. She was a few feet down the road when she heard a snatch of talking, in what sounded like Keely's voice. And then an engine started up some way behind her. By the time she'd turned, the four-wheel-drive was already pulling away from the pavement, its rear door slamming shut.

It passed her at growing speed, followed immediately by the Deliveroo driver, leaving the street empty.

She shouted Keely's name, knowing, even as she did it, that the girl was gone.

Jonah was only just inside CID when his phone vibrated in his pocket. He pulled it out, seeing a number he didn't recognise, and answered.

'DCI Sheens,' he said.

'This is Veronica, from social services,' a woman's voice said. There were street sounds in the background and she sounded panicked. Almost tearful. 'Keely Lennox is gone. She got into a car with someone. I think it was by arrangement.'

And Jonah wondered why he hadn't been expecting this.

Veronica arrived while he was still scrambling to inform the detective chief superintendent that their witness had vanished. The DCS took it with his usual calm, but Jonah was left feeling like a monumental failure after the call, nonetheless.

Lightman showed the social worker into Jonah's office. The middle-aged woman looked up at him with an expression of such shame when he arrived that he felt moved to comfort her.

'I'm very sorry about this,' Jonah said. 'I don't think you should feel responsible in any way. If anyone might have predicted it, it was me.'

Veronica pulled a wry expression. 'But you weren't the one there, letting yourself be lured away.'

He gave her as sympathetic a smile as he could manage. 'You said you were sent a message?'

'Yes.' Veronica pulled out her phone. 'It said "I'm parked outside". It came from a number I didn't have, and I just assumed it was the taxi I'd booked.'

'You don't know how someone got your number?'

'I don't,' Veronica said. And then she added, 'But . . .

Keely knew we were going to take a taxi, and she would have had ample opportunity to get hold of my phone and find out the number last night.' She gave an awkward shrug. 'I didn't think I had to guard it from her.'

'It wasn't part of your brief,' Jonah agreed, with a small smile. He took the phone and copied down the number. 'Do you think, looking back on what happened, that it came across like that? Like it was part of Keely's plan?'

'I don't know,' Veronica said, her expression troubled. 'I mean, she could have been snatched. But then it's difficult to know how they found us unless Keely told them. Someone could have followed us from the station last night, I suppose . . . But then how would they have my number?'

'Was there any sound of a struggle?' he asked, guiding her back to his original question.

Veronica sighed. 'It was very quick, all of it. I thought I heard her say something, but there was no shouting. No confrontation. She might have just opened the door and climbed in. Or there might have been multiple people, working together to drag her in, I suppose.'

Jonah nodded, easily able to imagine Keely's swift execution of a well-thought-out plan, but also remembering that she represented a threat to the three men she was determined to see put away. They couldn't work on the assumption that she'd chosen to go.

'We're seeing if we can find some CCTV,' he told Veronica, 'but can you tell me if you noticed anything about the vehicle she left in?'

Veronica's lips pursed. 'It was a four-wheel-drive. A Land Rover or something like that. Slightly old-looking but no plates, as I mentioned. I'm sorry, I – I know it's no help at all.'

'You didn't see anything of the driver?'

Veronica sighed. 'Nothing much. I have a vague impression of them being male. Short hair. Black jacket, I think. I didn't really have time . . .' She shook her head. 'I don't know . . . the only other thing was that there was a delivery driver. He was on his phone while we were waiting, and then he left straight after the van. I can't be sure, but it looked to me like he was part of it.'

'Driving a car?' Jonah asked.

'No,' Veronica said. 'No, it was a motorbike.'

Jonah gave her a sharp look. 'And what was the age of the driver?'

'I . . . I couldn't say for sure. But reasonably slim, and white. Maybe young.'

Jonah nodded to himself. They would check CCTV, but that sounded a lot like Callum Taylor, who had presumably been there as backup or distraction in case Veronica didn't turn away for long enough.

And if it had been Callum Taylor, then someone else had been driving the four-by-four. If Keely had planned it, she had more than one person on her side.

'So, things have moved on us,' Jonah said, perching on the table of the smaller meeting room. They had been bumped out of their favourite gathering spot to make room for the eight a.m. senior management meeting. Jonah would normally have been part of it, kicking off the week with caseload allocation, budget decisions and any staffing issues. But the DCS had immediately excused him. As far as Jonah was concerned, that was the biggest win of the morning. He'd rather be here, with his own team, any day of the week.

'Keely's disappearance is concerning, in part because we don't know whether she went willingly. Although I think her entirely capable of arranging it, she is also a very likely target for the men whose freedom she threatens.' He glanced at each of his team members. 'I think it's worth bearing in mind that Frank Pinder is still at large, and that we don't currently know for sure where Henry Murray-Watt is.'

'Where does that put us?' Hanson asked. 'Are we focusing on finding Keely now?'

'It unfortunately puts us in the situation of having two teenage girls to find urgently instead of one.' Jonah took a gulp of coffee. 'Nina's safety is if anything less certain now that Keely has vanished. We no longer have Keely here as a potential witness, for all the help that's been so far. Knowing that Keely more than likely was the victim of abuse doesn't rule out the possibility that she's put her sister in jeopardy. And, worse still, if she didn't go willingly, there is now nobody left to free Nina . . . or to feed her, give her water, and make sure she doesn't bleed to death.'

There was a brief pause, which felt longer with time ticking ever onwards.

'Assuming for a minute that Keely did choose to vanish,' Hanson eventually said, 'and ignoring the fact that you hate assumptions . . . If Keely really was leaving a trail that ultimately leads to Nina's location, isn't the implication that she's given us enough to work with?'

'Assuming that, then yes, it is,' Jonah agreed. 'Though it's also possible that the trail only leads us to her chosen three men, and she'll release Nina once we've arrested them.'

'I'm guessing Keely's phone's off,' Lightman chipped in.

'Yes, no signal from it after she left in the four-by-four,' Jonah said.

'And is Quick's team treating her disappearance as a kidnap?' Lightman asked.

'I think they're keeping an open mind,' Jonah replied.

He could see that Ben looked dissatisfied with that, but

before he could address it, Hanson asked, 'The unmarked four-by-four. Does it tell us anything?'

'Sally Murray-Watt owns a dark green Range Rover,' Lightman commented. 'Year of manufacture was ninety-eight. If she took the plates off it, then it would probably answer to Veronica's description.'

'You aren't even looking at any notes, you absolute swot,' O'Malley said.

'Who needs notes?' Lightman asked, with a small smile.

'So do we think Sally Murray-Watt is helping her, or that she and her husband have conspired to kidnap her?'

There was a brief silence, and then Jonah said, 'I think we need to visit the Murray-Watts, as a matter of priority. I'll take volunteers.'

'I'd like to work on additional clues left by Keely, if that's OK with you all,' Hanson offered.

'That's the opposite of volunteering, Juliette,' O'Malley said, with a laugh. 'But I'd like a scenic drive, so that suits me fine. Want to come, Ben?'

After a fractional pause, Lightman said, 'Fine with me.' Jonah wondered whether his hesitation was down to the flashes of tension between him and O'Malley, which seemed to have come out of nowhere. His two sergeants were usually firm friends as well as great colleagues. He'd never known them to fall out.

The change had clearly come from Lightman. The normally calm and unemotional younger sergeant was suddenly reacting with anger to a lot of what O'Malley had to say. It wasn't lost on Jonah that it all centred around whether or not to trust Keely Lennox's allegations, but experience had taught him that arguments weren't always about what they seemed to be. When you'd been dwelling on one source of anger for a while, it was all too easy to flip out about something else.

He and Jojo had developed a phrase for it after a client of hers had seemingly lost their mind over a hybrid geranium in a garden. The client had eventually admitted that hybrid geraniums were his mother's obsession, and that his fury had been the result of a deeply dysfunctional relationship with said mother.

'Hybrid geranium' moments had inevitably become their shorthand for arguments based on an unvoiced stress. It was a phrase he'd had to consciously stop using in front of Michelle out of a feeling of disloyalty.

The tricky bit for him now was working out whether Lightman was having a hybrid geranium moment, or whether he really did feel strongly about this particular investigation. A complex extra thread to untangle amid the many others.

'It strikes me,' Jonah eventually said, aware that he'd been silent for a while, 'that being certain of who the three men Keely Lennox wants sent down actually are is key at this point. If she's gone willingly and wants us to follow her trail, we need to know who we're looking at. And if she was taken against her will, those men are probably at the heart of it, too.'

'I think we can now be pretty confident that the first two men are Frank Pinder and Henry Murray-Watt,' O'Malley said.

Jonah nodded. 'Frank Pinder is a given. Her clues led us straight to him. And as Ben said last night, it's clear she sees Henry as responsible for a lot of her suffering, even if we have yet to find evidence against him. Does anyone disagree with that analysis?'

There was a short silence, and then Hanson asked, 'So what about man number three? Who is probably our Volvo driver. It's unlikely to be Jared Boula in that video. He has no family in the UK and few apparent friends. None of his

colleagues drives a Volvo and his girlfriend has no car at all.'
She glanced up at Jonah. 'I haven't picked up so far on anyone who might fit the role during Keely's interviews, either.
There are no specific school teachers mentioned. Or anyone else in a position of power. She made it clear all these
three men had power over her, so who fits that?'

'What about the social worker?' Lightman asked. 'Mark
Slatterworth. He only started working with them six months
before they left the Murray-Watts'.'

Jonah gave a slow nod. 'He would definitely have access to
them, though it looks from their record as though he barely
saw them. And the accent is wrong for the Volvo driver,
unless he was deliberately putting one on. He sounded local.'

'Slatterworth didn't seem remotely anxious coming in to
see us, either,' O'Malley said. 'And he's about as far from the
abusing type as you can imagine, based on the kind of folks
we've encountered before.'

'There is no abusing type,' Lightman shot back. 'That's
the whole point of looking for evidence.'

And there it was again, Jonah thought. The same touch-
point. But O'Malley immediately said, placatingly, 'Ah,
you're right, so,' and Ben visibly relaxed after a moment.

'So,' Jonah tried. 'We look for evidence. Where do we go?'

'I guess we start with the objective stuff,' O'Malley said,
glancing at Ben. 'Her care record shows their interactions . . .'

Lightman gave a short laugh. 'I think calling her care
record "objective" is fairly flawed.'

O'Malley looked slightly helplessly at Jonah. He wasn't to
any degree a confrontational man. He'd joke his way out of
conflict at any opportunity. Lightman's frustration was
clearly getting to him.

'OK, Ben,' Jonah said, quietly, 'what do you think our
way forward should be?'

'I think we should stop second-guessing everything Keely has told us, and trust her,' Lightman said, his voice unusually hoarse. 'I don't see the Lennox sisters as these manipulative teenagers you all seem ready to believe in. Not in any way. I see two young girls who've been drastically let down by the system, one or both of whom are clearly in real danger. So let's stop messing around with doubt and use what she's given us to find them both.'

There was a short silence, one made up of discomfort as well as sympathy. Seeing someone so detached suddenly becoming emotional was both strange and awkward.

'I agree that they've been let down,' Jonah said in the end, as gently as he could. 'Everyone should be believed when they make claims of that kind. But that doesn't mean we shouldn't look at this from every side. There's still a strong possibility that Keely chose to remove herself from us, and that she's continuing to play games, even if that's for the very best of reasons.'

It was the least confrontational way he could think of putting it, and so he was more than surprised when Ben stood quickly, and walked from the room, shutting the door firmly behind him.

There was total silence after his departure. None of them, Jonah thought, had been prepared for it.

But Jonah needed to deal with the situation. Keeping his team working was, beyond anything else, the job he was here to do.

'Sorry,' he ended up saying. 'You're all functioning on too little sleep, and I didn't do the best job of handling that.'

'Ah, I'm sure it was my fault,' O'Malley added. 'I'd spotted he disagreed with me. Should have kept my mouth shut. And I don't even disagree, really. I just, you know, want to make sure we're not having the wool pulled over our eyes.'

'I need you to tell us your thoughts on what's happening,' Jonah said, firmly. 'Whatever the fallout.'

O'Malley nodded, clearly relieved to hear it.

'I guess ... Ben's not wrong, though,' Hanson said, a moment later. 'We don't know whether Keely meant to vanish or not, but we do know that she's been telling us the truth.'

'Should we not be looking at any calls to and from Keely's phone now?' O'Malley suggested. 'If she arranged to disappear, it must have been done using her phone. Whereas if she was abducted, it's surely possible that she was tricked, like Veronica was. She could have been sent a message, too, telling her to get into the car.'

'That's a good point,' Jonah said. 'Let's look into it.' He glanced over at O'Malley. 'Do you want Juliette to go with you to the Murray-Watts instead?'

'Ah, no. I'll make things all right with Ben,' the sergeant said, with a return of his usual cheer. 'However annoying he finds me, he won't hate me for long if I buy him doughnuts.'

Hanson returned to her desk with her mind largely on what was going on with Ben. There was no sign of him in CID, and no message left for them to say where he'd gone, either.

She felt a strange surge of frustration towards him, one that was probably the result of a poor night's sleep. Why couldn't he tell her what was bothering him? It was so hard to help when he was unwilling to open up.

She pulled up her chair and sat, watching O'Malley pick up his keys. He was presumably on a peace-offering doughnut run.

She picked up her phone, and after three attempts, managed to send Ben a brief message saying she hoped he was doing all right, and apologising for not being much help.

It was only once she'd pressed send that she realised there was a package on her desk. A small Hermes parcel with her name and the address of the station.

She frowned at it, trying to remember what she'd ordered recently. She generally tried to send things to her house if they weren't work-related. Getting failed delivery attempts was generally less of a hassle than objects having to be checked by the duty staff for any threat. This one looked to have been deemed all right, however, and she tore off the packaging with a feeling of pleasant anticipation.

The box inside was plain, and the size of an A6 page, but a few centimetres deep. Lifting the lid, she found a memory stick packed in a layer of condensed polystyrene. Attached to it was a purple gift tag. She turned it over, and with a slightly strange feeling read the words.

For DC Juliette Hanson. From Keely xxx

She stood looking at it for a while, and then pulled out her own laptop. She disconnected it from the Wi-Fi, a move that the cyber team had instilled in her. She wasn't about to plug in an untested item on a machine that had access to the police systems. Viruses and Trojans were almost always spread by human error, the cyber team had said, and she'd prefer not to be the human who made the error.

The flash drive appeared in the My Computer bar, and she opened it to see a row of fifteen videos in MP4 format. The thumbnail stills were all, she saw, of Keely's face.

She felt strangely cold as she plugged in her headphones and pressed the play button on the first one.

'*Hello, detective constable,*' Keely said, her expression full of humour but her gaze as direct and unflinching as ever. '*I hope you enjoy the gift. It's a just-in-case situation, really. I didn't want you missing out on my story, whatever happens. So here it is. A backup for you.'* She paused for a moment, and then said, *'You don't get to choose your story. That's the thing I've learned more resoundingly than anything else . . .'*

Hanson could only watch blankly for some moments as the truth sank in. This was what Keely had told them. From the beginning. Every single part of her story, word for word the same.

20

It was easier than I'd thought, turning Ninny into a villain. And I mean that in all senses of the word 'easier'. It took remarkably little effort for a real sense of reward, and it gave me no guilt whatsoever. Not one flicker of it.

They didn't even question it when Ninny suddenly seemed to start misbehaving. When she stole Sally's signature burnt-orange lipstick and ruined her white sundress by getting smudges all over it. When she was found to have trodden mud right across the beautiful living-room carpet. When she somehow lost the necklace Henry had chosen for her birthday.

Every one of these crimes was designed to anger Henry as much as possible. To play on his hatred of his house or the women in it looking messy, or being disorganised.

They might have given Ninny the benefit of the doubt if they'd stopped to think about it. She had never been covetous or messy. She was obedient, dutiful and organised. In fact, her memory for things was as good as her memory for words. She never lost things.

But I'd made it all pretty persuasive. The smears on the dress as evidence of the lipstick theft. The fact that I'd used Ninny's shoes to muddy the carpet. And then taking that beautiful flowing horse-shaped necklace, the one they'd spent so much on, and throwing it into a neighbour's recycling bin. There was no way it was coming back, no matter how hard Ninny tried to find it.

She couldn't understand how any of it had happened.

She was incapable, back then, of suspecting me. Of thinking that her sister could ever do her wrong.

In a strangely satisfying but vastly unfair turn of events, she eventually went mad at Callum, accusing him of framing her and trying to ruin her life. She threw herself at him in the garden, raining down blow after blow, and I half expected him to lash out in return. I was waiting to see the violent boy who had been thrown out of his previous home.

But that boy never appeared. Callum just kept trying to calm her. To hush her. Telling her that they would hear and she'd be in trouble.

It didn't work. Ninny kept it up, and when Henry came and pulled her away, Callum stood looking at her with such pity that I wanted to hit him. To tear into him too. But instead, I gave him an expression of shock and asked, in a whisper, what they would do to her.

He thought, at that point, that I was afraid for her. He didn't know that I was feeling a rush of glorious anticipation.

You should have seen Ninny's face the first time she was punished. It's an expression I've seen on a lot of people since then. It always comes from people who've decided that their life is wonderful because they *deserve* it. The ones who never think anything bad will ever happen to them.

Well, Ninny was about to learn. It didn't matter how much she sobbed and pleaded, as it hadn't mattered with me. Punishment came, regardless.

The first time she was shut into the darkness, I crept downstairs once everyone was asleep, and padded through the rooms with a heart that pounded with excitement, trying to hear her. Trying to listen for her whimpers. Though after almost an hour of waiting, I had to admit defeat and return to bed.

After that, she began to lose privileges. She was denied

riding lessons for two weeks, and then was told she'd have to get herself to and from them. That Sally had too much to do. This despite Sally spending most of her time in the house, and the lessons being a full two miles outside Godshill.

I made everyone all the less suspicious by trying to plead her case to Sally. I did a lot more, I'd like to tell you, than Ninny had ever done for me. I told them she was good, really, and had just made a mistake. And I remember how Sally smiled at me, her eyes slightly teary, and said what a good sister I was. How much I'd grown up.

I also made sure to offer to walk with her to the stables each Saturday, and then spent the time running laps of the pasture. And afterwards I would insist on using my pocket money to treat Ninny to a hot chocolate once we'd hiked back into Godshill again.

The third time this happened, Ninny began to cry the moment the mug was in her hands.

'I don't know what to do,' she said. 'I'm trying so hard.'

'It'll be OK,' I told her, as if I were on her side instead of the reason for her downfall.

'It has to be. I can't keep feeling like this,' she told me.

I tried to ignore the squirming sense of guilt as we trudged back home down Godshill's pretty little streets. Streets that seemed somehow drabber today, no matter how many times I told myself that she deserved this.

Callum's insistence that there had to be a bad guy was proven absolutely right. The more Ninny was punished, the more we both seemed to slide past every difficult scenario. Callum started to fill out a little as Henry refrained from starving him in punishment.

And I, of course, did even better. I was suddenly their perfect child: the studious, clever, skinny little athlete who smiled and simpered and complimented them. And did

I mention how popular I was? Everyone at school wanted to be around me now, and none of them realised that I was dangling them all. That I was endlessly dancing them like puppets, because I'd finally learned where to find the strings. It was a golden season.

How ironic that it was the product of absolute darkness.

The only real moment of doubt I remember experiencing was when Callum finally realised what was happening. I did wonder if he'd started to get suspicious about Ninny's many mishaps and apparent bad behaviour, and realise that they weren't part of her character. Whatever the cause, one afternoon when I'd thought myself alone and free to wreak havoc, he suddenly appeared, as if from nowhere.

My plan for that day was simple. I'd seen Ninny playing with the neighbour's dog over the fence, encouraging it to jump up. I could see that she wanted its company. Something to cuddle and stroke. And perhaps she was enjoying the idea of rebellion, too, now that I look back.

The dog was too small and overfed to make it over the fence, however, and Ninny eventually wandered off into the garden. I smiled as I watched her leave. I'd seen my chance.

I slid open the French windows into the living room and made my way over to the coffee table in the corner, on which sat one of Sally's two prized Japanese lamps. They were a perfect pair, huge, lacquered things with cream shades. She'd bought them from Marquis Antiques in Lyndhurst a year before, and it had taken a lot to convince Henry that they were worth it.

She'd been obsessed with them ever since. She polished them at least weekly, and wouldn't let any of us go near them, even when we were tasked with cleaning.

I'd had my eye on them for weeks, and now I knew what to do. I would break one of them, and then run out into the garden, then into the kitchen to tell Sally that a dog had been in our house.

And what would a dog be doing there? Sally would ask, of course. And if she hadn't seen the damage by that point, she would see it later on. And want to know why the French windows were open.

And Ninny, who could never lie or hide anything, would incriminate herself. She would actually believe that it was all her fault.

My hand was already on the base of the lamp when Callum said, 'What are you doing?'

I froze where I was, and when I looked at him it was with fear and raging anger.

His own expression was horrified. Even if he'd suspected that I'd been behind Ninny's misfortunes, he hadn't been certain until he'd seen it. That much was clear.

'Go away,' I said, in a low hiss.

'No,' he said. 'I won't. You're going to break it, aren't you? And then you're going to blame her . . .'

'She deserves it,' I said.

'No, she doesn't,' he said. His voice was low but urgent. Harsh. 'She's a nice person, and they've already driven her to misery. How can you want to pile on more? She's your *sister*.'

I snorted at him. 'Did you see her worrying about me, when it was my turn to be punished?'

'She was just keeping her head down,' Callum said. 'Same as we all try to do.' He shook his head. 'I didn't think . . . I thought you were . . .'

He couldn't seem to finish his sentence, and I could feel fierce heat in my face.

'Well, maybe I'm not what you think. So you can start hating me, all right? If you didn't already.'

I'd let my hand fall from the lamp, but part of me wanted

to do it anyway. To throw it not at the floor but at him. I almost didn't care about getting caught.

'You can't do it,' he said. 'You know how much Henry hated spending the money. I was there, waiting for half an hour in that stupid shop in Lymington while she wheedled him into it. He'll go ballistic.' He swallowed, and then said, 'I'll tell them the truth if you do.'

I tried to take a breath. I knew what I needed to do. I needed to calm him down. To be sweet to him. To make him believe that I wasn't the person he'd finally seen. I needed to manipulate him as well as I'd manipulated every-one else.

But somehow I couldn't do it. I could only stand there, shaking with anger and a sense of burning shame.

'Maybe I won't do it,' I said in the end.

Callum nodded, and seemed to breathe at last.

'But if you tell anyone,' I said, leaning to speak close to his face, 'I'll get you thrown out. I swear. You know I can do it.'

I saw his expression change. The anger, the shock, the relief . . . all of them swept away. And he looked nothing but resigned. As if I'd turned out to be as terrible as he'd long suspected.

Callum turned away, and I knew that everything had changed now. That he was done with me.

I dug the nails of each hand into my arms, and bit down on my own teeth to stop from crying.

Stop being so fucking pathetic, I told myself. *He's just a stupid, naive boy*.

But even thoughts of how I would hurt Ninny next didn't make me feel better.

I gradually came to really understand myself, over seven long months of manipulation. I began to realise that this wasn't just about survival; it was about choosing my own happiness over someone else's.

Our second Christmas was almost the inverse of our first. Ninny was given almost nothing of any value, whereas this time I was showered with gifts. Only Callum remained a constant: the one in the middle who could never be as good as one of us or as bad as the other.

At school, as I became increasingly successful and popular, Ninny's fortunes dropped. She was struggling with friendships, ending up the outsider more often than not. She smiled less and resented those around her more. She would be irascible at times, and at other times cold. Detached. A little like me, though I was slow to see it.

She began to get in trouble, too. Which only made her life at home worse. Teachers would send her to the headmistress for refusing to do something or for answering back. I heard Sally explaining to Henry one night that she'd been given detention for ruining another girl's work and then flatly refusing to apologise for it.

It made my task a lot easier. I could take a few days off each time Sally was called in to see her teacher or, even better, the headmistress for something Ninny had genuinely done.

Callum was by now spending much more time with my sister. He had started offering her food and help as he had once done for me.

It was clear that my relationship with my foster brother had fractured, but its edges weren't neatly split. Some part of us was still uncomfortably and uselessly attached. So we would still approach each other from time to time, and talk to each other in a prickly, reluctant way.

In fact, Callum's remaining interest lay in reminding me how awful I was. He wasn't going to let me forget that he'd peeled away my surface layers and seen the truth. He seemed to want to prod at this side of me. To stir it up. But as he asked me time and again about the bad things I'd done, I began to realise that he was fascinated. I think, you know, that he saw the same potential for darkness in himself and felt an affinity for me even while he hated me for it.

But with Ninny he was simply kind, and I could see that she was growing increasingly dependent on him. He had begun gifting her tiny torches to keep on herself so she'd be able to see down in the cellar. He got them from a friend of his at school, he said, whose dad ran an eBay business.

It gave me a sick sense of rage whenever I saw them together, and a little after that second Christmas, I decided to do something about it.

I knew it was going to have to be subtle, this sabotage. Callum was wise to me, and Ninny was . . . well, she seemed increasingly hardened to me. At times, when I caught her looking at me, I felt a peculiar chiming. As if I was seeing the darkness reflected back at me.

I would turn away from her when it happened. I didn't want to see it. I wanted to be unique in the worst of my nature. Unmatched.

The easiest way to drive them apart, I realised, was to use other people. I knew enough pupils with sisters in Nina's year to feed poison to her. Rumours didn't need to be true in order to spread. And there were a few of my peers with older siblings in Callum's year at secondary school, too.

I did it gently, my little dripping of poison. A rumour rippled around Callum's year that Ninny thought her foster brother was a freak who'd never get a girlfriend. I embellished it a bit, saying she knew he clearly fancied her, which was gross as he was older. But maybe he was desperate.

And to Ninny's year, I spread the idea that Callum had called her an ugly ginger bitch. The terminology was crude, but I knew it would spread more easily the harsher it was. Those girls delighted in telling each other bad words, and delighted even more in passing them on to the once-popular Ninny.

I watched Ninny carefully that week, waiting for some reaction. Every time I saw her, my heart would thump with anticipation. I wondered if it would be obvious once she'd heard. Whether I'd see her crying. Whether I should pretend to comfort her.

When it finally happened, her reaction took me a little by surprise. I came to meet her after school on the Friday, one of the days when we took the bus together. Her face was not blotchy but drained of colour. Her jaw was set, and there was something blazing in her eyes. Something a little intimidating.

For the first time I could remember, she ignored me entirely when I went to speak to her. She stalked past me onto the bus, walking past the girls who increasingly talked about her instead of to her, and went to sit alone. She put her bag next to her so I couldn't join her, and then turned to stare out of the window.

I remember feeling uneasy. I had wanted to hurt her, not to cause this tight-lipped rage.

As we travelled the mile and a half till our drop-off, I watched her with a feeling of increasing worry. Did she know I'd started this? Was she going to do something irrational?

I followed her off the bus and into the empty house. It being Friday, Sally wasn't due home until four forty-five, after her Pilates session and a quick coffee with some of the other women who went. We would generally get on with any homework until she got back. Sally liked to find us settled quietly in the kitchen with our books out, in case Henry arrived home without warning. The picture of two perfect, studious girls.

But Ninny didn't go to the kitchen. She walked down the hall and into the living room. I trailed after her, as she usually trailed after me, and watched her pace up and down. And then, in a violent movement I would never have believed my sister capable of, she took one of Sally's precious Japanese lamps, and she hurled it at the wall.

It was strange, the fear that hit me. There was my perfect sister, her face a mask of rage, that smashed lamp in pieces on the table and around her feet.

Almost in the same breath of time came the unmistakable sound of Sally's key in the door, a good half-hour early.

I could see what was going to happen. Ninny had already become the perfect villain, and now she'd done something unforgiveable. Something monstrous.

And her punishment would be monstrous, too.

I remember being unable to look away from her face as Sally called out cheerfully, 'Where are you, girls?'

Before I could do anything, Ninny had called back, 'In the living room.'

Ninny stared right back at me, her cheeks flushed and a slight shake through her body. But she didn't seem to regret it. It was almost as if she was willing me to get her in trouble. For Sally to ask Henry to punish her.

I was still staring at her as Sally walked in, with a sunny, 'What are you up to?'

I turned to her first, and before Ninny could say anything, I said, 'I'm so sorry, Sally. I broke your lamp. Your favourite. I was showing off doing dancing and I kicked it.'

I kept my eyes away from my sister's face as Sally's expression changed. Instead of the usual disappointment or concern our foster mother showed when we did something wrong, she looked angry. Really, genuinely angry.

'You awful child!' she shouted, and she suddenly rushed forwards, bending to pick up the lampshade, and then scrabbling for the other pieces. 'How could you be so stupid?'

'I'm so sorry,' I told her again. 'It *was* stupid.'

She rounded on me after a minute, and there seemed to be tears in her eyes this time. Hurt, angry tears.

'Go to your room,' she said. 'When Henry gets back, you'll learn the meaning of sorry.'

I knew exactly why she was so angry. It wasn't just that these were her prized possessions; it was also that Henry would use it as an excuse to criticise her again. To tell her she should never have spent so much.

I nodded at her, feeling almost sorry for her, and only once she had turned away again did I look over at my sister.

Ninny's expression was caught in blank shock. She shook her head at me slightly, with her mouth open a little. She couldn't understand what I was doing.

I knew what was waiting for me. But as I climbed the stairs and waited in my room; as I endured the blindfolding and the whipping that came later; and through a long, dark, lonely two days in the cellar with none of Callum's torches to light my way; all through it all, I felt a burning warmth.

They aren't going to hurt my sister again, I thought. *Never, ever again.*

21

Despite her worry over Ben's state of mind, Hanson was still slow to notice him returning from wherever he'd been. After hurrying to alert the DCI about the memory stick Keely had sent, she had started skipping through the videos, finding herself both disturbed and impressed at the perfect match with what she'd told them in person.

But as Ben pulled his chair out from behind his desk and sat, she snapped out of her preoccupation and paused the video. He seemed calmer now, she thought, but clearly also ashamed.

'Hey,' she said, as an opening. And then found herself at a bit of a loss.

After a slightly agonising pause, Ben said, without making eye contact, 'So the storming out thing. Most stylish thing I've done? Yes or no.'

Hanson couldn't help laughing. 'I mean, I guess the bar was pretty low . . .'

'That's a yes, then,' he said. And then, after a beat, he added, 'Sorry. Guess I'd better apologise to Domnall and the chief.'

Hanson gave a small shrug. 'I think Domnall went to get you doughnuts, actually. I'm considering storming out of a meeting myself.'

'Told you it was a stylish move,' Ben said, with a small smile.

She was just grinning back at him when she caught sight of Jason Walker walking across CID. He was moving towards the kitchen, but there was no question that he was watching her. Something in his face dropped, as if seeing her smile at another man was painful to him.

Hanson tried a good-natured smile, but Jason did nothing but nod at her and go on his way.

'Do you think they'd consider moving the kitchen?' she muttered to herself. But when Ben asked what she'd said, she said a hurried, 'Nothing,' and went back to Keely's videos.

It was rare for Jonah to get really stuck in with investigative work, however much he might enjoy it. There were always too many meetings, workload considerations or obstacles to be moved out of his team's way. He was extremely lucky to get to conduct interviews, something that most of his peers had long ago given up, but he missed the grind of proper policing sometimes, too. The hungry urgency of looking for links or suspects.

Linda McCullough had come up trumps with the photos from the drama studio. She had sent him an enlarged photo of the computer screen they'd come from. The desktop showed a young woman standing on what looked like a mountain in Thailand, smiling at the camera.

He'd so far established that this wasn't a photo of a celebrity. It didn't appear in any reverse image searches. So if it wasn't a selfie, which seemed unlikely, she must be family, friend or partner to whoever owned the computer.

Digging online felt like playing a sport or an instrument after a gap. The muscles were a little untrained, but they were still there. He still knew how to swiftly and effectively compile himself a list of likely individuals and add to it as he stumbled on more and more names.

He had so far worked through a list of children's home workers. All of them had worked with Keely and Nina at some point, so he looked through their acquaintances using the gift of their social media profiles. Finding no matches with that desktop image, he had taken on board Lightman's suggestion of the social worker, Mark Slatterworth. Slatterworth had a fiancée, Jonah discovered. But one who looked nothing like the girl in the photograph, and who seemed to live with him. Which made it unlikely that this machine was his.

He started to look at Keely's and Nina's teachers. And then at parents of the students at their school. He was aware that the process was taking time and decided to restrict himself to the parents of those in their classes. It was extremely unlikely that Keely or Nina would have come into much contact with others.

To his relief, when he was eventually interrupted, it was by Lightman, who tapped on his door with what was clearly a remorseful expression.

'Ben,' Jonah said. 'Come in.'

Lightman entered, but though he closed the door, he didn't come to sit down opposite Jonah.

'I'm sorry for being . . .' Lightman swallowed. 'I shouldn't have left the room like that. I've apologised to Domnall.'

Jonah gave a shrug and a half-smile. 'We all have to walk away from things from time to time. And, right now, we're all under a lot of pressure. Although I'd prefer us to discuss things, I do understand.' He left a pause, wondering whether Ben would say more, and then added, 'But if there's anything you want to talk about, you know you can, don't you? I'll listen without judgement.' He grinned, and then added, 'Unless you tell me I'm doing a crap job, obviously. But even then, I'll do my best to pretend.'

Lightman gave a small smile. 'Noted, sir. I'll – try not to let it all get on top of me in future. Just a blip.'

There was another pause, in which Jonah made no move to say anything else. He knew it was sometimes better to give people space to talk, even if they didn't immediately feel able to.

But when Ben broke the silence, it was to say, 'In other news, there's no reply from the Murray-Watts. The landline rings out and both mobiles are switched off. Domnall and I are keen to head over there and get into the house, if we can.'

Jonah glanced at the clock on his computer. It was nearly eight forty-five. Still early enough that Sally and Henry might be sleeping in. They could also, equally well, be out exercising without their mobiles, or in Henry's case be en route to work. Many quite understandable reasons why they might not pick up immediately.

But something about that radio silence made him feel uneasy. The Murray-Watts had expressed concern for Nina, more so since gathering that Keely had turned up. Surely they would make sure they were contactable with any news.

'Take a method of entry team with you,' he said. 'If you can get sight of anything that implies either of the Lennox sisters are there, or have any intel from the neighbours to that effect, go in. If not, hold off, and we'll just have to do it the slow way.'

The slow way meant getting a warrant from the magistrates' court. It would involve showing enough intel to suggest that a search of the house would prove criminal activity. What Jonah was hoping for, instead, was enough evidence to use a Section 17 justification. That meant danger to life and limb, and if either of the two girls had been taken by force to the Murray-Watts' house, it was reasonable.

Once Lightman had ducked back out, Jonah checked his messages and felt a sharp twinge of guilt. He'd meant to prioritise finding Michelle help today. He'd barely thought about her so far this morning. Though, he realised, it was still early. Probably too early to ring anyone and beg for childcare.

He set himself an alarm for nine thirty to be sure he wouldn't forget, and returned his focus to his desktop.

He found himself thinking of Jared Boula once again. Their only reason for dismissing him at present from their investigations was the fact that he didn't seem to drive a Volvo. But there was still, Jonah thought, a reasonable chance that Keely wanted him brought to justice, and still more that she represented a threat to him.

The woman in the desktop picture looked a similar age to Keely's former keyworker, too. And although Jonah had already checked Jared's social media for any pictures of him with a girlfriend in recent times, he found himself returning to his Facebook page.

He scrolled back further this time, and his eye was caught by a relationship status announcement from two years before. It revealed, baldly, that Jared was no longer in a relationship, and several of his friends had reacted with sympathy. Jonah winced, wondering why anyone had ever thought public statuses were a good idea.

And then, a single screen-scroll further down, he came face-to-face with a picture of the same blonde girl who had featured on the computer desktop. The computer that contained a huge catalogue of violent child pornography.

The squad car drew up outside the Murray-Watts' house smoothly and quietly. It was still only nine thirty, and much cooler than it had been the evening before. With the windows down, O'Malley's Toyota had quickly become chilly. But it was bright and sunny in spite of the cooler air, and the scene was one of well-moneyed perfection, right up to the sheeny-looking Jaguar in the driveway.

Lightman climbed out of the car as the uniformed constables emerged, mentally preparing himself for a range of scenarios, including the Murray-Watts being in the house and outraged.

O'Malley gave him a wave and pulled away from the kerb. He'd been summoned to Jared Boula's house by the chief and would be meeting a couple of other uniforms there. It was quite possible that Boula would try to resist arrest, given they were bringing him in for possession of child pornography.

Ben glanced over at the method of entry team who were assisting him here. They were parked further down the road in front of a hedge. He'd asked them to keep well out of sight until he'd worked out whether they were needed.

He walked up the garden ahead of the two uniformed police constables from the squad car, passing large clumps of Michaelmas daisies in full flower. The garden was immaculately tidy. Orderly. Well cared for. Worlds away from the violence Keely had talked about. Which, of course, meant nothing. He knew too well that abuse wore a lot of different faces.

Lightman pressed on the doorbell. There was no sound from within, and he went on to knock vigorously. After waiting a full minute, he sent the constables round to the back of the house, which was easily accessed through the garden.

The constables reappeared, signalling no sign of any occupants. And without any sounds of a struggle, there was currently no firm justification for entering.

He was on the verge of going to knock on doors when he heard a woman's voice on the road behind them. He turned sharply, thinking momentarily that Sally Murray-Watt had just been out walking the neighbour's dog after all and had now returned.

But the woman standing on the pavement was black-haired, dressed in a business suit and had a baby on her hip. She was shifting from foot to foot, clearly impatient to be gone.

'Sorry, I'm about to leave, but I just wanted to let you know that they tore off in a hurry early this morning. I got woken by their engine.'

'You're a neighbour?' Lightman closed the gap between them a little. The baby, an almost spherical creature of probably three or four months, stared at him mutely.

'Yes, I live opposite,' the mother said.

'Did you see who was in the car?'

'No, I only saw them disappearing off up the road out of the village as I opened the curtains.' She glanced over at the Jaguar that was still on the driveway. 'But if it helps, I'd guess it was Henry driving. Terrible gear changes I could hear from over the road. Sally usually drives the Land Rover and she's pretty competent at it.'

'Do you know what time this was?' Ben asked.

'Early,' she said. 'It was only just light. So probably six or a bit after. I tried to go straight back to sleep and eventually gave up at just after seven.'

'And you say they were in a rush,' he said. 'What made you think that?'

'Well, it was totally unlike their normal way of coming or going,' she said. 'They're generally really quiet. Considerate. Whereas this was sprays of gravel and flooring it as soon as they hit the road. It was like the bloody house was on fire.'

Lightman nodded, mentally adding this to his map of events this morning. 'Have you seen much of them recently?'

The woman considered. 'Not a lot. But then I'm working stupid hours.'

'Any visitors at all?' he tried. 'Their foster kids . . .?'

'Well, the boy – Callum, I think? – comes and goes. Less so recently. I think he's got a job. But I did see one of the girls last week.'

Lightman blinked at her. 'Which girls do you mean?'

'The red-heads,' she said, shifting the child on her hip. 'Sally said one of them was moving back in?'

Lightman nodded, as though this was all as he'd expected. 'When was that?'

She let out a short sigh. 'Well . . . Wednesday, I think. Late on. The bloody dog got out and obviously decided to make a bolt for their house. The one place that isn't gated off. Fresh-scented dog heaven.' She shifted again, with the impression of someone who has just remembered the time. 'Anyway, I thought they must all be asleep as the lights were off, so I went round the back to find him, and was pretty embarrassed to look up from collaring him and find myself face to face with the girl.'

'She was outside?' Lightman asked.

'No, in the house,' the woman said. 'She was standing in the living room, looking out.'

Lightman nodded again. 'And how did she look?'

'Oh, just, you know, a bit horrified.' The woman laughed. 'I think I scared the life out of her.'

Jonah wasn't surprised when O'Malley rang to tell him there was no sign of Jared Boula. A man with a computer full of kiddie porn was likely to be spooked by a police interview. Jonah had the depressing suspicion that Boula had made a run for it, like Frank Pinder.

And probably like Henry Murray-Watt, too, he thought, considering what Lightman had reported.

Though he wasn't clear on what had motivated Henry to flee. If they'd had Nina in the house, maybe Keely wasn't in control. Or maybe Sally Murray-Watt had been the one to pick Keely up, and was actually helping her.

He told O'Malley that they were cleared for forcible entry to Jared Boula's house and then hung up. With a sudden thought, he looked back over his team's notes. It was Sally they'd spoken to the day before. And, in fact, Sally who the missing persons enquiry into Nina had contacted earlier in the week.

Had anyone actually seen or heard from Henry since the girls disappeared?

22

Sally and Henry locked me in that cellar for almost two days, the longest I had ever been left. It was unfortunate for me that Ninny had chosen to smash the lamp on a Friday, giving them two clear days to punish me without any missed school.

Everything had changed for me. Not during those two long days, but the moment I had shouldered the blame for my sister. It was as though I had suddenly seen everything I had become; and everything I could be instead.

And for the first time I saw Henry Murray-Watt for what he was, too. Not as the gatekeeper of goodness, or the father I desperately wanted to please. He was the enemy. A pathetic bully, who made Sally almost as miserable as he made us.

Sally actually looked anxious as she let me out. As though she wasn't sure if this had all gone too far. She asked me, as she drew me upstairs to see Henry and apologise, whether I was all right.

'I'm fine, thank you, Sally,' I told her, my mind full of my sister's anger, and everything I'd done to cause it. 'Don't worry about me.'

But I could see that she was worried. And Henry looked even more so when he realised that I wasn't tearful, broken and shaking. I'd chosen my punishment and I'd taken it gladly.

'Are you sorry for what you did?' Henry asked.

'Absolutely,' I said. 'I'll be much more careful next time.'

I didn't say it rebelliously, but I said it with my head up and an eager expression, and Henry clearly didn't know quite what to do. For a moment he actually looked towards Sally, who said, 'Perhaps she should go and join the others in the living room, then?'

'Yes,' Henry said. 'Yes, that sounds a good idea.'

I was half desperate to see Callum and my sister and half nervous. I remember the walk taking a good long while, during which I was very conscious of my bare feet on the boards of the hall, and the sensation of hunger in my stomach.

I don't know quite what I was afraid of. Maybe it was that they would reject what I'd done. See it as some kind of trick or manipulation. Or perhaps just ignore it. Make that sacrifice feel like it had been for nothing.

It doesn't matter, I remember telling myself. *You didn't do it for praise.*

And it was a strange, powerful thought.

They both froze as I walked in. They'd been in the middle of a game of Monopoly, Ninny with a bright set of notes clutched in her hand and Callum in the act of moving a counter. I had a good long moment to look at my sister properly for the first time in a while. To see how hard and closed off her expression was now. How the light seemed to have gone out of her. And I knew it had been my doing as much as Henry's.

I checked that Sally and Henry were still in the study, and then I said, quietly, 'I'm so sorry, Ninny. For everything I did before. I'm never, ever going to try to trip you up again. I'm going to protect you.' I nodded at Callum. 'And you, too. Even if you don't like it.'

My sister blinked at me for a moment, her gaze blank. And then she got up and launched herself at me. Her hug was ferocious, and I could feel the Monopoly money catching in my unwashed hair.

'I probably smell awful,' I said, with a laugh.

'You do,' she admitted. 'But I'll put up with it.'

She was almost the same height as I was now, thanks to our habit of never growing at the same speed, and it felt so comfortable to put my arms round her in return.

I saw Callum, over her shoulder, nod at me and then turn away, some kind of emotion in his expression that was too much for him to show.

Ninny finally let me go, and I checked the hall again before I said, barely above a whisper, 'You were right, Callum. We should hate them. And we should make it hard for them. Whatever they do to us, we should make them suffer for it.'

Callum stood, still looking away, and very carefully placed his counter down on Oxford Street. I could feel Ninny staring at me. But where once she might have looked shocked at this statement, she now looked exhilarated. Determined.

'We don't have the power, do we?' Callum muttered. 'I mean, what can we do? We can't do what they did. We can't lock them away or take their food.'

'No,' I said, 'we can do worse. We can turn them against each other, more than they did to us. We can make them doubt and make them rage.' I smiled at him. 'And maybe even make Sally see that she needs to stand up against him. I should have realised earlier what Henry really is. I understand now, and we're going to use it against him. All of it.'

And from that one short speech came the beginning of everything.

The revenge we took on Henry was subtle, seditious and glorious. Most of the ideas were mine, which probably won't surprise you. I have, it seems, a talent for the right sort of thinking. For patient, devious manipulation. And I put it to full use.

My first foray was actually aimed at Sally. I manufactured, on the school computers, a receipt for an astonishingly expensive new tack set, and then left it on the hall floor. I had noted, already, how much attention Henry paid to Sally's expenditure on riding. How he would check the cost of everything she brought up, and would sometimes descend into a silence that seemed to make Sally nervous.

It worked beautifully, with Sally proclaiming over and over that it wasn't hers. That she must have picked it up with something else when at the riding school. Henry grew more and more ominously quiet.

Later, Ninny played a wonderful part in comforting Sally, telling her Henry should believe her. That she was so careful with her money. And Sally seemed both touched and a little thoughtful at this. It was the first, marvellous wedge driven between them, and it was like opium for the three of us.

The next plan was bolder. It was clear that Sally was insecure about the way she looked, in more ways than one. If she were to distrust Henry, I knew it would be about other women, despite his profound lack of charm. And so we wove a complex web of phone calls to the house from female callers who hung up straight away. We dropped in mentions of a classmate whose father had had an affair, and occasionally queried how late Henry was working.

It began to weave its magic. Sally responded by eating less, wearing increasingly bizarre amounts of lipstick, and by behaving erratically around her husband. She would veer between coy smiles and sudden flares of temper. The pinnacle came after a full two months, when Callum left a single earring (from a pair bought at great expense through Ninny's paper rounds) in the passenger footwell of Henry's car. We waited days for her to find it, and when she did, it was a struggle for us all not to laugh.

It resulted in the first argument we'd ever heard between them; the first time Sally had harangued her husband instead of the other way around. We huddled together in Callum's room to listen to it, faces alight with malicious joy.

And, of course, we added more into the mix. We trod a path over Sally's gorgeous aquilegias from the back door of the garage where Henry liked to tinker with DIY projects. It was a risk, as we were likely to get blamed too, but since nobody actually went into the shed except Henry, it was clear that Sally believed him guilty and stewed on it silently. Another tick in the column of Henry's lack of love for her.

And then we went into that same garage on the day Sally had cleaned in there, and we hid his two most-used tools in a drawer, under a carefully folded duster. And by then, Henry was so on edge that he roasted her for it, bellowing at her until she cried.

None of it stopped the punishments that came our way, of course. Not those subtle sabotages or any of the many that came afterwards. We hadn't really expected it to, and if anything, trusting each other less made them both more irritable. And in Henry's case, more determined to exert control.

But none of the arbitrary punishments seemed to hurt as much. With the three of us all helping each other, and with glorious revenge to think about, we were protected. We found ways of hiding food and a little padding in our clothes for the times when the cellar beckoned. Callum smuggled four of those mini torches down into the cellar and hid them skilfully, so we would never have to be trapped in darkness. I managed to get a copy of *The Subtle Knife* down there, too, which we ended up reading ten or fifteen times each.

My end goal was always to get us all out of there, though. I wanted us free from having to worry about any of this stuff. Free to live.

The problem was always Callum. He was terrified of being separated from us, and still more terrified of being sent to some awful poverty-ridden house and a school where he would fail. He also thought that we wouldn't be believed, which I (ironically) dismissed. Callum told us to do what we had to and get out of there and not worry about him. We had a sympathetic social worker, he said. We would be fine.

'I want you to come with us,' I told him. 'To tell them it's happened to all of us.'

But Callum resisted, and I wasn't going to do anything without his agreement. I'd left the two of them to suffer enough in the past. I wasn't going to leave him there.

The situation went on for a full year. A full year of Sally and Henry slowly tearing each other apart, and tearing into us, too. We all continued to flourish at school, though Ninny still struggled to make and keep friends. She'd lost the carefree air that had made her so popular and couldn't seem to bring herself to fake it. I, contrastingly, began to see friends as irrelevancies. They were simply puppets who could be made to do what I wanted. Experiments in control. I only really cared about Callum and my sister.

Things might have gone on like that, with Callum too stubborn to back down, and me equally so, if one of our hiding places hadn't been found in the cellar.

I suppose we'd been expecting it. It could only be so long before they poked about in there enough to find our stashes.

But when Sally found two full bags of sweets in there, smuggled down inside Callum's hoodie pocket, she and Henry lost all sense of perspective.

They seemed to know, without being told, that it had been Callum. I tried to take the blame, but for once they saw through it. And so Callum was dragged down there, with Sally for the first time actually screaming at him about being a greedy, thieving devil, and Henry's face tight with anger. It sent fear thrilling through me.

We didn't see Callum for three full days, and I don't think any days of my life have ever felt longer. I couldn't settle to anything and kept making excuses to prowl around the house so I could try again and again to find that hidden cellar.

After so many blindfolded trips down there, I was certain that the cellar opened off Henry's study. I had paid careful attention to the floor I was walking on, and no matter how many times they spun me around, I knew that the floor surfaces and the sounds of the various rooms never changed. I never left that room once I entered it.

It being in the study made locating it hugely difficult. Henry's bolthole was so often locked, and it was occupied most of the time that it wasn't. Entry was strictly forbidden, of course, so on the odd occasion when I found it unlocked, I was sometimes forced to retreat by Sally's presence. If they had been angry about sweet smuggling, there was no question they would have been incandescent over an attempt to sneak into Henry's sanctuary.

On the second night, I lay awake imagining Callum bleeding to death from his wounds and dreamed of his ghost. I woke as pale as if I had spent the night in the cellar with him. And I felt little better when I finally saw him at dinner time.

He hadn't bled to death, but he was barely able to walk.

He limped up the stairs, his face an awful deathly white, and lowered himself down onto a kitchen chair.

I expected Sally to look worried, as she often did when we were released from the basement. But as I watched her face, I realised with a sick dread that there was no concern there at all. She was satisfied. Glad that Callum had been so badly beaten.

We met up that night, the three of us. It was a risk, but one I thought was worth taking. We chose my room for its distance from the master bedroom, and we spoke in voices that were lower than a whisper.

'I'm not going to let them keep doing this,' I told Callum. I couldn't hiss at him or speak loudly, so instead, I used my eyes to tell him how serious I was. 'Whether you back us up or not, I'm going to get them in trouble.'

There was a pause, and then Callum said, 'All right.' And I wanted, fiercely, to hug him.

'OK. We need our social workers to see how bad it is,' I said. 'It's not good enough to tell them. You know how easy it'll be for Henry to use Sally. She'll believe anything he says, and they'll believe her. We need proof.'

'Callum has the marks on his legs,' Ninny said.

But Callum shook his head, bitterly. 'Sally's already explained to the school that I fell down the stairs and landed hard. It's why I was supposed to be off today. It's so clever. It's just what the bruises look like.'

If Sally had been there just then, I think I might have gone for her. Hit her. Torn into her with my nails. Even though I knew it was Henry who had caused all this. Even though she was a victim, too.

'We could film them doing something,' I tried. 'I'm sure our social worker would want to see how they bully us. He seems like he'd care, too.'

In the time since we'd arrived at the Murray-Watts, we'd had a change of personnel. It was a common occurrence, we were told, but they'd try to keep us with our new social worker for as long as possible. I liked the new guy, Mark. He was positive and sympathetic, and easy to talk to. I was sure he'd take our side.

'But the bullying is really hard to describe, isn't it?' Callum argued. 'I've thought about it a lot. You could watch one of those conversations that tears into you and it would just look like them being slightly strict parents. The rest is always downstairs.'

'Which we can't even find,' I said, glumly.

There was a silence, and then, to my surprise, Ninny said, 'We need injuries. Obvious ones. That's the stuff they look for in abused kids. There was a talk about it at school. How to look out for our friends.'

Callum looked doubtful, but I saw, straight away, the logic of what she said. 'She's right,' I said. 'We need one of us to be injured in a way that couldn't have been anything else.' I looked straight at Callum then, my face absolutely set. 'It should be me. You can hit me.'

'No fucking way,' Callum said, and I was surprised not only that he'd sworn, but by quite how fierce he looked. Quite how much conviction there was in his almost-whisper. 'It's going to be me. I don't care how many times you ask, I'm not going to hurt either of you, or let you hurt each other. It'll be me.'

I sighed. 'It's not about being a boy . . .'

'No, it isn't,' he shot back. 'It's about being an older brother.'

And no matter what I said, Callum insisted. And so he won, in the end.

You probably know the outcome already: Callum being

beaten by a tennis racquet. Though not before we'd spent a full two days preparing everything. Rehearsing it all with each other.

I wasn't too worried about what I would say. I was confident that I could tell our social worker and the police everything that had happened. Ninny was a different matter.

'I'll mess it up,' she told me, her eyes full of fear. 'Tell me what to say. Please tell me what to say.'

So I rehearsed it with her. I told her what she needed to say. And I told her twice, even though I only needed to say it once.

I remember being hugely grateful for my sister's extraordinary memory. It was going to help us, I thought. She'd know what to say.

It never even occurred to me that this talent of hers would be used against us. That her words would be seen as fake because they were too similar to mine. However clever I was, I still had a lot to learn.

Anyway. Two days later, we were ready to beat Callum. The bit you won't know is that I was fully intending on doing it myself, but when it came to it, I found that I couldn't. Somehow, with that racquet gripped in my hand and my jaw clenched so hard that it hurt, I couldn't swing it. I tried, but I kept pulling back. Swinging away.

Ninny held out her hand, and said, quietly, 'I'll do it. It's going to help him in the long run. I'll do it.'

I didn't really believe, when I gave it to her, that she could. That she would. But she took the racquet and she swung it so hard that I reached out in shock to try and stop her.

Callum made only the smallest sound as the racquet connected with his face. It's a source of enormous wonder to me, even now, that he didn't flinch. I don't know how he can have been that strong.

There was a moment when he stood there with his eyes wet and his lip twisting. And then he held his hands up to his face and caught the flow of blood that started pouring from his nose.

There were tears in Ninny's eyes, and she reached out to touch his shoulder.

'I'm sorry,' she whispered.

But Callum shook his head.

'You need to do another one,' he said. 'On my cheek.'

23

Hanson was absorbed in Keely's videos once again, alert for inconsistencies as she listened onwards. She knew she needed to go back and find more in the earlier recordings at some point. They had only found three clues out of a possible seven, assuming there really was one clue hidden in each clip.

But the greater part of her was simply absorbed by what the older Lennox sister was saying. By the sea change that seemed to have happened after she'd stepped in to save Nina, and by the plans the three children had made to undo their foster parents.

She found herself genuinely liking Keely at last, too. It was somehow easy to warm to her now, instead of feeling caught between suspicion and frustration.

Bizarre though it might at first have seemed, it was clear that all of this was about justice. And if those three kids had taken their ability to manipulate, and had used it to assemble piece after piece of evidence against the guilty, she could only admire them.

Once or twice, she found herself going back to check earlier details in the previous tapes, and it was during one of those checks that she stumbled on something they had all missed entirely.

Keely had been describing how she and her sister had caught the bus to and from school. The stop had been on Purlieu Lane, Keely told them. And then, as Hanson skipped forwards in the tape, there it was.

'*Pearl Lane*,' Hanson muttered to herself.

It had been a difficult one to spot, even with Keely's careful enunciation, but Hanson was sure of it. She'd called it Pearl Lane, just once.

She pulled out her headphones with a feeling of triumph and rose to tell the chief.

Lightman was intrigued to finally step into the Murray-Watts' house. Let loose on the place, the method of entry team made short work of the door. Their shouts of 'Police, police!' were met with silence, and Lightman followed them inside.

The hallway was just as large and beautifully decorated as he'd imagined. It stretched almost the full width of the house, all of it oak-floored, though with occasional expensive-looking rugs. Cream walls were punctuated by uplighting and carefully placed art prints.

The uniformed officers spread out through the house. Lightman thought about going to the living room, where Keely or her sister had been seen. He was certain that the Lennox sisters had been accumulating evidence of some kind. It would probably be simplest to go and find that evidence for himself.

But he found himself walking past the living room and searching instead for Henry Murray-Watt's study. He remembered Keely's account. How she had been certain that the cellar opened off the one locked room in the house.

Having walked the length of the hall, he found a single locked door at the end. Called over, the method of entry guys made quick work of it with the ram, hitting it hard enough to splinter the door frame and then standing back to let him through. He regretted the destruction, but the super had cleared them to search.

The room was large, and classically furnished as if it were some kind of library. It stretched from the very front of the house to the very back, dominated by a massive oak and leather desk, which had the only signs of mess or clutter he had seen anywhere in the house. Notebooks, papers and scientific journals were scattered across the top of it, and Lightman glanced over them all, trying to recall exactly what Henry specialised in. It was some kind of biology, he thought. Presumably well paid, though he supposed Henry's wealth might be inherited.

Every wall was covered by slightly hectic bookcases, too, with gaps only for a window onto the garden, a full-length mirror and a single door in the wall at the end of the house. Lightman moved immediately to the door, but discovered only a bathroom on the other side of it instead of a cellar: a recent extension bolted on to the end of the house, by the look of it. A veritable palace of a place, with marble-effect tiles, a freestanding bathtub and a shower.

Back out in the study, Lightman looked carefully at the bookcases that lined the walls, and then at the individual books. He thought of all those murder mysteries with secret passages behind the bookshelves, and he laughed at himself. Was he expecting to be able to tilt the right book and find it?

One of the constables came to find him at that point.

'Sir? The house looks like it's empty.'

Lightman wondered whether he ought to employ their help in looking for the cellar. The Murray-Watts' hasty departure that morning implied that there would be nobody to find even if they did, but it seemed only right that he should try to prove Keely right at long last.

He was on the verge of instructing them to search when his phone began to buzz, insistently.

'We've got another location left as a clue by Keely,' the DCI said, 'and it's right near you. The bus stop next to Purlieu Lane.'

O'Malley had a fondness for raids that was born out of years spent in the army. Everything about them was familiar. The clear hierarchy. The practised movements. The sense of being a machine in the process of doing what it did best.

There had been a short while in his policing career when reminders such as this had been painful. Early on, when his dismissal from the army had still been full of a sense of shame, anything that brought it to mind had felt like a jab from something sharp. It had taken a good few years to come to the conclusion that he was a much better copper than he had ever been a foot soldier, and that he enjoyed this life far more.

This particular raid was technically a kidnap squad operation, overseen by DI Quick and involving two of his constables. Murray Quick reminded O'Malley strongly of one of the army captains he had served under, too. The humourlessness was the main feature, but he was also without any apparent ego. He was more than happy for O'Malley to go in before him once they were ready.

Domnall had dragged his stab vest on just for the occasion and was now feeling slightly suffocated by it. It was embarrassing to note that it was much tighter than it had been, and he wondered how much he weighed right now. He usually lost weight over the summer, and put it on over the winter. It was a little worrying to be heavy in September.

'Boula's phone is currently off,' Quick had told O'Malley as they gathered just up the road. 'It hasn't pinged any masts since five this morning, which is an interesting time for him to be up and about.'

'Where was that?' O'Malley asked.

'Here,' the DI had said, zipping up his vest.

'Let's just hope he isn't out for a quiet jog and run out of phone charge,' O'Malley said, with a grin.

'He would be likely to have returned home and recharged the phone by now, if so,' Quick said, taking O'Malley's point entirely seriously. O'Malley decided not to attempt any humour with him from now on.

There was no reply at the door. DI Quick hefted the big red key and gave the door a sharp blow close to the lock. It popped open with surprising ease, which O'Malley thought was probably more down to Quick's skill than the flimsiness of the door.

O'Malley gave the 'Police!' shout and trod quickly into the hallway.

It wasn't a particularly large house, unsurprisingly, given that Boula worked in care. By the time four officers had moved in, it felt crowded.

O'Malley peeled off into the living room, looking for signs of recent occupation. A shout came from upstairs that the place was empty. O'Malley was staring at an empty desk, noting three rectangular outlines of different sizes in the dust, and an empty four-way adaptor below.

'He's taken the computer,' he said to Quick, as the DI came to find him. 'There goes our easy conviction.'

The bus stop at the end of Purlieu Lane was empty, its small shelter backing onto greenery, but positioned to give a view out over the fields on the far side of the road. It was a quiet, single-lane road that ran up to the nature reserve known as Godshill Inclosure.

It was, he thought, an intensely rural scene, made all the more idyllic by the country pub back down the road. The verges were running wild with flowers, and the single bus stop looked like it was being reclaimed by the bushes behind it.

Lightman had spent a few minutes looking it up on his phone and discovered that the bus Keely and Nina had taken to school diverted up here briefly from the main road, turning at the little triangle of green at the end of Purlieu Lane, and then departing the same way.

It was clear that there was nothing sitting within the bus shelter, but Lightman wouldn't have expected there to be. With no telling what time he or the team might arrive, Keely must have left her piece of evidence out of sight.

Glancing back down the road towards the pub, which had yet to open, he made his way round the back of the shelter. The greenery behind had grown right up to it. It would be easy to hide something there.

He started pushing some of the branches aside, quickly finding the spikes on an acacia that stood in the midst of it. But the moment he had them out of the way, he saw it: a small cardboard box nestled on the ground right behind the shelter.

It was a slightly awkward manoeuvre to lift it out without ending up with a face full of thorns, but he managed to grab it and extract himself without injury. It was extremely light, making him wonder fleetingly whether it might actually be an empty box of rubbish. But a closer look showed him a label, with Juliette's name on it. Which was in itself interesting.

Taking the box over to the car, he gloved up and rested it on the bonnet to peel it open. He saw immediately why it had been so light. It contained only expanded polystyrene with some glossy photos resting on top.

Twisting his head, he could make out text on them. They

were screenshots of a WhatsApp conversation, between someone without a photograph named Chuck and someone named Sarah. The first one, from Chuck to Sarah, read:

> I can't wait to see you. I want to bury
> myself inside you and belong to you totally.

Lightman tried to stamp down on a rush of nausea. He could feel his heart rate rising, and he took a few breaths to bring it back under control.

It was a good thing. They had real, hard evidence now. Because there was no question that these were messages between Frank Pinder and Sarah Mallard, and that they were going to be the nail in his coffin the moment they found the guy.

24

I couldn't blame Callum for what he said to the police. Aside from an initial rush of betrayal, my overwhelming feeling was one of inevitability. I had known how frightened he was of leaving. I just hadn't understood how susceptible he'd be to manipulation. I'd also underestimated his desire to please Sally, who wasn't a bad person, and who probably did love him.

I hadn't predicted, either, how easily his honesty could be used against him. I think I grew up a lot as that part of it hit home.

You don't need to hear about how hard we fought to get the Murray-Watts charged. There was an inevitability to our failure in this, too. Though I did sometimes wonder if it could have gone differently with our old social worker. The one who'd known Ninny when she still had an aura of innocence. Who'd been thoroughly charmed by me, instead of all the charm being Sally and Henry's. It was clear to me that he was listening to us as if we were a couple of fantasists, and it began to make me angry. And I don't think that helped, either.

But anyway. On to what matters. We may have lost our battle for justice, but we were free of them.

We spent several months back at Henley Road Children's Home, waiting to see what foster parents the system might spit out at us. And as featureless and grubby as the place still was, as cruel as some of the other kids seemed, it felt like safety.

And, in fact, the cruelty wasn't so bad now. Ninny and I were hardened to it, and we'd learned a lot about how to deflect. How to intimidate. They mostly left us alone. Though I saw that Ninny, still struggling with her school-friends, would sometimes look at them all wistfully when they messed around together.

Her favourite keyworker, Jared, had gone off travelling, which was another source of disappointment to her. She had no allies among the staff, and no close friends there. I found myself caught halfway between my old role as her champion and an instinctive need to let her find her own feet. Though perhaps it was less about wanting her to learn, than a feeling of weary cynicism and sadness at how I'd let her down.

One afternoon, a few weeks after we'd arrived, once it had become apparent that Sally and Henry were going to escape charges, I found her crying in her room. I went to sit next to her on her bed, wondering whether she'd cried a lot recently. We'd been put in separate rooms, now that we were older, and I sometimes missed the closeness of the cramped twin beds.

I sat quietly there with her for a while, until in the end the tears slowed, and she said, 'Do you think we'll ever see him again?'

I didn't have to ask her who she meant. It gave me a strange, possessive little feeling to know that she was talking about Callum.

'I don't know,' I told her. I should have found some way of comforting her. I thought of saying something, but for some reason I heard myself tell her, 'He might not be allowed to talk to us. If he even wants to.'

A fresh rush of tears squeezed its way out, and I felt guilty. Awful.

'That's only for now,' I said. 'I'm sure one day he will. But maybe we need to find other friends like him.'

She cried, hard, for a minute, and then said, 'I don't know how to make friends.'

'Yes, you do,' I told her. 'You were brilliant at it before Henry made you feel awful. You just need to remember how you were before.' I gave her a squeeze round the shoulders. 'I'll help you.'

Though actually, I wasn't the one who helped her. That was left to Jared Boula on his return, and later to Frank Pinder. The men who offered acceptance, before taking far more than either of us had ever offered.

Jared returned only a few weeks after we had. He'd changed a bit, since we'd last seen him. I thought at the time that he seemed more like a man. More adult and reserved. More confident.

He'd changed physically, too. Puppy fat had given way to lean strength, and his months of travel had left him tanned. Roughened. Appealing.

I remember washing up after dinner with him, once, and feeling strangely embarrassed at having him talk to me. There was something of the popular boy at school about him now.

At one point, I remember him putting an arm round me, and then laughing at me when I blushed. There was a glimmer of what I thought might be cruelty in it as he said, 'Aww, do you fancy me? Is that why you're blushing?'

I remember denying it, furiously, blushing ever more deeply. And then rushing out as quickly as I could, to hide from him in confusion.

I was to find out later that a lot had happened to change Jared. That he hadn't just travelled abroad, but had spent time in England, too, being moulded. Being hardened.

And yet he was all sunshine with Ninny once again. He brightened her life and made her radiant.

I watched the two of them carefully, at first. I would find excuses to be where they were, not quite trusting his kindness. I suppose I had recognised enough of myself in him to be wary. I'd glimpsed the darkness and was no longer blinded by the light.

But I had to admit that he was kind to her. Patient. Warm. Understanding. And that it was doing her the world of good.

And more than that: I found myself envying it. Something in Jared's eyes, face and body made me feel unexpected rushes of fascination. I ended up watching them, not in order to protect her, but in order to torture myself.

In the end, I had to stop my spying. It became clear that Jared was more aware of it than I'd realised.

On a particular Saturday, I'd followed them down to the newsagent's. They'd gone to buy ice creams for everyone, and the little shop was the one place we were all allowed to go without being accompanied.

It was a simple local store with a hideously bright neon sign that read EXPRESS – OPEN SEVEN DAYS. Half the confectionary was out of date, but the kids gorged themselves on it anyway, saving up everything they had.

I was the only one who rarely went there. It was a cave of wonders to me as well, but one that I was afraid of. I was afraid that I really was the greedy girl Henry had thought me. I imagined going in there and losing control, gorging on Mars Bars and Maltesers, and having to be dragged out.

The worst thing was how the possibility of visiting it nagged at me. Six days a week, I would feel the temptation, and have to resist it. I would go and stand in front of the mirror instead, looking myself over as Henry might have done. Seeing every soft part and telling myself to get rid of it.

Sundays were the only day where I felt free of it. Without the temptation, my fear of myself would drop away, leaving me twenty-four hours of glorious calm.

But today, with Ninny and Jared inside, I knew I had to go in. I needed to see what they were doing. To keep watch until the real nature of their friendship came out into the open.

I waited until they'd gone inside and turned their backs towards the door to reach into the big, colourful chest freezer. And then I walked quickly inside and down one of the aisles.

It was easy to loop round and end up at the far side of the shop, with a full view of what they were doing. I thought myself well enough screened behind a rack of cards; their attention was clearly on choosing for everyone.

But Jared, who I now realise knew a lot about conceal-ment, looked up at me, suddenly. It was so clear, as he shook his head, that he'd expected me to be there. That he had known about every other time. He turned to Ninny and, laughing, asked whether I was jealous.

'Does she always follow you around? Or is it me she's obsessed with?'

I felt the burn of total humiliation, and without any dig-nity, I rushed back across the shop and out of the door. Ninny's laughter followed me on to the street.

I returned to the home feeling powerless, and resentful, and rejected all over again. That feeling chiselled away at the lock I'd put on my worst feelings; the feelings the Murray-Watts had so expertly stirred up.

I'd thought myself protected against it all. I'd thought that I understood manipulation. But the flicker of desire that Jared was able to ignite in me had confused everything. It was as though even the tiniest hint of sexuality could shut down all rational thought.

Isn't it sad, how easily controlled we are? How simple it was for one of the three to divide us all over again? And how pathetically quickly I forgot my vow to protect my sister, no matter what?

25

Hanson was desperate to move on with Keely's story. To find out about Jared Boula. About Frank Pinder. But part of her mind was still thinking of inconsistencies. Of the trail Keely wanted them to follow.

So she listened again, her mind on whatever clue Keely had planted. And it was easy, this time, to see it. To hear it. As Keely told them about the Express Shop that was open seven days, and yet somehow closed on Sundays.

With that revelation, it felt impossible to sit still, in spite of the rest of the story that she wanted to hear. She needed to be up and moving. Finding the next part of the trail.

She went quickly to the chief's office and tapped on his door. He was so deeply immersed in something on his computer that it took a second, louder knock to get his attention.

'I think Keely's left us something at the newsagent's on Henley Road, too,' she explained. 'I'd like to get over there and see what it is, but I'm also conscious that the story itself may tell us more. It feels important to be listening to it.'

'I'll take on the videos,' the chief said, with a grin. 'It's been hours since I pitted my wits against Keely Lennox and lost.'

'Thanks, chief,' Hanson said. She paused for a moment, and then she asked, 'Do you think we should put out an alert for the two girls? On social media? And in time to make the lunchtime news? It's been such a long time since Nina vanished . . .'

The DCI's expression became serious. 'I've been thinking about that, too. The only thing that concerns me is those three men getting to hear about it. It tells them that the girls are out there somewhere, if they haven't already got either of them. But I think it's worth that risk. We need to get the public on this, too. If you can send something over to intelligence before you go, I'll make sure it gets distributed.'

'Thanks,' Hanson said, with a feeling of relief. It meant something, knowing that others beyond their team and Quick's kidnap squad would be looking for the sisters.

She was turning to go when the DCI suddenly said, 'You don't know any babysitters, do you? Childminders? Someone who might be free during the day?' He gave her a slightly awkward smile. 'I know it's a long shot.'

Hanson was about to say that she didn't, but then she thought of what Ben had said a few weeks before about his sister.

'You should ask Ben,' she said. 'His sister, Sammy, is a mum. Loves kids, but they're at school now, and she's delayed going back to work to be around a bit more for her dad.'

'Thank you,' the chief said. 'Let's hope she can rescue me.'

Sammy turned out to be exactly what Jonah needed. Genuinely enthusiastic about the idea of taking Milly, and unfazed at having never met her. She was also, even more importantly, happy to head over to the house and pick Milly up.

'I can have her until evening,' she said. 'I miss the baby stage. I mean, I obviously hated it at the time and was dying to get back to work. But now that I'm here, I feel a bit wistful. Renting a kid sounds a great idea.'

Michelle answered him in what sounded like a state of full-on tearfulness.

'She's not having a good morning,' she said. Jonah could hear periodic wailing from Milly in the background and felt for her.

'My DS's sister is going to take her for the rest of the day, if you'd like her to,' he said. 'Give you a break.'

There was a brief pause, and then Michelle said, in a thick voice, 'Thank you. That's . . . you're amazing.'

Jonah realised that this was the first genuinely positive thing Michelle had said to him for some time and hung up feeling both a lot better and a lot worse. It was clear that he needed to help her more. Michelle's negativity about everything was probably the product of misery. It made the way he'd been thinking about Jojo feel unforgivable.

But he would have to fix his screw-ups later. With Sammy taking over, Jonah could once again have his mind on finding Nina Lennox.

His hope for Nina's safety had been shaken by Keely's disappearance, as much as Hanson's had. If it was true that Keely had run, then she had done so at the precise moment when she might have simply explained everything to them. It left them still having to play the game she had created, and dance when she said 'dance'. And it left Nina hanging, in whatever situation Keely had chosen to leave her in.

If she really had planned all this, was it as simple as an attempt to gain power, or was it more than that? Was there something she needed time for? Did they need to work something out?

Or, he thought, had she left the tapes because she knew someone would come for her?

Hanson was halfway to Henley Road, pulling away from a leafy junction in Bevois Valley, when a motorcyclist roared past her. Expecting to see them vanish into the distance, she almost failed to brake quickly enough when the motorbike slowed down drastically just in front of her bumper.

She was still swearing as the bike moved right and then

slewed round to the left, coming to a total stop diagonally across the lane ahead.

Hanson stopped too, adrenaline buzzing through her. She found herself mentally going over the last few minutes of the journey and wondered whether she'd done something to piss the motorcyclist off.

They at least didn't look too big to her. A slightly bulky leather jacket covered a slim frame. But there was something that looked like a piece of hardboard attached to their back, and none of their actions seemed entirely sane.

She watched the rider reach up for their helmet, and wondered whether she should be trying to drive away. There were no cars behind her, and only a few coming the other way. She could move round and avoid whatever was going on here.

And then the helmet came away, revealing waves of red hair.

For a brief moment, she thought that Keely had staged a return, before she took in the different shape to the jaw. The slighter build. The warmer eye colour.

She was looking at Nina.

Keely's sister looked at her steadily for a moment, and then, as Hanson was on the verge of opening the car door, she held up a hand.

With her other hand, Nina reached behind her to the hardboard. It came free, and she swung it round until it was in front of her.

There were letters inked onto it in blocky capitals, to make a sign.

NOW FIND
MY SISTER

Hanson had just long enough to read it and to look back up at Nina, before the girl dropped the hardboard, shoved her helmet back on, and drove the bike straight up the slope at the edge of the road. She was immediately lost among the trees.

Despite the fact that Hanson knew should try to pursue her – and despite a blast on the horn from a driver now sitting behind her, too – Hanson found herself unable to move. Because she'd finally remembered where she'd seen Nina before.

Lightman was only a few minutes off rejoining the A31 when a call came through on his mobile. It was clearly a Southampton Central number, and he wasn't surprised when the voice that came through was Murray Quick's.

'Your chief says you're out towards the New Forest,' he said.

'Just passed Brook on my way back,' Lightman told him, slowing the car as he saw a layby ahead. 'Do you need me for something?'

'If you can,' Quick said. 'My team has just found the car used to pick up Keely Lennox. It's been abandoned in a car park at the wildlife centre on Deerleap Lane. Your chief wanted to check whether it belongs to Sally Murray-Watt.'

Lightman started to accelerate again. 'Already on my way,' he said.

The CCTV recording from outside the refuge arrived in Jonah's inbox some while before he'd been expecting it. He'd become used to huge delays in getting at footage in his years of work.

He clicked on the file immediately and was overwhelmed with gratitude to see that the intelligence officer who had sent it had cropped it to the time of Keely's disappearance.

Keely was suddenly there, onscreen, standing alongside Veronica. The view was from a short way down the road.

It was a good angle, he thought. One that would show exactly what had happened in those moments before she left.

The whole sequence took only a few seconds, as Veronica had said. The social worker moved off slowly down the road, away from the camera, with her phone in her hand. After a moment, Keely turned towards the four-by-four. After a brief pause, she took four rapid steps, opened the door, and climbed into the car. The four-by-four was already moving by the time she closed it after her.

He let out a long sigh as he rewound it and watched again. There was no hint of panic on Keely's face. No sense of threat. It looked like Veronica's instincts had been right, and that she'd set the whole thing up.

He finished the clip and was still staring into space when Hanson called him. He could hear the stress in her voice as she said, 'I've just seen Nina Lennox. And I think all of this might be my fault.'

26

The confusion of desire, distrust, envy and loneliness I felt whenever Ninny and Jared were together made it almost impossible to be around my sister once again. It was infuriating and satisfying at once that Ninny only seemed to notice on his days off, when she would suddenly become needy.

I remember how she came to find me one Thursday evening. I'd buried myself in work, which had increasingly become my habit even though I was already miles ahead of all my classmates.

Ninny knocked and came in before I could answer. Not deterred by the sight of me at my desk, immersed in an essay on Bismarck, she flopped down on the bed behind me.

'Can we do something together?' she asked. 'I feel like I haven't seen you.'

'You've clearly had other things to do,' I said, not looking at her.

There was a pause, and then she said, 'But I'd like to see you too. I miss you.'

I didn't say anything for a moment. It would have been a great opportunity to talk to her properly, about my own loneliness, and about my worries over Jared. I might have told her that it was less jealousy than it was concern.

But the fact of her only wanting to see me now, when her favourite wasn't here, was too much at the forefront of my thoughts. It was like a swelling in my throat that would only let certain words past.

'Well, I'm working just now,' I told her. 'Why don't you

go and talk to your own keyworker, instead of constantly stealing someone else's?'

It was deliberately harsh. I knew that Ninny worried about this, sometimes: about the two boys who were supposed to be Jared Boula's main responsibility. Neither of them really got a look in, but somehow the manager seemed oblivious. He looked past the situation as Jared looked past those boys.

There was total silence from my sister. I thought about turning to see Ninny's expression, but I couldn't bring myself to face her.

The silence went on, and then my sister rose and left.

I sat where I was for a while, staring at my half-finished essay. For some reason I was imagining Jared returning the next day and speaking to *me*, instead of her. Reaching out to touch my hand. And the idea filled me with a confused mixture of fear and desire.

I withdrew from her further after that. And I found myself withdrawing from others, too. From the friends I'd deliberately made at school. From the teachers who had been excited by my intelligence and my willingness to learn. I spent longer within my head, imagining alternative versions of my life. Of the world we lived in. Versions where Callum had sided with us, or where he came to find me and told me how wrong he'd been.

I slid into a world of fantasy, and, in short, became a perfect victim for the wiles of Frank Pinder.

With the advent of our new foster placement, it seemed as though the universe had finally delivered me something good. A handsome, athletic, effortlessly cool man was suddenly part of our lives and telling us that he loved us. That he loved *me*.

I remember the very first time we visited him and Evelyn, on a sunny May bank holiday weekend. Frank had set chairs and tables up in the garden and put out a huge tub of iced drinks and lollies on the patio. He ran around after us all, making us laugh with constant banter, and it was the most normal and relaxed I'd felt in years.

I could see how torn Ninny was when Mark, our social worker, asked us whether we'd like to go and live with the Pinders. She was clearly as smitten with her potential foster father as I was, but to move meant leaving Jared, her best buddy. Her not-quite-boyfriend.

I was the one who talked her into it. Isn't that a kicker? When we had a chance of holding off, and neatly avoiding one of the three men who overturned everything we might have been.

I told her that we'd have to move on from the home at some point. That Jared would probably move on soon, too. And then we'd have to take wherever they could get us, instead of somewhere fun. Somewhere that felt like home.

And so, one September afternoon, we packed up our rooms at Henley Road, and moved to the Pinders' ugly little bungalow, a place that seemed all the more reassuring for its ordinariness. For its distance from the rich austerity of the Murray-Watts' house.

For a long time, I thought we'd made the right decision. Frank was wonderful. Funny, generous and endlessly, endlessly patient. He never got angry if we were late, or told us off for swearing. He actually encouraged a little bad behaviour, to the amused horror of Evelyn.

He saw all the ways that I didn't quite fit in, and he fixed them. He taught me slang and encouraged me to join the football team he coached, and somehow lent me a glow of popularity even there. I could see how much the other girls envied me, even snotty, wealthy Rhiannon, who was transparently in love with him.

It had a profound effect on me. I stopped controlling everything so completely, even my food intake, and started to make better friends. I began to feel actually liked, and I even found myself a boyfriend. A nice, earnest geek who loved how smart I was. Though of course Ninny found herself a cooler boyfriend. A year older than she was and devastatingly handsome.

But being outdone by my beautiful sister worried me less now. I'd shrugged on a new version of myself: one who learned to call things *lit* instead of great. Who would *throw shade* at someone instead of insulting them, and declare anything said back to me *savage*. Who would tell my friends that they'd *slayed* when they'd achieved something, and discuss exactly how *cray cray* some of the girls were.

I sounded, in fact, as little like the Murray-Watts' pet as I could have done. But as much as I might have pretended to be that person, I knew even then that it was skin-deep. That I didn't really care about their *lit* parties or their *sic* hairstyles. As time went on, I would sometimes imagine just walking away from them all, or telling them exactly how little I cared about their dramas. Savage, right?

But for a while I was happy enough with it. I really did like Evelyn, too. She was a terrible cook, and hopelessly disorganised, and also incredibly kind. Which made it all the more confusing when Frank was suddenly touching me and kissing me and telling me that he loved me.

I don't think I need to go into much detail about what happened, do I? You have my statements about all of it. My sister's statements, too. Perhaps you even believe them by now.

The only part of it I want to focus on is the blindingly

obvious fact that he had it all planned out. The fact that he had so clearly done it before, now that I look back. From the encouragements to drink, to the physical affection, right up to the gradual erosion of boundaries.

On the first night that he raped me – because it was rape, however you look at it, however much I might have thought I was consenting – on that first night, Ninny was away at a showjumping championship with Evelyn. And I felt lucky to have him to myself. Even luckier that he wanted to watch *Gossip Girl* with me, even though he was surely too adult for it, and to order in pizza.

Of course it never occurred to me at the time that the TV show had been chosen carefully. It was the episode where the young Blair loses her virginity to a man who is not her boyfriend.

It was during that scene that Frank began stroking my leg.

It may interest you to know the exact feelings that made me go along with it. There was a feeling of pride that this handsome man was interested in me. Not in my sister, as Jared had been, or in any of the drop-dead gorgeous girls on the football team.

And there was arousal, too. The straightforward response to an unfamiliar and much-craved feeling of touch.

And, finally, there was guilt. Guilt that somehow I couldn't refuse him without it being unfair. Without it letting him down.

It all seemed to carry me away, the whole thing, so that even while I was terrified of it happening, I didn't feel I could stop it.

Afterwards, he told me how long he'd been thinking about that. That what we had done was absolutely right, because we loved each other, and I should never let anyone tell me otherwise. And of course he told me I couldn't tell anyone. That it would get me thrown out.

I felt a little rush of doubt just then. Because this was so very much like what the Murray-Watts had told us. It sounded, suddenly, like manipulation, and I turned away from him.

I think Frank saw that in my expression, because he put a hand on my face and turned it gently until I was looking at him again. And he said, 'I'd never let it happen, though. I'd never let them take you away from me. Even if it meant I lost everything.'

I was stupid enough to fall for it. And so our relationship continued, built on snatched opportunities for closeness. When Evelyn was on night shifts, I would wait for him to tell me whether to come and see him. He would often ask me to sneak into his room at exactly one a.m, doing everything I could not to wake Ninny. At other times, he would tell me, privately, that we shouldn't risk it that night, or that he was too tired. I remember feeling somewhere between relieved and disappointed each time he told me not to come.

A few weeks after Frank and I had started sleeping together, I finally saw Callum again. He was waiting for me outside the school gates. Well, waiting for us. For me and Ninny. I was just the one who happened to emerge first.

It was the first time I'd seen Callum since the fallout at Sally and Henry's, and I remember vividly how full of shame he looked. And how his shame was the mirror of mine.

Faced with my former foster brother, I suddenly felt dirty. I imagined that he could see Frank's touch on me and would recoil.

But seeing him was a relief, too. He looked well. Less emaciated. No hollows under his eyes. And he looked a little older. He was almost sixteen now and had gained what looked like a foot in height. He was starting to look more like a man.

'I just wanted to . . .' He stopped, clearly trying to find the words to say that he was sorry.

'To apologise?' I asked, trying to help him. But for some reason it came out wrong, perhaps because I was so practised at being angry with him. It sounded sarcastic. Harsh.

His expression changed, the old belligerence rising. 'To explain about what happened. I should have done it before, but it's . . . I wasn't ready.' He shook his head, looking away. 'I just want you to know that I felt like I had no choice. I want you both to understand how hard it was. You've never had to – you've never had to lie in front of Sally.'

'Except every time I claimed you hadn't done something when you had,' I snapped back. 'Every time I suggested to her that Henry was cheating, or angry with her, or –'

'It's not the same,' he said, his voice rough. Loud.

Two of the girls from my year paused in the act of walking past, exchanged a look, and then carried on. I saw them looking back at the two of us as they went on, unsure whether to be impressed or worried by this older boy.

My face felt hot. I hadn't meant to argue with him. I wanted to tell him that I understood him. That I forgave him. But all I could do was to stand there and glower back.

I heard a call from somewhere behind me. Callum's name, said in the warm tones I could never seem to manage.

Callum looked past me, and I saw him smile at last.

Ninny was suddenly there, hugging him, asking him how he was. If he was all right. Her face was alight, and I could see the reflection of that light in Callum, too. And it made something twist inside me.

'I'm OK,' Callum told her. 'Things are all OK.'

'What happened after we left?' Ninny asked, withdrawing and looking at him keenly. Piercingly. 'Did they punish you?'

'No,' he said. And then, awkwardly, he added, 'It was actually pretty good for a few months after you left. They were on their best behaviour in case social services came back again. I think it all scared Henry shitless. He backed right off and left me alone.' He paused, and then, in a much lower voice, he added, 'And obviously they both wanted to make sure I was properly back in their fucking net.'

He looked so angry with himself, for a moment, that I felt the strangest urge to hug him. But though it might have been hard when I'd first known him, it was impossible now. I could still feel Frank's caresses on me and it seemed like an infection of some kind that I might pass on.

'So it got worse again?' I asked, trying to phrase it as a simple question, instead of an accusation. To avoid sounding like I was telling him I'd been right all along.

'For a while,' he said, glancing at me and then away. 'Things are . . . sort of OK now. I'm almost as tall as Henry these days. And I started working out at the school gym . . . and doing press-ups and squats whenever they shut me in the cellar. They realised they couldn't overpower me any more.' He gave a small smile. 'They still say some fucking awful things. And they still love to deprive me of food. But I have a proper weekend job now, at the pub. The Cuttings. It's still Pa Rewzi running it.'

I shook my head at him slightly, finding the memory of the village strange. 'Isn't Pa Rewzi about a hundred and five?'

'About that,' he said. And he almost smiled. 'It's freedom, anyway. When I'm hungry, I just buy myself something.' He paused, for a moment. 'They actually want to adopt me, and

I'm . . . I could do it, you know. I could manage another couple of years with them until I'm a legal adult, and then . . . and then be their legal heir. End up with all that, once they're gone.'

It made my stomach drop. 'Callum, no!' I said, unable to help myself. 'They'll dangle that inheritance over you for the rest of their lives. They'll use it to make you keep doing what they want. They might live for decades, and then leave it all to charity. You'll be their prisoner –'

'I'm not a child any more,' he said, rounding on me. 'They can't control me like they used to.'

'It's OK,' Ninny said, putting a hand on his arm. 'You've got to do what's best for you.'

Callum's expression calmed as he looked at her, and he nodded. 'Yeah, I have. I need to think about the future.'

'We have to catch the bus,' Ninny said next. 'But let us have your number. You can have mine.'

Callum glanced over at me, and I shrugged.

I watched them exchange numbers, half wondering whether I should get my phone out, too. For someone who had become so practised at getting what I wanted out of people, I felt strangely powerless when it came to Callum. Though perhaps the problem was that I didn't know what I wanted.

I knew one place I could find him, at least. If I needed to. He would be working away at the Cuttings, helping ancient Pa Lewzi restock the bar or serve a plate of soggy food. For some reason the quiet, rural little ideal made my eyes sting slightly. It felt such a long way away from where I was.

I watched Ninny hug him again, while I folded my arms across myself, tightly. Callum nodded at me, his eyes not quite meeting mine, and I ducked down to pick up my school bag. And then I followed Ninny to the bus.

I found it hard to talk to her during the bus ride home. Seeing Callum had clearly made her happy. Happier than she'd been in a long time. She asked a hundred different questions about him, and made a hundred conjectures about his life now. She didn't seem to care that I said nothing in return.

I shut myself away when we got back home to the Pinders' house, and for the first time in years I cried into my pillow. When Frank came in to see if I was OK, and put his arms round me and gave me a single kiss behind my ear, I didn't know whether I wanted to sink into the cuddle or tell him never to touch me again.

27

'It was seven or eight months ago. Nina got hit by a careless driver,' Hanson explained, her voice a little strangled even to her own ears. She was in the small meeting room, sitting in a triangle with the chief and O'Malley.

'He drove straight through a pedestrian crossing while messing around with his phone,' she went on. 'I was driving the other way and saw him clip Nina. I got out to help and ended up staying with her. A couple of guys were making sure the driver didn't leave. She had a possible broken wrist and had taken a lot of skin off her leg and was clearly in a state of shock. So I started chatting to her.' Hanson made herself glance over at the DCI, who was looking into the distance, thoughtfully. It was impossible to tell whether he was disappointed in her or not. 'She told me her name was Nathalie. Which I'm guessing, based on what we know, was down to an innate distrust of people in authority of any kind.'

'And you told her your name,' the chief said, his tone so neutral that he may as well have been Ben.

'Yes.' Hanson nodded, and then grimaced. 'I also told her what I did. Which station I was from.' She gave a short laugh. 'She was intelligent and curious and it seemed a good idea to take her mind off things. I think I probably even told her what areas we covered. I'm not sure. But the bit that – the bit that may have kicked things off was when she asked why I'd joined the police. I remember that bit pretty clearly now I've . . . now I've worked it out.'

The DCI lifted his head, and said, 'You told her you liked

to help people, but it was really the puzzle you enjoyed most. The feeling of all the pieces arriving scattered, and you putting them together. How you have to solve it by holding it all in your head and being ready to totally shift your view when something new arrives to fight with your pet theory. How it's somewhere between a crossword and a Rubik's cube.'

Hanson found herself staring at him, her face a hot red. 'Did you . . . did Keely . . . say something?'

The chief shook his head, his expression slightly amused. 'It's what you told me, the first time you got drunk at the pub.' He smiled at her. 'I've been wondering why Keely came to me, and I now understand why. None of it was about me, which I should have realised when she challenged me on it.' He gave a humorous shrug. 'I'll admit that I underestimated her. Both early on, and multiple times afterwards.'

O'Malley grinned, his expression sympathetic. 'I think you'll find we all did. So . . . Nina told Keely all about this nice policewoman she'd met, and . . .'

'And Keely decided Juliette was the one person likely to listen to her,' the DCI said. 'Specifically, to look past the three apparent fabricated cases of abuse and accept that the CAIT and social services had failed her three times over.' He gave her a slightly wry smile. 'And it's possible that what you said gave her the idea of planting clues. It would suit what we know of Keely to plan everything around one person's thinking.'

'I'm really sorry,' Hanson said, feeling the heat in her cheeks increase.

The chief laughed. 'I don't think you can take any blame for giving a kid a nice answer about why you wanted to be in the police,' he said. 'Though I do hope you've realised, since, that the job is actually about doing boring shit.'

Hanson felt a rush of relief. The chief was in no way a hard taskmaster, but she'd expected a lecture on not giving out personal information.

She nodded at him, mock seriously. 'It has come to my attention a few times, yes.'

'Then there's hope for your management career, after all,' the chief said.

'He never says that kind of thing to me,' O'Malley said, cheerfully.

'So,' the chief went on, in a slightly more serious voice. 'Going back to your encounter with Nina this morning. What impression were you left with? Did she look healthy? And did you feel that she was doing it all willingly?'

'She didn't look injured, or in any way like she was suffering physically,' Hanson said. 'As to whether she's being manipulated, I don't know. I mean, she was very much alone, on what was presumably Callum's bike. She could easily have driven somewhere else or come and talked to me properly if she'd wanted to. And she seemed very collected but very focused in the way she looked at me. I'd say she wanted me to take her seriously.'

'Which makes it likely that she and Keely have been working together, even if we can't be certain of that,' the DCI said, quietly. 'Particularly given the probability that Keely arranged her own disappearance from the refuge.'

'What's beyond the trees she drove into?' O'Malley asked.

'A few industrial units that let onto houses,' Hanson replied.

'Quick's team are already looking to see if they can trace where she went,' the chief confirmed.

'If anyone would like a wager, I'm happy to stake quite a lot on her not being traceable,' O'Malley said.

'No deal,' Hanson answered, shaking her head. 'It was

too carefully done. She knew exactly where I'd be, and where to stop to make her exit easy. I'd say this was another part of the game.'

'It seems like it,' the DCI said. 'But I keep coming back to the question of why. Why suddenly tell us to find Keely, and show herself? It weakens her position. It makes it clear that there's no threat.'

'Maybe because it's not just about justice?' O'Malley said, with a shrug. 'Or maybe we were getting too close to finding Nina, too soon.'

The chief nodded, slowly, his eyes unfocused. 'I've been wondering about whether time plays a part in all this. Can we think of some reason we shouldn't find Nina quickly? What's the benefit of a delay, once we've got to the point where we believe her?'

'Could she be somewhere that helps her with bringing these men to justice?' O'Malley suggested.

'But she's already bringing them to justice,' Hanson argued, 'through her interviews, and the evidence she's left us.'

'Well, there must be a reason,' O'Malley said, with a shrug. 'Doing this risks making us give up all together because we suspect they're wasting our time.'

The DCI lifted his head. 'Of the evidence we have so far, we've had photographs of Jared Boula's hard drive, a letter from Frank Pinder, and Nina's phone placed at his house. Along with one video of an unidentified man. None of it has pointed to Henry Murray-Watt, has it?'

Hanson shook her head. 'No, but there's a lot more to find. Whatever she's left at the newsagent's could be evidence against Henry.' She glanced up at the clock. 'Should I get over there now?'

'Yes,' the chief said, thoughtfully. 'I think that would be a good idea. We know that one of the two Lennox sisters was at the Murray-Watts' house last week, according to the neighbour. That strongly implies that they were there to photograph or take something in particular.'

Hanson put her pen away and rose, wondering whether Keely had another plan in getting them to pursue her. Was she trying to lead them to one of her abusers, as she had with Frank Pinder?

She felt a momentary run of cold up her spine. Or was she, in fact, trying to tempt one of those abusers into doing something? Was she challenging those three men to find her, too?

28

I don't know why it never occurred to me that Frank was also screwing my sister. I suppose it was part of his manipulation, to make me feel like I was the only one who meant anything to him. That I was special, even while he was sleeping with his wife most nights of the week. His narration had become my reality, and I was stupid – so stupid – about all of it.

I didn't have a clue until the morning I saw Ninny creeping back to her room at six, an hour before we were all supposed to be up. I'd only got up to use the bathroom, and I kept the light off because I didn't want the harsh brightness. I hadn't bothered to shut the door fully, so it was easy to see Ninny out in the hallway, where a single orange night light was kept plugged in.

I recognised what she was doing. It was a little ritual I was familiar with, that breathless creep back to bed. Only it had always been me doing it, and I'd been going to a room further away.

I should have experienced a rush of sympathy for my sister. For vulnerable Ninny. I know I should. But all I could feel was searing hot anger. That she'd had Jared to herself, and her gorgeous boyfriend, who she'd somehow managed to keep when I'd ended up pushing mine away repeatedly until he stayed away. She'd met up with Callum twice in the last fortnight, too. She had everything, and yet she still wanted Frank, too.

And he must love her, I realised. Worse: he might actually love her more.

It was crushing, the realisation. I felt my world crumbling. And it only increased all the shame that was eating at me. I felt more corrupted, more *wrong* than I had ever felt.

During the two days I kept silent about it all, I found myself washing my hands, face, body constantly. Over and over. Desperately trying to be cleaner.

I felt like walking up to Frank and demanding an answer, all the while. But in my confused mind, I was afraid of him being angry with me about it. I was afraid that it might tip him into choosing my sister for good.

But to keep quiet was unbearable. And so I chose to confront my sister instead. To ask her, angrily, what was going on.

People often talk about someone going pale. I've only seen it actually happen a few times, and when I shut myself into Ninny's bedroom and accused her of sleeping with Frank, it was the real thing. A strange and total draining of colour out of her face.

'It's wrong,' she said, staring at me with a look that made me feel uncomfortable, even through the anger. 'It's so wrong. I don't . . . I felt so grateful to him, for being kind. But it's so wrong. I don't know what to do.'

She looked up at me as if I could guide her. She's looked at me like that so many times. She's so often laid a crisis at my feet in the expectation that I'll work it all out. But I was too angry with her to play the caring sister. I couldn't think about her feelings when I was brimful of hurt and anger.

'You have a boyfriend!' I hissed. 'Why do you . . . why did you have to take him?'

I hadn't meant to cry. I was going to be collected. Firm. I'd thought I could manipulate her into backing down. Into letting me have this, at least. This thing that I somehow wanted even though it made me hate myself. But I found myself sobbing. There are times when the way you feel is too much for your mind to handle. However strong I like to think myself, it happens to me, too.

Ninny watched me for a moment, and then I saw it. The horror in her expression. The same thing I had felt when I realised I wasn't the only one.

'He's . . . doing it to you, too?'

'It was me first!' I said. 'I didn't . . . He does love me. He really does.'

I stalked across the room away from her, my fists clenching and unclenching and my head full of fury. And it was Ninny – guileless, fragile Ninny – who somehow understood better than I did.

'Listen. I . . . I don't think he loves either of us.' I wheeled to shout at her, but she rose and said, 'It's wrong. What he's doing. It's so wrong. I feel . . . It isn't love. It's not the same as love.' She shook her head. 'You know that really. He shouldn't say he loves a fourteen-year-old and a twelve-year-old.'

'It is love,' I said. 'Why else would he want to kiss me and touch me?'

There was a long silence, and then Ninny said, solemnly, 'Because there's something wrong with him.'

It took half an hour of conversation for me to begin to agree with her, and several days of agonised reflection to bring me round fully. The very next time Frank went to hug me after driving us home from school, I almost crumbled. But then I imagined him hugging Ninny, instead, and I realised that everything about all of it was wrong.

Evelyn had a night shift once more that Wednesday, and Frank asked me to come and see him that night. I found myself shaking slightly as I told him I couldn't, because it was my period and I felt sick and bloated. As you probably realise, I'm a good liar, even under pressure, and he backed off quickly.

In spite of the way I now felt, it still took a major falling-out to convince me to report him. I had been stung too hard by our failure with the Murray-Watts to want to consider it, at first. But Frank managed to argue with each of us in the space of a week. He made it suddenly, abundantly clear that he saw us both as his possessions.

I dealt with the way he spoke to me, but strangely it was the sight of him up in my sister's face, telling her she wasn't going to whore herself out any more, that decided me.

We reported him the next day, Ninny and I. It took all of our combined courage. And that courage was needed again and again, as we told our story. To social worker. Detective constable. Detective inspector. A constant round of police officers whose names I barely had time to learn.

And what good did it do us? None, except to drive us both harder towards the man who took the tatters of what we'd been and unravelled them.

With a feeling of inevitability, we returned to our tatty, bleach-odoured children's home. And we found it changed.

Unimaginably, it had actually become a worse place. It wasn't like we'd been expecting Shangri-La, but, after Frank, we'd hoped for some kind of peace, at least. But that was decidedly not on the cards.

Two strong, aggressive fifteen-year-old boys had arrived and made a swift and vicious friendship. Tom and Brandon were now the unquestioned rulers of the place, and it was clear that most of the staff were as incapable of standing up to them as the other kids were. We watched in horror as they mortified and bullied the littlest ones, taking everything they could from them with grim satisfaction. And when either of us tried to protest, they would turn the searchlight of their sadism on us, instead.

It became clear pretty quickly that one of the members of staff had leaked our accusations about Frank Pinder. Tom and Brandon began asking questions about what our daddy had liked to do to us, which quickly became sexual taunts. It was hideous to see the girls joining in, too. Teenagers who were as often their victims, but who would wade in in an attempt to win some kind of popularity with them.

Ninny had at least been looking forward to seeing Jared again, and was delighted to find that he was now her keyworker. But it was no longer easy for her to hang around with him, his arm slung across her shoulder. Frank's perversions had made her brittle and frightened. She would flinch, now, each time he touched her, and I could see that it amused Jared.

It worried me, too, that Jared seemed to like Tom and Brandon. He would joke with them, rarely discipline them, and at times even laugh along as they victimised someone. With clearer eyes, I now saw the ugliness of Jared beneath his tanned skin. I saw the cruelty for what it was, and I was relieved that Ninny seemed to recognise some of it too.

But it didn't protect her. Not really. And it did nothing to help her against our fifteen-year-old tormentors, who drove her to shaking, white fury every few days with their taunts. Their unwelcome touch. Their sexualised threats.

After the twentieth time they'd cornered one or other of us, and with no help coming from anyone within the home's staff, I decided to put an end to it.

I made a point of hanging around the games room alone for most of Saturday, and was rewarded when Brandon approached me. He was the more dominant of the two.

He had such a swagger on him, did Brandon. It's a walk I've learned to interpret. It isn't confidence but fear. Fear of the world; of someone bigger or stronger; of not having enough status to survive.

But that doesn't make me want to trip the swaggerers up any less. I know what a boy like that is capable of.

'Hey, ginger,' he said, as he rolled his way over to me. I don't think he'd ever used my name. Not once.

He came right up to me where I was pretending to read at one corner of the sofa, and sat, looming, on the edge of the arm. 'Would you like to help me out with something? I hear you like to use your mouth, and I could use a bit of a clean.'

I looked up at him as if considering, and then I closed the book and gave him a very predatory smile.

'All right.' I started to kneel up on the sofa, so I was on a level with him. He moved backwards slightly, clearly startled. Willing acceptance obviously hadn't been part of his plan. 'I can show you what Frank liked, if you want.'

I saw a rush of genuine fear on his face, and then a rush of what I knew was excitement. It was very clear that, for all his talk, he was totally inexperienced. Innocent. But where, for me, experience meant I was tainted, for him it would mean respect. Street cred.

There is such a world of difference in the lives of girls and boys, however hard we fight.

He glanced towards the door, and said, 'All right.'

I started to run my hand slowly up his leg, with a sick, strangely sad memory of doing this with Frank.

'He called what I'm about to do "Shangri-La". Do you know what that means?'

Brandon shook his head, his eyes on my hands.

'It means a plane of pure pleasure. He was a bit of a

masochist, was Frank,' I said, in a very low voice. 'So he really loved it . . . when I did this.'

And I grabbed at where I knew his balls must be, under his loose tracksuit trousers, and I twisted.

He doubled over before doing anything else, and then gave me a shove so hard that I fell and whacked my head on the far arm of the sofa. Luckily, Brandon's own pain was too much for him to do a lot more. He scuttled out, bent double and calling me a bitch in a fierce, low voice, tears pouring from his eyes.

The poor boy, I thought. Expecting paradise and getting agony. He wouldn't even be able to tell anyone about it. Not without ruining his reputation.

What I didn't know then was how easy it would be for him to twist the truth. To tell an entirely different version of it that would damage me and – more significantly – my sister. That would mean that for the third time we would neither of us be believed.

But at the time it felt like a victory. In the short term, we were left alone. I don't know quite what Brandon said to his equally awful friend, but neither of them approached us again.

And that cemented in me the idea that justice only happened when you took it into your own hands. None of these institutions designed to care for us had ever stepped in to help. If I wanted to protect myself – and to protect Ninny – it was going to be up to me.

29

Jonah was trying to catch at the straws of everything before they eluded him. The strings of Keely Lennox's net were as elaborately woven as they were methodical, but he was still struggling to understand her newest move.

Sending Nina in on that motorbike made no obvious sense. Keely had apparently chosen her moment to depart, and had left videos to make sure that he and his team had the clues they needed. Clues that they were gradually following. They had already been eager to find Nina, and with the discovery of Sarah Mallard at the Pinder house, had become even more motivated.

So why show her hand? Why reveal that Nina was fine, and ask them to focus instead on following her? What was it that he was missing?

He was certain, in the way he often was, that he was overlooking something profoundly significant. It felt as though he'd got stuck looking at a painting from only millimetres away, seeing random shapes that made no sense. He was certain that he would realise what he was looking at if only he could step back far enough.

Now find my sister . . .

What did she want them to do?

He was still going in circles when O'Malley came to find him.

'I've given a call to the football club treasurer where Frank Pinder coaches, and I'd lay money he's hiding something about Frank,' he said. 'I'd like to go and see him in person.'

'OK,' Jonah replied, half his mind still on Nina. 'But make sure you have a squad car on standby in case Frank's hiding out there.'

It took Hanson less than five minutes to retrieve Keely's clue from the newsagent's. It had been left by an apparent courier, who had presumably been Callum Taylor.

Asked her name by the shop assistant, Hanson gave her own – which had turned out to be exactly the right answer.

'Oh, it's the big ones,' the assistant said. 'I'll have to get you to come round and carry them. One of them's bastard-heavy.'

Hanson waited until she'd hefted the boxes out to the car one at a time, and then slid on a pair of surgical gloves. It took several goes with one of her more robust keys to slit the tape on the heavier box, but it then came open easily.

Inside, nestled in eclectic pieces of expanded polystyrene, was a computer. And although she had no immediate way of confirming the theory, Hanson would have bet money it belonged to Jared Boula.

The treasurer of the Southampton Tigers football club lived in a house that had obviously cost a great deal more than Frank Pinder's. It was a white-rendered cottage amid a mismatch of houses on Welland Road, close to the picturesque centre of Lyndhurst.

The treasurer's name, O'Malley knew, was Colin Sergeant. His overly formal headshot on the club's website showed him as a forty-something man who radiated a good opinion of himself. Colin had already assured both O'Malley and Quick that he'd heard nothing from Frank since the previous weekend. But unlike Quick, O'Malley hadn't believed him.

Following the chief's advice, he'd brought a pair of uniforms with him, and had hopes that the presence of a squad car and those who were clearly officers would produce some kind of tangible effect.

The photographs of Sarah Mallard's text messages that Lightman had sent over were very much on his mind as he made his way to the front door. Even as photographs of a photograph of a screenshot, they had packed a punch, and O'Malley felt a burning need to bring Frank Pinder in. It was made all the stronger by the fact that he hadn't believed Keely earlier.

He was slightly taken aback to find the door opened by a teenage girl in pearl earrings and a Jack Wills hoodie.

'Oh, I see.' She folded her arms. 'You've come to quiz us about Frank, haven't you?' She glared from him to the constables in challenge. Her accent was unmistakably public school, and her disdain for them apparently limitless.

'Rhiannon.' It was a man's voice, coming from the hallway behind. It was Colin Sergeant himself, the headshot brought to life, who put his hands on her upper arms and steered her out of the way. He stepped into the doorway himself, but Rhiannon remained just behind, hovering with malevolent intensity.

'Right,' Colin said, with an easy smile. 'What's going on? I thought we'd already been through everything?'

O'Malley wondered, fleetingly, what Colin did in his day job. He gave the overwhelming impression of a working-class man made good. His accent was the kind you'd usually find in one of the lads from the Thornhill estate, but his clothes were Crew Clothing, a match for his pricey house. And his daughter had clearly been educated somewhere a marked step up from a city comprehensive.

'I'm Detective Sergeant Domnall O'Malley,' he began.

'We spoke a short while ago. We now have reason to believe that Frank Pinder might be in Lyndhurst, after all.' He gave Colin his own easy smile. 'I wondered if you were certain you haven't seen him.'

Colin shook his head and gave a good-natured sigh. 'Seriously, I'd have told you if I thought I knew anything helpful.'

'So he hasn't visited you, either last night or today?' O'Malley asked.

'No, he hasn't.'

O'Malley nodded. Smiled again. 'Would you mind showing us round the house?'

There was just the briefest hesitation before Colin said, 'Of course.'

'Dad!' It was Rhiannon speaking, and the word was sharp. A protest.

'It's fine, it's fine,' he said, stepping back to let the three of them inside.

Rhiannon stood frozen for a moment, and then turned and ran up the stairs two at a time.

O'Malley entered the slightly narrow hallway ahead of the two constables and found his eye drawn to a kitbag that was lying on the floor. It still had a price tag on it but it was clearly full. Colin hastily moved himself to block O'Malley's view.

'Would that be a possession of Frank's, Mr Sergeant?' he asked.

There was a brief pause, and then Colin said, 'All right, look. I did lend Frank some money this morning and let him leave some stuff here for later. He was desperate. And the thing is, you need to leave him alone. I know all about the manipulations of that girl. Nothing that she said happened was true. He was cleared in full, and all this blowing up again . . .' He shook his head. 'I'm going to protect my mate when I know that mate's a good bloke, all right?'

O'Malley sighed. 'Do you know where Frank is now?'

'No clue, I'm afraid,' Colin said. 'He dropped in at eleven. I gave him a couple of hundred in cash, and he left again.'

'He didn't say when he'd be back to pick up the bag?'

'No, but I said any time,' Colin said, firmly.

'Do you mind if we have a poke about, then?'

'Be my guest,' Colin said, smiling expansively as though he weren't aiding and abetting a wanted criminal.

O'Malley dispatched the constables to search the ground floor and made his way deliberately upstairs. It was clear that Rhiannon hadn't wanted the police here, and O'Malley suspected there were reasons for that beyond the kitbag.

He found the daughter quickly enough. She was in a very large, very blue room, and was lying on her bed with her back to the door. It was clear from where he stood that she was messaging someone.

'Do you mind if I look around in here?' O'Malley asked her.

The moment she heard his voice, she fumbled with the phone, which bounced off the bed and onto the floor. She scrambled off the bed to retrieve it, and then glared at him and stalked out onto the landing.

O'Malley watched her go, and then glanced around her bedroom, seeing nothing else that might obviously belong to Frank Pinder. As he was on the point of leaving, however, Rhiannon staged a return. She stomped up to the doorway, and said, 'You shouldn't listen to any bullshit from Sarah Mallard. There's no way Frank would touch her. She's a bloody freak with no friends.'

'So you know it's Sarah he was with last night?' O'Malley said. 'How did you find that out?'

Colin appeared behind her and put a placating hand onto her shoulder. 'Frank explained earlier today.'

O'Malley walked past the two of them onto the landing, allowing Rhiannon to return to her room and slam the door. The moment it was shut, O'Malley turned to Colin Sergeant and said, 'I think we should have a word together downstairs.'

'We managed to follow the vehicle's progress out of the city after it picked Keely Lennox up,' Quick's constable was saying. She was hovering next to the empty four-by-four, which had been parked neatly in a corner space at the wildlife centre. Lightman had positioned himself a little further away, letting his eyes follow the lines of the vehicle. 'They came pretty much straight here. We haven't managed to get any clear view of a driver. They were in a cap and balaclava.'

Lightman nodded to her, loading up an image of Sally Murray-Watt's Range Rover onto his iPad. It was fairly clear to him already what the answer was here, but he still looked carefully at the outline of the car in front of him. At the ridged bonnet. The bull-bars. The dented paintwork. The lack of insignia.

'So you think you know whose it is?' the constable asked.

He glanced at her, recognising the type of smile she was giving him. It was the sort of smile that he only had one response to: one of careful neutrality.

'We had an idea,' he said, 'but it turns out not to be right.'

This car, in which Keely had left the refuge, might share a rough shape and colour with the one in the photos he had, but that was as far as the similarity went. It was an early-nineties Land Rover Discovery, not a Range Rover from almost a decade later. It wasn't Sally Murray-Watt's.

'Well, good to check,' the constable said. And then, with another one of those smiles, 'Do you want to take a look at the stuff on the back seat?'

'It's a hard thing finding someone you like accused,' O'Malley said, picking up the mug of coffee Colin had suddenly decided to make for him. 'I've had it myself, with a lieutenant of mine in the forces. I liked the fella well enough. Thought him a good man. I'd seen no bad behaviour from him, and I said so. Which I think is the only thing you can do in those circumstances. You have to be honest in your opinion.'

Colin sat back, folding his arms over his chest. 'So you see my point. I know Frank. I've known him eight years. And I'd trust him with any kid.'

'Of course, of course,' O'Malley said. 'Including your daughter.'

'She's a huge fan of his,' Colin agreed. 'For good reason. The work he does with her team – and the positivity he brings – is unique.'

O'Malley nodded. 'The football team, is it? So he's a supportive coach.'

'He is.'

'Do they communicate?' he asked, lifting his mug again. 'Frank and your daughter?'

Colin's smile grew slightly fixed. 'Only occasionally.'

'I guess it's the only way of keeping in touch with teenagers, really,' O'Malley went on. 'Text messages. FaceTime.'

'Exactly,' Colin agreed.

O'Malley took a great gulp of coffee. It was bloody good, he thought. Almost worth the wait while Colin had faffed with a machine on the counter. 'I suppose she shows you the messages, when they're from him?'

There was a pause, and then Colin said, 'Come on. I respect her privacy.'

O'Malley nodded. 'Probably just the usual stuff, anyway.'

Colin, O'Malley noted, had yet to drink any of his own coffee. He was nodding to himself, his expression a little distant.

'Do you know what he was sending to Sarah Mallard? Frank?' O'Malley said, after a moment.

Colin sighed. 'I'm sure it was the usual stuff. Training chat. Encouragement.'

O'Malley gave another nod. 'I've seen some of it now. Lucky to be able to see it, as he'd asked her to delete it all.'

There was another pause, one that O'Malley was quite happy to let go on as he continued to make his way slowly through the coffee.

'What . . . kinds of things was he sending?' Colin asked, at last, and O'Malley was very careful to show no reaction at all.

'I can't be too specific, you know?' he said, quietly. 'It's evidence that's going to be used against him. But . . . it was graphic. And there were photographs. Ones he'd sent, and ones he'd asked for. It's not surprising he ran.' He looked away, shaking his head. 'In all honesty, Colin, I'd be worried for my daughter. I think that's more important than where Frank is, or how you feel about him.'

'You're sure it's genuine?' Colin asked. 'It could be fake.'

'We're fairly sure,' O'Malley said. 'The number used was for a burner that we recovered from a bag in Frank's house. We think he now has another one, that he's been using since.'

There was a pause, and then Colin surprised him by asking, 'What happened with your mate in the army? The lieutenant?'

O'Malley grimaced. 'I saw a lot of evidence in the end that changed my mind about him. He'd been in there, abusing all the new recruits, the moment they set foot in the barracks. All while I thought he was a good officer. A friend.'

He rose a moment later, satisfied to note that Colin looked a great deal paler than he had done.

Jonah had retreated to his office, and with a feeling of inevitability, loaded up Keely's interview tapes once again. He'd started again at the beginning, skipping through them to find the sections he wanted.

He wrote down inconsistency after inconsistency, each one undeniable. And surely, surely intentional. They lay in the horse riding Keely had said her sister had been so good at. In the descriptions of her sister's incredible memory. In her obvious attraction to Callum Taylor, who had ended up dating Nina. And in her comments about her running.

He found himself flicking backwards and forwards, from care report to interview, and at last he found himself able to stand back. To see it all.

He pulled up the database. It took him only a minute to locate what he wanted: the photographs he and Lightman had taken of the Lennox house.

He scrolled through until he found it. There, in the living room, was something almost as significant as the video she'd left on the iPad. Next to a family photo was a child's drawing.

It had been taped to the wall instead of being properly hung. It showed a three-person family, with two crudely drawn girls and one woman. And in childish writing, next to each, a name: Ninny, Mummy, Nina.

Into the sudden realisation that he'd been wrong about

virtually everything came the urgent buzzing of his mobile. He answered it to Lightman, who said succinctly, 'The car Keely Lennox disappeared in has her overnight bag still in it. There's also a dummy, dressed up to look like Nina, along with a used roll of gaffer tape and some cable ties. I don't think Keely went willingly.'

30

The day I saw Ninny with Callum Taylor changed a lot of things for me. It was the final piece in the puzzle of my own nature. In coming to terms with the reality of who I was, and how every promise to be different – to be better – was empty.

My life had shrunk by this time. I'd been denied the promise of a foster family who might actually love me, after two bitter failures. Denied the idea of a just world after our treatment by the law. Denied close friendships and a chance of a normal relationship with one of the boys at school, because of the awfulness of what I knew I'd become.

I suppose it was inevitable that the result of all this was a closing down. A failure of *feeling*. The landing of blow after blow had acted on a nature that was already inclined to coldness and had closed it off entirely.

I remember being at school one day when Leanne, a girl in my class I was supposedly best friends with at the time, fell badly on the playground. It was clear as she raised her head that she had really hurt herself. There was blood already pouring from her nose, and as she opened her mouth in an effort to breathe, I saw two of her teeth dislodge themselves from the front of her gums.

She looked up at me for help. In pain, and distress, and fear.

And although I bent down after a moment and started to help her, I felt nothing. I reached for a real, human reaction, and found emptiness instead.

But it turned out that it was possible for me to feel. I just needed something to stir up strong enough jealousy, and a burning desire for revenge.

I'd gone to the cinema with Leanne on a Saturday afternoon. It was something I didn't get to do all that often, now that I'd started a job at a fusty ladies' fashion shop on Saturdays. I only had one Saturday off in every six, and Sundays were my only chance for a really long run and then an afternoon spent collapsed in a chair reading.

I think Ninny must have forgotten that I might be around on that particular day. Or perhaps she just assumed that she wouldn't be seen. It's not as though Southampton is some tiny village where everything you do is under observation. And we were a little off the beaten path, too, having decided to watch an arthouse film at the Picturehouse in Ocean Village instead of something glossy at the Odeon.

Whatever she thought, anyway, Ninny ended up at the same bus stop on Canute Road that I was headed for, her rich, blazing hair making her obvious from right down the road. I recognised the figure next to her in a heartbeat, too. His form was as familiar to me as the shape of mine.

I faltered the moment I saw them and stepped into an alcove next to the doorway of the Wetherspoons. I'd long known that they'd been meeting up frequently without me, but had been incapable of confronting Ninny about it. Of even asking gently about it. I couldn't admit to my sister that I wanted to know every single detail about Callum, while hating to hear his name.

I was too far away to hear what they were saying to each other, but that almost made their movements clearer. Everything about them was a dance of intimacy, and I stood frozen, something strange happening in my heart as I tried to tell whether they had tipped over into romance, or whether it might be possible to stop it.

And then the number 17 bus drew up alongside the kerb, and Callum leaned in and kissed her, their mouths together and arms hooked lightly round each other as though this was a habit. A routine.

I felt as though something was cracking open inside me, letting streams of heat and cold meet each other. The part of me that wanted to look away – to walk away – found itself overwhelmed by the hot, furious part that wanted to watch and then to approach and to tear into them both with my hands.

The kiss ended as Ninny disentangled herself and hurried to board the bus. Callum waited for her to take a seat, and then waved her off as it pulled away.

Without any conscious thought, I followed him as he moved off. It didn't feel like me walking those roads. I was nothing more than a mass of witness. A single painfully beating heart somehow connected to my vision.

Callum moved quickly down Canute Road, his gaze fixed ahead of him. It was lucky for me that it was. I didn't seem capable of hiding.

He crossed until we were alongside Queen's Park, and then he ducked through a gate, the long shadows of the trees falling on him and making him indistinct. It seemed natural to follow him into the shadows.

I saw him stop to light up a cigarette, and then suddenly turn to sit on one of the few benches that were still in the sunshine.

I fought to come back to myself somehow, then. Fought for awareness of my body, in order to change course. To move off the path. But he had already seen me, his eyes somehow drawn to me as if he'd known I was coming.

He shook his head at me, his face half angry, half resigned.

'What are you doing here?' he asked. It wasn't quite accusatory, but it wasn't quite friendly, either.

'I followed you,' I said. With anyone else, I might have pretended that it had been a coincidence. That I'd just happened to be strolling among the trees of King's Park, and why not? But I knew that wouldn't work with him. Callum knew who I was. What I was.

He sighed, and took another drag on the cigarette.

I moved towards him, half expecting him to stand up and leave. But he sat where he was, and asked, 'Why would you want to follow me? You don't even like me.'

I thought of asking about Ninny. He must have known that I'd seen them together. But instead I found myself saying, 'Don't let them adopt you. Don't do it.'

His face grew momentarily tight, and then he said, 'It's too late. I've done it.'

It was somehow clear to me that they had already used it against him. That they'd already harmed him in a new and terrible way. I felt my heart squeeze, and without really meaning to, I sat down next to him.

'What did they do?' I asked.

He looked away, and I could see that he was fighting not to tear up. Fighting not to break down in front of me. 'They filled out all my university forms with their income like good little parents, and now . . . they're saying they won't give me a penny.' He threw the cigarette violently away from himself, even though it was nowhere near done. 'And I can't get a bloody grant because they earn too much and stated they'd pay it, and now I have six months to earn enough to pay fees and rent and food for the first term. And I don't know what I'll do after that, if I even make it that far.'

I could imagine Henry's self-righteous expression as he told Callum that he didn't deserve their support, and I cringed.

'Can't you report them to the university?'

'They aren't stupid,' he said, harshly. 'And neither am I, even if you like to pretend I am. They transferred the full amount into my account, lifted my bank card and withdrew it all, to make it look like I'd spent it.'

My familiar rage against them surfaced again. As angry as I was with Callum, I wanted to go to them, right now, and tear the money from them. More than just the money. I wanted revenge for everything they'd done.

'There must be something you can do,' I said.

'Well, I'm all out of ideas,' he said, bitterly. 'At the moment all I've got is spending every free minute working for bloody Deliveroo.'

Not every spare minute, I found myself wanting to say. He'd had enough time to see my sister. But as I watched his face, his body, my eyes following the familiar lines of him, I realised that he looked exhausted. Resigned. Defeated.

'We need to stop them,' I said, quietly, and then, before he could answer that he'd already tried, I said, 'I don't mean just this. I mean that we need to stop them. From doing everything they do.'

He looked at me, then, in what was almost amusement as well as frustration. 'That worked really well last time.'

'We failed because we didn't have proof,' I said. 'And because we believed in a system that was essentially fair. If we want to take them down, we need to have so much proof that it's overwhelming.'

'Nobody's going to listen to you again,' he said, his voice tight. I could see the guilt in him. The knowledge that it was partly his fault. 'Not even if I say it too. It'll seem like revenge, or manipulation, or, I don't know . . . like you two have . . . *issues.*'

I knew, then, that Ninny had told him about Frank. I could feel my cheeks burning, but I still returned his gaze, flatly and unflinchingly this time. 'Of course they will,' I said. 'If we set something up that *makes* them listen.'

'Like what?' he said.

And the truth was, I hadn't known what I meant until I said it. Until I had to give him an answer. But hearing myself forming the words made it clear to me, and I gave him a small smile. 'Even the law will look into something if there's a threat.'

For a moment, I thought he was going to agree. I could see the surge of hope in him. The gleam of it in his eyes.

But then he gave a short, exasperated sigh, and turned away.

'We aren't the bloody Avengers. We're going to end up getting screwed over, or worse.' He shook his head. 'I'm not going to do anything that makes them want to get revenge. I've got too much to lose.' He stood up, angrily, but instead of leaving immediately, he hesitated, and said, 'And you should be careful, too. They hate you. The two of you. I don't think you have any idea how much. They'll find a way of getting you back for leaving them, and you need to have the sense to be afraid.'

I made my way home from Queen's Park on foot, burning with the idea of revenge. However dismissive Callum had been, I knew I could do it. Not alone, but with help. With his help.

Perhaps if it had just been about stopping Henry Murray-Watt, I might have gone ahead by myself. I was sure I was smart enough to bring him down. It would just take time. Patience. Calculation.

But as I walked, and I burned, I began to think about Frank Pinder, too. About what he was probably now inflicting on other young girls. And I saw, in a moment of blinding revelation, exactly how it could be.

I didn't know, then, about Jared Boula. I didn't know that the way my sister had begun reacting to him was based on fear of him, and not on past experience. I didn't know that he'd pinned her up against a wall and put his hands inside her, because she hadn't been able to bring herself to tell me or Callum.

So here's a small confession for you, one that I hope you find illuminating: Jared Boula never touched me. It was my sister he assaulted. It was Ninny.

31

After visiting Colin Sergeant, O'Malley had sent the constables away and spent some time writing up his notes in the car. He'd left the driver's door ajar, which happened to be on the same side as the house. An unassuming picture, he thought. A copper just getting on with his paperwork.

He felt no small rush of satisfaction when the door to Colin's house opened, fifteen minutes after he'd left.

Colin looked a very different man from the one who had greeted him a short while ago. The smile, and the aura of certainty, were both gone, and his forehead was creased with anxiety.

He was holding a mobile phone in his hand, one with a pastel blue cover on it.

'Sergeant, I think . . .' He cleared his throat. 'There's something I think you should see.'

He held the phone out. O'Malley took it without asking how it was in his possession. He strongly suspected that Rhiannon didn't yet know that her father had it.

The screen showed just three messages between Rhiannon and a person whose number had been saved as 'C xx'.

> The police are here, looking for you. They know about the money and the bag. You can't come back here. If you need anything, I'll find a way of bringing it. Missing you. Xx

C, who was transparently Frank Pinder, had replied:

Shit, OK. I'll have to stay away, no matter how hard it is.
Your honestly the only thing keeping me going. I'm going to
prove I haven't done anything but it might take a while. Might
need a few things from you too but you can't tell anyone I can't
have you wrapped up in this too, its such a mess. Make sure you
delete everything, for your own sake. Love you xx

Rhiannon had sent another message, which read:

I'll be here whenever you need me. The psycho bitch
won't win. I promise. I'm going to keep telling them it's
all lies until they listen. Love you so much xx

Frank had read the message, it seemed, but hadn't sent a
reply.

O'Malley glanced up at Colin. 'What he's doing . . . what
he's done,' he said quietly, 'you weren't to know. And thank
you for this. I think it's going to be the way we track him
down and stop him.'

The chief was already on his feet when Hanson arrived at
his office door.

'We have an active mobile phone belonging to Frank
Pinder,' she said. 'It pinged a mast in Lyndhurst, and then
one further west. Quick's looking to pin down exactly
where he is now.'

'That's good news,' the chief replied, in such a vague
tone of voice that Hanson almost laughed. Sometimes the
major breakthroughs didn't quite make it past his thoughts.
It was an occurrence she was at least reasonably used to.

'We also have Samantha Wild here,' she went on. 'Keely and
Nina's friend from the children's home. She wants to talk to us.'

Jonah's reaction was one of those odd little nods of his that were directed somewhere off into the distance.

'Let's talk to her,' he said. 'I think she might help us convince Murray and his team about what's going on.'

He began to walk across CID, and Hanson took a few rapid steps to keep up.

'What will they need convincing of?' she asked.

'The fact that Keely hasn't been stage-managing any of this,' he said.

Samantha – or, she offered, Sam – was in one of the big armchairs of the comfort suite, curled up in it as if she were trying to blend in with the fabric. Jonah was reminded inescapably of a young owl in a nest, an effect helped by Samantha's large, round glasses.

'I think . . . there are some things you don't know,' Sam said, her voice unsteady but surprisingly loud. 'I know you've been looking for Nina, and – and Keely's gone now, too. But it isn't as simple as you think.'

Jonah smiled. Nodded. 'No, we're definitely beginning to learn as much,' he said. 'But it's a slow process. Anything you have to add would be incredibly helpful.'

'Look, I'm really – scared for Keely.' She looked between Jonah and Hanson. 'You probably don't realise that she isn't this tough, cold person.'

Jonah nodded again. 'I do realise, though I'm afraid it took me a while.' He glanced at Hanson. 'Do you think you know where she might have been taken?'

Samantha pressed her lips together, as if she was still not sure about what to say. And then she said, 'No, I . . . I'm sorry, I don't. But Nina – she came to see me.' Her forehead creased, with an effort of concentration. 'The two of them came. She told me I needed to help you follow Keely's trail.

Look, she doesn't want to put a few people away. She wants revenge. On everyone. Before they left, she said . . .' Samantha shifted, rubbing her hands together, as if she didn't like to remember this. 'She was talking about going away, and she suddenly didn't sound like herself. She said she probably wouldn't see me again. And then she said that she'd finally worked out what the shadowy part of herself was for.' Samantha took a breath. 'I told her I'd miss her, and she said . . . she said, "There's nothing in here to miss. It's all rotten from the inside out."'

Jonah felt a wave of unease surge through him. He heard Hanson ask, 'Keely?' But he didn't need to wait for Samantha to answer to know what she was going to say.

'No, Nina. It was Nina.'

He knew Hanson was waiting for him to explain. The two of them were back in CID, where Jonah had drifted without intending to.

'You remember right at the start,' he said, 'what Keely said to us. She said if we wanted to find Nina, we needed to try looking in the mirror.' He gave a short laugh. 'It wasn't just about examining our own prejudices and facing up to our responsibilities to them. It was about inversion, too.'

It had all been so very, very clever. In thirty years of this job, Jonah didn't think he'd met anyone as clever as Nina Lennox.

'We obviously thought that everything Keely was telling us was her story,' he said. 'It's not an unreasonable assumption. She was there, dripping with scorn, and clearly devastatingly sharp. And she was telling us the story of a young woman who'd learned to manipulate everyone around her.' He shrugged. 'Only it wasn't her story. The truth of it all was hidden by the casual use of that nickname, Ninny.

Even when I'd seen her house, and the drawings on the walls, I didn't understand it. Ninny wasn't a nickname for Nina. It was what Nina and her mother called Keely, the sweet, slightly dappy older girl. Everything that's happened has been Nina's doing.'

And Keely did what she told her, Jonah thought. A willing participant in her sister's plans. Because as bright as Keely Lennox clearly was, she had nothing on her sister's extraordinary mind. He'd drawn down their school reports, and finally seen it. That it was Nina who had won maths, English and science prizes. That it was Nina who had been called brilliant.

By contrast, it was Keely who had gone from being a sunny, open girl to a closed-off, rebellious teenager. It was a defence mechanism to hide her fragility. She might be so used to defending herself that she seemed haughty, but she was in no way tough.

Where she wore the obvious marks of abuse, Nina's were far more subtle. It had driven the younger Lennox sister to pretend. To fake smiling innocence, and to learn manipulation. He'd been painfully slow to realise that he was seeing the inversion, because the best manipulation was invisible.

And of course it had been Nina who had wanted Callum Taylor from the start. The one who had recognised something of herself in him. And Keely had been the one standing in her way.

He could see that Hanson was with him now. That her mind was racing ahead as fast as his was. He felt his phone buzz in his pocket and felt tempted to ignore it, but the chance that it was part of this made him pull it out.

'Linda,' he said, recognising McCullough's extension.

'We've got your results back from the swabs we took off Keely Lennox,' she said. 'And it isn't either of the Lennox sisters. In an unusual moment of the fates aligning, though, we do actually have DNA from the relevant person on file from an old incident. The blood she was covered in belongs to Callum Taylor.'

'So you believe Keely Lennox to be under threat,' Murray Quick said, once the chief had finished speaking.

The two teams were crammed together into one of the smaller meeting rooms, Quick having brought two constables and a DS to the briefing.

Hanson had been watching Quick carefully as the DCI spoke, alert for signs of disbelief. She was intensely aware that what the chief was saying sounded more than a little bonkers. The idea that the two sisters had not only set up a trail of evidence in order to bring three men to justice, but had also performed an elaborate switch, seemed cracked when said out loud.

And of course, it *was* slightly cracked. It was the kind of thinking that came out of serious intelligence combined with desperation and a hefty dose of fantasy.

Yet there had been a logic to all of it. Hanson could see that now. Nina had needed a strong bargaining chip in order to get the police interested, and what better chip could there be than a sister under threat?

But although it was Nina who had arranged every part of it, it could never have been her sitting there and implying that she'd abducted her older sister. Not when the world thought Keely the strong, strange, cold one, and Nina the slightly built, sunny innocent. There was only one of them who came across as a sociopath, and it was quite definitely Keely.

'It's possible that she is under threat,' the chief was saying to Quick. 'I no longer believe Keely planned to go, or went willingly. The items recovered from the car are one factor in that conclusion, and, in particular, another dummy made to look like Nina.'

'The other dummy was used as a clue,' Lightman said, quietly. 'It seems as though it should signify something this time, as well.'

'It could just be a way of showing us that Nina's in control now,' Hanson suggested. 'For whatever reason, she feels like she needs it.'

'Do we really believe that Nina's a threat to her sister, though?' O'Malley asked.

'We can't know that for sure, which means we need to assume that Keely is in danger,' the chief said. 'It's now clear that Nina has been managing all this from the start. The one thing that isn't clear is exactly what she plans on doing with her sister now, and why.'

'What about Callum Taylor?' Quick asked. 'Is there any indication of how Keely ended up covered in his blood?'

'That's still unclear,' the chief said. 'It seems unlikely that Nina would injure Callum, but it concerns me that we haven't necessarily seen him since this started. We assumed he was on the motorbike in the allotments and when Keely was snatched, but we've now seen Nina riding a bike like that. He might be wherever Keely is, and we have no way of telling whether he willingly provided his blood or not.'

As the DCI finished, Hanson couldn't help thinking of those later videos. The ones where it became clear that Nina would do anything to have Callum Taylor to herself.

Had Keely's existence got in the way of that? And had Callum himself rejected her?

32

I spent days deciding how I'd convince Callum to help me. I knew that I needed him on board to stand a chance of convincing my sister, and that his help was the more important. He was older, and far more independent. He had a motorbike and wasn't going to be questioned about being out alone. I needed him.

And you'll probably have understood by now that I felt as little able to keep away from him as I felt able to suddenly spread wings and fly. I wasn't quite willing to admit to myself that I was looking for a reason to be around him, but deep down, I knew that was as much my motive as the idea of revenge.

I decided that I should steal Ninny's phone and message him, pretending to be her. It seemed the only way of making sure he turned up to talk to me.

But before I could execute this particular plan, Callum actually came to me.

I saw him waiting on his motorbike outside the school gates at four o'clock on a sun-and-clouds Thursday afternoon. He must have known, I realised, that Ninny had History Club until five. He was here to see me, not her, and the idea gave me a strange twist of fear and excitement.

The girls I'd been walking with, Leanne and Casey, watched me with bright interest as I approached him. I was aware that they could finally see what I saw in him, now that he was eighteen and grown into himself. They saw the brooding handsomeness. The aura of unexplored depths. The slight hint of danger. And I knew that, for that moment, they envied me.

He held a helmet out to me, wordlessly, and although I wanted to protest that I'd never ridden on a motorbike, I found myself taking it.

'Where are we going?' I asked him.

'Somewhere we can talk in private,' he said.

I climbed on behind him, uncertain whether I should touch him, but needing to hold on. We didn't go quickly or far, but I remember being intensely aware of my arms being round his waist. My body having to touch his.

He steered us to Hollybrook Cemetery, where he pulled the bike up under a tree and then climbed off. He watched me scramble off inelegantly, a faint smile on his mouth, and I wanted so much to shove him. To hit him.

To kiss him.

His smile faded slightly a moment later. He looked away from me, and then said, 'They're in discussions about fostering another girl. A twelve-year-old. One with no defences at all. She came to the house last week.'

I felt the same twist inside me that I knew he must have felt.

'We can't let them do it,' I told him.

'That's why I . . .' He gave a frustrated sigh. 'I know we can't. I've been trying to work out what to do, but . . .'

'If she's already visited, it might happen soon,' I said, thinking back to the process we'd been through with the Murray-Watts. With Frank. 'I'll have to do something quickly.'

'You can't prove what they've done in a few days or weeks,' he argued.

I was thinking of what he'd said before. Of how much Henry hated that I'd got away from them. And I looked up at Callum with a grin.

'I don't think we need to. I just need to ask to come back to stay with them. To be adopted.'

Callum blinked, and then shook his head with a wry smile. 'The shit you gave me for going through with that . . .'

'We'll have months before it happens,' I told him. 'I can dangle it and get them to take the bait. And then I can delay. I can suddenly have doubts about leaving my sister . . . I can string it out until we have enough to put Henry away.'

He shook his head again, but there was a twist of a smile to his mouth. An expression that might have been something like hope.

'You keep saying "we",' he said, after a moment.

I found myself moving towards him, my breath tight in my chest.

'Yes,' I said. 'We'll do it together. Take revenge on all of them, and stop them from ever poisoning anyone again. I know you have it in you.'

'How do you know that?' he asked, looking up at me with that messy, troubled gaze of his almost overflowing.

'Because somewhere underneath it all, we're made of the same thing, aren't we?' I put a hand out to his stomach, and watched where my fingers touched his T-shirt. 'There's the same shadow under here. And everything you do to cover it up is pointless. It's pointless. I can feel it every time I'm near you.' I closed the gap a little more. 'It burns to be let loose, doesn't it?'

He didn't step away. I could feel his breath coming and going in his abdomen, its pace quick and off-beat. I lifted my head to meet his eyes again.

He gave one slight protest, then. Just 'Nina . . .'

But I knew it was nothing more than the echo of a protest. The last, hopeless effort to pretend we hadn't stepped into each other's shadows.

And then he pulled me the final inches towards him, and was kissing me, so fiercely-softly that I felt like I'd been taken apart from inside.

And that's all I have to tell you for now. There's more, of course. A lot more. But I won't be telling it to you until you find me.

I think you must have realised by now what that means. Who I really am. So you know what you have to do.

33

Jonah finished watching with a sense of huge frustration. Nina's story cut off abruptly. Pointlessly. It wasn't even a cliffhanger as such. Just a non-ending. A taunt.

Why leave them dangling? Why not go on to say more? To give them the solution to her puzzle, or at least point towards it? Why was she once again taunting them, if she really wanted these three men brought to justice?

He wished he'd met Nina herself. Though of course every story, every comment that Keely had made in that interview room had really been Nina's. In some ways, he supposed he knew her well.

He needed to understand what she wanted. That had become very clear to Jonah now. Without really knowing, they all risked making a wrong move, and it was clear that such a mistake could have serious consequences.

It now looked overwhelmingly likely that Nina had arranged for her sister to be grabbed, in collaboration with the unknown driver. It was also, he thought, crucial to identify that driver.

Jonah's thoughts circled back to Sally Murray-Watt once again. Could she somehow have become Nina's accomplice? She, like her husband, hadn't been seen in days, and it was clear that she was victim material. Henry had wrapped her up in his coercive control for years. It wasn't hard to believe that Nina might have now done the same.

He sent a swift email to Quick's team, asking them for any update on Sally Murray-Watt from her communication devices, and then sat thinking about Nina's appearance on the motorbike.

Now find my sister . . .

Everything he had learned about Keely now applied to Nina. She had been telling them the truth for a long time. She had suffered and been unable to convince anyone of the truth. She was just as likely to have taken Keely for good reasons as for bad.

But why tell them to find her? What did this next part of the game benefit her?

Unless it's no longer a game . . . He thought, with a sudden twist to his stomach.

'Sir.'

It was Lightman, Jonah saw, as he blinked his way out of his thoughts.

'Sorry, Ben. Fire away.'

'We've picked Nina up leaving the city on the A336 towards Totton, shortly after she intercepted Juliette in Bevois Valley,' he said. 'We're looking for her on other traffic cameras and CCTV from there.'

'That's good,' Jonah said, a little distantly. He felt as though Lightman was speaking through a fog, but that what he was saying was important. 'We need to find her.'

'We'll do our best.' Lightman hesitated, and then said, 'Could I have a couple of minutes of your time?'

'Of course you can.'

In spite of his mind being a million miles from the conversation, Jonah felt a rush of curiosity as Ben shut the door. The last time his unflappable sergeant had asked for a private talk had been when he'd explained about his father's illness.

Ben sat slightly formally in the chair opposite him, and said, 'I'm uncomfortable with the line of enquiry we're following.'

Jonah gave him a half-smile. 'How so?'

'We're only looking at one possibility right now: this idea that Nina Lennox is responsible for the kidnapping of her sister. Which seems to be ignoring a lot of very significant factors in this.'

Jonah nodded, realising that Ben's thoughts had followed the same path as his. 'It does ignore them, and that's exactly what's started to concern me, too.' He focused on his sergeant fully. 'The dummy was the thing that tipped it for me, but it's possible it has nothing to do with the one Nina left in the drama studio. If you wanted to lure Keely Lennox into a car, what better way than making it look like her sister was in the back?'

Lightman nodded, his expression unmistakably relieved. 'So Nina wasn't playing a game when she turned up on that motorbike.'

'No, I don't think she was. I think she was asking for help.'

'And if it wasn't Nina who took Keely,' Lightman went on, 'it was one of those three men. And they somehow knew where Keely was.'

'Yes,' Jonah agreed. 'Which means that someone here or in social services must have told them where to find her.'

'Henley Road,' Hanson said, triumphantly, pulling her earphones out.

'Er, yes,' Ben said, with a quizzical look. He was just returning to his desk, and he gave her a small smile as he sat. Everything about him looked more relaxed, and she wondered what he'd been talking to the chief about.

'On the videos,' she said, deciding to park that question, 'Keely calls it Henley *Street* Children's Home, just once.' She gave him a grin. 'It's more evidence. And, you never know, it could be something that leads us to one of them.'

She might have said more, but the chief emerged at that point, his movements swift.

'We need a briefing.' He turned as if to go, and then swung back to say, 'And if anyone has any food they can give me, it's probably worth a promotion.'

'I have carrot sticks and hummus,' she said, just as O'Malley shouted, 'Chocolate Hobnobs, and you can keep your promotion.'

'Sorry, Juliette,' the chief said, going to grab the packet of Hobnobs. 'I just don't think you're the right fit for senior management just yet. Maybe think about offering a bit more sugar.'

'I'll work on it.'

She followed the other three into the larger meeting room, which had mercifully become free.

As soon as the door was shut, the chief swallowed a mouthful of biscuit and said, 'Ben and I both believe we've been on the wrong track for the last hour or so. It seems much more likely that Keely was taken by one of the three men whose freedom she threatened, rather than by her sister. And what we now need to do, urgently, is to work out which of them has taken her, and track them down.'

Hanson glanced over at Ben, who nodded in satisfaction.

'Frank Pinder is the only one we've made any ground with,' O'Malley said, his voice concerned. 'If she's been taken by one of the others, we're seriously lacking in leads.'

'So we need to go over what we have,' the chief said. 'Work out what there is. What it might signal.'

'Jared Boula has been off-grid since this morning,' Lightman began. 'We've made no headway with the staff at the children's home, and the manager there seems slack to the point of negligence. Boula has family in France, but his passport hasn't been used since last year. No other particular friends that we've identified.' He paused, checked his iPad, and then continued, 'We've pulled his phone records and there are very few texts and calls that aren't to centre staff or the kids he's worked with. Nothing on his social media to suggest a strong friendship group of any kind. Most photos seem to be with colleagues, who've said they're only casual friends.'

Hanson absorbed this, and then said, 'He still has that photo of his ex-girlfriend on his desktop. Might he still be in touch with her?'

'There's nothing on his phone to suggest that,' Ben said, thoughtfully. 'But it's obviously possible that he has an unregistered mobile. Given the radio silence today, that might fit. No reply from the girlfriend to a call this morning, but I'm happy to try her again. I can head over there if we can't raise her. She's local.'

'If she hasn't heard from him, I'd like you to push her for possible contacts and locations,' the chief said. 'If he's currently relying on someone he trusts, she might fit the bill.' He rose, and went to grab another biscuit from the packet, which he then held out to the rest of them. Hanson took one, despite knowing she'd had too much sugar this morning. 'What about Henry Murray-Watt?' he asked next.

'Depressingly little information,' O'Malley said. 'Neither his bank cards or his phone have been used since last weekend. He's not a frequent caller or texter, but even for him, that's a long time without having sent something. He's on sabbatical at the moment, which means the uni haven't been expecting to see him and the department aren't sure when he was last in.'

'He was potentially at the house yesterday evening,' Hanson chipped in. 'There was some talking in the background when I called Sally, and she said she had to go and help him.

345

But she could well have had the TV on and have been covering for him.'

'And nothing from Sally, either?' Jonah asked. 'No calls? No sightings?'

O'Malley shook his head. 'She's even more of a hermit than he is. From what the neighbours say, she only tends to go out to shop, to her Pilates class or to have a haircut. Occasionally to ride at the stables, but even that's rare now. She doesn't actually seem to use her mobile. Just a couple of calls from Callum, but largely nothing. The mobile seems to be both off but inaccessible, too.'

'And that in itself is odd,' the DCI said. 'Isn't it? We have three individuals all seemingly aware of how to hide their location, or happening by luck not to give it away.'

There was a brief pause, and then O'Malley said, 'Which I guess is more worrying when it comes to the abduction. Because as well as understanding how to avoid being traced, they had to know where she was, didn't they?'

'Yes, they did,' the chief agreed. 'And that means that from here on in, despite the benefits of information sharing, we need to keep everything to ourselves. We tell social services nothing. We keep information off the database. If you have anything to share with the team, send it via email. *Just* to the team.'

Hanson glanced round at O'Malley and Lightman, and then looked back at the chief. 'So . . . you're saying you think it's possible someone on Quick's team is informing whoever took Keely?'

'Yes,' the chief said. 'That's exactly what I'm saying.'

34

Hanson arrived at Henley Road Children's Home at one p.m., though it felt like late evening. It wasn't just how long their day had been. It was also the panicky feeling of time draining away.

They've had Keely for six and a half hours, she thought, and a trickle of cold ran down her spine. Six and a half hours was enough time to cause her a lot of pain, if they wanted. Or to silence her for good.

She shoved that unproductive thought aside and headed for the front door. There was something here for them to find, and she was bloody well going to find it.

Look for the patterns, Jonah thought to himself, as he ran through video after video. Nina had a method in all this, and it should have become obvious by now. In each case, it was two correct versions of a place, and a wrong one. The others should surely be obvious now.

And yet he found himself struggling. Focusing on the tapes where they'd found nothing so far, he couldn't hear those deliberate slips. Nothing was jumping out at him.

Some of it, he thought, might be the effects of Nina's slightly odd language. Her very un-teenage vocabulary, and the way the style of it was enhanced by Keely's cold delivery. It meant that words would jump out at him, and he would find himself pausing the tape, before realising that none of them referred to a place.

And then, in a video where she described, in detail, her

revenge on fifteen-year-old Brandon for his merciless bullying of her sister, he found himself snagging on a repetition.

Shangri-La . . .

She'd used the phrase twice, he realised. Twice in the same segment. And then, right at the end, she'd said *paradise* instead. Two different terms for heaven, with that same pattern of two right, and one wrong. So 'Shangri-La' must mean something.

He found his heart accelerating as he double-checked it, though it seemed, at first, to be mystifying. What was Shangri-La? Might it be some kind of a curry house?

A quick google showed him that there was no restaurant within Southampton with that name. And somehow that didn't feel right, anyway. It needed to be somewhere that meant something to Nina.

He began searching for addresses with that name, instead. And there, within the New Forest, he found one. A farmhouse with an address near Beaulieu.

His heart still hammering, he ran a search for the deeds of the house through the Land Registry. The registry had a set of deeds for the right address and post code, and as Jonah read them, he felt a slow smile spread across his face.

They were owned by a Mr Pierre Boula. A man Jonah would have bet good money was Jared's father.

Hanson had wasted a good fifteen minutes in a fruitless search of Nina's old room at Henley Road. The manager had explained, a little rudely, that there would be nothing in there, because the rooms were scoured when a resident left. There had been two different girls in that room since, he said, and it been empty again since. There was no way Nina had left anything.

But Hanson had looked anyway, thinking of photos hidden beneath floorboards, or memory sticks attached to the frame of the bed. She'd been stubbornly determined to prove him wrong, but that had ultimately faded as she checked every inch of the room. It was clearly empty.

'Where did Nina like to go, here at the home?' she asked. 'What were her favourite haunts? Games room? Dining room . . .?'

The manager, a scruffily dressed man of forty or so, gave a sigh. 'She didn't really hang out much anyway. She liked being in her room. She wasn't very sociable.' He paused for a second. 'Though actually, she did sometimes hide out in the shed. When it was wet, and she wanted to get away to read.'

And despite her misgivings about searching a shed that was half full of run-down sports equipment, Hanson had actually found what she was looking for quickly. A small box taped to the wall behind the door.

She was gratified to open it and find another memory stick inside.

Come on, Nina, she thought. *Solve this for us.*

Jonah went to find Lightman, the one team member still within CID. With Jared Boula's house now pinned down, they had a firm lead for the first time.

Ben was just finishing up on a call and waved to him as he approached.

'Quick's team has found Sally Murray-Watt's car,' he said, the moment he'd put the phone down. 'It was hidden in the allotments right next to the house. It looks like Henry might not have gone far.'

Jonah thought of the cellar that had never been found. He gave a sigh. 'If he went anywhere at all. What better place to hide than somewhere nobody believes exists? Take a squad car over there. O'Malley's already en route to Jared Boula's.'

35

I'm hoping this video won't be needed. It's just insurance, really. In case our intricately laid plans go wrong. There are none of the usual clues for you to follow, but there are a few things you really need to know.

I decided to do this one myself. After the particular cruelty of making Ninny – Keely – describe the moment I betrayed her with Callum, I thought it was probably time to face the camera.

It is a source of immense wonder to me that she ever forgave me for that betrayal. Though it shouldn't surprise me. I've always known that she is a profoundly better and kinder person than I am.

Somehow, we drew back together, the three of us, in our new formation. The one driving force became revenge, though I suppose it was also about justice. Perhaps the two of them are interchangeable, sometimes.

I could see how much my relationship with Callum hurt Keely. It was clear from the paleness of her face, and the occasional glimmer in her eyes. It made me choose to sit apart from Callum whenever we were together, when at every other time I wanted desperately to be wrapped round him.

A good person would have called it all off to spare her. But as you'll know by now, I didn't. I pursued what I wanted, as helplessly and as single-mindedly as a fired bullet. I imagined myself, sometimes, tearing straight through everyone I came into contact with. Hot, and metallic, and terrible. And it made me feel a sick sense of triumph. As if I'd realised an ambition to become the worst possible version of myself.

We finally moved into a new children's home during this process, and it was the first change that had genuinely made our lives better. Cedar Avenue was a world away from the Henley Road home. The way the staff dealt with us, and the way they squashed anything that looked like bullying, gave us both freedom and a feeling of value.

But all of that was only a backdrop to what we'd set out to do. What I'd persuaded the other two to do. I knew what we needed. Film footage. Documents. Things that nobody could argue with. Those things, and an opportunity to destroy each and every one of them.

'Frank Pinder,' Callum told us, a few weeks after we first met, 'is seeing one of the girls on the football team. We don't need to do any more than send the police round while he's with her.'

'But we should try to get documents anyway,' I told him. 'Letters. Screenshots of text messages.'

'How are we going to do that?'

'I'll make friends with her,' I said. 'Pretend to be someone else, online. He targets the lonely ones. The ones who are desperate for some love. She'll be easy enough to bring round if I set up a good enough fake profile.'

'All right. I believe you,' Callum said.

It went exactly as I'd planned, the lonely Sarah Mallard so desperate to talk about her secret romance that she'd confided in a faceless stranger. She trusted me enough to send screenshots of messages, and with encouragement, even of their most sexual ones.

'Jared worries me,' I said, a few days later. 'All that shit he told his ex-girlfriend . . . As much as I hate to admit it,

I think we need to be careful. If he realises we're following him, I think he could get genuinely violent.'

'I've been thinking about that,' Keely said, slowly. 'If Jared's been looking at things online, we can use it against him without having to go near him.' She looked up at me. 'You need to hack him.'

And of course she was right. I think I often give Keely less credit than she deserves, and this was one of the times she saw everything clearly. I could easily learn how to hack him. I'd already successfully dug out addresses, phone numbers, schedules and a few private communications. I'd enjoyed it, too, the power I had over people through their devices. The illicit pleasure in seeing what I shouldn't have.

'You should both learn to ride a bike, too,' Callum said. 'I've been thinking it over. There will be times when one of you needs to get around, quickly and easily. You can learn on my Yamaha while I put together a second bike from parts. Now I have the flat, I've got somewhere I can keep it.'

'Are you really going to let us borrow the Yamaha?' I asked him. 'What if I break it?'

'Then you'll have to have some lessons in repairing it, too,' he said, with a grin.

It was strange how easy both of these things turned out to be. I'd been privately worried that I might find the motorbike scary, but it was actually liberating to tear across rural tracks and paths at high speed. I would finish each lesson breathless and desperate for the next.

As for hacking Jared Boula, you'd have thought that a man with a hard drive full of kiddie porn would be more careful about clicking on links sent in emails. But he opened and executed the very first piece of Malware I sent, and it was a doozy. A gorgeous little piece of trickery that gave me full control of his computer. It even deleted its own icon from the desktop before it could be spotted.

I had to be careful, of course. I had to make sure I left a clear trail of what I had and hadn't done, so nobody could accuse me of having planted anything. I filmed myself doing most of it and made sure I showed the dates each file had been created. Many of those awful images were, luckily, downloaded to his machine years before we'd even met him.

So that was Jared Boula, delivered to us by his own wrongdoings, and Frank Pinder being gradually drawn in. My only misgivings were over Sarah Mallard. I had to sit and watch as she was tangled further and further in Frank's web. But I knew it had to be this way. That he needed stopping for good.

And then, of course, there was Henry Murray-Watt.

He and Sally had immediately taken the bait of adopting me. I could see that it would be the ultimate win for them. They wanted to take back control. And I began to realise that that they genuinely saw themselves as in the right. The messages I had from them were full of imagery of me returning to the fold. Of how they could help me to find my way again, having become lost. Because they knew I was a good girl, really.

It was nauseating.

The trouble we had with Henry, however, was one of proof. We'd already tried and failed to show what he'd done, and we were no longer in a position to gather actual evidence of abuse. He had left off doing anything directly to Callum, and there was frustratingly little chance of us proving what he'd done in the past.

We spent a lot of time trailing one or other of them, trying to find something. Some fragment of intelligence that could prove what he was, and what he'd made Sally become. But by the time we'd finished assembling a body of evidence against the other two men, we still had nothing substantial on Henry. Only a pointer as to why he'd got away with so much of it – an illuminating thing in itself – but nothing that proved his guilt.

It was into the midst of our most intense time of frustration that my chance meeting with DC Juliette Hanson happened. An event that let me see, in a flash, not only how to ensure that we were taken seriously, but also what we needed to do to bring Henry down along with the others.

I felt molten with excitement as I went to tell Callum and my sister. I laid it all out before them and let them come to see that I was right.

'But can we be sure that one of them will give in?' Ninny asked.

'We'll have days to work on them,' I said. 'And if neither of them has cracked by the time I go to the police, then we'll still have time. And you'll have the incentive that I'm off explaining everything, and that they won't get away with it, which will probably be persuasive.'

'We can break them,' Callum said, with iron in his voice. 'They've never been subjected to what they dished out to us. They'll crack.'

My sister nodded, very slowly, and then said, 'I don't think it can be you who goes to the police. Nobody will believe that you're capable of hurting me. It'll have to be me, and you'll just have to tell me what to say.'

36

'Ben,' Hanson said, pulling her earphones out once again. 'I don't think Henry Murray-Watt is hiding out at his house. I think Nina has been keeping him prisoner there.'

She saw Lightman pause in the act of picking up his car keys. He was about to leave for the Murray-Watts' home, alongside a squad car full of constables.

'The backup video she left,' Hanson explained. 'She pretty much says it. That they needed to find a way of making them confess. And locking them both in the cellar, just like they were locked away, sounds pretty effective to me. I don't think it was Sally Murray-Watt I spoke to at all last night. I think it was Nina.'

Ben opened his mouth to reply, but then looked past her, and she turned to see the chief striding towards them.

'We've got a location on Frank Pinder,' he said. 'Let's go before he moves.'

The door swung open again, and Keely could feel her heart rate picking up.

You need to think your way out of this, she told herself, pushing both the wish and the fear away. *Play your way out.*

She owed it to Nina to do this. She'd been so stupid, getting into that car with him. The moment she'd taken a proper look at the dummy, she'd realised that it wasn't her sister.

And then she'd been even more stupid, when he'd started to ask her questions. She'd felt fear rise up in her, and in her panic, she'd made it painfully obvious that Nina was the one he wanted.

But it's going to be OK, she thought. *You can trick him into thinking she's somewhere else. He won't find her, but the detectives will. They'll get there.*

'Now you've had time for a little think,' Jared said, 'it's time to tell us where your sister is. And what she's done with my computer.'

It was only by an effort of will that she kept her smile in place. 'I don't . . . I don't know where she is but . . .' she said, her mind working furiously. Fiercely. Looking for the one way she could turn all this around. 'I know she took some things to our old house. It might be there. In the cottage on Furzley Lane.'

Jared's smile turned sickly, and she couldn't help flinching as he put a hand on her knee. 'See,' he said, 'if I were Nina, I'd have hung on to that computer. If you're going to try and blackmail someone, you keep your evidence close.'

Keely shook her head. 'She was never going to blackmail you. The computer was just a distraction, in case you tried to stop us. It'll be sitting untouched in a box somewhere.' She gave a little sigh, reminding herself that she could do this. That she'd put on a performance for the police, for hour after hour. She could do this.

She could see the beginnings of belief on Jared's face. He wanted to believe her, she knew. To think that he was safe.

'She doesn't actually want to go after you,' Keely went on. 'You never touched her. Never hurt her. And I never told her about . . . what happened. I was confused over it, that's all. This – all of this – is all about our foster parents. She wants them put away, and I'd like to see it too. That's why we called the police on Frank Pinder, and why

356

Nina's – why we're going to get the Murray-Watts locked up as well.'

She could feel her heart thumping in her chest. She had slipped up, but she hoped not enough for him to realise. He needed to latch on to the old house. That was all he needed to do.

But he was smiling at her. 'So Nina's at Henry's house, then?' he asked.

And Keely felt her heart drop, beyond her stomach, right down to somewhere in her feet.

Nina glanced over at Callum, seeing the same anxiety in him that she felt. The same desperate urge to be moving, instead of waiting. Endlessly waiting.

She could see a little dried blood in his hair, still, from where Henry had briefly fought back. He'd knocked Callum violently into a kitchen shelf when they'd first burst in on the two of them having dinner, and the resulting wound had bled profusely. It had got to the point where Nina had told Callum to go to the hospital.

Henry, who by then had been subdued by the threat of the gun out of his own desk drawer, had suddenly said, tetchily, 'Oh, don't be silly. Head wounds always bleed a lot. It'll stop with a little cold water on it.' As Nina had turned to stare at him, in his uncomfortable, bound position on a chair, he'd added, 'You shouldn't have attacked us like that. You have only yourselves to blame.'

She'd wondered, not for the first time, if Henry was just not quite right. Anyone who could play the angry, self-righteous father while faced with a gun was surely more than sadistic. And Callum going to the hospital would only have worked in his favour.

But Nina hadn't dwelt much further on Henry's mental

state. She had turned her attention to Sally, certain that converting her was the answer to everything. It hadn't gone that well so far.

After Sally had given up on her initial, pitiful cries for help, she and Callum had been grimly certain that their former foster mother would choose her own safety over her husband's freedom. It had turned out that this had been to underestimate a woman capable of starving herself to please him. Capable of moulding her entire life around his unbalanced and erratic pronouncements. His warped sense of right and wrong.

The question Nina most wanted to ask Sally was whether she knew, deep down, that everything they'd done was wrong. Nina suspected that she did. It had been there in her pained looks when she'd locked them down here, and in her teary-eyed hugs once they'd been allowed back upstairs. It was that part of Sally that Nina wished she could appeal to, somehow.

And she'd tried. My god, but she'd tried. Nina had approached her persuasions with every power of manipulation she knew. She'd called into question how much Henry loved her. Talked about what would happen to Sally in jail. Reminisced about the times when Sally had treated her well.

But there had been nothing. Not a flicker. Not a moment of doubt. All she had said, whenever she hadn't been crying for help, was that Nina was a wicked, warped, twisted child. Which Nina had smiled at.

'Yes,' she'd said to Sally. 'I know. But you helped make me that way.'

Sally hadn't replied.

Their former foster mother was staring at the floor now. At a spot not far from where she'd made Nina, Keely and Callum sleep for nights at a time.

Nina sighed. She'd worked hard to give the impression

that there was no urgency to any of this. That there was no limit to how long she and Callum were willing to hold them down here.

But, in truth, urgency was coursing through her. Callum had returned half an hour ago to say that there was nothing on the news about a hostage being rescued, and no other sign that Keely had been found.

Letting herself think about what they might be doing to her sister made Nina nauseous. Furious. Terrified.

If the police couldn't find Keely, then Nina needed to go and tell them more. Give them more. Make it easier, even though she'd thought it *would* be easy. They had so much evidence now. And they had all that technology, and manpower, and experience.

But if she needed to go and help them, then she and Callum were out of time. They still didn't have the confession that they needed. The camera that had been running for hours, streaming all of this to Callum's laptop via the Wi-Fi they had just managed to pick up down here, had caught nothing that would stand up in court.

Nina looked over at Callum, suddenly decided. 'Go to the police station. Tell them everything we know about Jared and Frank. Help them find her.' She rose and picked up the scissors they had brought down from the kitchen. 'I'm going to take Sally upstairs.'

Shangri-La was not well named. The idea of the place as any kind of paradise was laughable.

It was, in fact, one of the few rural properties O'Malley had seen in the New Forest that was genuinely ugly. A run-down red-brick farmhouse with small windows sat in a yard that was part mud, part riotous growth of weeds. It was clear that the place had not been a working farm in some time, and that the lands around it had been sold off to people who knew how to manage them. But the largest barn to the rear looked as though it had been done up a little more recently. There was also a very shiny new padlock on it.

The armed response team made quick work of the farmhouse, and then moved smoothly on to the outbuildings. O'Malley waited with as much patience as he could muster outside the larger barn until one of the team gave a call from inside. He didn't need Quick's nod to tell him it was time to go in.

It was dim inside, and it took him a few seconds to be certain that the main part of the barn was essentially empty. It had fairly modern wooden flooring, and there were easels and art equipment stored along the walls. But no people, and nowhere for anyone to hide.

He felt a drop of disappointment, before he realised that there was a partition wall at the far end, and in the middle of it, a door.

He followed the method of entry team through into a much smaller space. It had two beds in it, each covered with a single duvet and a pillow. They were both empty.

But there was a figure sitting on the floor, against the wall. A hunched-up red-haired girl.

They'd used cable ties to attach her to a metal-coated electrical duct, he saw, and he felt a rush of anxiety as he realised that she wasn't moving. There was no lift of the head. No response. And there was a large bruise spread across her cheekbone and much of her jaw.

He moved rapidly over to her while one of the armed response team cut the cable ties.

'We have a pulse,' one of the others said. 'She's breathing fine. Just unresponsive.'

O'Malley leaned down. 'Keely, it's DS O'Malley. Domnall O'Malley. Can you hear me?'

But there was no response at all.

Nina let Sally go up the cellar steps ahead of her. Her former foster mother moved slowly. Stiffly. The effects of days spent tied to a chair were clear.

And strangely, Nina found herself feeling something for her. An unusual rush of empathy that caught her off guard.

It wasn't justice, she thought, to submit Sally to what they had suffered. Justice was all about Henry being locked away, and Sally being helped to free herself of his influence.

She was moving up to offer Sally help when her former foster mother kicked back, hard and viciously. Her foot caught Nina in the groin, and she had no chance to so much as grab for the handrail. She fell backwards, missing the stairs completely and landing so hard on the cellar floor that she couldn't seem to breathe afterwards.

She heard Sally's voice through the dizzying pain. Her refined, softly-spoken foster mother was shouting, 'You can rot down there, you little bitch!' And then the door to the cellar slammed.

Jonah picked up the call from O'Malley after only half a ring.

'We've got her, and she's alive,' O'Malley said, briefly. 'But she's unconscious. He's used something to knock her out. We've got an ambulance on the way, but she can't tell us anything right now. There's no sign of Jared Boula.'

Jonah felt his heart kick, painfully. 'OK,' he said. 'We're heading to the Murray-Watt house now, which is where we think Nina is.'

It should have occurred to him earlier, he realised. That

at some point, Keely would admit that none of it had been her idea. Which would drive Jared towards Nina.

And it was Jared who worried him now. Not Frank Pinder or Henry Murray-Watt. It was the one who hadn't just seduced young girls but collected image after image of their pain and humiliation.

'We need to go to the Murray-Watts' house,' he said, turning the flashing blues on. 'Frank Pinder can wait.'

Nina felt unable to move. Unable to do anything except bend herself double with the pain radiating up from her backside and her right arm.

It's just pain, she thought, trying to think her way back to control. *You're not damaged. You'll be able to get out of here.*

Sally had locked the door. She'd heard her do it. But Nina had the laptop and an internet connection. She could call for help, even if they had to wait for a while.

She pushed herself up into a sitting position, using her left arm. As she rocked forwards, the pain increased in a surge, and she was unable to keep from giving a small whimper.

'It's probably your coccyx,' Henry said, from his seat across the room. Nina found herself looking at him, dazed, as he nodded at her in a matter-of-fact way. 'It might be a bruise or a fracture. It's very sensitive, thanks to all the nerve endings, and can be quite painful as it heals, too.'

'Right,' Nina said, easing her legs underneath herself, and then standing very slowly. It was agonising, but it felt a little better once she was upright.

'I think you may have angered Sally,' Henry went on.

Nina actually laughed. 'Do you think so?'

'I've sometimes experienced it,' Henry said. 'When she felt I wasn't disciplining the three of you as I should have been, or when she thought I was cheating on her.'

Half distracted by the pain, she found herself only understanding what he was saying slowly.

'She . . . do you really expect me to believe that she was the one asking for more discipline?' And she laughed again, even while she felt shaky. Unsteady.

'Oh, I thought you understood that,' Henry said, his face creased in a frown. 'I don't know anything about parenting. I was brought up alone by parents who didn't really want the difficulties, and sent me to boarding school. Sally was quite different. She had lots of siblings, and she brought the younger ones up. She understood how to make sure you all became good, successful people.' He nodded. 'We agreed right at the start that she would be in charge of all the parenting decisions. Obviously, I was there to be a strong father figure when she needed it. And to keep her in line, as she wanted.' He sighed. 'Though it was you three who needed most of the discipline.'

Nina hadn't thought that anything Henry said could shock her. She had gone into this expecting anger, denials of wrong-doing, or the total lack of engagement with them that they'd experienced so far.

What she hadn't expected was to have her faith in everything she knew about the two of them shattered.

'But you beat us,' she said, hoarsely. 'You must have taken pleasure in that.'

'I didn't beat you,' Henry said. 'We blindfolded you so you wouldn't know it was her, but Sally was adamant she should be the one to do it.'

Nina wanted to argue. She wanted to say that she *knew* it had been him.

But she had nothing to argue with. She'd never seen Henry beat her, or either of the others.

And she remembered, now, the occasional sounds of

satisfaction that had come from the person doing the beating. Slightly high-pitched, and, at times, horrifyingly sensual.

Sally was adamant she should be the one to do it . . .

She raised her head to Henry, with a rush of fierce anger. 'It doesn't even matter if she did it. You let her. You were part of it, even though you must have seen that it was awful for us. We begged and pleaded with you not to do it.'

'I wasn't going to listen to histrionics,' he said, sternly. 'I lived through just the same at boarding school. They weren't allowed to beat us, but they asked the older boys to discipline us. And so they should have done. It made us all strong.'

Nina shook her head, slowly. 'But did it make you happy, Henry?' she asked. 'Are you honestly happy with who you are now?'

And for the first time, she saw Henry's expression become pained.

Hanson hadn't left the station. There was too much to do. Too much that felt pressingly urgent.

It all came down to the cellar. They needed to find it, in order to find Nina. Because, she thought, if Keely had told Jared Boula where to find her sister, then he would head straight down there.

She was positive that Nina would have left them a clue to that cellar. She and Keely had made the videos in the Murray-Watts' house, she was sure of it. They must have trapped Sally and Henry and then filmed the videos upstairs. That was why their neighbour had seen one of them there.

Please, she thought, as she clicked on the first video again. *Please tell us where to find you.*

There were footsteps, above. Distant sounds of movement that travelled through the cellar ceiling. They must be close,

Nina thought, to be so audible. Sally and Henry's secretly constructed basement was quite impressively well insulated against noise. Though if anyone really yelled down here, they might be faintly audible.

Nina glanced towards Henry, though he'd shown no inclination to call for help so far.

She listened, wondering for a moment whether it was Callum. Whether he'd returned for some reason.

Or Sally, she thought. *It could be Sally . . .*

And it occurred to her, then, that Sally might have gone after Callum. And although he was much stronger than Sally was, his adoptive mother must be a lot cleverer than any of them had given her credit for. And a lot more damaged.

There was a sudden buzz against her leg, a sensation that startled her so much that she nearly dropped the gun. But it was just her phone in her pocket. The burner phone she used to communicate with Callum and Keely and which would occasionally get enough signal to receive a message.

She pulled it out, and saw, with a squeeze of her heart, that it was from Keely.

The police have found her, she thought. *She's safe.*

But as she opened the message, she felt the rush of relief twist into horror.

> I've got your sister's phone. I'm in the house,
> and you need to come out, Nina. I've run out of patience.

Nina put the phone back in the pocket of her skirt, telling herself that they were safe down here. That Jared couldn't find her. But fear lanced through her anyway.

And she was certain that Jared was the one up there. The one who'd taken her sister. She'd known, the moment Callum told her about the kidnap, that it had been Jared.

The knowledge had almost undone her. She had run to

the hall and grabbed Sally's car keys. There had been no time to walk to where the Yamaha was concealed in the allotment. She'd jumped up behind the wheel of the four-by-four, grimly determined to drive the stupid great machine somehow.

And of course it had got her nowhere. By the time she'd made it to the motorway, Jared had been long gone. Nina had endured a terrifying few minutes attempting to drive at seventy miles per hour before exiting back onto an A road and limping back to the allotments. She'd swapped the car for the bike, vowing not to be caught without transport again.

The bike wasn't going to do her any good now, though. It was in the garage, at the far end of the house, while she was locked down here, and Jared was up there, prowling. But it was clear that he didn't know where she was. Which meant they were safe for now. And maybe, even, that there would be time for the police to find them.

Unless he threatens to hurt Keely, she thought.

But then she breathed in a long, shaking breath. Jared didn't have Keely with him. He'd just said he had the phone, not her sister. Which meant she must be all right. He would have told her if he'd harmed her. He would have delighted in it.

The phone buzzed again in her hand, as a second message appeared.

If you won't come out, I'll fucking smoke you out.

37

They were five minutes away from the house, and Jonah was repeating a strange little pleading mantra to himself. *Just get there in time. You have to be in time. Get there in time.*

They had turned on to the long, gently bending road that led into Godshill, and between scattered trees, the Murray-Watt house swung into and out of view.

'Sir,' Lightman said.

It took him a few moments to realise what Ben was pointing at. As they came round another bend, the view opened out, and he saw smoke. A dirty, black pillar of it, rising into the air.

There was no question that it was coming from Sally and Henry's house.

It hadn't taken long for the smell of burning to reach the cellar. Jared must have made good on his promise pretty quickly.

He's assuming I have all the evidence in here with me, she thought grimly. *So if I don't come out, it'll all be destroyed anyway.*

She moved over to the laptop, still wincing from the pain in her backside. The screen briefly showed her own face in close-up, as well as Henry's form in the background. The webcam was still recording. They had what she'd come for now, in Henry's bemused confession.

'Who is that up there?' Henry asked. 'Have they set fire to my house?'

'It's Keely's former keyworker, a man called Jared Boula, and I'm afraid he has,' Nina told him.

'Why would he want to endanger you?' Henry asked, his expression genuinely puzzled. He seemed almost unconcerned about the danger itself, as if understanding Jared's motivation mattered more to him.

'I suppose for the same reason you and your wife locked us in a cellar, starved us of food and beat us,' she replied. 'Because some people are just messed up.'

A white van was parked across Sally Murray-Watt's perfect rose garden. The side door was open, and the vehicle was empty.

Jonah launched himself out of the Mondeo and began to run for the front door of the house.

'Get round to the garden,' he called to Lightman. 'And call for a fire engine.'

'Chief?' Lightman said. 'You aren't going in there, are you?'

But Jonah was already moving towards the house.

Hanson felt slack with relief, and for some reason, overwhelmingly inclined to laugh.

She pulled up the photographs that had been taken of Henry Murray-Watt's study that morning, flicking through until she could see the full-length mirror on the wall.

You have to look in the mirror . . .

Keely had done exactly as she'd said and told them where to find her sister. They'd only had to listen.

Jonah quickly began to regret stepping into the building. There was impossible heat coming at him, both from the left-hand end and from above. Part of the house must be completely engulfed, and it was clear that the fire was spreading.

The smoke in the hall was so thick that he could only see

by ducking down to floor level, and it felt as though it was clawing at his throat as he breathed in. He had the vaguest grasp of the geography of this place from what Keely had said and wasn't sure how to get to the study. Assuming that it hadn't already been overwhelmed by flames.

He staggered through a doorway and found comparative peace. The kitchen, which was as yet miraculously untouched and had only a cloud of smoke up at ceiling level. There was a cloth folded up next to the sink, and he ran it under the tap and then put it over his nose and mouth.

As he tried to think what to do, he heard a sound, from somewhere further into the house. It had come from along the hall. But that hallway was all but impossible to traverse.

He looked over at the back door. He remembered Keely talking about French windows in the living room. He might be able to make his way round the worst of it. And, regardless of anything, the fresh air might give him a clear enough head to actually think.

He made it to the door, then wasted several seconds trying to work out how it unlocked, before realising that it was unlocked already and just needed a firmer shove of the handle. Suddenly he was outside, in a garden that seemed absurdly quiet and still.

'Can we unlock the door from down here?' Nina called to Henry.

She was standing at the top of the stairs. It had been a painful climb, but she was relieved to discover that she could still make it. Her wrist, too, seemed to be unbroken. It hurt like hell, but she could still just about use it.

She didn't know why she was asking Henry about getting out. As a younger girl, trapped down here, she'd spent hours running her hands over the inside of the cellar door. She'd never found a lock, or a catch, or anything but a slight indentation around the frame.

'No,' Henry said. 'Only from up there, I'm afraid.'

There was a sudden shout from outside. One loud enough to make it through the door. 'You're going to fucking burn, Nina, and I'm going to enjoy watching it.'

She felt a shiver run the length of her spine. Even if they could get out, Jared was there. Waiting.

There was smoke drifting into the cellar already. Despite the well-sealed door, it was still making its way through.

A heavy, awful thought hit her then. That she would die in here, alongside Henry, and that it would be better in some ways if she did.

There's nothing left in here that isn't rotten, she thought.

She'd imagined that bringing the three men to justice might make up for every awful thing she'd done. For the way she'd stamped down on her sister's happiness to save herself. For the hurt she'd caused the people she'd manipulated. For how her revenge on Brandon had rebounded on Keely. And maybe, even, for taking Callum from her. Even for that.

But everything she'd worked towards had gone wrong. Jared was here, and very much free. Frank had escaped the police. And Henry . . . Henry hadn't even been the force behind those years of unhappiness. She'd had the real culprit right here, and she'd let her go.

And she knew why it had all gone this way. She knew it was because she didn't deserve anything better. She'd gone into this for revenge, not justice. Out of obsession instead of care for anyone else. She was too much shadow, and she'd poisoned the others with it, too.

She imagined just going to sleep down here, made heavy and stupid by smoke. And she thought about what would happen to Keely. To Callum.

They'd be together, she thought. *Without me to mess it up.*

'We need to get out,' Henry said, matter-of-factly. It was somehow enraging that he was interested in living when she was letting go of her life.

'I don't know if I deserve to get out,' she said, leaning her head against the door.

There was a surprised noise from Henry. 'Of course you do. Everyone deserves to live. And you've done nothing unforgiveable.'

'I stole Callum from my sister,' she told him, twisting her head so she could see him down on the basement floor. He looked so much less frightening now, she thought. Without Sally there to guide him, and with his height neutralised by the angle, he looked almost human.

Henry gave a short laugh. 'I've been abandoned by many young women I thought I loved, and I got over it. I didn't find my wife until I was forty, and now that twelve years have passed, I find I can look back on our relationship and see that it wasn't right. She didn't really care for me, I think. It's terribly sad, but I'll survive again. And your sister will move on in a short while.'

There was something so ridiculous about relationship advice from Henry Murray-Watt, the man she'd come to force a confession out of, that Nina found herself laughing. And somehow it broke the fatalistic clouds that had been hanging over her.

'You might be right,' she said.

She turned, and climbed down the stairs as carefully as she could, leaning on the handrail with her still-functioning right arm, and twisting to avoid too much movement around her coccyx. She lifted the scissors and approached Henry.

'You're going to have to try kicking the door down,' she

said, firmly. 'I'll be ready with the gun, because I think he's waiting out there for us.'

Jonah was almost at the window of the study when a hand and a foot appeared on the edge of the frame. He'd heard savage yelling and was half braced for some kind of attack.

He skidded to a stop on the paving and waited just long enough for Jared Boula to make it halfway out of the window, and then he stepped forwards, and hauled him out and downwards onto the grass.

The move gave him a momentary but strong advantage. Boula landed heavily on his outstretched arm, which collapsed on him in what looked like a painful twist.

Boula made no move to fight. He rolled over onto his back and started to laugh.

'I'm arresting you for the kidnap of Keely Lennox,' Jonah said. 'You do not have to say anything, but it may harm your defence if you do not mention when questioned something which you later rely on in court. Anything you do say may be given in evidence.' And then, getting properly to his feet, he said, 'Tell us where Nina is.'

But Jared Boula just shrugged, the laughter still in his voice.

'I have no fucking idea.'

Hanson heard the call end in her ear, and with a feeling of intense frustration, rang Ben again instead. She'd tried each of them three times already and got nothing. Was he in some kind of difficulty? Or had he already found her?

She could easily imagine at least three different scenarios, and in two of those Nina was in serious trouble. And in at least one of them, so were the chief and Ben.

To her huge relief, Ben answered this time, four rings in.

'Juliette,' he said, a little breathlessly.

'It's the mirror,' Hanson said. 'The door to the cellar. It's the mirror.'

Henry had made his stiff way up the stairs and was examining the door and its surroundings. She could see him thinking of this as a physics problem, working out where to stand to get the best leverage.

Nina was suddenly desperate to live. Desperate to get past everything that she'd been and become something else. She hoped, fervently, that he would find some kind of solution.

He shifted, wrapping an arm round the bannister. He was bracing himself to kick the door when they heard a muffled call from the other side.

'Nina! This is DCI Jonah Sheens. Can you tell me how to open this door, please?'

Jonah was alongside Lightman as the door opened. A slightly pale but otherwise healthy-looking Henry Murray-Watt stepped out into the study. Jonah decided to save arresting him until he was out of the burning building. He nodded to Lightman to escort him out.

He could see Nina just within the doorway, her flaming hair and pale skin brilliant in the dimness. Her gaze settled on him for a moment, and he smiled, and said, 'I'm glad to meet you at last, Nina.'

Nina held her hand out to him, and he felt a wash of euphoric relief flood through him. But as he helped her to climb slightly stiffly out of the door, she said, 'Sally made a run for it. I think I know where she's gone. Can you help me?'

38

'We found out about it by following her,' Nina told him during the slightly hobbling walk out into the old allotments. 'I thought she must have realised, deep down, that Henry was an abuser, and decided to make herself a place to run to if she had to get out. I saw it as a sign that she was redeemable, which is a bit embarrassing now I think about it.' Nina paused for a moment to cough, and Jonah could hear the same dry rasp to her airways he could feel in his own. They'd both inhaled more smoke than was good for them.

We should be on our way to the hospital, he thought, and a glance at Lightman just behind him was enough to show that his sergeant thought so too. But Jonah couldn't help feeling the same urge to pin Sally down that was clearly driving Nina. They needed to find her before it was too late.

Sally's bolthole turned out to be a tiny little shack at the far end of the allotments. It was overshadowed by the encroaching forest and was all but invisible until they were right on top of it. It wasn't in perfect condition, but the evergreen clematis growing over it looked well tended.

They hadn't even come to a stop before the front door swung open. Sally, her expression so much colder and more calculating than Jonah had expected, looked between him and the four other officers, and then, without hesitation, she ran.

It was a stupid decision, he thought, as he broke straight into a run in turn. She was one woman, against four officers, and they had backup a few hundred yards away back at the house.

To do Sally credit, she gave them a decent run for their money. She was fitter than Jonah had anticipated, and her very light frame made her whippet-fast. But with four of them on her heels, she eventually ran out of places to go. It was Ben who made the last move, circling round as she tried to dodge right, and grabbing her in a bear hug.

Jonah arrested her and then let two of the constables take her back to the shed. Nina was waiting there with the remaining officer, her eyes wide with anticipation.

'Thank you,' she said to Jonah.

And somehow, the moment was absolutely complete, in spite of Sally saying, 'I don't know why you're looking so smug. We aren't done, Nina.'

But, in fact, Sally had looked well and truly done only a few minutes later. Escorted back to the house and the waiting squad cars, she had stared in naked horror at the sight of her beautiful home on fire. Her expression confirmed to Jonah why she'd chosen a hideaway that was very close to their home. She hadn't been ready to give up her apparently perfect life. Though today, she was just in time to see much of it collapse in on itself in a sudden tumbling rush.

Callum Taylor missed the collapse by moments. Nina must, Jonah thought, have messaged him. He roared up outside, left the Suzuki parked up next to the road and all but ran over to where Nina was being looked over by an ambulance crew. He looked, Jonah thought, almost angry.

Nina gazed at him with a sardonic smile not unlike Keely's. 'It was Sally, not Henry. How did I miss that it was all coming from her?'

'Guess you're just not as smart as you think,' Callum said, and then, ignoring the attending paramedic, he grabbed her up into a fierce hug.

'Guess not,' Nina replied, and Jonah turned away at that point, for fear of ending up as emotional as she was.

They found Frank Pinder in an attractive little farm cottage close to Brockenhurst. It looked as though his friend the treasurer had stumped up for a nice little holiday rental. This, Jonah thought, was doing fugitive-from-justice in style.

Frank made a brief effort to resist arrest as Jonah and Lightman arrived with a squad car in tow, and then seemed to understand that he was caught at last. He said nothing to them on the drive to the station, and whenever Jonah looked in the rear-view mirror, it was to see him staring out at the scenery around him with bitter tears glittering in his eyes.

The first round of interviews began at five, with Henry Murray-Watt's extraordinary, open confession of everything he and his wife had done. He seemed to see nothing wrong in most of it, though he did admit that he should have questioned his wife further over some of her decisions.

O'Malley and the DCI had been the principal beneficiaries of it all, though Hanson had stationed herself in the viewing room for much of it.

O'Malley had shaken his head at the chief in disbelief once they'd stepped outside.

'If all policing was that easy,' he said, 'even I'd have made DCI by now.'

Sally Murray-Watt, however, had refused to comment at all. Hanson had been expecting her to turn the charm on. To convince and manipulate. But she seemed to have lost some of her certainty along the way. Hanson wasn't sure whether it had been Henry's about-turn that had done it, or the sight of her beautiful, perfectly tended house collapsing in on itself. But the fight had gone out of her, leaving her only with silence, for now.

Next door to Sally Murray-Watt sat Jared Boula, who had begun by telling them they'd got everything wrong.

'All this is just some sick fabrication by those two girls,' he said. 'They're fantasists. And they've nearly got a lot of innocent people in trouble already.'

'It seems that what they actually did was to try and get guilty people in trouble,' Jonah replied. 'Would you like to explain to us the images on your hard drive? Over thirty-five thousand pictures of child pornography and abuse, saved over a period of years.'

There was total silence, and then Boula said, without the smile, 'They put that on there. They're framing me.'

'It's interesting that that material predates you meeting them,' Jonah said, 'and also ties in with what you told your ex-girlfriend in April of this year.'

There was another silence, and Jonah let Hanson take over.

'On the evening of April twelfth, after the two of you had tried to rekindle your relationship, she confronted you because she'd found videos made on your phone. Videos of young girls taken without their consent, and in which you'd made a point of intimidating or harassing them. You told her that it wasn't your fault you were this way. That your father had been forcing you to do this stuff since you were a teenager.' Hanson looked up from her notes, and asked, 'What else did he force you to do, Jared? What was that room in the barn for?'

Like all the other pieces of evidence pointing towards their suspects' guilt, the recording of a conversation with Jared's girlfriend had been provided by Nina Lennox. They'd had to ask for instructions for how to find the last items, and although Nina had backups, they'd still gone to gather them all up: from the antiques shop in Lyndhurst. From close to the sports track marked out on the village rec. From the village pub just up the road from the Murray-Watts' house, and from under a bench in Queen's Park. The only one they'd had to leave, for now, was what Callum had hidden in Henry Murray-Watt's garage. But Jonah had hopes of picking it up once the fire crew was done. The single-storey garage hadn't caught as well as the rest of the house.

Amongst these additional pieces of evidence had been footage of Nina first finding the files on Jared's computer. There were also photographs of bragging messages he'd sent to some of the boys in the children's home, and finally a recording of the conversation with his ex-girlfriend.

Off the back of that tape, Jonah had been able to approach Jared's ex-girlfriend and ask her to provide them with information.

Jonah watched carefully as Boula's hands began to shake. It didn't surprise him when he began to sob.

'I'm sorry,' he said. 'I'm sorry. It was my – my dad. He made me the way I am.'

He'd gone on to detail the abuse he'd suffered. The constant poison Pierre Boula had dripped at his son for being pathetic. Unmanly. How he'd explained that women needed to be kept in their place. He had little by little pushed him to abuse them for himself.

His solicitor had remained silent through most of this, and despite everything Boula had done, Jonah couldn't help feeling for him. To hear that the father had passed on his own damage to his son couldn't help but chime somewhere within him. Jonah, the son of an abusive, controlling narcissist, who had learned to imitate those terrible interrogations when he needed to.

But he would hold Jared Boula accountable nonetheless, as he tried to hold himself.

Frank Pinder's case had been handed to DCI Suresh Acharya's team, though there was likely to be a great deal of collaboration between them. Acharya was set on reinvestigating Keely and Nina Lennox's allegations and securing a conviction there, too, if possible.

'So that's us done, then, on preliminary interviews,' Hanson said, once they were finished with Jared Boula. 'Now just on to the endless job of evidence.'

'Actually,' Jonah told her, 'there's one more interview to go.'

Their conversation with Mark Slatterworth became one of Hanson's all-time favourites, in a long list of immensely satisfying interviews. Whatever his other skills, there really was nobody to match the chief when it came to getting what he wanted out of a witness. Hanson always enjoyed being part of it.

The social worker arrived as warm and cheerful as he'd been on his last visit. He'd swapped his check shirt for a different one in light blue and white, but otherwise looked unchanged. He insisted on being called 'Mark' for this interview, and so the chief smiled, nodded, and said, 'Well, Mark. I think you have a few things to tell us.'

Slatterworth looked at Hanson and then back to the DCI, with a slightly forced expression of humour. When he spoke, it was with as much of his Edinburgh lilt as he seemed able to muster. 'I think there's probably more for you to tell me. But I'm happy to help with anything you need.'

'That's excellent news,' Jonah said. 'Because I think you can be of enormous help. I'd like to know, first of all, how you first met Sally and Henry Murray-Watt.'

Mark gave an odd, slightly explosive laugh, and then adopted an expression of confusion. 'I suppose probably – the first time I went to the house to see Keely and Nina.'

The DCI gave him a smile, and then said, 'No.' He started tapping his pen on the table, in what was clearly designed to be an irritatingly casual way. 'When I interviewed you yesterday evening, you mentioned how well Callum had progressed as a student, referencing how he had been when they first took him on. That despite the fact that he isn't and never has been your responsibility.'

'Oh, come on,' Mark said, with another laugh. 'It's all in his notes.'

'Strange that the notes should have included references to the car that Mr Murray-Watt used to drive,' Hanson said, glancing at the DCI. 'Henry swapped his Porsche for a Jaguar before the Lennox sisters arrived there. And yet you talked about Henry having a Porsche on the drive. How did you know what car he'd driven several years before?'

There was a brief silence, and then Mark said, 'He must have told me.'

'It's also strange,' the chief went on, 'that you should have formed such a strong view of the couple after only two months of knowing them. A strong enough opinion to be able to speak assertively to the Child Abuse Investigation Team about their good character.' He looked up at Mark. 'On how many occasions did you visit the Lennox sisters during that time?'

Mark frowned, shrugged, and said, 'Well . . . twice, including when I went in response to Keely's emergency call.'

'So, in fact,' the chief said, 'you'd been to the house in the role of social worker exactly once before the incident where she accused them of abuse. Strange that you were so absolutely convinced they were innocent.'

Mark opened his mouth, hesitated, and then said, 'It was . . . it was clear what they were like. I mean, maybe I went a little bit too far when I was talking to you yesterday, in hindsight.'

'And at the time, too,' Sheens said. 'When you gave your thoughts in detail to the investigating officer and didn't mention that you had barely met the Murray-Watts in an official capacity.'

There was a brief silence, and Mark said, 'I don't really remember that, but if you're saying I spoke too strongly in support of them, then I think you should bear in mind all the other factors at the time. And the police –'

'My colleagues conducted a case as well as they could with the evidence that was provided to them,' Sheens said, and then immediately asked, 'When was this photograph taken?'

He handed a glossy-printed snap across the table, and Hanson felt a rush of absolute glee.

The photo showed Mark Slatterworth in sunglasses at what looked like a picnic, with Sally Murray-Watt waving at the camera alongside him. The chief described it for the camera.

'I . . . I don't recognise this,' Mark said. His throat sounded dry and tight with panic.

'That's strange, considering it came from your house,' the DCI said, and handed him a second image. This showed a pinboard full of photographs, with the snap of him and Sally up in one corner. Again, the DCI described it, flatly.

'What are you . . .?' Mark looked up at him. 'What were you doing in my house? I never gave permission –'

'We have yet to request a warrant,' the chief said, 'but will be doing so. These were not taken by an officer. They were sent to us by an interested party.'

Hanson knew, of course, exactly who the interested party was. The photo was one of the many pieces of evidence Nina had left for them.

There was a long silence, which the chief seemed to be enjoying. Mark swallowed three times. Four. And then he said, 'I don't know them that well. They were just in – an am-dram group I'm part of. This was just one of the socials.'

'Did you declare to your employers that you knew them before agreeing to become Keely and Nina's social worker?' the chief asked.

'No, I . . .'

'Thank you. On to my constable's next questions.'

Hanson was ready for this. She handed him two transcripts, one from his summary of Keely's accusations about Frank Pinder, and the other the initial police report from Keely's interview with the CAIT's DI.

'In the investigation into allegations against Frank Pinder,' she said, 'you said Keely specified the weekend of the eighteenth of November as a definite date that Frank had raped her. But it later emerged that Evelyn Pinder hadn't been on call that weekend and had, in fact, been in the house.'

'Yes,' Mark said, the sound strangled. 'That's right. Keely had lied about it.' He nodded. 'She tried to change her story later. I told you.'

'But,' Hanson continued, 'in the initial police interview she gave, she said, "The weekend before last," which backs up the date she later said she had meant. And when interviewed again about it, she maintained that she had never given the date of the eighteenth. That was only what you passed on.'

The DCI chipped in, his voice almost bored, 'I have already put in a request for access to Frank Pinder's phone records for that time period, which I am positive will be granted, so why don't you tell me about the private phone call between you and Frank the afternoon Keely confessed?'

'But I . . .' Mark gave another, strange laugh. 'I had to tell him that the girls wouldn't be returned to him, and that this was now a police investigation.'

'But you also shared details of the case,' the chief said. 'And while doing that, you tipped him off about the dates he stood accused of rape.'

'No!' Mark said, and then, in slight anguish, 'I just gave him the bare bones.'

'You then,' the DCI continued, 'went on to change your account of what she had said to cast doubt on all her claims.'

'I just wrote up what she said!' Mark protested.

'In 2012, you also assisted Jared Boula by squashing Keely's claims and feeding him exactly the right lines to get away with assault,' Hanson put in. 'We have records of the calls to him. Do you want to tell us about the call you also made to him last night, disclosing the refuge Keely had been taken to?'

There was another silence, which told Hanson everything she'd wanted to know. And then the DCI said, 'Did the Murray-Watts pay you? Was that it? And Frank, and Jared? Was it really enough to make you break every promise you'd made to the children in your care and offer them up for systematic abuse?'

'Nobody – was abusing – anyone,' Mark said, suddenly shouting. He pressed his forefinger into the table as he spoke. 'Keely is an out-and-out liar. Henry and Sally never laid a finger on her, and it was all about revenge. About control.' He shook his head. 'You can see it in her the moment you meet her! She's twisted, and wrong, and I wasn't about to let her bring down good people.'

'People like Frank Pinder?' the chief asked, his voice iron. 'A man who was found with a thirteen-year-old girl naked in his bed last night, as you must by now be aware?'

Slatterworth's face twisted.

'Perverts like Jared Boula?' Sheens added.

'Jared never did a thing,' Mark said, dismissively. 'That was clear from the first.'

'Based on what?' the chief asked. 'On your bizarre prejudice against Keely Lennox?' He shook his head, and despite the nature of what he was saying, was suddenly conversational again. 'You might be interested to see the extremely graphic contents of Jared Boula's computer. It might make it harder for you to be so self-righteous. Though perhaps you and he have something in common. Perhaps you enjoy seeing young girls beaten and abused.'

'You can't say that,' Mark said, his voice hoarse. 'I don't – I'm going to – I want my solicitor.'

'I'm more than happy to begin the process of interviewing you as a suspect,' the chief said, his voice absolutely courteous, 'but before we do that, I'd like to give you the opportunity to explain just how Jared Boula threatened you into disclosing Keely's location.'

Mark looked as though he might talk, but seemed to have lost the capacity. The DCI nodded, and rose. 'Do get in touch with your solicitor.'

With the official interviews done, Hanson went with the chief to see Keely and Nina, both of whom had agreed to come to the station. They had each spent a little while in the hospital, having blood tests in Keely's case to determine how she'd been knocked out, and being checked for smoke inhalation and fractures in Nina's.

Hanson suspected the chief should be getting his lungs

384

checked, too. He'd had to take several water breaks during the interviews, and she'd heard him coughing in the corridor when she'd left the interview room. But the chief being the chief, she guessed he would be leaving that for another day.

The Lennox sisters had been declared fit within a couple of hours, at any rate. They would ultimately be sent to a safe location arranged directly by the chief himself. Callum would go with them until it was clear that none of them was under any kind of threat. There would be no leaks through social services this time. No social worker actually working against them, either.

Hanson felt a surge of gratitude as she walked into the comfort suite. The Lennox sisters were watching some kind of cooking programme on TV, Nina perched slightly peculiarly on a cushion – presumably to avoid pressure on her bruised coccyx – and with her wrist in a support.

Callum Taylor was, of course, there as well, sitting close enough to Nina that it was hard to tell their limbs apart. He looked a lot cleaner than he had back in Godshill, with his head wound stitched and a clean T-shirt and jeans on him.

Nina paused the programme and looked directly at Hanson. 'It's good to see you again, detective constable,' she said.

Hanson saw a sudden, striking similarity between the two sisters. It went beyond the hair, the skin tone and the cheekbones. It lay in the cool intelligence they shared, and in the way they so instinctively masked what they really felt.

'It's definitely Juliette,' Hanson said, firmly. 'And I apologise for having led you to believe that catching criminals was a lot more fun than it actually is.'

Nina's smile turned crooked. 'Oh, I don't know. I'd say it's been entertaining.'

There was a momentary silence, and then the chief said, 'I'm sorry as well. For the length of time it's taken for all of us to listen to you. To all of you.' He gave a half-smile. 'It should be the case that every officer begins with an assumption that people are telling the truth when they bring accusations. You should never have had to go through all this just to get where you now are.'

Nina's ironic grin had widened, but she looked away at Callum for a moment, and Hanson knew that there was real emotion there. That this meant something to her.

Callum lifted her hand and squeezed it. 'About time,' he said.

'Will they go to prison? Frank Pinder, Jared Boula, the Murray-Watts . . .' It was Keely who asked, her gaze piercing. Searching. A gaze that no longer made Hanson's hackles rise.

'I hope so,' the chief replied. 'To be realistic, there's always a chance of any case failing. It's one of the most frustrating things about this job – when you do your utmost to bring someone to justice, but it fails.'

Keely shook her head, her expression dissatisfied.

'But,' the DCI went on, 'everything you've given us has been – well, it's an exceptionally compelling body of evidence that I feel has the best possible chance of success.'

'You've got all of it, now,' Keely said, with a nod. 'And even if it was Juliette who was supposed to solve it, I'm glad we got you, too.'

Hanson couldn't help grinning as the chief reacted with visible emotion. He tried to cover it by saying gruffly, 'Well, also for what it's worth, I think all three of you should consider becoming detectives one day.'

'We were thinking more along vigilante lines,' Keely said, coolly, and Hanson out and out laughed.

On their way out, Nina suddenly called out, 'Juliette?'

They both turned, and Nina threw something to her. A small, circular black object.

'Callum found it on your car, a couple of weeks ago,' she said. 'It's a tracking device. You can buy them online, if you know where to look.'

Hanson found herself staring at Nina, feeling the weight of it in her hand.

'I saw who put it on there, in case it helps,' Callum told her.

'Would that be a fairly hefty, dark-haired guy with a five o'clock shadow?' Hanson asked.

'It was,' Callum agreed. 'I got him on camera. I missed him putting it on, but I caught him leaving. I'll send the video to you, if you like. I had some fun with that one, by the way. I attached it to Henry's car and then to my motorbike, just to mess with the guy.'

Hanson grinned, and nodded, wondering if there was much point in pursuing this. And then she thought of how Nina had roared up to her on her motorbike in Bevois Valley, and she narrowed her eyes. 'Would there be any other tracking devices on my car? Or on any of the team's?'

Nina gave her a beautifully innocent smile. 'I'm sure there won't be. In a day or so.'

Keely looked curiously at Hanson. 'The guy who put the tracker on, he's been hanging around you quite a lot. Who is he?'

Hanson thought about the professionalism of sharing this information with them, but she felt as if she owed them an answer. 'Just a bloody ex-boyfriend,' she said. Which was as much of a description as she felt Damian deserved.

39

The chief called time at nine p.m. They had, he said, all been up for far too long, on far too little sleep. Though he looked lively, even upbeat as he returned to his office to pack up. His cough seemed to be waning, too, and he had eaten an entire Domino's pizza while filling in paperwork.

'I sort of don't want to go home,' Hanson said to Ben and Domnall, as she switched off her machine. 'I mean, I'm knackered, but I'm also wired.'

'You'll feel better after a drink or two,' O'Malley said. 'I, for one, am going straight to the pub.'

Hanson gave him a grin. 'OK. I'm in.'

'So hard to convince,' O'Malley said. 'Ben?'

'I'm obviously in,' Lightman said. 'Who are you going to take the piss out of if I go home?'

'Good point,' Hanson said, with a grin. 'I'll ask the chief along too.'

Jonah was anxious to pick Milly up and return home to Michelle. His brief visit earlier had made it clear to him that he'd been failing his partner.

With a whole day to herself, he'd expected to find Michelle playing the piano, or reading – two things she enjoyed hugely and almost never managed to do with Milly around. Instead, he found her curled up in bed. Her eyes were oozing tears, and it was clear that this had been going on for some time.

He had sat next to her, and pulled her into a hug, hoping he didn't smell too much of smoke.

'I think – I think you need some time to yourself,' he said. 'And to see someone. This has all been . . . You're feeling overwhelmed, aren't you?'

She looked up at him, and it was shocking how much she had changed, now he really came to see it. The outgoing, positive woman he had once proposed to was now lost in sadness. How could he have failed to notice?

'I can't do it, Jonah,' she said, through a sob. 'I'm the world's most terrible mother.'

She buried her face into his chest, and he felt his own eyes filling.

'You are no such thing,' he said, unsteadily. He put a hand up and stroked her hair. 'You're a wonderful mother who needs some bloody help. Which I'm going to get you, and also give you.' He squeezed her more tightly. 'We're going to make this all OK. All right?'

She'd nodded, after a minute, and he'd stayed in the hug for a while.

It struck him, then, that what she needed was her friends around her. And he knew of at least one close friend of Michelle's who would be free.

'Why don't you ring Kerry?' he asked. 'Get her to come round. She doesn't have appointments on a Monday, does she? Or I can call her, if you like. Company, and a takeaway, and some wine . . . You'll feel a little more like the alcoholic I know and love.'

Michelle had given a brief laugh. 'OK.' She'd rubbed at her eyes, and then said, 'Thank you.'

It had struck him, forcefully, that his family was the most important thing. More important, even, than his work. And he'd carried that knowledge back to CID with him.

So as the team began planning their pub trip, he excused himself, and called Sammy to give her an ETA.

'Oh, you don't need to rush,' Sammy replied. 'I've done the nine o'clock bottle and put Milly down to sleep. You can pick her up any time before eleven.'

Jonah wasn't certain what he should do, but in the end decided that giving Michelle a little more time with her friend was probably the fairest thing. She'd been starved of company and of time without responsibility. That much was clear. So he agreed to a short trip to the pub. After all, he thought, helping his team to wind down after a case was important too.

Hanson watched the others talk for a while without really engaging. The chief and O'Malley were having some good-natured banter about politics, but she found herself watching Ben, who seemed full of relief but also, underneath it all, angry.

She suddenly rose, and said, 'Come on, Ben. My round, but you're helping me carry it.'

'Yes, sir,' he said, with the tiniest of smiles.

He followed her to the bar, and Hanson could feel a ball of nerves in her stomach as she said, 'You don't have to tell me everything. Or anything, really, unless it helps. But . . . something about all this has been getting to you, hasn't it?'

Ben looked away, leaning his elbows carefully onto the bar so that his head was down. A defensive pose.

'It . . . has. For a few reasons.'

'It's something to do with those two girls, isn't it?' she asked. 'Do they remind you of someone?'

There was a pause, and then Ben said, very quietly, 'Yes, that's . . . They remind me of me.'

Hanson looked away, too. She could see discomfort in

every line of him, and she thought she understood what he meant.

'You mean you've experienced something like what they've been through?' she asked, even more quietly.

Ben nodded, and she felt a flood of sadness for him.

One of the bar staff arrived to take their order, and Hanson guessed that this would shut the conversation down. But once they'd ordered, Ben added, 'It was my piano teacher.'

He grabbed up the first pint that had been put on the bar, and drank almost half of it straight off. Hanson suddenly understood that this was too much for him.

But it didn't feel like a judgement on her, now, that he didn't want to talk. She supposed it never had been. He'd clearly just learned to shut everything away.

She took a breath, feeling overwhelmingly sad and angry for him. 'It probably isn't . . . the time or the place. And I know you might not want to talk about it at all. I won't . . . I'll avoid interrogating you. But I'm here any time you want to chat, you know?'

She reached out and squeezed his shoulder. He nodded. And the silence afterwards felt all right, she realised. It was all right.

Jonah managed to tear his mind away from the Lennox sisters just enough to make actual conversation with his team. He watched Ben and Juliette's interactions with interest. It was clear to him that there was some undercurrent there, this evening, and he guessed it might be connected to the way Ben had been behaving.

He regretted, sometimes, that Ben wasn't an easier man to read. Even after years of working together, there was a lot he didn't know.

But they came back from the bar cheerfully enough, and pressed another low-alcohol pint on him.

He was midway through it when his phone buzzed. He glanced at the screen and saw that it was a message from Jojo.

As he looked up, he caught Hanson's eyes leaving his phone a little guiltily. She'd obviously seen Jojo's name.

Hanson picked up her drink, and he wondered if she was thinking badly of him. It was quite possible that Ben had told her what had happened last night, on Furzley Lane. It had probably looked like he was trying to get Jojo back. Which was even more awful now he understood the way Michelle had been feeling.

But when Hanson looked up at him again, her eyes were warm with sympathy.

Jonah gave her a small smile. 'I'll be back in a minute,' he said, and took his phone over to the bar.

He opened the message with a squeeze of an emotion he couldn't quite place and read.

> Jonah, I'm sorry. I'm really sorry for everything I said last night. I was just drunk, and angry after having to get out of the cab, and I suppose I'd bottled up a lot of things I wanted to say before. I'm actually doing fine, when not mad drunk. I've landed on my feet, and I've even started dating someone. Someone who seems nice, and stable, and even climbs now and then. So you don't need to worry about me. I really don't want you to have any anxiety about it all. I'll be fine. J xx

Jonah felt an awful deadness as he finished reading. As if he was waving something off.

The urge to reply to her was overwhelming. He wanted to tell her something of what he felt about it all. He began typing quickly. Unsteadily.

> Please don't apologise. It was so good to see you,
> and I know you will be fine. More than fine. Wonderful.
> You're the toughest person I know. It's me I'm worried
> about. I don't actually know how I'm going to survive
> without you in my life, even though I know I have to.
> I can't walk out on the woman who is mother to my
> child and who is struggling and desperately needs me.
> But I still miss you like bloody oxygen.

He stopped there, and looked at it for a while.

And then he deleted everything except the first sentence. After which he wrote:

> I'm glad you said it, and got old hurts off your chest.
> And I'm glad that you're doing well. I will always,
> always wish you well.

He pressed send and went back to find his team.

Acknowledgments

It becomes clearer to me with every book that each one owes a huge amount to a huge number of people. Those people stand together to make a mountain of wonderful industry. I just get to stand on top of it with my name on everything.

So, this is to thank my simply wonderful agenting and editing team of Felicity Blunt, Rosie Pierce, Joel Richardson and Grace Long. Your insight and patience when I wrote a daft second half of this (TWICE) were immense, and you are such fun, warm-hearted people to work with.

To Jen Breslin and Ella Watkins, who work tirelessly to create wonderful proofs, marketing materials and publicity opportunities, and generally make it possible for people to actually know the book exists.

To the wonderful Deirdre O'Connell and the Sales team at Penguin, who have done simply incredible things in getting Jonah Sheens onto shelves across the country.

To the brilliant Rights team and my amazing international publishers. Knowing that Jonah and team continue to reach readers in many languages is such a huge, huge privilege and I am overwhelmed with gratitude.

To Beatrix McIntyre, Jennie Roman and the brilliant copy-editing team. I am so sorry for making your lives SO difficult with this one, but thank you, thank you, thank you for being simply brilliant at engaging with it and helping me see the non-deliberate mistakes!

To Chris Haines for his ever-patient replies to my queries about police procedure. Please be in no doubt that there will still be errors, but that they will be mine — and that Chris is nice enough never to make me feel terrible for them.

To Hampshire Constabulary for allowing me to insert my own fictional CID into Southampton Central (not that I ever gave you a choice . . .)

To the LKs for listening to my whinges and being a source of constant fun. You are such a fantastic bunch and I love you all dearly.

To all those wonderful authors who were kind enough to not only read but to offer an endorsement. You really are the best humans on the planet.

To Gillian McAllister for the awesome voice memos and plot discussions — bright points in my day or week, always — as well as for your kindness.

To the incredible booksellers of Waterstones, Heffers, Blackwell's, Topping and Company, Book-Ish, Bert's Books, Forum Books, and every other fabulous independent that has not only stocked, but also recommended my books. Love you.

To Vic and Simon of Bay Tales for your wonderful, tireless support of me and so many other crime writers. You do wonderful things.

And overwhelmingly, to all the bloggers, reviewers and readers who recommended, championed and shouted about this book from the first. You are absolute marvels and I want to set up statues to each and every one of you.

Nail-biting cases that hook you in, and heart that keeps you coming back for more...

GYTHA LODGE

Read on for an exclusive extract from the next instalment

Coming 2023

Lindsay

Lindsay was laughing – really, genuinely laughing – for the first time in months. And possibly even for the first time in years.

This wasn't the kind of thing she did. The car. The man. The intoxicated flight through crowded streets.

She hadn't been out on New Year's Eve for decades. Not since Peter. And even then, it had only happened in the early years. The year that they'd met, at a party neither of them had quite wanted to go to. And for three or four years afterwards as they'd each forced themselves out for the sake of the other, with a babysitter booked to look after the child neither of them had planned on but both of them adored.

They'd each eventually admitted that the kitchen table and a game of Risk held more appeal than the fireworks and the crowds. And from then on they'd stayed in, as a couple at first, and later with Dylan too, always begging to stay up until midnight. To get the Twister mat out or dance around to Pink Floyd.

And then, after Peter's slow dwindling and loss and Dylan's departure for university in Dublin, it had mostly been Lindsay alone. Her not even forty, left to ring in the New Year with a jigsaw, and the TV, and a lot more wine than she was used to. Every year had been the same: a flood of memories from that first night, when she had fizzed with the hope that Peter might kiss her at midnight, and a sense of profound loss that she was moving into a new year without him.

It might have been easier if Dylan had chosen to stay within easy visiting distance. But he'd met the woman of his dreams, and decided to start a new life in Dublin. And so each New Year's Eve had been marked, for Lindsay, by an aching loneliness she managed to deny on almost every other day of the year.

Any other year, she would have been out for the count by now, numbed into oblivion by the wine. She wouldn't have been in an unfamiliar car, going to watch fireworks with a man she barely knew.

She glanced over at him, this other man. Watched the intelligent, attractive lines of his face as he manoeuvred the big vehicle past a crowd of revellers that had spilled onto the road from the pavement. And she felt a sense of huge serendipity in everything. In her long walk that had left her tired but also, somehow, enlivened. In her realisation that she had no wine in the house. In her decision to put on her nicest black sweater and jeans with the heeled boots she hardly ever wore and walk to the wine shop on South Parade.

Those decisions had sent her straight into his path. And him into hers. There had been no question in her mind that this was what was meant to happen: for her to meet someone on another New Year's Eve, somewhere else she'd never really intended to go, and for the two of them to be the obvious outsiders. Clear soulmates.

And somehow, only an hour or two later, she felt as though she'd known this man for years. It had only intensified the feeling that this was meant to be. He'd led a life so different from hers, and yet they shared so many strange points of similarity. Their taste in music. Their favourite films. The places they had visited, and in particular their love of book after book.

He'd shared so much about his life, his family, as he'd bought her three drinks one after the other, with most of his being tonic as he'd brought his car with him. So many stories of his own shortcomings told with a laugh, and so many of hers listened to with clear fascination.

'You've got so much strength,' he'd said, after some long and yet short amount of time. 'A lot more than I have. But you're not – brittle. You're warm, and kind-hearted. It's . . .' He'd lifted his glass, and swallowed, his eyes slightly over-bright. Something he clearly found embarrassing. 'It's – so rare, that.'

And Lindsay, who was by now fuzzy with drunkenness and filled with a feeling of absolute contentment, had leaned forwards and pressed her lips into his. His mouth had still been wet with lager from the one pint he'd allowed himself, and it had tasted like being a teenager again, only sweeter.

She'd barely thought about the significant age gap, or wondered about details like his surname. The connection between them seemed to make it all irrelevant.

It hadn't seemed strange to spend the next while with her body pressed up against him, as everything had grown busier and busier, the music louder. And it hadn't seemed strange, either, when he'd looked around at the crush and then said, 'Do you want to get out of here and watch the fireworks?'

Lindsay didn't know exactly where they were driving to, and it didn't worry her. He'd told her he knew exactly where to get the best view, his voice full of energy and a delight at sharing, and she believed him.

She felt a wave of joy at the trust she felt towards him. At the fact that she'd at last, *at last* felt that same warmth and willingness she'd felt towards Peter. A hot, gut-deep excitement. A feeling of wanting to give someone else control.

'Here,' he said, as he pulled up at a temporary red traffic light. He was holding a small thermos flask out to her, and she took it with a smile. Tipped it back without needing to think.

'Spiced rum and apple,' he said. 'Is that ok?'

'Definitely,' she said. It was strong but comforting. She could feel the heat of it spreading down and into her stomach, adding a sense of comfort to the jubilant feeling that had built in her all evening.

She glanced out of the car at a ruckus going on. There was a group of twenty-somethings on the pavement, drinking out of cans and yelling at each other instead of talking. On any other night she would have felt irritated by them. Threatened, maybe. Whereas tonight, she was part of an exuberant whole. She raised the flask to them and drank again.

He grinned, and said, 'I might have some soon. If you're OK to stay out a while so I don't have to drive for a bit.'

'I am,' she said, without hesitation. And this, again, wasn't the Lindsay who had spent the last seven years making excuses to be alone. This was the Lindsay of her past life. And perhaps a bolder version still.

He lifted his hand from the gearstick and squeezed her fingers just as the lights changed. They moved off, away from the hubbub. The bypass was quiet as they joined it and began to fly past illuminated houses. Just their car and one further ahead.

It wasn't far off midnight, and everyone who wasn't spilling out of pubs was at parties or on sofas; on riverbanks or clustered in gardens.

She realised she should send something to Dylan, before the mobile networks jammed up. Her son would scoff at any suggestion he was sentimental, but he would mention it if he didn't get a message from her tonight.

She pulled her phone out of her jeans pocket and found it surprisingly hard to focus on the screen. It made her laugh.

'God, I can hardly read,' she said.

'Are you calling someone?'

He asked it lightly. Without jealousy.

'Just messaging Dylan.'

She glanced over to see him smiling. 'I'd like to meet him sometime.'

'He'd love you,' she said. 'You're just his kind of person.'

And then her focus was on the screen for a few minutes as she laboriously typed:

Happy New Year! Hope you're all having a great time.

She scrolled for a while until she'd found a few celebratory emojis. They weren't in her most frequently used list, something she found herself thinking firmly, happily, that she was going to change. She was going to be the sort of person who was excited, happy, and celebratory again. She'd never believed in New Year's resolutions, but she was making one now.

And then, in a determined move, she turned the phone off. The rest of the night was going to be about her, and him, and nothing else. She could catch up with Dylan in the morning.

By the time she looked up again, they'd left the town and were driving between trees, the road dark on either side. She squinted out through the windscreen, disorientated, until she recognised a junction. They were already at Ashurst. Had it really taken her that long to write the message?

They turned a slight bend in the road, and Lindsay's phone slid off her lap, and down into the gap between the seat and the central console.

'Bugger.'

She heard him laugh gently. 'What's up?'

'My phone is . . .' She waved, her hands feeling only vaguely connected to her. God, she was drunk.

She reached over to get it, just as he lifted his arm to look underneath it, and her head collided with his elbow, hard.

'Eesh,' he said.

Lindsay found herself laughing. 'Sorry.'

'You shouldn't be apologising.' He shook his arm, glancing at her. 'That must have hurt. You OK?'

'I'm fine,' she said, grinning at him. 'I can't even feel it.'

'OK,' he said, shaking his head slightly as he looked back at the road. 'You're clearly tougher than I am.'

She reached down for the phone again, her fingers finding it, but not able to grasp it. She succeeded only in shoving it backwards, until it was pushed out of the space and into the rear of the car

'Sorry. Hang on.'

She pulled on the seatbelt to give herself more room, and half-turned in her seat. Twisting her right arm, she could just about reach down to where the phone now sat.

In this contorted position, she could see into the rear of the car, and at first it meant nothing to her: the neatly bound piles of wood. The can of kerosene. They were just things. The sorts of things people had in their cars sometimes.

But then she found herself thinking about a woman, and a murder, and a bonfire. A lonely forty-something woman whose photo had appeared again and again in the papers and online. A woman who had reminded Lindsay of herself in painful ways. A woman whose killer hadn't yet been found, though everybody had tried.

And the happy, detached contentment suddenly shifted. She felt it for what it was: a fog of confusion that was descending, and overtaking her, as he drove her God knew where. And with it came the most crushing sense of disappointment.

He's drugged you, she thought, angry with herself. Though less angry than she should have been through the haze that was wrapping itself around her. *You shouldn't have taken the drink.*

And then she thought about the three drinks she'd already taken from him, and how he'd carried each one out to her. And she realised that he might have been drugging her for hours.

She briefly imagined the other woman, Jacqueline, drinking with him too. Getting into the car with him and taking the flask. And then being unable to defend herself as he dragged her out into the middle of the woods.

And still there was a part of her that wanted to stay, and let him kiss her. That hoped she was wrong.

You have to get out. You have to get out now.

The thought was almost enough to keep her focused. She needed to do something to make him pull over.

But she might not be able to make him stop. She needed the phone. It was her one chance to call for help. And if he knew she had, then maybe she'd be safe.

She reached further, ignoring the kerosene and the wood and stretching out with her fingers. She could feel how close he was to her, now. How vulnerable she was. It was no longer exciting.

But somehow it was hard to hold on to her fear. Even to concentrate. She found herself staring into nothing, even while her body was twisted uncomfortably, her arm out towards the phone.

'You OK?' he asked, his voice rumbling close to her. It jolted her, kicking a little fear back into the haze.

'Just trying to reach it,' she said. And she tried to laugh. And then she found herself laughing for real, for some reason. It was so stupid, not being able to get her hands on the bloody phone. What a ridiculous way to end up dead.

The tips of her fingers slid on it, barely able to grip. She'd only shoved it further away.

'It's OK, we're nearly there,' he said.

She became aware that the car was jolting, now. That it was tipping and rolling over something bumpy. The phone vanished out of her sight.

She slid back round until she was properly in her seat, trying to remember to be afraid as she saw that they were driving down a high, open track over heathland.

'We'll get a great view up here,' he said.

She found herself looking at him, and saw that he was smiling. It was a surprisingly warm smile.

You need to get away, she thought. *Get away from him, Lindsay.*

She sure as hell couldn't fight, with her limbs feeling loose and her thoughts foggy. And she wouldn't have stood much chance, anyway. As fit as she was, he was clearly stronger, his muscles used to activity.

There was a stand of gorse ahead of them, suddenly, and he swung the car around to park next to it. They were on the brow of a hill, looking out over woodland below. And it was familiar to her. Lindsay had walked here.

'Lyndhurst Heath,' she said out loud, unclipping her seatbelt clumsily and letting it slide across her.

'I love it up here,' he said, turning to her.

He looked as though he might kiss her. And for a moment, a surge of longing in her made her hesitate.

What if he meant everything he said? What if he really feels this?

But even through the haze, she saw a flicker of something

cross his face then. Something anticipatory. Faltering. Something that wasn't adoration.

And suddenly Lindsay wanted nothing less than his kiss. She opened the door and slid out. And then she ran for the woods, down a path she knew well.

She heard the car door opening a way behind her. And then heard his shout. She just had to make it to the trees. That was all.

She looked up at them, their shadowy shapes seeming close but also impossibly distant, and she could feel the fuzziness closing in further. Her legs were almost entirely without feeling as she hurled them at the ground, every bump in the ground sending her bouncing over it.

'Lindsay!'

He was behind her, and he was closer. So much closer.

Lindsay tried to focus on the blurring trees, fighting the exhaustion, and the part of her that told her to give up.

No, no, no, the stronger, more stubborn part of her repeated. And as she tripped, and stumbled to her knees, it was that part of her that let out a howl of fury at the unfairness of it all.

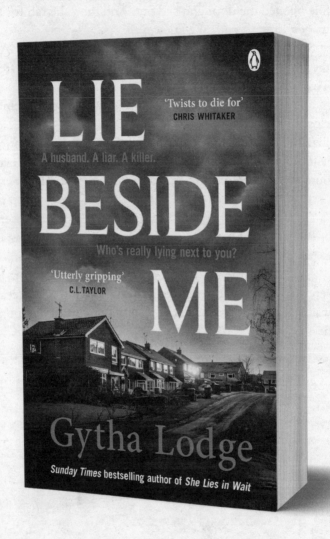

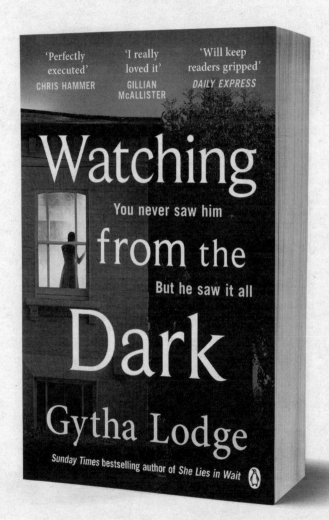

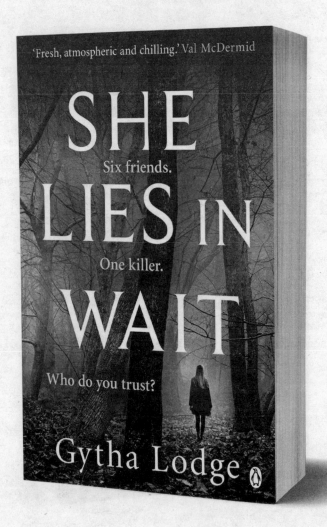